From HELL to HOME

THE FINAL VIETNAM STORY

DJ Power -Author

DORRANCE
PUBLISHING CO
EST. 1920
PITTSBURGH, PENNSYLVANIA 15238

The contents of this work, including, but not limited to, the accuracy of events, people, and places depicted; opinions expressed; permission to use previously published materials included; and any advice given or actions advocated are solely the responsibility of the author, who assumes all liability for said work and indemnifies the publisher against any claims stemming from publication of the work.

The content of this work is fictional and does not depict any actual person or event.

All Rights Reserved
Copyright © 2022 by DJ POWER

No part of this book may be reproduced or transmitted, downloaded, distributed, reverse engineered, or stored in or introduced into any information storage and retrieval system, in any form or by any means, including photocopying and recording, whether electronic or mechanical, now known or hereinafter invented without permission in writing from the publisher.

Dorrance Publishing Co
585 Alpha Drive
Pittsburgh, PA 15238
Visit our website at *www.dorrancebookstore.com*

ISBN: 979-8-8852-7057-1
eISBN: 979-8-8852-7786-0

From HELL to HOME

THE FINAL VIETNAM STORY

DJ Power -Author

TABLE OF CONTENTS

THE CANADIAN MISSION   7
THANK GOD SOMEONE HEARS ME   24
MAKE THE CALL   39
HE IS HERE   53
PREPARE THE RIDE   56
ON MY WAY (but to where?)   68
MY HEALTH IS BETTER, BUT NOT MY LOVE LIFE   77
TIME TO GO   82
ALWAYS EXPECT THE UNEXPECTED   88
DIDN'T SEE THIS COMING   98
A BIG ONE COMING UP   101
TIME TO JUMP OFF   113
YES or NO!   122
CAPTURED AND ARROGANT   127
ON THE RUN AGAIN   132
THANK GOD FOR FRIENDS   140
RELAXING WITH JUST THE WAR   143
THE DEVASTATION HITS HOME   148
BACK ON THE HORSE   161
A MISSION OF A LIFETIME   163
THE RUG IS PULLED FROM UNDER ME   170
WINDOW SEAT ON THE LEFT, PLEASE   178
VIETNAM ISN'T THE ONLY WAR   186
EL TORO to LOS ANGELES AIRPORT   237
ONE MORE FLIGHT THEN HEAVEN   231
FINALLY, EVERYTHING IS GREAT OR IS IT?   240

THE CANADIAN MISSION

I could feel someone punching my chest. Stop it. That hurts! Where is my mother? Why is the Corpsman pushing up and down on my chest? I am so cold. I need a blanket because I am about to turn to ice. I know that I'm yelling at them but they don't seem to be paying any attention to me. The damn blades on this noisy helicopter seem to be causing them not to hear me.

"Give me a blanket or get my mother, please. Die? Who's dying? I know Dewey is dead but who else is in that bad a shape for them to die? For God's sake get me a blanket. I'm freezing here. Isn't anyone on this piece of shit cold? What the hell is this guy doing with his hand on my neck? My neck is starting to hurt like hell and he won't stop squeezing. God, I'm tired, I need to go to sleep."

"Stay with me, Corporal. Don't close your eyes. Stay with me, damnit." The Corpsman is yelling at the body lying in front of him.

"Come on, Doc. Do something. He's too good a guy to die like this. He's indestructible, Captain America, Super Marine, he can't die," as tears started to come to Tomelli's eyes.

The Corpsman was still pushing on Coleman's chest and Seu was holding his neck trying to stop the blood shooting from the massive wound in his head. "Doc" continued to work on Coleman for what seemed hours, but it was only minutes when the two men on the floor of the helicopter finally stopped.

Ten minutes had gone by with them working on Jim. The blood that was spurting out seconds ago had suddenly stopped. The Corpsman reached over and lifted Seu's hand from its position. The "Doc" finally sits up away from the body, looking around and finally he yells over the helicopter noise. "It doesn't matter anymore. Your friend is dead." looking right at Joe.

"No! He can't be dead. Bring him back. Do something to make him better." Joe now has a hold of the Corpsman's blouse and yelling.

"Why is Joe screaming at the "Doc?" I can't hear him over the sound of the helicopter. I can't see anything and it's so cold. The sound is slowly going away. I can't hear the sound of the blades anymore. The helicopter sound is far off in the distance now. What is going on? We must have landed because it is now super silent.

"It is very dark in here. I cannot see anything and I am having trouble breathing. What kind of blankets are these? It feels like rubber but it can't be. It's been a while since we landed and we haven't started the debrief yet. Where is the Commander? Where am I?"

My head is hurting terribly and I'm trying to yell to get this damn blanket off me. What the hell is happening?

As I am trying not to think of my predicament, a name pops into my head. Ken Marceau. Why am I thinking of him? It was so long ago. This was one of my first missions just after I returned from the debacle in Cuba.

Kenneth Pierre Marceau, one of the most wanted men on the face of the earth. He was chief advisor to Fidel Castro of Cuba and an expert in South American Revolutions. Right hand man to the king of revolutionaries, Ernesto "Che" Guevara. Marceau, a French Canadian National, educated in Moscow, involved in the coup that overthrew Brazilian President Joao Goulart in April of '64'. Prior to that, he was involved and still is with the IRA (Irish Republican Army) uprising in Northern Ireland during the late 50's and early 60's.

The Commander had called and ordered me to report to his office no later than fifteen hundred hours on Friday, June 21, 1964. I'm right in the middle of Recon training at Marine Base, Camp Lejeune, Jacksonville, North Carolina. I am coming to realize that no matter what I have going in my life, it doesn't matter to him. I know when you are ordered to do something, especially by the Commander, you do it. Going over to headquarters on Wednesday, I receive my orders and I am off to Langley, Virginia.

Arriving at Langley, McLean, Virginia (the home of the Central Intelligence Agency) is always interesting. I have an ID that says that I am a Field Agent in the Clandestine Service. I show my ID to the guard at the gate who never smiles but looks at it and then waves me in.

Parking my car across from the main entrance, I get out and enter this hallowed place. To my left is the ever-present wall with name and badges of agents who have given their lives in service to the CIA. I enter the elevator directly in front of me and push the button that says 3. It always amazes me when the elevator door opens on the third floor, there is always someone waiting to escort me to the Commander's office. (Someday I must ask how they know I'm on the elevator.) As usual, there is never any waiting, I just go into the office without an announcement. This time as I enter, I notice another man sitting in the back of the room out of the sunlight.

"How was your trip up here from North Carolina?" as the Commander motioned me to sit down in front of his desk.

"Not bad, no traffic. Took only about seven hours to get here." I knew he didn't care but I thought I'd throw it in anyway trying to ease the tension that comes with reporting to him.

"Let's get down to business. Kenneth Pierre Marceau. I know you have never heard of him but you are going to know him better than you know yourself. He is wanted by the authorities in several countries for organizing revolutions and participating in mass murders. He is an associate of "Che" Guevara, right hand man to Castro and takes responsibility for conducting uprisings in many Central and South American countries these past five years. We want you to kill him before he can start anymore shit in this part of the world." Never has the Commander given such a direct order to kill someone. Usually, he beats around the bush for a while and then the orders."

Grasping for the opportunity to interrupt, I asked, "Where am I to find this guy? Who am I going to be working with?"

"You will find Marceau in a small town outside of Quebec, Canada. He was born and raised on a farm in Shawinigan Falls. He will be there from this coming Tuesday until whenever. His mother is dying and he is extremely close to her and wants to see her one last time before she croaks. We are sure that he will be there Tuesday because he is booked on a BOAC jet from London to Montreal. We know when and where he'll be for a while but he could leave any time after her death." The ever-present pitcher of water and a glass was on his desk as he poured the liquid into the glass and sipped, never taking his eyes from me.

"Will he be alone or does he have bodyguards with him?" getting my question in between the sips he was taking.

"Right now, we don't know how many will be with him but he never travels without a minimum of two guards. We do know he is in Belfast; Northern Ireland and he has his reservation on that plane. It is exactly one hundred and four miles from Montreal to Shawinigan Falls. We have no idea what he will be doing at the farm outside of seeing his mother. We have maps of his hometown, the farm and the area surrounding both," again stopping to sip some more water."

"You didn't answer my other question. Am I going to have support or will I be doing this alone?" again staring right into his eyes.

"Field Agent Simon will be going with you. You are familiar with *him I know. You two went on a little weekend visit to your fiancé's hometown about a year ago. You will be the shooter and he will be your bodyguard. You're going to take his Galaxy 500 to Canada acting as two guys going fishing,"* once again taking a sip of the liquid in front of him.

Josiah Simon, Senior Field Agent with the CIA, and former All-American football player with the Florida State University Seminoles. Josey, as he likes to be called, came home with me a year or so before because the Commander felt that anywhere I was going at the time I needed a babysitter. There were many questions about why he was with me because Josey was different than any of my existing friends because he is extremely colored. He is black as coal, to the point that he is almost purple. Many in the company have told me that he was going to be the first colored football player to play for the legendary and in-famous football coach at the University of Alabama, Paul "Bear" Bryant. Something happened that changed Josey's mind about going to 'Bama and he decided to go play for the "Seminoles." I would never ask Josey about why he changed his mind, but I would guess that Bryant went out in the sunlight with him and found out Josey wasn't white. I bet he was kicking himself many times for the loss Alabama suffered when Josey decided to go to Florida State.

One reason I love working with Josey is his 1964 Ford Galaxy 500, two-door hardtop with a SOHC 427 Cammer Challenger engine automobile. This is the fastest car I have ever ridden in but have never driven. It would be exceedingly difficult not to have a good relationship with Agent Simon because he is extremely easy going. There is no doubt in anyone's mind that he will take a bullet intended for you to make sure you're safe. Also, and this is quite important, when he is with you, there is no doubt who is in charge.

As we continued the briefing, the man sitting in the dark decided to join us. It was Sean Callahan, my CIA handler on my first mission to Vietnam. Why was he hiding in the dark? What did he have to contribute to this mission? Why the secrecy?

The Commander started to speak. "I asked Sean to join us regarding Marceau. He is doing this against his will because he is still dedicated to the IRA cause and he feels that betraying Marceau is going against his beliefs in Northern Ireland. He has received pertinent information regarding Marceau leaving England and arriving in Canada. He has refused to go with you on this mission and that's why Agent Simon is going instead," taking his usual sip of water before continuing.

Turning to Sean, the Commander nodded, letting the Irishman con-
tinue with the briefing. "Marceau will arrive in Montreal on BOAC
flight 127 at 1146. It will take about forty-five minutes for him and his
bodyguards to retrieve their bags and clear customs. I would expect
him to have a car at the front entrance that will take him directly to
the farm. Now his mother's house is five miles outside of the town to
the north. It is a small farm with the main house in the middle with a
large barn to the northwest side of the main house. The land around
the main house was cleared of all trees and bushes for one hundred
yards on all sides. Just outside the clearing are woods and marsh as far
as the eye can see. There are no other roads or paths into the farm other
than from the main road," with this Sean finished his part in the briefing
and the Commander started to speak again.

"Excuse me, sir. I don't want to be a pain in the ass and Sean we
were in on a successful mission, but I am concerned that you won't be
on this one. I know you are loyal to the people back in Northern Ireland
but even when you speak of Marceau, you have a kind of reference to
him. My question is that you are giving us all sorts of vital information,
how do I know you won't be doing the same thing with him in a couple
of days?" looking directly into his eyes.

As I glanced at the Commander, he had that look as if his head was
going to explode. He went to say something but Sean interrupted.

"It's all right Forrest. I'll handle this. Jim, we do go a little way back
because of your first mission and if I do say so myself, I helped you
and your team get out of there alive. I am committed to the cause back
home and if anyone gets in the way of that then we will have problems.
Marceau has done that. He has committed too many revolutions with
Che and he has forgotten our battle and that is just not acceptable. I
will give you as much information about him that I can but I will not
be there when you kill him. He has done some good things for the cause
so I will honor him by not accompanying you." trying to show a slight
smile when he finished.

As the Commander stared daggers at me, he spoke up, "I don't want
the mother hurt. Bodyguards and Marceau, I don't care about but you
are to leave her alone. Let her die in peace," again taking another sip
of the water.

"How quick do you want this mission done," a simple but strange
question as I looked directly at Sean.

"As quickly as you want. I don't know how long he will be staying
at the farm. I would imagine if the old lady were on her last legs then

he will remain until she is dead. Best plan would be wait until she dies and then take him out." looking at me with a little bit of hatred in his eyes.

We stayed in the meeting for another hour. Josey came in to join us and Sean brought out the latest pictures of Marceau. I know how much the Commander respects Sean and he would never expect him to turn on us. I have looked at Sean's face as he speaks about Marceau. I have this feeling that this murderer is something more to Sean than just a "freedom fighter."

Marceau is five feet, ten inches in height and he weighs approximately two hundred pounds. He has black hair, blue eyes, and a fair complexion. There is a scar over his right eye which causes the lid to droop. He speaks several languages but English and French are the ones he uses the most.

Kenneth Pierre Marceau was born in Shawinigan Falls, Quebec on May 14, 1930, to mother, Marie Theresa and father, Jacques Pierre Marceau. Father was a leader in the "Mouvement Souverainiste du Quebec." (Quebec Sovereignty Movement) He was shot dead when police tried to arrest him for anti-government activities when Kenneth was only nine years old. Marceau quit school in his hometown when he was fourteen years old to help work on the family farm. He became involved in the sovereignty movement and when he was fifteen, he was the main suspect in the bombings of government buildings in and around Quebec City. At age sixteen he left Canada, went to Moscow, and attended the General Staff Academy. Founded in 1936, it is intended for the best and brightest officers in the Soviet Armed Forces. Most attendees had to have previous military experience, but with Kenneth they made an exception. Upon graduation, he was sent to Cuba to work with the newly established Dictator, Fidel Castro, and his second in command, Ernesto "Che" Guevara. Guevara and Marceau became immediate friends and they were seen everywhere together in Havana. They even traveled to and from South America many times where they were in constant touch with the revolutionaries in Brazil. Marceau is credited with the overthrow of Brazilian President Joao Goulart and for the establishment of the Revolutionary junta led by future president, General Rene Barrientos Ortuno. From the success they had in Brazil, Guevara and Marceau went to the Republic of the Congo and formed the revolutionary group known as "Simbas," from the Kiswahili language meaning "lion." The rebels under the direction of future Prime Minister Patrice Lumumba created the rebel state called. "The People's Republic of the Congo," with the capital being Stanleyville and named Christopher Gbenye as President. Once the Congo fell, Marceau set up the revolutionary tribunals which had tens of thousands of loyalist murdered.

From the Congo, Guevara moved onto several small revolutions in Central and South American and Marceau went back to Moscow. He then traveled back and forth to Cuba from the USSR and participated in the "Cuban Missile Crisis" and the showdown between then 1st Secretary of the Communist Party Nikita Khrushchev and then President of the United States John F. Kennedy. After the crisis was over and everyone seemed to "stand down," Marceau disappeared, with many thinking he had been purged because of Cuba. From the assassination of Kennedy to about nine months ago, no one heard or saw Marceau until a picture of him was in the local newspaper in Belfast. It was rumored that he was involved again with several bombings to many British Army barracks in and around the Northern Ireland capital.

Once we were finished with the briefing, I went out to my car and started to put together everything I thought I would need for our trip. The Commander told me that I wouldn't have to check into HQMC (Headquarters Marine Corps) because he has us leaving in two hours. As Josey brought his big car around and parked next to mine, I got a little jealous because here was an agent with one sweet ride and me with a 58 Plymouth Fury.

As the big engine roared down the highway, we were passing the big East Coast cities, such as Philadelphia, Newark, and finally New York City. We decided to go into the city and get something to eat. There is a fascinating restaurant in Times Square called the Automat. They have a wall that has all sorts of doors on it that when you put in some money, the door unlocks and you take out your food. I remember going there when I was young with my mother and father. Finishing our meal, we got back on the highway and it was no time at all when we entered the State of Connecticut. Passing the capital of Hartford, we then entered my home state of Massachusetts. Springfield and then Worcester came roaring past on Route 9 and coming into Sturbridge. Memories came flashing back of how our 4th grade class came to "Old Sturbridge Village" on a class trip. Sturbridge Village is an actual town that operates as if they were back in the Revolutionary time. As I just sat there and thought, "How everything in my life has changed with the stroke of an M14 rifle"

"You want to stop and see your folks while we are up this way?"

Josey asked as the skyline of Boston came into view.

"No, not today. They will ask too many questions on what we are doing here and where we are going and what we will be doing in Canada. I just don't want to lie to them again, but thanks for asking." looking at him like a big, big brother.

Getting off the Mass Pike and onto the Southeast Expressway just south of downtown, we proceed north past the Boston Garden, home of the Celtics and Bruins and into Charlestown.

"I remember this road. You want to stop and say hi to Linda or do you just want to keep going?" He never turned to look at me but stared straight ahead.

"No, for the same reason I don't want to see my folks, too many questions to answer and not sure she'd believe me this time. The last time you were with me she just couldn't understand why you were there, even after I explained things to her."

Now he turned and looked at me for a split second.

"What things?" was all he said.

I told her that I was learning something new about our job, surveillance and you were with me to teach me the ropes."

He giggled as I explained.

"And she bought that shit?" was the only thing he said.

"Hook, line and sinker. What can I say, she loves me and believes every lie I've ever told her and there have been a few." I then went on and told him about me going to Disneyland before reporting to Pendleton and missing her graduation.

When I finished, he just kept shaking his head and saying, "I can't believe she still is with you after that or that you actually want to get married. This was her big day and you would rather go to a kid's amusement park than see her graduate. You are a piece of work, my man." He didn't sound as if he approved of what I did but it's past now and I can't take it back.

The highway stopped on the other side of the Mystic River Bridge as we were approaching the border of New Hampshire on a two-lane road. Continuing into New Hampshire we decided to stop for the night in the capital, Concord. The next day we traversed onto smaller roads into Maine. These roads would take us to every small town from Bath to the border of Canada. As we entered the state of Maine, we decided to stop to eat in Bangor. When we finished, we got onto US Route 201N to the Canadian border. It is amazing when you cross the border between the United States and Canada that the two towns change *names. At the border crossing on the US side, it is Jackman, Maine and when you cross, not three feet from the US border you are now in Armstrong, Quebec, Canada.*

"What brings you gentlemen to our country?" the Royal Canadian Mountie asked leaning over and looking through the driver's window.

"Just on vacation, sir. Hope to do some fishing up around Shawinigan Falls. We want to camp out and play a little golf also. No real plans just trying to get some rest from the humdrum in the States." Josey is one person who thinks fast.

"Shawinigan Falls, you say. Yes, they have all those things you are looking for. I hope you have a great vacation and then you tell your friends. How long are you staying up here?" The Mountie starting to finish his conversation.

I don't know why I answered and didn't just let Josey continue his conversation with the officer seeing he was doing so well. Josey went to say a week and I for some unknown reason blurted out, "No more than a month."

"Well, what is it? A week or a month? You fellas don't seem to have the times down to well. Why don't you pull your car over by the shack and we can discuss your answers." As he stood up and put his right hand on the handle of the pistol that was in his holster.

"No need to get to alarmed, Sergeant. My friend here has just broken up with his fiancé. I should say she dumped him. He's kind of out of it as you can expect." Giving a little wink at the end of the sentence.

"I've been married three times so I know exactly how that is," looking through Josey's window at me. "What happened young fella? Another guy?"

"I really don't know. Everything was going great and we were going to get married in the fall. Suddenly I get this letter telling me it's over and she never wants to see me again. It's awful, just awful." Suddenly unexpectedly I start to cry for effect and that sealed the deal.

"Sorry about that, young fella. Remember there are more fish in the sea, just get back out there and drop your hook. Okay fellas, you can go and enjoy Canada," waving us through without another glance.

As we pulled straight ahead, I looked at Josey and said, "I am so sorry about **opening** *my big mouth. I don't know what made me do that because you were doing so well. From now on, whoever is driving is the one who speaks. That okay with you?" I said patting him on the shoulder.*

Turning southwest on QC-173N, we take this highway all the way to Quebec City. Josey says that we should spend the night here and in the morning head toward Shawinigan Falls. We decide to eat at the hotel instead of going out in the city. This way we can avoid any questions local gentry may ask. After supper we decide to go back to our room and get our gear in order. I have taken my haversack into the hotel when we checked in but left the other equipment in the trunk of the Galaxy. Closing the door to our room, I proceed to take the Remington out and start to clean it. When I finish with the rifle, I start cleaning the scope. Usually for a job like this one I only take between five to ten bullets, but for some reason I have taken a whole box and I now start cleaning all that's in the box. This means that I now have fifty rounds to my disposal and in my mind, I am hoping upon hope I won't need them all.

The next morning, I awake early or should I have said early for me. It is still dark as we head toward the car and Marceau's farm. Driving on the QC-40W out of the city there is hardly any traffic on the road. Approaching Trois-Revieres (Three Rivers) we turn onto QC-155N and head toward the farmhouse. Past the town of Shawinigan Falls is a turn off 153Rue. We decide to take this and drive through the village of Grand-Mere and approach the farm from the north. Parking deep in the woods, we head for the farm through the fields of the few farms in this area. One good thing about Marceau's mother's farm is that it is the only property on the north side of the road.

As we approach the farm through the fields, the sun is just coming up from the east. Not only did the farm have a lot of land but it also has an overabundance of creeks and rivers. By the time we got to the edge of the field that overlooks the farmhouse, Josey and I were both soaked from the waist down. Approaching, we start to crawl to the edge of the field where we can get a look at the farm. I put my clenched fist up to stop. Using the binoculars that Josey brought, I could see at least eight men standing out front of the main house. The alarming thing about them is they were wearing the uniforms of the Royal Canadian Mounted Police. Passing the binoculars to him to check out what I have just seen, I motion to him to fall back into the woods.

"What do you make of this?" as we come to a clearing in the woods. "They have more Mounties in front of that house than cops at Police Headquarters in Boston." shaking my head while whispering.

"I wonder what they are doing there. Do you think they are here to arrest Marceau when he arrives?" Josey asked, making a great point.

"They looked too relaxed to be an arresting squad. They would have men out on the road to warn them that he was arriving. When we passed a few hours ago I didn't see anyone out there. No, they are a greeting unit or even a squad to protect him. We will need to wait to see what happens when he arrives. He should be here within a few hours. Let's just check out the reception he gets and then we can go from there." whispering to Josey but in my mind, I was thinking of a worse outcome.

We made our way back to the spot at the edge of the field. Lying on the cold ground for over an hour, I motioned for him to move back but suddenly a disturbance started at the front of the main house. Men started to run around until they were lined up in a straight line. As a large Oldsmobile came up the road, the front door of the farmhouse opened and out stepped a senior officer of the Canadian Mounties. He was all "spit and polish" and acted as if he was the official greeter for this despicable human being.

As the car came to a stop in front of the house, the officer and another police officer opened both rear doors. A dark-haired individual came from the rear right door. As soon as half the man's silhouette was through the opening, I knew immediately that it was Kenneth Pierre Marceau

Snapping to attention and saluting, the senior officer shook Marceau's hand profusely. Turning, he started to wave his arms everywhere, saying something that made Marceau smile. As I continued to watch this homecoming process, Josey has taken out a little black box and headphones. Placing the headphones on just one ear, he points the box toward Marceau. As the two continue speaking to each other, Josey is telling me what they are saying.

"Excellency, we have a dozen men throughout the farmland for your protection. No one will be able to get in or out without us knowing. You may remain here with your mother as long as you wish." speaking to Marceau and waving his arms giving orders to his minions.

I motioned to Josey to move back to our position in the woods. I needed to speak to him right away, but I also wanted to be in a place that we couldn't be seen or heard. The woods and clearing were like huge sound speakers. Sound carries further than anyone might imagine. As we got to the place we both thought safe, Josey walked about thirty paces in all directions making sure we wouldn't be seen. Returning in over fifteen minutes we both sat down, and I started to speak in a loud whisper.

"What do you make of this whole mess? What the hell is that Mountie calling him Your Excellency for? I need you to get out of here quick and get somewhere that you can contact the Commander. Tell him everything that is happening and that we will need at least ten if not twenty agents here by tomorrow afternoon. I will also need more bullets for the Remington and a machine gun, like the ones we used in Cuba. Also, find out why Marceau is portraying someone that he can be called 'Your Excellency.' Do you think you can get out of here and be back by tomorrow afternoon? I don't want to wait any longer than that because we don't know how long the old lady will last," trying to act less anxious than I actually felt.

Josey emphatically stated that he could do this. I then explained to him why I wanted the agents. After explaining everything to him over and over, I told him to make sure the Commander knew that these are real Mounted Police and killing just one of them could cause an international incident. I also told him that I would need at least two to three grenades but didn't tell him why. After explaining everything that I could think of and having Josey repeat it back to me, I shook his hand and he was off.

I decided to stay where I was and see if anything out of the ordinary was going to happen. I took the binoculars out of the sack that Josey had left behind and scoped out the area in front of me, but nothing out of the ordinary was happening. As the hours rolled by, still nothing unusual was happening. They changed the roving guards every two hours, but Marceau never came out of the house. His two bodyguards that accompanied him from London did come out every so often to kind of stretch and look around, but he was never with him. As night came, it became quite cold, but I did have an extra amount of cloths on, which Josey suggested I take as we packed for the trip. Night turned into day with the sun coming up in the east but again nothing out of the ordinary was going on at the farmhouse. As the sun came up over the tree line, Ken Marceau decided to come out of the main house. Looking around for a second and then almost sprinting toward the barn, he approached the side door which was next to the large white barn door. One of his guards rolled the big door back and he started to walk into the barn through that opening. I lost sight of him, but he wasn't in there for long. He reappeared in about ten minutes holding a wire basket which was full of white eggs. Lying in the field about four hundred yards from my target thinking, "You can take the boy out of the country, but you definitely can't take the country out of the boy." Hopefully, he'll do this whole thing again tomorrow, but he will be getting bullets instead of eggs.

The day slowly went by and again it was the same as the previous days, nothing. The Royal Canadian Mounted Police changed security every two hours to the minute. I started to write down somethings I thought I could use in the future. After a while I dozed off but I really didn't get much sleep because when there was a noise, I was fully awake.

I could tell the afternoon was ending by the sun in the sky. As the sun slowly went down over the trees to the west, Josey suddenly appeared. He was all smiles, but I decided I'd wait till we got to our place in the woods before I started questioning him.

As we got to the edge of the woods, the first thing he handed me was a cloth bag with five grenades in it. He went on to tell me that ten agents had come up from Boston yesterday and were in place on the other side of the farm. He also told me that the Commander had discovered that Marceau had a Russian passport and he was impersonating a high-ranking Russian Politburo executive, thus "Your Excellency." Josey took out of his "bag of tricks" a walkie-talkie. This would allow us to speak with the agents on the other side of the farm. Josey said that the lead agent knows exactly what I want, and he'll be waiting for further instructions. I went on to tell him about Marceau going into the barn earlier this morning to get eggs. As we were speaking, the radio made some noise. Josey put it to his ear and listened. The person on the other end was speaking loud enough for me to hear the conversation.

"Agent Simon. A hearse or station wagon from town is pulling into the driveway. It looks as if the old lady has "bought the farm." [I thought this was a terrible remark to use seeing where we were] Will this hinder our plans on getting the others out of the area?" the agent on the other end asked.

Josey looked at me for an answer, but I signaled that I'd speak with the agent.

"This is Sergeant Coleman. Whom am I speaking with?"

"This is Agent John Tracy from the Boston office, Sergeant. What do you want us to do now that the hearse is here?" which was the correct question to ask.

"I'm sure they will take her body away, but I'm not sure he'll accompany her. If he does accompany her, there is no guarantee that he'll return to the farm. If it looks as if he's going to go with the hearse, then we will have to accelerate our plans. Have your men spread out and be ready for anything. If he stays here this evening and plans to go out tomorrow morning, then we will proceed with the original objective. I can't imagine it will take long for them to load the old lady into the car. We should have an idea within the next hour or so, what he's going to do." as I was finishing, I could see the hearse coming up the drive.

Josey and I went back to our original viewpoint and waited. The two men who were in the hearse had gone into the house by now. About an hour later one of the men from the funeral home came out and retrieved the gurney from the back of the wagon. He rolled it inside and less than fifteen minutes they both came out pushing the gurney to the back of the hearse. Loading the body didn't take much time and then the driver spoke briefly to the RCMP officer, got into the wagon, and drove off. No one else moved so it looked as if Marceau was here for the evening.

Josey went off a little way and relayed the news to our Boston agents. As the evening came, the movement on the outside of the house seemed to diminish. They didn't change the guards as often as before and two cars with two policemen in each left the farm about midnight.

"What do you make of that? Two cars left and no replacements have shown up. Very strange if you ask me." whispering to Josey on what was going on.

We then went back to our little place at the edge of the woods so I could explain what we were going to do once the sun came up. The agents on the other side of the farm were going to make a racket as if it were the beginning of WWIII. I would then throw a few grenades into the garden of the main house making the bodyguards come out of the house. I would then take them out and wait for Marceau to show his face. Once he did, I would put a bullet in his head and off we go. While I'm doing this, Josey would get our car and bring it up to where I was shooting. Everything was perfect on paper but as we both knew nothing is ever that perfect in real time.

"What if he doesn't come out? What if he wants to make a stand in the house?" Josey always had questions that put a damper on my plans.

"Then we go into the house after him. We definitely can't leave until we know he's dead."

Just then the radio again made the same noise as before.

"What's happening on your end, Tracy?" I said into the speaker.

"May have a problem here, Sergeant. A military truck is coming up the highway. Hopefully, it will keep on going, but it's slowing down so I don't think it's going to pass," the agent was yelling into the radio.

Just as he stopped speaking, I could hear gunfire coming from the other side of the farm.

"What's happening over there?" I yelled into the speaker.

"We are taking heavy ground fire coming from where the truck has stopped," Agent Tracy was yelling back.

"Can you see who's firing at you?" Why I asked that I don't know because it doesn't matter in a fire fight like this.

"Try to keep them engaged while I work from this end. I'll be in touch," shutting off my speaker.

Just as I did that, the front door of the house came flying open and the two bodyguards came running out. They were both carrying AK-47 semi-automatic rifles. Fortunately, I was ready for them. I picked up the Remington and sighting in on the guard on the left I squeezed off a round. I didn't even look to see where I hit him because I knew he was dead. I took another round from the pocket of my shirt, put it in the chamber, snapped it shut and sighted in on the other guard, who was now starting to run toward the barn. Just as I was squeezing off the round, gunfire started coming at us from behind. Josey spun around to fire back just as the rifle recoiled in my shoulder. The second guard dropped just as he was reaching for the door of the barn.

I looked around to see who was firing at us, but as I turned, I caught a glimpse out of the corner of my eye a face in the window. It was Marceau, looking out but not too closely. He was about three feet from the glass which would make an exceedingly difficult shot.

"I'll be right back," I yelled to Josey who had his machine gun firing double time. He was firing in all sorts of directions but not aiming at anyone or anything.

I started to crawl out of the protection we had established and headed toward the farmhouse. As I crawled, I wondered who that was behind us shooting like crazy but not really hitting anything. Crawling leaves anyone vulnerable to ground fire and it doesn't give anyone the capability to go in any direction with speed.

"What am I going to do if Marceau has a grenade?" as I kept crawling and trying to get those kinds of thoughts out of my head.

As I approached the farmhouse, I had at least fifteen more yards to go. I stopped and rolled over onto my back. I was facing the side of the house with the front door on my right. Still carrying the cloth bag with the grenades, I take one out and now turning on my left side, I pull the pin and lob the heavy object toward the right window in front of me. The grenade hits the sill of the window and bounces down in the dirt but had exploded before it hit the ground. The explosion blows out the window and the bottom part below the sill, leaving a gaping hole. Immediately I roll onto my stomach and having the Remington at the ready with a round in the chamber, I wait, pointing the rifle directly at the front door of the farmhouse.

Waiting for Marceau to come out seemed to take forever. No return fire is coming from the house but neither did Marceau appear. Again, I roll on my left side, taking out another grenade from my little pouch. I start to move a little closer for my next throw. Suddenly small arm fire starts coming from the farmhouse. Rounds were hitting in front of me and to my right. I could see him in the window, but he was further back, which made his firing at me hard.

Taking a grenade from my pouch, I pull the pin, wait for a second and then launch the heavy object toward the hole in the side of the house. Again, it hits the top of what remained of the sill but this time it goes forward into the room. Seconds later the explosion blows out the remainder of the window and the front of the house.

Rolling on my stomach and aiming at the front door I wait, knowing that he had to come out sooner or later. I didn't have to wait that long. Marceau comes out of the house, hitting the front door screen dazed and bloody. His left arm just hangs to his side with blood running down from his shoulder. His face is bloody and distorted with his left eye completely closed and disfigured. Disorientated and not knowing where he is going, he has nothing in his hand. Staggering he brings his right arm up to block the light that now was shining directly into his face. As he did this, he left his right side vulnerable and I squeeze the trigger. The jolt was expected but lying in the prone position it seemed a lot more exaggerated. I knew exactly where the round was going and it hit him in the temple, right beside his right ear. I knew he was dead before he hit the ground, so I turned and started to crawl back to where I left Josey. I stood and started to run bent over, but the firing suddenly stopped as quickly as it had started. As I reached Josey, I could see men retreating into the deeper part of the woods.

Josey got on the radio to see how the agents out front were faring. Agent Tracy was yelling that the firing had diminished but there was still firing going on, but all his people seemed all in one piece. I yelled for him to get his men out of harm's way as soon as possible. He was to take his men and head southwest toward Montreal. I assumed the

RCMP had contacted Quebec and told them they were taking fire and needed assistance, so reinforcements would be coming up the road at any minute. Rather than go back the way Tracy's people had come, I decided it would be better going the other way, heading toward Shawinigan Falls and then toward the border.

As I was telling Tracy what to do, Josey had run into the woods to retrieve his car. Pulling up to where I was, we put our weapons in the trunk. I got into the passenger side and we headed right down the driveway and out onto 15 Rue.

As we traveled down the highway, the radio once again made that strange noise. I picked it up and just said "hello" into the receiver.

"Sergeant, I hope our little charade didn't hinder your mission. We were aware who Kenneth Marceau was and what it meant to your country. We got notice a few days back from Washington asking for our assistance. We put on the rouse that we were there to protect him because he had a diplomatic passport, which we knew was false. The men in the truck were also RCMP and were shooting blanks as were the men in the woods. We will go back to the farm in an hour or so and find the bodies. We will blame the French renegades for this and let them explain to their superiors how they had nothing to do with it. You can now slow down and have a very save trip home. God Bless and do come back to Canada when you can actually enjoy our country," with this he disconnected.

Looking at Josey, I just shook my head and we both started to laugh.

Turning onto QC-1555W, I finally tried to relax, thinking that we were on our way back home to "God Knows What Would Be Next."

"What the hell is that noise?" I can hear something that's loud in the distance, but I don't recognize it. I'm yelling as loud as I can, but no one can hear me. This blanket or whatever it is isn't moving. I'm pushing as hard as I can against the top but nothing. The noise outside is getting louder and I still can't figure out what it is. Louder and louder like it's going to come right into where I'm lying. Breathing is becoming quite difficult and the noise is becoming unbearable.

THANK GOD SOMEONE HEARS ME

As the plane was taxiing into position, a Catholic chaplain was walking around all the dark black bags that were on the ground. He was blessing all the bags and would stop and say a few words over each body which lay inside. As Captain Andy Prete approached the bag in which Jim Coleman's body lay, he dipped the aspergillum into the container, scooping up some holy water and was about to toss it on Jim's bag.

"What the hell was that?" he said to himself. "Did I see what I thought I saw or have I been out here in the heat and humidity all day that I'm starting to imagine things?"

"David, come over here for a second," the captain yelled at his assistant who was putting the bags into the bleak wooden coffins.

"Yes, sir, what can I do for you, Captain?" Religious Affairs Specialist David Opfer was really bored in what he was doing and he was getting tired of lifting dead bodies and putting them into the boxes. He's been in country for over four months and this is all he's been doing since arriving. As a chaplain's assistant, this was his main job along with being Captain Prete's altar server.

"David, I know this sounds crazy but I think I saw this bag move. Is there a doctor around so we may check on the body?" he was almost yelling at his assistant.

"Father, sir. Sometimes the bodies, which are dead, will move on their own. It has something to do with the nerves becoming relaxed. Like they are moving into place for the last time," Specialist Opfer said with conviction.

Dave Opfer had no idea what he was talking about but he thought, "It will move this chaplain on his way. He's a hell of a nice guy and he's been great to work for but why in hell do I always have the one chaplain in this man's Army who is holier than thou." thinking to himself and shaking his head.

"David, just humor me for a minute will you. I really think I saw this bag move and I don't think it was just a bodily reaction. Can you get someone to come and check it out? Please." Chaplain Prete was almost begging his subordinate to do what should have been an order.

"If it will make you happy, Father, no problem. I'll get a stethoscope, open this bag, and check out the body myself. Now remember, Father, sometimes there isn't a body in the bag, just parts of a body, like a leg or arm, not even a head." the specialist sounding sarcastic and trying to have the chaplain change his mind.

Seeing that the chaplain wasn't going to change his mind, David muttered something under his breath and turned and went to find someone with a stethoscope.

He returned just a few minutes later with a Practical Nursing Specialist who was wearing a white jacket and had a stethoscope hanging around his neck.

"Be careful, Captain. I'd stand back if I were you. The smell can be overwhelming at times, especially in this heat. He's been in this bag for a while so the body is starting to rot," now turning toward the bag and pulling down the zipper.

Opening Jim's shirt, he placed the scope where his heart would be and listened. Nothing. He moved the scope around Jim's chest but again he could hear nothing.

"Sorry, Captain. I can't hear a thing. I checked his heart and around it and heard nothing. Not a sound at all. I'll check his neck to see if there is a pulse there," moving the scope to Coleman's neck.

"I told you, Cap" stopping in mid-sentence and holding up his hand.

"What's the matter? Do you hear something?" Father Prete was asking the Practical Nursing Specialist.

"I hear something, a beat. Don't talk, sir. Let me listen." bending down closer to the body thinking this made it sound clearer.

Suddenly, he straightened up and yelled over to some others standing by the other coffins. "Hey, one of you guys get the doctor. Make it snappy. I need him right away."

The chaplain was now pacing back and forth beside the open bag with Jim Coleman's body just lying there.

"What did you hear? Is he still alive?" He was almost pleading for an answer.

"I don't really know what I hear, sir. I think I can hear a faint heartbeat but I'm not sure. That's why I want one of the doctors to listen." He was chalk white with fright.

In less than a minute an Army Lieutenant Colonel was running toward them.

"What you got Bruce?" as he took the stethoscope from around his neck and put both ends into his ears. As he bent over Coleman's lifeless body, Jim's eyes came wide open.

"Motherfucker." Colonel Wallace jumped about three feet

backwards. "Sorry about that, Chaplain. This man is alive. Get a gurney and take him out of that bag immediately. Do you know his name?"

The Colonel was now starting to bark orders as fast as he could. "Get me an ambulance. We need to get this man to the hospital as quickly as possible. What's his name? Check the toe tag it'll be on it. Padre, you just saved this man's life." as the Colonel went to Coleman's feet to look for the toe tag but there was none.

"All the manifest says about him, sir is 'Cia.' His last name must be Cia. I'll get the original manifest and check for his name," Specialist Opfer finally spoke up. He turned and started running toward the large shack that was not too far from where they were standing.

"How did you know he was alive?" the Colonel turned to speak with Chaplain Prete.

"I saw the bag move or a least I thought I did. I called over Mr. Opfer and he got someone with a stethoscope. He checked thoroughly and all at once he heard a sound of a heartbeat. He was the one who saved his life, not me." The Chaplain was trying to give David some credit for what they had done.

As the Chaplain was looking all around Corporal Coleman's body, he could hear the sirens of the ambulance coming. A drab green truck with a huge red cross on its sides with United States Army printed underneath came pulling up to where they were standing.

The medics jumped out of the truck and pulled a gurney from the rear. They rolled it to where Coleman's body was lying on the ground. Gently, they picked him up and placed him on the gurney. Without waiting for any orders, they started running toward the truck but were careful not to tip the gurney over. As they fixed the gurney in place, Chaplain Prete got into the back with Jim. Before he could sit down, the ambulance started up quickly, knocking him against the closed door of the truck. He finally sat down, took a hold of Jim's hand, and started to pray all the way to the hospital.

As the ambulance came into the loading zone for the hospital, it suddenly turned, knocking the Chaplain to the floor. Stopping, the driver put the vehicle in reverse and started to back in. Chaplain Prete looked out the back window and read the sign above the door, "61st Medical Battalion, Cam Ranh Bay, Republic of South Vietnam."

As the ambulance came to a stop, the back doors came flying open and two nurses, two orderlies and a doctor were waiting. Once the orderlies got the gurney out of the ambulance, one of the nurses put an oxygen mask on Coleman. Without hesitation, they started to push the gurney in to the hospital at a very quick pace. All the way into the operating room, with Chaplain Prete still holding Jim's hand. As they were going to enter the operating theatre, one of the nurses said, "This is as far as you go, Chaplain. He's in our hands now."

"No, my dear. He's always been in the good Lord's hands. You are just his handmaiden." Smiling, he let go of the Jim's hand and made the sign of the cross on Jim's forehead. Leaning over the body he whispered, "He will take good care of you, son. I'll see you when you come out. Don't give up the fight." With that he straightened up and wiped away his tears. Quickly, the ones who had been waiting wheeled Coleman's body into the operating room.

The chaplain walked outside of the hospital and started toward the Army compound. He went through the main gate and gave a half salute to the MPs stationed there. He went past a number of tents with three-foot high wooden floors. He passed the communication tower which was in charge of all the comings and goings at this huge base. He walked for another hundred yards until he came to the building he was looking for. He walked up the four steps and opened the door. As he entered, he looked above the door, seeing the sign which read, "Chapel."

"David, we are going to say a mass for that young man who is in the operating room fighting for his life." He spoke to the young corporal who also just came into the building from the flight line. Specialist Opfer just smiled and started to prepare for the Mass.

"Did you ever find out what his name was, Dave?" as the Chaplain started to put on his vestments.

"I think he's Mexican or Filipino, maybe even Italian with a last name like Cia," as the chaplain's assistant got the water and wine in place.

Suddenly the Chaplain's Assistant Opfer turned to the chaplain, shaking a little saying, "Did you ever think of what would have happened to Cia if you hadn't seen the bag move? He would have been buried alive," shaking his head as his whole body continued shaking. Chills went up the chaplain's spine and he shook his head saying, "I never really thought about that. What a horrible way to die. Let's get cracking. We'll say this Mass while he's still in surgery. After we are finished, I want to go back to the hospital and be there when he opens his eyes and wakes up." talking directly to his assistant.

"I know you have thought of this, but what if he doesn't wake up? What if he dies on the table?" trying to prepare the new chaplain of the horrors of war. "I know that could very well happen, but I don't believe he will die because he's been through so much already and I know the good Lord will take care of him. I just wonder what outfit he's with and who left him there on the tarmac? Whoever it was must have thought he was dead. He had been shot in the head and it looked as if he lost a ton of blood. His uniform or black pajamas were soaked with blood, his own. Come to think of it, he didn't have a uniform. He's dressed like the Viet Cong. Do you think that he's one of those "White Russians" that everyone's been talking about?"

(It was well known that the Russians had personnel that spoke and acted like American soldiers. They would infiltrate behind American lines and even enter American bases to get intel for the North Vietnamese. This went on for most of the war.)

"I don't know, sir. When he wakes up, I would imagine he'll have a lot of questions to answer and he will expect a lot of questions of his answered. I would think the big brass will be coming down to talk to Mr. Cia." He helped the priest into his vestments and they went to start the mass for their unknown person in the operating room.

When the mass finished and Chaplain Prete got out of his vestments, he immediately started to walk back to the hospital and check on his new "friend." Was he a "White Russian" as the Chaplain had said earlier in the day? According to the debriefing he got when he first arrived in country, there weren't that many American personnel here. This stranger could be with some "special unit." He's heard a lot of talk about these "special, highly trained, special operation units" that free wheel not only in the south but also up in North Vietnam also. No one knows who they are, what country they belong to or where their main base is, but rumor has it that they are highly trained killers. Could this man be one of them? He's now starting to think about the Green Berets who were operating up north in the mountain region near the DMZ and Pleiku. Whoever this man is, the chaplain felt obligated to contact his family immediately, if he has one.

As he entered the hospital, Captain Andy looked around to see if he recognized anyone he would know from a few hours before. He keeps walking toward the operating rooms, when a nurse that he had seen at last Sunday's mass comes out the door.

"Excuse me, Lieutenant. I'm looking for the young man that was brought in a couple of hours ago. He was found alive on the tarmac in a body bag. They were going to operate on him immediately and I was wondering how he is doing? Do you know his condition or could you find out for me?" asking these many questions of this Army nurse.

"He's still in surgery, Father. I don't know his condition and it's very tough to find out while it's still going on. I will have the chief surgeon see you when they are finished. Better still, I'll have him call you at the Chapel when he is done. Is that okay?" With that she turned and went back through the door she just came out of.

"Typical Army. Never can get a straight answer from anyone," talking to himself as he left the hospital to go back to his dismal office.

Jim could hear voices but he couldn't see anything. He could feel something inside his head that was rubbing against his skull. A male voice was asking for all sorts of things which he hadn't the faintest idea what they were. There was a light coming through his closed eyes. Suddenly his eyes opened and when he could see, there was a Vietnamese doctor standing over him.

"You cock-sucker. I've been captured," shouting loudly, as his right hand moved quickly and grabbed the doctor by the throat.

"Get him off me" the doctor shouted. "Grab his arm. Be careful of his head." Major Thomas Lee kept shouting and trying to get Jim's hand from his throat while not trying to injure any more of his patients open wound.

A nurse dropped the tray that she was working from and two orderlies came running up to the table to grab Jim's arms. They forced them back to his side but it took both to hold him down. As one held his arm, the other orderly got a piece of linen and tied his free hand down to the operating table. His left arm had not moved that much, but to be safe, the surgeon yelled for them to tie the other down, also. As Jim was cussing obscenities toward the surgeon, the anesthetist was trying to put the ether mask back on his patient's face. Each time he'd get the mask in position, Jim would shake his head violently and it would come off. Jim was still cursing and calling the Major all sorts of names, yelling about being captured by the VC and something about Dr. Lee's ethnic background. Finally, the anesthetist got the mask secured in place and Jim was starting to go to sleep again.

During all this, the surgeon kept saying to the man on the table, "Easy, fella. We're all in the same Army. I'm Major Lee of the 61st Medical Battalion here in Cam Ranh Bay. You've been seriously wounded and I'm trying to take a bullet out of your head. The wound is still wide open and we need to put you back to sleep again so I can continue. I'm sorry you must go through this, but I have about another two hours here before I'm done. Do you understand what I'm saying to you?"

Jim was almost asleep, but he really didn't hear anything the doctor was saying to him except that his name was Lee and he was in Vietnam, somewhere. He tried to move around but he couldn't and his mind was quickly going to a place he didn't want to be in, dreaming of Linda.

"How in God's name did that happen?" the Major was now screaming.

"Freak thing, sir. He just came out of it suddenly. There was no indication that he was waking up" the anesthetist said, shaking his head.

"Do you realize if he had awakened while I was in his skull what could have happened? I could have ruptured an artery or something worse. His brain is completely exposed. Someone's going to be accountable for this," looking directly at the captain at the end of the table with his hand on the mask.

Chaplain Prete was quite uneasy while waiting for the operation to be finished. While waiting he fiddled around his office and chapel and said the rosary at least three times. There were two other desks in this office which he shared with two other chaplains. He was assigned with an Episcopal minister and a young Jewish fellow from Minnesota just out of rabbinical school. He thought that he didn't just help Catholics but all of them helped each other when it came to soldiers needing solace from a religious.

Andrew Prete grew up in Cranston, Rhode Island to a medium size family. He had a sister and a younger brother both still living back home with his parents. He attended public high school in Cranston where he was quite a football and baseball player. He was so good that his senior year in football, he was chosen all-state and received a full sports scholarship to the University of Notre Dame in Indiana, where he graduated cum laude. While playing baseball for the university, he was approached by the St. Louis Cardinals and offered a contract to play major league baseball. During his time at Notre Dame, he became close friends with one of his professors, a Holy Cross priest Clifford Wirtz. While his friendship grew with the good priest, a transformation happened and he received a call to the religious life.

A major problem though, he was engaged to his high school sweetheart, Barbara Mills. He left one weekend for home, told his mother and father, and then went to see Barbara. As he finished explaining everything to her, she hugged him, said she understood and he left thinking, "Maybe she has another boyfriend." but just one year later Barbara Mills entered the convent.

After graduating from Notre Dame, Andy enrolled at Marquette

University in Chicago to get his degree in theology. After being taught by the Jesuits while attending Marquette, he decided to attend the St. Mark's Seminary in Erie, PA. Rather than be a Jesuit he became a Diocesan priest and was ordained in 1961.

His first assignment was a small parish in Erie named St. Rose of Lima. He enjoyed parish life but deep down he really wanted to do something more as a priest. While hearing confessions one Saturday afternoon, he ran into an Army sergeant who was home on leave. This sergeant changed Father Prete's life forever. He told him about when he was in Korea in 1952 and how the chaplains were the greatest people ever, especially during the war. He told the priest that the chaplains would go out on patrol with all units and comfort the wounded and pray for the dead or dying. How back on base, the chaplains would be there if anyone had any problems no matter how slight they seemed to be. As the sergeant spoke, Father Prete was getting this feeling that he couldn't let go. A week later he was in Pittsburgh to discuss his desire to become a chaplain with his regional bishop. He was surprised to find that his bishop had been a Navy chaplain during World War II. After getting permission from the bishop to go into the chaplain corps, he contacted the head of the chaplain training unit at Fort Benning, Georgia and within three months, Father Andrew Prete said goodbye to his parish in Erie and headed for his basic training in Georgia. Upon finishing his training, Father Prete was sworn in as a Captain in the United States Army. After graduating from basic, and a brand-new Captain, Chaplain Prete was given orders to report to Fort Bragg, right down the road from Fort Benning. When arriving at his new duty station, he was assigned to the 1st Calvary Division and in particular the 11th Airborne Division which was stationed in Seoul, South Korea. After a brief leave, he was ready to depart for Seoul, when his orders were changed and his new assignment was the 61st Medical Battalion, Cam Ranh Bay in the Republic of South Vietnam, arriving in country on October 27, 1963.

As Chaplain Andy, as he loved being called by the men, was saying his daily prayers, the phone on his desk started to ring.

"Chaplains office, Chaplain Prete speaking." as he always answered the phone.

A female voice was on the other end, "Chaplain, this is Lieutenant Finocchi, Rosemary Finocchi from the base hospital. We spoke just a few hours ago regarding the young man that was having brain surgery." She had an incredibly soft voice.

"Yes, Rosemary. How is everything going over there?" as he held his breath fearing the worse.

"Everything went fine, Father. The bullet cut an artery in his head but there was no brain damage. The bullet went around his skull and not into it. The doctor removed all the bullet fragments, but there are still some minute fragments still left in there. The doctor told me to tell you that there is nothing to worry about and the remaining fragments will pass within months. Mr. Cia had lost a lot of blood and his blood pressure went so low you could not get a pulse. That's why whoever left him assumed he was dead."

'Such a reassuring sounding voice.' he thought as he continued speaking with her. "Is he awake? Do we know who he is and what unit he's with? I would like to notify his next of kin as soon as possible." groping for anything positive.

"We had a little problem during surgery. He woke up in the middle of it and attacked Dr. Lee, the surgeon. He's quite strong even in his condition and he also has quite a mouth on him. Called the doctor everything you could think of. By what he was yelling it sounded as if he thought he was captured by the enemy and the doctor was one of them," trying not to laugh.

"Is he going to be in trouble for doing that? You know, hitting an officer." not knowing the protocol when it comes to such things.

"I don't think so because he was still under anesthesia and groggy. It all depends on Major Lee, I suppose. He's kind of a stickler for military protocol. At least I hope he's not going to be in trouble. We still don't know who he is or where he comes from, meaning what unit he belongs too. As you know he wasn't wearing any kind of Army uniform, just the black pajamas as all Vietnamese seem to wear. Have you found out anything about him, Father?" she sounded quite concerned.

"Rosemary, I really don't know where to begin. I know they took his fingerprints upon arrival at the hospital but nothing has come back yet. His last name was on his toe tag and that was Cia. It could be Spanish, Italian, or even Arabic. Oh, my God, I just had a thought. His tag spelled Cia but it was in all capital letters. What if his name isn't Cia but he works for the CIA, the Central Intelligence Agency." Thinking now about the way he was dressed, not in uniform but the way the Viet Cong dress. I know there is a CIA compound in DaNang. I could call down there and find out if they are missing anyone. They won't tell me anything, seeing they are spies themselves, but it's worth the effort.

"Rosemary, thank you for keeping me in the loop. If anything, out of the ordinary comes up or he is ready for visitors, will you let me know?" hanging up as he as finished speaking.

Sitting at his desk, Chaplain Prete was contemplating who to call in DaNang. He knew no one there, not even his counterparts in the Chaplain Corps. Who could he call and what would he say when he got someone? He just kept thinking about it even when he left the Chapel and started walking back to the hospital.

As he entered the ward, he started to look around for Mr. Cia. The Lieutenant he spoke with on the phone was not on duty. As he approached the orderly on duty, he noticed a young man in the bed next to the duty desk. His head and right eye were covered by bandages and there were tubes going in and out of both arms.

"Excuse me. I wonder if you can tell me what bed a Mr. Cia is in?" he said with as much authority that he could muster. "He's right here, Padre." Pointing to the bed next to his desk.

As the chaplain approached the bed, he could see Jim's left eye was closed. He took a chair and moved it closer to the head of the bed to where Jim's face was.

"What do you want?" a voice came from the patient but the lips didn't move and the eye still was closed.

"I came to see how you are doing. My name is Andy Prete. I am the Catholic chaplain here in Cam Ranh Bay." as he started to introduce himself and get comfortable.

"I don't care what your name is and I definitely don't need a Catholic chaplain. You can leave now." Still the left eye has not opened.

"Before I leave can you tell me your full name?" trying to get some much-needed information.

"Why? It's none of your business. If I wanted anyone to know my name, I'd have a name tag." still not opening his eye.

"When you were in the bag, the only name on your toe was Cia. No first name, no unit number or identification code," explaining to someone who really didn't care.

"What the hell are you talking about? What bag? What toe? Are you trying to tell me that they thought I was dead and they put me in a body bag?" With this Jim's left eye opened.

"I was going around blessing all the bags and I saw the one you were in move. I got a medic to open the bag and we discovered you were still very much alive. You just got out of surgery after nine hours," smiling and trying to have Jim relax.

"Did some "gook" doctor operate on me?" Jim's voice started to get very loud.

"Dr. Lee operated on you. He's a Major in the US Army and Chinese American from San Francisco. He said you will make a full recovery." smiling as he spoke.

"Tell me something if you know. Did I grab him by the throat and try to strangle him? I remember something but I thought I was captured by the NVA. We have been trained to resist at any cost." trying to make sense of any of this.

"To answer your question, yes, you did grab the Major by the throat. No one can blame you though. You woke up in the middle of your surgery, not knowing where you were and you went a little crazy. They got you settled down and Dr. Lee continued finishing an exceptionally long and tedious operation. He's one of the best surgeons in the Army."

Jim didn't know what to say and was a little concerned with what the Asian doctor what he was going to say and do to him once he was feeling better.

"So, I owe you for saving my life? Thanks," turning and closing his left eye.

"Can you tell me your real name? I know it's not Cia," trying to make the question sound like a joke.

"No, it's not and no, I won't tell you my name. I need to get back to my unit. I need to get out of here, now." trying to move out of the bed but not really moving at all.

"Is there anyone you need me to call to let them know your alive and that you are here?"

"Nice try, Padre. I give you a name then you know where I'm coming from. No thank you, I can wait. It can't be that long for me to get out of here," sounding more belligerent than usual.

"Don't you want your unit to know you're alive? You must have meant something to them because they brought you back instead of leaving you out in the bush," still trying to gain Jim's trust.

Without thinking Jim yelled out, "Marines don't leave anyone behind. Oh, shit," he said without thinking.

"So, you're a Marine. Are you stationed in DaNang?" asking still more questions.

"You are really a nosey son of a bitch, aren't you?" Jim not caring about his rank.

"That's the trouble with priests. We try to help people who don't want to be helped and they think we are being nosey." The chaplain thought that was the best comeback. "About you getting out of here. I heard the doctors talking to the nurses and they said they were going to send you to Japan to recuperate. They also said you'd be there for a few months then you'd be sent home. What do you think of that?" the chaplain continued talking.

"I'm not going anywhere accept back to my unit. I can't go home if they don't know where I live. I haven't finished what I came here to do. Now get me a secured phone." He hesitated then said, "Please."

"I don't know if the phones here are secure but the phone in my office is. As soon as you're allowed to get out of bed and walk, come to the chapel, and make your phone call. I know you don't trust me, but if you give me the name of the person you want to contact and where he's located, I can make the call," looking into Jim's one good eye.

"I can't wait that long to be able to get out of bed. I need to contact someone in country, DaNang. If I tell you something secret is it like me going to confession?" Jim knew now he needed to trust the chaplain.

"You're a Catholic? Not too many people outside the religion know anything about the sanctity of the confessional. Yes, to answer your question. If you tell me as if we were in confession, then I can't divulge anything you said to me. I'm bound by my faith and orders as a priest not to tell anyone about your confession. This is under the pain of excommunication." He now was serious.

"Let me think about this for a while. Will you come back tomorrow to see me? I'd like that." trying to be as sincere as he could muster.

"You want me to come back tomorrow morning?" Now the padre was trying to play coy.

"Yes, Father, I would like that very much. Before you go, thanks again for saving my life," trying to hold out his hand so the priest could shake it.

"The priest took his hand and squeezed it. "I'll see you tomorrow morning, Mr. Cia."

"It's Jim, Father. Just Jim for now. See you tomorrow." He closed his left eye and started to think of what he would say to the Commander once he got here.

After the priest had left, Jim was in excruciating pain. He started to think of what had just transpired and then he started to talk to himself.

"He doesn't know who I am or what I have done. He does not really know that I am working with the CIA. He knows now that I am a Marine but that was my mistake; he did not figure it out. I want to trust

him, but I do not know if I can. If I tell him anything I must make sure it is in a confession type of atmosphere. That way he cannot tell anyone anything that I have told him. I must contact the Commander; he will know what to do to get me out of here. That son of a bitch let them leave me here, not knowing whether I was dead or alive. I will never forgive him or any of the others for that. I was yelling all the time but they did not pay a bit of attention to me. God, I am in a lot of pain. My head is beating like a bass drum. I got to get something for this pain. I should have told the priest about how much it hurts but what is the sense? He couldn't do anything about it anyway. He would have told the nurses and they could have got me something. God, I wish he were back here now. God, please make the pain stop." as he slowly fell into a coma.

As he lay in his bed, a senior nurse came by to check on him. "What can I do for you?" just talking to him thinking his eyes were just closed but he is awake. As she bent down to check his bandages, she noticed that he hadn't moved and she started to talk directly to him. "Can you hear me, son? Are you okay? Are you having any pain?" now aware that there is no response from her patient.

"My head is killing me. Can I get something for the pain? I feel as if my head is going to explode." talking directly to the nurse but no one can hear him.

"Code Blue, code blue," the nurse is yelling for an adult medical emergency.

Suddenly the ward was in an uproar. Nurses, doctors, and corpsmen were running up to where the nurse was bending over Jim. Stethoscopes were everywhere; both nurses and doctors were listening to whatever was causing Jim to be in this predicament.

As the medical people were working on him, Jim was still talking. *"What is wrong with these people. All I need is a couple of aspirins to get rid of this awful headache. It reminds me of when I was in the helicopter, no one heard me. Oh, my God, am I dying again? Get me the hell out of here."* as his body started to shake out of control.

The doctor that was on duty was going all over Jim's chest with his stethoscope when Jim suddenly started to convulse. Standing straight up, he turned to the nurse and yelled in her ear, "Get me 5cc's of phenobarbital, stat." Then turning back to his patient, he tried to grab both of Jim's shoulders to hold him down. Losing his grip on the right shoulder, Corporal Jamison, one of the orderlies that was standing at bedside, pushed the doctor's hand away and he placed both his hands on the patient's shoulder.

The nurse returned within seconds with the drug that the doctor had ordered. Having the orderly hold down Jim's right arm, the nurse quickly injected the needle into Jim's upper part. Within what seemed like seconds, Jim quickly calmed down and just laid there on his bed.

As Jim was starting to become alert and open his eyes, he looked around at all the people that were at his bed. As his eyes passed by everyone, he suddenly stopped at the small officer that was standing at the foot of his bed, with the gold oak leaf on his color, which is the designator that this man is a Major. Thinking hard, Jim tried to smile at the little man, saying,

"Are you the surgeon who operated on me? Major Lee?" as he mumbled his name in embarrassment.

"Yes, I am Major Lee, and what is your name, son?" smiling at his patient.

"Jim, sir. My name is Jim. Doc, I'm sorry for anything I did or said during the operation. The chaplain told me that I was salty in the operating room. I wasn't myself, sir, and I do apologize. I thought you were the enemy and we are taught always to resist," trying not to seem too bigoted. "You came out of the ether before you should have. I would have done the same thing, not realizing where or who I was. Now Nurse Spinelli tells me that you had quite a time a few minutes ago. Do you remember anything that went on?" moving from the front of the bed to the side where Jim's good eye was open.

"I remember that I was telling the nurse that my head really hurt and I asked for some aspirins. For some reason, she didn't do what I asked and just started to rip my clothes. I started to yell but nothing. It's quite frustrating that this always seems to happen to me," looking right at the doctor he insulted a few hours ago.

"Jim, has this happened to you before?" The doctor now was leaning toward his patient's mouth so he could hear him better.

"Yes, sir. It happened when I got shot and I was in the helicopter. I remember" suddenly stopping remembering that there were people around the bed who shouldn't hear what he was saying.

"Is something the matter, Jim?" the doctor said to his patient." I have nothing more to say, sir. I'm a little tired so I'd like to go to sleep now if that's all right with you." trying to turn away from the doctor.

"Before you go to sleep, let me ask you one more question. These headaches you are having, how severe are they? On a scale from one to ten, ten being the most painful, what is your pain level?" As he is talking, he is looking into the left eye of his patient.

Jim didn't say anything right away because his head was hurting so much and he was having "Fifteen. My pain level is off the charts. I would love to have it just ten, but it's worse. I am also having trouble with my good eye seeing you, Doc. Everything is blurry but my eye isn't watering. Other than these things, I feel great." Jim is now wondering if the doctor could tell he was lying.

Jim not only has headaches but the pain in his head is almost unbearable. The pain lasts for two to three minutes, starting from the place where the wound is and traveling right to the back of his eyes. He can't move his head at all and if he does, the pain shoots all the way to the end of his fingers. He doesn't want to tell the truth about the pain because he knows this would be the end of his career as an "assassin." All he has been doing since the chaplain found him in the body bag is trying to figure a way he can contact the Commander. In his mind, he feels he needs to talk to someone about what went on in the last mission and how he ended up in the hospital. He knows he has no access to a phone and even if he did, he doesn't know the Commander's phone number. He thinks that he can talk to the chaplain about anything, even the most confidential of matters and he won't or can't tell anyone else because he's a priest. He still wasn't sure of this but deep down he really wanted to believe this. He knew if he made a mistake in trusting him and things suddenly went "south" then he'd be in a lot of trouble. It's been five days since he got out of the body bag and he's starting to get "antsy." He wants to get out of here but he knows he can't even stand up yet, let alone start walking toward Da-Nang.

MAKE THE CALL

"How are you feeling today, Jim?" as Chaplain Andy pulled the chair closer to Jim Coleman's bed.

"I've been in this god forsaken place, cooped up for almost two weeks now and I want to get out of here." Jim was careful not to cuss in front of the priest.

"Jim, you were seriously shot and it's going to take some time to heal. I heard the doctors saying that they may just recommend you get out of the Marines on a medical discharge." With this news Jim's face turned chalk white.

"How can they do that? They don't even know who I am. Only thing they know is my first name and that I am a Marine. Father, you can't let them do that to me. The Marine Corps is all I have. I need to stay over here and finish what I started." Jim was in tears as he spoke directly to the chaplain.

"They took your fingerprints, Jim. Everyone in the service has their fingerprints on file. They will know who you are any day now." stating the obvious.

"Padre, you're starting to sound like "007," giving out a little laugh but cringing with the pain that came with this joke.

"Jim, you know you're not anywhere near going back in the bush. As the doctors said last week, it's going to take you at least three to four months in rehabilitation to get back to where you were before getting shot. That's not even a guarantee. I'm not trying to upset you but you have to face reality. Is there anything I can do for you right now?" the chaplain asked one more time.

"Why do you care so much about me? You don't even know me or what I've done. Maybe if you knew half of what I have done, you wouldn't be coming around asking all your "nosey" questions. I'm not the guy you think I am." trying to figure out what the chaplain really wanted.

"Jim, I know you have a lot on your mind and you trust no one. I can tell just the way you look at me and how you look around the room every time you talk. I'm here for two reasons. I am a priest and I need to comfort you in your time of need, and secondly, I like you and I want to help. I want to be your friend," leaning in as close as he thought Jim would permit.

"I want to trust you, Father, I really do. Remember a couple of weeks ago, when I first got out of surgery and we were talking and you said it was just like in the confessional? You said if I told you some things that were highly secretive that it could be considered confession and you couldn't tell anyone? Does that still stand?" looking into the chaplain's eyes to see if he was telling the truth.

"Absolutely, Jim. Anything you tell me can and will be considered to have the rights of the confessional. I am bound by my vows as a priest not to divulge anything to anyone under the pain of excommunication. That means that I can be stripped of being a priest forever. Anything and I mean anything is just between you and me and that can never be broken, no matter what." Jim saw in his eyes that this man was not lying. He came to the decision to trust him and God help him if he's wrong. "Well, Father, I am going to trust you. What I'm about to tell you may give you nightmares for the rest of your life. Where should I start?" Jim tried to sit up against the two pillows that were on his neck.

"Well, let's start with your name?" With that question, Father Andrew Prete reached into his front right pocket and took out his purple stole, the symbol of a priest ready to hear confession. He unrolled it, kissed the middle where a cross is stitched and put it around his neck.

"What are you doing?" Jim asked with a little confusion in his voice.

"You want this to be like you're in confession, then I have to put on my stole because when a priest hears confession, he has to wear it. Now if anyone sees us they will know that I'm hearing your confession. No questions will ever be asked." continuing to straighten out his stole.

Jim was thinking as the priest was talking, "This guy isn't that stupid. He's clever. In another time and another place, we really could have been friends. I will just tell him enough so he'll contact the Commander," smiling as the priest kept on talking. "James Coleman, my name is James Coleman. I am a Corporal in the United States Marine Corps. My main MOS is that I am a Scout/Sniper. I have been on temporary duty with the Central Intelligence Agency since I got out of boot camp at Parris Island. That's why my toe tag read CIA. I am based in DaNang and Padre, I need to contact my boss there. His name is Commander Forrest Damon, and he is the military liaison for the CIA. I have no idea what his phone number is and I think it will be hard contacting him and believe me Father, he doesn't trust anyone. He'll ask you a thousand questions to get what he wants to know and he won't answer one of yours. I need to let him know that I am still alive." Jim was getting quite anxious as he spoke to his new "friend."

"Jim, you have to relax. I will contact this Commander Damon and tell him you're here and alive. A few more questions, please, if you don't mind." Now he was going to try to press him for some personal answers.

"Not right now, Padre. I have a splitting headache and it's hard for me to concentrate. We can pick this up later. Don't forget about contacting the Commander. This is important to me." closing his eyes and hoping the priest would leave.

Chaplain Prete pushed back the chair and stood up. "Well, I have to get ready for evening Mass. Is there anyone you want me to pray for?" hoping he'd get a little more information on who this Marine actually is.

With nothing being said by Jim, he said his goodbyes and turned and headed for the exit of the first-floor ward.

The next day, Father Andy started back to the hospital at around 1000 hours. He had said his morning mass and then he called DaNang. He thought he'd be able to contact this Commander without any trouble, but unfortunately it was not meant to be. It took him the whole rest of the morning to get to the higher ups in the Marine Detachment that was now based in DaNang. They didn't even know a Corporal James Coleman and while talking to them it sounded as if they didn't care to know him. When asked if they knew the Commander, they told the priest that they as Marines do not keep track of any Navy personnel, then hung up abruptly. Luckily, Lieutenant Andrew Prete was not the type of person, whether being a priest or not to give up.

As he was approaching the hospital, he stopped short and started talking to himself. *"I'll call my friend Morey Greenberg. He has been stationed in DaNang since the Air Force got there, being assigned to the 476th Tactical Fighter Squadron. If anyone is in DaNang, he'll know where to find him"* They met in chaplain school. His folks wanted him to be a rabbi in some nice synagogue in the suburbs of Detroit, but Morey had different ideas. When he graduated from rabbinical school, he enlisted in the Air Force. A terrific guy and very, very funny. He is the type of man that can find the Commander even if he doesn't want to be found.

The chaplain turned suddenly and rushed back to his office. As he sat down, he took a book out of his desk and started to thumb through it. This was the telephone book of all the numbers of military personnel in South Vietnam. Last night he looked in it to see if he could locate a Commander Forrest Damon, but he found nothing. He decided to thumb through the DaNang section when he saw the name Captain M. Greenberg, Chaplain, USAF, and his phone number. As he dialed, he thought of what he was going to say to Morey. Just as he thought to hang up, a familiar voice came on the other end of the phone.

"Morey, is that you? Andy Prete in Cam Ranh Bay. I am fine and, how are you? Morey, we can catch up later, but right now I need a really big favor." He told his old friend what he needed and about trying to reach a Commander in the Navy, named Damon.

Captain Greenberg told the priest that sometimes units around Da-Nang do not have phones. He said that if this Commander is in DaNang he would find him. He also asked when he found him what was he supposed to say? The priest told him that all he wanted was his phone number. After a few more minutes of catching up, Captain Greenberg said he would get back to him in a couple of days, if it took that long and he hung up.

The priest once again left his office and headed toward the hospital. As he entered, he noticed Lieutenant Finocchi, the surgical nurse that was taking care of Jim.

"Good morning, Rosemary. How are you this fine and wonderful morning?" he said with a huge smile.

"I'm fine, Father. Have you heard about your boy? They are going to send him to the Army hospital in the Philippines. I overheard that it may be sometime this afternoon or tomorrow. He needs some special care and he can't get it here." She was always one step ahead explaining the facts before you ask.

"Well, if that's what he needs then that's what should be done. You people did such a terrific job bringing him back to life. I know he'll heal perfectly and live a fruitful life because of all of you," trying not to look down in the dumps.

Turning away from the nurse, Father Prete made his way down the long corridor to Jim's ward where he was the only patient. As he came up to Jim's bed, he grabbed the chair, pulled it up to the bed and went to sit down.

"I have someone in DaNang trying to find your Commander. I also heard from one of the nurses that you may be transferred to a hospital in the Philippines today or tomorrow. So, we got a lot to do before then," trying to sound non-committal as Jim seemed to like this scenario.

"Anything you want to know is okay with me." Jim said lying right to the priest's face.

"What were you doing when you got shot?" A very normal question in these circumstances or at least Father Andy thought so.

"We were on a routine patrol up by the DMZ when we ran into an NVA patrol and a fire fight started and a lot of us got shot. We were being extracted by helicopter when I got it. I remember a corpsman was holding my neck trying to make my wound stop bleeding. Nothing sinister in this, just a routine patrol." As Jim was explaining he was trying to figure out what the priest really wanted.

"I thought you said you wouldn't lie to me because this was like confession. Why are you lying to me now?" not upset but quite direct.

"I'm not lying. That's how I got here," feeling a little foolish getting caught lying this quickly.

"I believe you were shot. I believe you were administered by a corpsman. I do not believe you when you say it was routine. I don't know anything about the CIA, but I would imagine that anything they do isn't just routine," sounding a little disgusted with the man lying across from him.

"Padre don't be mad at me. There are some things that I just cannot tell you. I won't lie to you if you don't ask," trying to stay on the good side of the chaplain.

"How can I not ask if I don't know what I'm asking is so secret? Rather than lie just tell me you cannot discuss this question. That way I will not try to figure if you are bull shitting me or not." He finished; Jim had this look on his face. "What's wrong? Haven't you ever heard a priest cuss like you do?" smiling as Jim still looked shocked.

"I just didn't expect it. I used to hang with a priest when I was fifteen or sixteen. He is a great guy. Used to cuss occasionally, but nothing bad. My friend Jack, me and Father Jim Hutchinson were inseparable. I was an altar server and he started having me instruct the younger kids who wanted to be altar boys. In fact, I ended up dating his kid sister, Maureen, when I was a senior in high school. The three of us would go to Red Sox games and movies. So, I've heard a priest cuss a little, but you caught me off guard. Not something I really like to hear." Jim was trying to explain a little of his life while he was a civilian.

"You were an altar boy?" leaning forward in his chair.

"Now why would you want to know that? That question has

nothing to do with my getting back to my unit. You wouldn't be thinking of trying to find my parents, would you?" not upset but thinking that he'd have to be on his toes with this guy.

"Jim, don't you want your parents to know that you're still alive? Also, do you have a wife or a girlfriend who would be worried about you?" still trying to get inside Jim's mind.

"Father, I have no one. My folks have been dead for years and I have no wife or girlfriend. The adage that the Marine Corps tells you, "If you're not issued it, then it doesn't exist." A big wide smile came to Jim's face, as the priest just shook his head.

Sitting there listening to the Corporal lie to his face was something Father Andy was struggling with. He just knew that Coleman had a mother and father, but he was not sure if he had a wife or girlfriend, but he knew it was one or the other. He just did not understand why this man, a step away from deaths door, would want to lay here and not want at least his parents to know where he was and what he has been going through.

"Okay, you win. No personal questions about your family or if you do or do not have a wife or girlfriend. Sorry to get so personal but it is part of being a priest. I'm just trying to ease your suffering," his sarcasm coming through in his apology.

"Father, there are just things I can't and won't talk about. Those are the ground rules and if you can follow them, that is great. If not, we might as well stop right now and go on our separate ways. I will not change my mind, no matter what you say or do." Jim was getting profoundly serious while looking directly into the priest's eyes.

"How will I know what to talk about unless I ask?"

"You can ask but if I say, "move on or I don't want to talk about that," then you have to honor my request and not ask again. That is the way this thing is going to work. If you do not like the guidelines, then let's stop right now." again Jim being really serious in his demands.

"Jim, I understand or at least I think I do regarding what you want or don't want. You are the one who asked if this would be like being in a confessional. If you want this to be a confession between you and your priest, then there cannot be any boundaries. If you just want to talk about general stuff, then that's fine also. Then there will not be any questions from me. You can just talk about whatever you want, and you will not have to worry about anything. If you are looking for something different than that, there must be dialogue. Do you understand what I saying to you?" Captain Prete being as calm as he could.

Jim just laid on his bed, looking up at the ceiling. His head is throbbing, and his eye feels like it is going to come right through the bandages that are covering the side of his face. He did not want any medicine right now because he wanted to keep his head clear. He wanted to do this. He wanted to tell the priest everything, but he is having trouble getting his head around someone knowing what he's done for the past few months. He kept thinking to himself, "I know I can trust this man. I know as a priest he cannot just go out and tell everyone he meets about me and what I've done. What would the Commander say if he knew I was going to do this? I know what he would do. He would have me put in front of a firing squad and have me shot as a traitor. I don't care what he'd say, I must tell someone about the past or I will go crazy." Jim smiled knowing exactly what the Commander would do. He would come in here like he was attacking the beach on Iwo Jima, raising hell everywhere he turned.

"You can ask me anything you want, no holds barred. The only thing you must tell me one more time, on your honor being a Catholic priest and such, that you will never divulge anything I tell you. I don't need it to come back and bite me in the ass." looking a little embarrassed with the last word spoken.

"Jim, on my honor and with the fear of excommunication from the church, I promise to you this will never be repeated. Also, you have been shot up badly and I wouldn't want one part of your body that hasn't been damaged be bit." the priest trying to lighten up a very tense situation.

"Okay, then let's begin," grabbing hold of the priest's hand and squeezing it.

With this Captain Andrew Prete took out his "stole" and kissing it in the middle where the cross was stitched into the fabric, he placed it around his neck. As he was sitting there looking directly into the Corporal's eye, he started to think of the first question.

"Jim, what is your last name?"

"Coleman, James Coleman from Massachusetts," answering without hesitation.

"Very good, Mr. Coleman. Are you married?"

Jim was taken aback by this question. Of all the things that was hinted about by Jim to the priest in prior conversations all the time he said to the priest about top secret stuff, he didn't expect this question to be the second one asked. Why is this so important to him?

"No, I am not married. I have a girlfriend and we have spoken about getting married, but the answer is no to having a wife." Jim was feeling a load was being taken off his shoulders.

"What is her name?" still sticking with the same kind of questions.

Blinking uncontrollably, Jim tries to answer, "Linda, Linda Collins. She lives in Medford, Massachusetts. I have known her since she was five. I have not spoken to her for over seven months. We plan on getting married once I leave here and get back to the world."

"Are your parents deceased as you said they were?" again asking a personal question instead of a military one.

"No, they are very much alive. They live on the South Shore of Boston in a small town of Hingham. That is where I grew up and graduated from high school. I went to a parochial high school for three years taught by the Xavierian Brothers. I had some problems with a few of the teachers. We did not agree completely on a few things, so my mother took me out of there and put me back in Hingham High School. I always said being taught by the Xaverian Brothers made going to Parris Island easy. The Brothers were just like the drill instructors. I think they were harder on us that the DIs." He let out a little laugh with this and the priest thought that was a good sign.

"Yes, I know the Xavierian Brothers reputation, on how hard they are on their students. They can be very demanding. What was the name of the school you attended with them?"

"Mission High School. Went there for over three and a half years but because of what was happening, if I did not leave, I would have never graduated. The school is in the Mission Hill district of Roxbury, which is a part of Boston. It was a small parish school with only eighty students in my senior class. It was one large building but it was segregated. Boys on one side and girls on the other. That is why it was called a "boys school.""

"Now after you graduated high school, did you go directly into the Marines?" the priest was fixated with these types of questions.

"No, I went to work for a friend of my brother, Bobby, for one year. I went to Parris Island the last day of May in 1962." With that Jim's head really started to hurt.

"You said your brother? Do you have any other brothers or sisters back home?"

"No, sir, just my older brother. He is six and a half years older. He is married and has a little girl, name is Mary Louise, named after my mother, but they call her "Marylou." Jim was not feeling great but he wanted to get this done.

"How did you like Parris Island? Did you have any trouble dealing with things while you were there?" trying to see the reaction on Jim's face with these questions.

"Dealing with what things, Father? I don't know what you are referring to," trying not to show that he knew exactly what the good father was talking about.

"The discipline and the harassment. Every Marine I speak to tells me that it is almost unbearable," trying not to laugh with the lie he is telling.

"Now who's lying Padre? No Marine worth his salt would tell anyone that never went to PI, there was anything bad about the island." Trying not to laugh at the chaplain who was looking quite embarrassed. "To answer your question, no, I got along fine or as well as anyone else. It's not a country club, you know. I especially excelled on the rifle range. I shot perfect all the time I was there. First time ever done by a recruit. That's how I got put with the CIA." Now Jim wanted to see the reaction of the priest but there was absolutely no reaction on his face.

"How long after graduation from PI did you go to work for the CIA?"

"Almost immediately. I was sent to HQMC in Washington, DC to march in the Drum and Bugle Corps. This was something I really wanted to do but after arriving at Headquarters, everything seemed to change. I was sent to Quantico and then I met the Commander." opening up like it was nothing special.

"I'm sorry, Jim. Remember I am new in the military. What does HQMC mean?" looking a little sheepish with that question.

"No, Father, I am sorry. HQMC means Headquarters Marine Corps at 8th and I Barracks in DC. It is the oldest standing building in Washington. During the War of 1812, the British burned down the White House and other government buildings. But due to the way the Marines fought in that war and how impressed the British were, they left Headquarters Marine Corps stand and never tried to destroy it. That's a little free history lesson about HQMC," trying to smile but it hurt so much.

"Now you said something about Drum and Bugle Corps and how you wanted to march with the Marine Drum and Bugle Corps. Why?" looking a little quizzical.

"When I was eight years, I got involved with the Church Drum and Bugle Corps. It was a recent activity the CYO was starting in all the Catholic churches around Boston. I joined because my brother was involved and I would do anything to be with my brother. We were drummers. He was much better than me, but I loved it because I was with him. We went from drum corps to drum corps all through Southern Massachusetts.

"When I signed up with my recruiter, I got this thing that said I was guaranteed this MOS 5593 for at least two years after boot camp. Seems they lied to me also, because when I arrived at HQMC, I was assigned to the Marine Corps Drum Corps for about a week and then everything changed." With his head hurting so badly, Jim was having trouble concentrating.

"Now the Commander is with the CIA?" The priest once again got back on point.

"He is supposed to be the liaison between the military and the CIA. The only military I have ever seen are Marines. I can get into that later but at the beginning I seemed to be the only one, along with my spotter, Joe. The Commander was and still is all controlling." Jim was starting to look around as if he thought someone was listening to him and the priest. He finally said to the chaplain, "I don't like talking about this so much in the open. Is there any other place we can go that someone can't listen in?" really starting to get a little more paranoid than he was at the beginning.

"Jim, you're the only one that's in this ward. We are at the far end and there are no windows or stairwells on this side of the building. You cannot be moved right now because of your wounds. I really think this is as safe as you can get," not trying to scare him into thinking he doesn't care.

"Okay, I guess you're right. There was a lot of crazy stuff happening both in Washington and Quantico in the beginning. They had me and another Marine going all over the western part of the country evaluating this one sniper rifle. That lasted about two months. This is when we finally learned what they really had in mind for us." Jim started to blink more than usual and his eyes were starting to roll toward the top of his head.

"Are you all right, Jim? Should I call someone to come and check you out?" the chaplain was now standing and ringing his hands in near panic.

Just then Jim started to shake uncontrollably and white foam started to come out of his mouth. The chaplain started to scream for assistance, and he started to run down the middle of the ward toward the exit. The nurse that was at her station was coming toward him, having heard him screaming uncontrollably. She ran right past Chaplain Andy not waiting for an explanation and went directly to Jim's bed. He was still shaking violently. The nurse went directly to the stand next to his bed and pulled open the draw. Taking a large and long needle from the compartment, she tore off the plastic wrap that was protecting the head of the needle. Holding the needle up in front of her face, she pushed the plunger until a little liquid shot out. She then put some alcohol on Jim's right arm and without much finesse she stabbed Jim's upper arm and proceeded to push all the liquid into the arm. Within seconds Jim's contortions started to subside and minutes later he was sleeping as if he just came out of his mother's womb. The confessional was now closed and the chaplain was thinking that it may be a long time before it is open again for this Marine.

As Captain Andrew Prete returned to the chapel, he walked past the pews that lined both sides of this small building. In the rear was his office and as he approached, he could hear the phone ringing.

Chaplain Prete, Cam Ranh Bay, may I help you?" was the typical way Father Andy answered the phone.

"This is Commander Forrest Damon in DaNang, Chaplain. I got a message that you needed to speak with me. Make it quick, I am a busy man. What do you want?" Jim did not lie when he said the Commander could be abrupt and direct.

"What I want, Commander, is a little respect. I have someone here in this hospital that you might want to see," dragging it out just to see if he could upset this pompous ass.

"I doubt that Chaplain. I do apologize for the curtness but I am busy and do not have time for give and take. Who is this person that you think I would waste my time and come to Cam Rahn Bay?" again trying not to be rude but failing miserably.

"Well, Commander, I'm sure you'll make time in your so-called busy schedule to come down here and look in on an old friend of yours," still drawing this out as much as he could because he could tell he was getting under the skin of this arrogant Naval officer.

"Really. And who would that be? All my people are accounted for. So, whoever it is that wants to see me, I think he's playing games with you," again being very direct and condescending.

"So, but he knew where you were. I'll just go back to his ward and tell him that you don't have anyone missing and you don't have the time to come down here and see who it is," trying again to be as sarcastic as possible.

"All right, I don't have a lot of time for your little games. Who the hell, sorry, who is this person who knows me?" getting a little more aggravated with every word.

"If I were you, Commander, I'd sit down right now. He says that you and he go back a long way," drawing it out ever further to see how far he could go until this pompous ass blows his top.

"For God's sakes, Captain, what is this puke's name?" now yelling into the phone.

"James Coleman," saying nothing at all as the phone on the other end went uncharacteristically silent.

"The phone continued to be silent. Nothing was coming from Da-Nang. The chaplain could hear breathing on the other end of the phone but nothing was said. It must have lasted a good two to three minutes before the Commander said something.

"Who did you say it was?" was the only question he had and his demeanor was quite changed.

"Jim Coleman, Corporal in the United States Marine Corps," again waiting for something to be said on the other side.

"That cannot be, Padre. Jim was killed over a month and a half ago on the DMZ. Does this person have any identification on him?" A clever question from someone who deals in things like this.

"Commander, I am a Catholic priest. You know what that means, don't you? Jim and I have been talking and that's how I got your name and where you are stationed." He could hear the Commander start to stammer on the other end.

"If this person is who you say he is, what has he told you?" starting to get his voice and gall back.

"I just told you who and what I am. I cannot divulge anything that was said to me from the sacrament of penance," giving his best message about confession.

"Yeh, yeh, I get it. I am a Catholic or at least I used to be when I was growing up. How do I know that this is the same James Coleman that I use to know? Is there anything that you can tell me that isn't part of his confession?"

Trying not to yell at this obstinate, old Naval officer. "Linda," the one word that the Captain knew would get Damon on a plane immediately.

"I'll be there in the morning. Please, Father, do not let anyone talk to him before I get there. It is especially important that Jim doesn't speak to anyone but yourself and me. Thank you for calling me and I'll see you at first light." as the Commander disconnected the phone connection.

Commander Damon was torn between being exuberant that Jim was alive and anxious that Jim may have talked too much. He started to talk to himself, *"I know Jim and that is the last thing he would do. They said he was dead in the helicopter when they were leaving "Dog-patch." Jim was dead when they landed in DaNang. I saw the flight crew put him in a body bag. How could he be alive? He has a gash in the side of his head that I could put my hand in. He stopped bleeding halfway to DaNang. Isn't that the sure sign that his heart stopped pumping blood? It could not be Jim. If it is not then how did this chaplain know about Linda? That was the one name that I would know it was really Coleman. I wonder how much he told this priest. I must get down there first thing. I must make sure that Jim does not say another word to anyone. I will deal with this "holy roller" at a later time."*

"I need a helicopter to take me to Cam Ranh Bay first thing in the morning." Damon screamed into the phone. "I don't give one rat's ass who you take orders from. This is an emergency. I need to be there no later than 0800. I will be on the tarmac at 0500, so make it happen. Make sure it is the fastest chopper you have. It doesn't matter why I have to be there, it's way above your paygrade." With that final statement he slammed the phone back in its cradle.

Sitting in his hooch and looking out at the guys who were still alive, he wondered if he should tell them about the telephone call. He thinks that he should tell Tomelli because ever since it happened, Joe's been really down and this would definitely pick him up. Thinking if he does tell him, then Joe will want to go with him to see Jim.

Now his thoughts were going to what has happened since they landed back from "Dogpatch." He started to talk to himself again, "Torres and Nichols came back all shot up but with a little "tender loving care" they will be fine once they get out of the hospital. Brand went to the Philippines and the Montagnards and Koreans, were still with us. Only two CIA operatives, including Sean came back alive. Now if Jim is alive that will make an even dozen that came back from thirty that went on that mission, not counting the one pilot that survived. Not the best average, if you think about it but we got the pilots back, even if one was dead. Strong, who would have gone a long way in the Marine Corps or even the CIA was killed. Roosevelt Woodrow Wilson turned out to be a hero, but as he knew, no one will ever know about it. Wilson saved four lives in that battle at "Dogpatch" but no bigger life than his number one nemesis Brand. Too bad they cannot receive medals because Wilson, Coleman, Tomelli and Strong would be up for at least the Navy Cross, if not the Congressional Medal of Honor." Shaking his head, the Commander stands and walks out of his hooch toward the remaining members of his unit. No one can see the tears flowing down his cheek.

HE IS HERE!

The next morning, Chaplain Prete decided to make his rounds at the hospital, immediately following morning mass and to forgo his breakfast. For some reason in the back of his mind he knew today would be so much more different than any other day while he's been in Vietnam. As he went from bed to bed saying prayers with the soldiers lying there, he could not get his mind off his number one patient, Jim Coleman. He knew he had to get to him soon and continue his "confession" before that bombastic Commander showed up. As he finished the second ward, he started to go toward the ICU ward. Suddenly, the front door came flying open and standing in the doorway was a large man, in green utilities with a cigar in the corner of his mouth. He looked like something out of "Central Casting." Saying nothing, this hulk of a man kept his head going from right to left, just like a lighthouse. Finally, after what seemed an eternity he stepped forward and walked right up to Captain Prete. Looking him up and down, trying to intimidate the chaplain, putting his face as close to the priest as possible, he shouted.

"You're the son of a bitch I'm looking for. Where is he?" not moving an inch from the front of the priest's face.

"Commander Damon, I suppose?" as the chaplain put out his hand.

"I'll get to you later. Where is he?" not bothering to even look at the outstretched hand.

"If you will follow me, Commander, I'll get his doctor. He can ex"

"Chaplain. You listen to me and listen well. When I tell you that I want to see someone do not give me any bullshit about someone else. I want to see Corporal Coleman, and I want to see him now. If he is the right person then I'll talk to his doctor or anyone else you have in mind. If he is not then I've wasted the government's money flying up here on a wild goose chase. I will be gone and it will be as if I was never here. Do you understand me, Chaplain?" He was enunciating every syllable as slow as he could.

Prete could feel the hair start to move in the back of his neck. He knew that this man outranked him and could kill him or have someone do it without thinking twice about it. But he knew if he cowered in front of this large man, he would never get the respect that he wanted and deserved.

"Who in the Lord's name do you think you are talking to? I am a man of the cloth, not one of your flunkies' that you can scream at without consequences. You know this and the disrespect you are showing me just can't and will not be tolerated," thinking to himself while this senior officer is screaming at him. "One thing, Commander. You will not talk to me in this manner. I am an officer in the United States Army and I am also a chaplain. You will show me respect or you will do what you should do by yourself. Is that understood? You will not bully these people and you will calm down and ask questions in a civil manner," shaking like a leaf as he spoke to this Commander. "Okay, Father, you win. I am sorry about the way I acted but if this is the right person, I need to see him and then arrange for him to be moved to another facility. Would you please take me to him," putting his hand out for the priest to shake.

As he took his hand to shake, Father Andy says, "If you will follow me. He's in the ICU ward, just around the corner. He's all the way in the back of the ward and he's the only patient there," as he let go of the hand, turned and proceeded to the door, just down the main hall.

"He's in terrible shape. He lost a lot of blood and his wounds were not that deep. The bullet went around his skull and fragmented. He is having terrible headaches but the doctors are optimistic and say once stable, he will have a quick recovery. I just have this feeling that he has been so alone, I know he'll be excited when he sees you. I know you being here will cheer him up," as they came to Jim's bed.

Coleman was lying on his side, away from where the two men were approaching. He could hear the footsteps but thinking that it was just the doctors who were coming to prod and poke him, he did not turn over.

"Straighten up, Marine." This was the one voice that Jim could never forget.

Turning around quickly to face the one person he wanted to see in the entire world was not the best thing for him. His head felt like it would explode and his eyes started to roll up in his head.

"You all right, Jim?" was the one question Jim did not expect to hear out of him.

"Yes, sir, I'm fine. How are you?" looking at the Commander and trying to smile.

"How am I? What kind of question is that? You are the one in the bed with tubes all over you. How are you feeling, son? We all thought you bought the farm. I could not believe it when the chaplain here called me and told me you were still alive. You look like shit, Corporal." This is the language that Jim expected to hear from his boss.

Half smiling, Coleman moved his left hand and held it out. He did not want to shake his hand but just wanted to hold it, to finally be with someone who understood.

As the Commander grabbed his hand, Jim noticed tears coming down the big man's face. If he did not know better, he would think the Commander was crying. He knew the Commander better so it must be sweat from this hot Vietnam morning. He would never cry in public or anywhere else, especially over one of his own.

"Commander, it's great seeing you. Get me the hell out of here. I am going nuts. I'll be ready to return to duty within a week or so," trying to sound as confident as he could muster.

"We can talk about that in a few minutes but I need to talk to your doctors first. I just cannot believe that they thought you were dead and left you on the tarmac. I'll have to check on that when I get back to the unit."

"Chaplain, I need to talk to Corporal Coleman alone now. Would you please excuse us? Also, thank you again for doing what you did for Jim. If it were not for you, he wouldn't be here now. Again, thank you and you have wonderful day," a subtle way to dismiss the man who saved his man.

"Jim, I will look in on you later. You have a good day and thank you, Commander, for getting here so quickly," standing and starting to turn.

"That will not be necessary, Chaplain. From this point on, Corporal Coleman is not your worry and he is off limits to everyone but the medical staff. Until I can plan for him to leave here no one and I mean no one is to come in contact with him. Is that understood, Chaplain?" The niceties have suddenly vanished from the Commander's vocabulary.

The chaplain just stood there dumbfounded, wanting to say something but the look in Jim's eyes was saying, "Please don't." A very awkward few moments went by and then Chaplain Andrew Prete from Rhode Island nodded and walked away, never to see Jim again. The one person who Jim could really talk to was gone from his life, forever.

PREPARE THE RIDE

The Commander mentioned that he would be in Cam Ranh Bay for as long as it took Jim to be relocated. He told him that he would have to find a hospital that did not have "nosey chaplains hanging around asking stupid questions."

When the Commander was finally alone with Jim, he sat in the chair and said matter of fact. "What did you say to the chaplain? Did you tell him anything about the mission that got you shot?" No such thing as starting out with "how you feeling" or "where does it hurt? No, not him. Right down to business, no small talk or delaying the inevitable.

"I didn't tell him anything about the mission. I told him what we are supposed to tell anyone outside of our unit. We were on a routine assignment on the DMZ and encountered the NVA. That is all there was to it. I did have to tell him my name and other things so he would try to contact you. He's a good guy and he contacted you, which I thought was going to be impossible," stretching the truth just a little so this man wouldn't go crazy if he only knew.

"Tell me about the operation if you can remember." the Commander getting down to business wondering if Jim knew only twelve, not counting the one pilot, came back alive.

As he kept asking him questions, Jim figured out if he did not want to answer he would feign a headache and for once, the Commander would stop the interrogation.

Days went bye and every time the Commander would start to ask about the operation, Jim would have a relapse.

Just as the Commander was leaving after the third day, two Navy SPs came in front of Jim's bed. The Commander assigned them to stand guard and make sure no one came to interrogate Jim.

"How would you like to be stationed in Hawaii? Due to the injuries that were occurred on your last mission and the rehabilitation that you would have to go through, this would be the ideal recovery billet." the Commander said one morning.

"Will my family be able to come out and visit me?" hoping for a positive answer.

"No, you'll still be isolated to anyone from the outside. In a few months when you are healed, we can think of making some arrangements. Again, I must ask. You mentioned your family many times these past few days but you never mentioned anything about Linda. Is that over? What's the story?" surprising Jim that he sounded interested where he was never interested before.

"No, we're good. I just don't think she could or would manage seeing me like this. I am only trying to protect her. Parents can manage most anything, but I am sure she could not. It's better this way," trying not to make direct eye contact with him while lying to his face.

"I know this is your business and I don't mean to pry, but have you written to her since you've been shot?"

"I started to the other day but it's really difficult with just one eye and a head that wants to explode at any time," trying to be honest as possible.

"You know the nurses will write any letter for you. You don't have to do it yourself if you're not able," again trying to be helpful, which is not his style.

"If I have them write it, she would start to ask questions about the different handwriting. That would open up a bigger box of worms than I think I can stand at this time."

"It sounds as if you have some decisions to make in your young life. It is not my business what goes on as long as it does not interfere with you getting better and back to the unit. If it does come between her and the unit, then I will get involved. Is that understood? Jim, if you ever want to talk about any of these things that are coming down, you know you can talk to me." Now who is lying to whom?

Days went bye and Jim had not seen the Commander at all. Asking the guards where he was did not help either. All they said was he went back to DaNang but they said he would be back before you left.

"Where am I going? No one told me that I was being moved. The Commander asked me what I thought of Hawaii but he never said that was definite," asking these two sailors to answer for the Commander.

"Don't know where you're going but it's going to be very soon. To-morrow or Wednesday. I guess it's up to the doctors and when your transportation gets here," one SP answered.

"Tell me how you can be so sure that it's tomorrow or Wednesday?"

"That's when we were told that our assignment here would be over. We are to report back to DaNang no later than 2200 on Wednesday. We already have our ride out of here confirmed. We were sure the Commander had already briefed you," again just trying to answer Jim's questions honestly.

"When you deal with the Commander, you get used to the way he operates. Everything always is top secret. Are you sure you don't know where I am supposed to be going?" looking for a direct answer.

"The other guard finally spoke up. "I heard a couple of locations. Subic Bay in the Philippines, Okinawa, or Guam. They all have Navy hospitals there. I know they have a special military AirVac to take you out of here. We never really got to talk to you while the Commander was here. Can we ask you a few questions?" trying to be a friendly voice in this conversation.

"Sure, you can ask me anything. It does not mean that I can answer because some answers to your questions may be confidential but go ahead, let's try. Ask away," knowing that they wanted to know who he was and why was a Marine Corporal so special to the Navy Commander.

"Who are you? You are a corporal in the Marine Corps but he treats you as if you were the Commandant of the Corps. Our orders are that absolutely no one comes to talk to you without the Commander's permission. Even the chaplain cannot come near you and they usually can go anywhere they want. What gives?" as one of them pulls the chair out and sits down.

"Remember, I just said some things are confidential. Well, everything you just asked me falls under that umbrella. Sorry, but I cannot answer your questions. I will tell you that I am not the Commandant of the Marine Corps." With that, Jim tries to let out a big laugh but his head is really hurting now.

The doctors and nurses come every half hour to make note of his dressing and stitches. Removing the tubes from his body, giving him a couple of shots, which Jim didn't care for because he hates needles. It all came down to something that happened back when he was a kid, 8 or 9 years old. It seemed this dentist, Dr. Copeland used a huge needle when giving Novocain to numb Jim's mouth. What he would do is hold this needle in front of Jim's face and say in a terrifying voice, "This is really going to hurt," which it did every time he did inject Jim's mouth. To say Jim was terrified of needles would be an understatement.

As Jim was settling in for the morning, two nurses in flight suits and a doctor in scrubs came up to his bed. The two SP's looked at each other and moved away from the bed, walking down the ward about twenty feet away.

"Good morning, Jim. Are you ready to travel? Did anyone explain what is happening this morning? the doctor, who had the insignia of a full Navy captain, was talking as if Jim and he were long lost friends.

As he was telling Jim a few things about his trip and how they were going to monitor his every breath, Jim was looking at one of the nurses who was standing in the back. "Ronnie, is that you? It's me, Jimmy Coleman," almost screaming out her name.

"Commander, do you know this Marine?" the captain turned and looked at this one nurse.

"As she moved closer to the bed, she gasped and said, "Oh, my god. It is Jimmy. What have they done to you? Are you all right?" then remembering where she was she said. "Yes, sir, I met the Corporal when I was stationed at Bethesda over a year ago. He came into the emergency room with a bullet in his leg. Seems things just never changed with you, do they, Jimmy?" looking right at Coleman without changing expression.

Jim just stared at this nurse that he had not seen since being stationed in HQMC. Veronica "Ronnie" White was the emergency room nurse when he was brought into the hospital after suffering being shot during his mission in Baton Rouge in late 1962. When they arrived at the ER, the Commander met them and went in to explain to the doctors and nurses that he got shot in a hunting accident, somewhere in Maryland. Jim and Ronnie went out a couple of times when he was at Headquarters. She is originally from the Boston area and he had a lot of fun with her. The last time Jim heard from her; she was trying to get assigned to a Naval hospital near Boston.

"What are you doing here? I thought you were going to be assigned to the Newport Naval Hospital in Rhode Island." Jim asked, ignoring the prodding the captain was doing with his stethoscope.

"Just do what the doctor tells you to do, Corporal." Ronnie speaking in a very military manner.

"Commander, it's already been established that the two of you know each other. No need to be uninterested now," not looking up but moving his stethoscope around Jim's body.

"We heard yesterday that there was a Marine in Vietnam that needed medical evacuation right away. I am the senior officer of the Medevac units. It was explained to me what you needed and I picked my best team and left Hawaii late yesterday afternoon and we just arrived. We will be preparing you for transport this evening for evacuation sometime tomorrow. We will be taking you back to Tripler Army Medical Center in Honolulu, where you will be evaluated," the captain, still poking with his scope was explaining to the Corporal. "Commanders, prepare our patient for a complete examination. I want to look at that wound more closely before we ever think of moving him. I don't need him hemorrhaging half-way back to Hawaii," smiling at Ronnie as he was talking.

As the two nurses came to the bed and started fussing around a medical tray, Jim noticed something on Ronnie's ring finger. "What is that the rock of Gibraltar? Are you engaged? Who's the lucky stiff?" embarrassed with the last question.

"You were just talking to him. His full name is Captain Benjamin Pfister and we met when I transferred to Tripler a year ago. He is the head of the trauma center there, Jimmy, and he's great at what he does. You are in the best of hands." "I bet he's great at what he does and not just to me," trying not to sound jealous but it did not work.

"James Coleman, how dare you. I have not heard a word from you once you left Washington and now you start talking like it was just yesterday that we saw each other. I did not know if you were dead or alive, and the way you look, it's apparent that you were closer to death. I thought you went back to Boston, married that child that you were dating in Medford. Are you married?" finishing rambling on.

"No, still single but I am still involved with Linda. We have talked about marriage but I really can't see me getting married now or any time in the future. I don't know what's going to happen to me and the rest of my time in the Marines because of this injury," considering the look on her face and knowing he had just poked the bear.

"Is it you never want to get married or you just don't want to marry her?"

Jim is thinking as she is talking, "Here come the fangs."

"To be honest, I don't know. I want to get married to her but then I think I would just like to get married. To whom, it does not matter. Then I think of what I am doing here and how she couldn't manage it. She does not even know where I am at or if I am dead or alive, just like you. So, you see it just was not you I did not contact, it's everyone that I know."

"Jimmy, is it true that you were in a body bag ready to go into a coffin and a chaplain saw the bag move and got you out? We heard that when we were leaving Hawaii. You and your story are famous and no one even knows who you are," smiling and grabbing his hand.

The captain interrupted their conversation. "Ronnie, how are his vitals? Do you think he will be ready to go in the morning or even as early as tonight? I am going to talk to our pilot now and see when he will be ready to leave. I know the pilots need sleep, so it may be tonight. If that's all right with you, Coleman?" as he said his last name it sounded as if he were spitting it out.

"His blood pressure is a little high but his heart sounds good. He is running a little fever, 100.6 and his skin feels a little clammy. Do they have a lab here? I can draw blood and have it analyzed to see if there is an infection. I can tell you more when I get his blood examined, Captain," turning and winking at Coleman.

One of the nurses that was stationed at Cam Ranh Bay piped up and said that there was a lab on base. She also said that at times the technician was hard to find.

"Ronnie, draw some blood from your boy there and then go with the lieutenant. She can show you where the lab is. Lieutenant, the Commander is a qualified lab technician so she will run the tests even if your tech is there. Ronnie, make sure you check for all the infections you can think of. Also, there is something new about Hepatitis B in the blood that we may have to be aware of. Make sure you check for that, also. Hopefully, your boy here will not have anything that will keep him from traveling. The fever is something we must be aware of and keep a close eye on for the next few hours. Corporal, how you doing? Ronnie will be taking good care of you while you catch up on old times," with "your boy" and "catching up" the captain sounded as if he was getting jealous of the attention Ronnie was giving to the Corporal.

"Simply great, Doc. Why can't I travel even though I'm a little hot?" asking what he thought was an intelligent question.

"We are going non-stop to Honolulu and if your fever starts to go up significantly and we are half-way across the Pacific, it will be difficult to find somewhere to land. I want that fever gone before we even think of leaving. You, my boy, have no say in this." just as he finished the double doors to the ward came crashing open.

"What the hell is going on here? Doesn't anyone have the smallest inkling to contact me when you arrived? Who the hell is in charge here, anyway?" turning and looking directly at Ronnie, the Commander continued, "Don't I know you from somewhere, Commander?"

"I'm in charge, Commander and may I ask, who the hell are you?" Jim lying on his bed could just tell this was going to be good between his Commander and a full bird conceited Navy Captain.

"I am this Corporal's commanding officer. That's who." putting his chest out like a little toy soldier.

"There better be a "sir" behind the "that's who, Commander. For whom I am? I am Captain Benjamin Pfister and I am this man's doctor. If that isn't enough, I outrank you." turning and again concentrating on Coleman.

"Listen, Captain. I'm the one who arranged for you to get him. I'm just saying that someone should have got me." sounding a little embarrassed for being shown up by this "doctor."

Again, the Commander turns and looks at Ronnie and says, "Are you sure we don't know each other?"

"Commander, we need to get "my" patient out of here as soon as possible. If his fever doesn't go down in the next few hours, I will transfer him to the USS Repose." turning to the Commander and saying, "That's the hospital ship that's of the coast of Korea. Hopefully, with the drugs we are giving him, the fever should break soon," turning and walking down the ward toward the exit.

"This is driving me crazy" ignoring anything the captain had said. "I'm known for my memory and I know we have met. Did we ever go out on a date?"

As the Commander was talking, Jim wanted to laugh out loud but he knew that it would hurt too much.

"If you have that great of a memory as you say you do, then you'd remember," turning away from him and coming over to Jim's bed.

"I know we never slept together because I'd never forget that" really getting down to the "nitty gritty."

"God, no. I'd try to forget that if we had. Jimmy, I need you to move your legs over, one on top of the other and then lay on your side," grabbing his right leg and helping him turn.

"I got it now. I'll be damned. Boston accent, calling him Jimmy. You're the emergency room nurse that was on duty that night at Bethesda Hospital," smiling like he just won the Irish Derby.

"Give that man a kewpie doll," Ronnie coming across very sarcastically.

"I thought you got out of the Navy. Jim told me you went back to Boston and went to work for a big hospital back there," again puffing his chest out because he remembered something about her.

"How do you know that? I got out for about six months and went to work at the South Shore Hospital in Weymouth. I didn't care for civilian life, so I decided to come back in the Navy. I got assigned to the Philadelphia Naval Hospital and after four months, I was told Hawaii was available. I was transferred to the Army hospital and was put in charge of the trauma center for the Navy. We're you investigating me because I dated Jimmy. How dare you." Ronnie couldn't speak due to the fact she was so angry and wanted to slap this "pig" across his arrogant face.

"Calm down, Lieutenant. It's my job to investigate everyone who meets any of the men under my command. Just so you know, you passed with flying colors. So, there is nothing to be upset about," as he thought this will get her out of his face.

"It's Commander, you pompous ass. How dare you do anything about me without my permission. We're in the same Navy. Get out of my sight. This patient just became off limits to you," again moving Jim's legs but not as gentle as she usually did.

Captain Pfister came back and was standing to the right of the bed and in the shadows but he was smiling and couldn't help it. As the Commander turned to him for some assistance, the captain said, "You heard her, Commander. This patient is hers and she has the authority to do what is best for her patient. I'd leave if I were you. You can come back in an hour or two, but I would change my attitude if I were you," trying not to laugh.

"I'd say closer to three hours." Ronnie was still fuming but she finished with Jim's legs and then moved toward his head.

"Did you know anything about what he was talking about?" leaning over and whispering in his ear.

Jim thought and saying to himself, "If I did, which I didn't, I would say no anyway." "No, nothing. He has done stuff like this before. He's put surveillance on my folks and my brother's family, including his in-laws and I don't even know them. When I found out, all he would say was that it was for the good of the nation," not lying to her but spreading the truth a little.

It took Ronnie about thirty minutes to calm down. It seemed every time she'd look at Jim, she'd go into another tirade about the Commander. Finally, Captain Pfister turned to her and said, "Commander, it's time you put everything in the past and just get over it. You do know you're in the Navy and as you are aware anything goes in this man's Navy." Captain Pfister would never say another truer word.

"I know Ben, but it just irks me that way he's so smug. He knows he can get away with anything and he has no-limits," as she spoke she was in tears.

"Well, right now we have a patient that we must get his fever down. We have to do this in a hurry, so I can either get him on our plane back to Hawaii or on the hospital ship sitting offshore. What's his temperature now?" sounding a lot more concerned that when he was talking to the Commander.

"An even 100 degrees. Still a little too high to fly. We can try some penicillin to see if that would bring it down. It's going to be another two to three hours until we can really get it where it should be. What do you want to do, Ben?" informal for a military meeting of the minds.

"Commander, when we are working its Captain or Doctor. Never first names. Is that understood?" sounding a little out of sorts with the informality.

"I'm sorry, sir. It won't happen again," showing the embarrassment that she was trying to hide.

As the doctor finished up, there was no small talk between he and the two nurses. As he left the area, the other nurse, named Bridget, came up to Ronnie. "I know you two are engaged or at least you are and forgive me for what I'm about to say. What the hell do you see in that guy? He's a pompous ass. The way he speaks to you in front of me is embarrassing. I'm your subordinate and he can't talk to you like that in front of a mere Lieutenant. That's against the rules. You can have your pick of anyone in the Navy. Why him?" She sounded as if she really didn't care for the captain.

"He's not that bad. He is just Navy more than I am. I was wrong using his first name and he was right to call me on it. Let's drop it, Bridge. Okay?" turning her back to her friend and Jim.

Jim had his eyes closed, hoping they would think he was asleep.

"Another thing" Bridget Murphy started to ask, "what is the story with you and the Marine in the bed?"

"There's no story. I met him over a year ago when he came into the Bethesda Hospital Emergency Room. He had a bullet in his leg. He said he was on a hunting trip in Pennsylvania and he was cleaning his gun when it went off by accident. Now this Marine is an excellent sharpshooter and to say he shot himself was something I never bought. He also came in the hospital with a civilian who sounded as if he just got off the boat from Ireland. He was a lot older than Jimmy and you could hardly understand him with his accent so thick. Jimmy and I got to talking in the operating room and we discovered that we were both from the Boston area. He was cute and not at all like some of the Marines I've met. He really is a good guy. Only thing wrong is that he's enlisted and he's got baggage."

As Ronnie spoke, Bridget looked at her with a quizzical look at her final sentence. "What do you mean baggage? Is he married?"

"No, it's even worse than being married. It's that Commander that was here an hour ago. Jimmy can't do a thing without that idiot being involved. We would go out when he was based in DC and the Commander would go crazy. I don't know what he has on Jimmy. I tried to find out something about the Commander from people I knew in Washington but every time I'd try I'd hit a roadblock. Once I got a call from Naval Intelligence wanting to know why I was interested in him. Never found out why they wanted to know," sounding as if a big weight was lifted off her shoulders.

"I really liked Jimmy. I even thought that something was really going to happen between us and I was willing to give up my commission for him. We only went out a few times but there was a spark there or at least I felt it," wiping the Corporal's forehead with a sponge.

"What happened? Why didn't you connect?" Bridget was really getting into this real-life soap opera.

"Everything was going great. I mean everything. Jimmy is so kind, courteous, gentle, and just wonderful. He was transferred to Lejeune but he'd come up every other weekend. He could have stayed with me but he is such a gentleman that he'd get a motel room, just for himself. He's quite religious, also. One weekend he was supposed to come up to DC but he didn't show and never called. He finally called a few days later and said that he'd been transferred but he couldn't or wouldn't tell me where he was going. He left and I never heard from him again. I thought we were happy. I even had my papers prepared for when he got back from where he was and we'd get married. I knew he was seeing some young girl in the Boston area. I guess he'd known her for most of his life. She was still in high school but he really liked her. When he didn't write I tried again to find out what happened to him but it was worse this time. I couldn't even find anyone who would even tell me that James Coleman was in the Marine Corps. It was a dead end. That was about ten months ago. I met Ben about a month after and he was nice and an excellent surgeon. The only trouble is, he's not Jimmy," turning away and walking down the hall.

After Ronnie walked out ear shot, Bridget leaned over to Jim and said, "I know you're awake. I saw you move a couple of times when she mentioned you. What's wrong with you? She's a wonderful girl and I think she still has a thing for you. Go for it, Marine. The fool she's engaged to can't see her through the "birds" on his collar. An officer who thinks the only thing important in life is being an Admiral is just full of himself and has no room for anyone else." As she spoke she straightened up her patient's bed. Jim opened his eyes as she continued, "Do you need anything right now Jimmy? I'm going to go out and have a smoke and a cup of coffee. Can I bring you something back?" As Jim shook his head, she turned and almost ran down the center of the ward toward the outside world.

Jim had no idea that Ronnie felt that way about him. He lay there thinking that he should have called her about his leaving. He thought they were just friends. Back then, all he thought about was Linda but now he hasn't thought of her since Ronnie arrived. One thing about Linda, she could not manage the idea that he was proclaimed dead, in a body bag and ready for the coffin. She will really freak out if or when he ever tells her.

Lying alone in this empty ward with guards at the doors was the loneliest he had ever felt. He was awake and all he could do was look at the ceiling inside this ward feeling like a prisoner. What was worse was to watch the ceiling fan going around in slow motion.

Jim thought to himself that he didn't feel hot or feverish anymore but he also didn't feel that great either. He was very anxious and couldn't wait to get out of this confinement. The Commander hadn't come back and that really surprised him.

Suddenly the doors slammed open once again. Here comes the Commander striding down the hall in all his glory and a huge smirk on his face. "Jimmy, my boy, how you doing? You're getting out of here in a couple of hours. I have a transport on the way. You'll be going to Subic Bay in the Philippines and when you're feeling a lot better, you'll transfer to a hospital in Guam. After a couple of months there rehabilitating, you'll be back here, fit as a fiddle, ready to resume your job. How's that sound to you?" One thing about this whole tirade that he's started, never has he ever called him "Jimmy." He has always been about rank, but this was different; something was in the works and Jim knew he was going to be in the middle of this mess.

"What happened to Hawaii?" he asked but he knew the answer.

"No two-bit Captain or doctor is going to tell me what I can and can't do with my boy." Here he goes again with the "my boy."

"I thought the doctor outranked anyone when it comes to the safety of his patient. How are you going to get around that?" he asked knowing the Commander was ready to tell him.

"I got this Admiral friend of mine to counteract his orders. You'll be in the Philippines for a couple of weeks, then you'll will be transferred to Guam for two to three months. You'll be getting your strength back. Because of the disaster of the last mission and how many men we lost, I will be forming new units. While you're in Guam, the new people will go through the same training you did. I'm not sure right now if they will be going to the same place you Marines did but they will be isolated and the Brits will be their trainers. I hope you get better quickly because I could use your expertise in this training." He knows Jim loves to do that. Just another push to get him to agree to what he has in mind.

Just as the Commander was finishing up, the ward door flung open and in walked the doctor, with the two nurses right behind him. Behind Ronnie and Bridget were two Navy corpsmen pushing a gurney.

"Nice try, Commander. You almost got what you wanted, but I have higher contacts in the Navy than you do. Corporal Coleman is being prepared to take a flight to Honolulu, Hawaii. There will be no further interruptions from you. If you can keep your mouth shut, I will allow you to stay and walk with him to the flight line. If not, then you're dismissed," getting about two inches from the Commander's face.

"Sir, how long will he be in Hawaii?" the Commander asking very sheepishly.

"He'll be there until I say he can leave. I don't want you trying to pull strings to get him out any sooner than he's able to resume his duties. If you do Commander, you'll find out how powerful a Navy surgeon and a Captain are. Have I made myself perfectly clear?" knowing damn well that this is definitely not the end but just the beginning of this story.

As the Commander stood at the foot of the bed he looked like a kid that just got caught eating a cookie that he was told he couldn't have. The two nurses were working quickly and quietly on the Corporal. Jim was trying to say something to Ronnie but as she bent over she whispered, "Not now," as she just kept moving the tubes around and tying them to each other with tape.

"I want this patient on the plane immediately. We are working on a time crunch and we are starting to lose." The captain turned and started walking toward the exit.

"Commander White. May I ask what time crunch time is?" Commander Damon asked kind of sheepishly.

"I will tell you on our way out, Commander. I have work to do right now and I can't be disturbed. When we leave, you may walk with me," never looking up but working the tubes all around Jim's body.

ON MY WAY (BUT TO WHERE?)

As they were transferring Jim to the gurney, a terrible pain started in his lower back. Not wanting to say anything because he didn't want to go to any hospital ship. With every small bump the gurney hit on the way to the plane, his back began to hurt more. The two corpsmen were trying to be as gentle as they could but they could hear him grown when the bumps occurred. Every time the gurney hit something, Commander Ronnie White would yell to be very gentle and to slow down and watch the bumps.

"What's wrong with Coleman, Commander?" Commander Damon asked as he walked with the head nurse toward the plane.

"What makes you think there is something wrong with him? He still has a piece of the bullet in his head. Bumps can cause a lot of discomfort to patients in his condition," answering as well as she could or as she wanted to.

"Commander, I'm not new to this sort of thing. I've had a lot of Marines and sailors under my command get shot. You people always take great care of them but this is different. I've never seen so many tubes in a body as is in Jim's. The extra special care that's being taken. The thing with the fever. I've had others who had fevers of 102 and they traveled with no problem. What I'm asking, Ronnie, is he dying?" The Commander was in tears as he asked his question but didn't want the answer he knew was coming.

"Commander, I'm not really at liberty to discuss his condition. What I will tell you, if we don't get him to Hawaii within the next twenty-four hours he will be dead. His kidneys are starting to shut down. We've filled him with all sorts of antibiotics but they don't seem to be working." Ronnie answered with tears running down her cheeks.

"You've got to save him. He's the best man I've ever had. Is there anything that I can do? Is there anyone I can call?" stopping and pleading with the nurse.

"Commander, if you have any kind of religion left in that body of yours, get down on your knees and pray to God to save him. He's the only one that can right now." still walking toward the plane and looking down on her patient and her love.

Stopping short on the tarmac, Commander Damon reflects on what

Ronnie had just said to him. "Call God. In my line of work, I'm the last one he wants to hear from," starting up again, walking to the far right of the gurney but close enough to know that this may be the last time he sees his protégé alive.

As they approached the plane, the back end was down just like a C-130 transport. Suddenly, they stopped short as Captain Pfister came down the ramp of the plane.

"How are you feeling, Corporal? Now when we get into the plane, you'll be transferred to a hospital bed which will be bolted to the floor. If you should have any kind of discomfort en route, you are to tell the nurses immediately. We didn't come all this way to lose you on the way back because you didn't say anything," squeezing Jim's hand as he turned and walked back up the ramp.

As they were still at the back of the plane, Commander Damon came over to the gurney and grabbed Jim's hand.

"Remember one thing, Marine. You're the best I've ever had. There will never be anyone better than you. You go to Hawaii, get better and then you come back to me here as quick as they will let you. There is always a spot open for you." With this said, he did something that no one thought he would ever do. He leaned over and kissed the corporal's forehead and said in a low voice, "I love you, Jim. " Tears were coming down his face as he turned and started to walk away, never looking back.

Jim couldn't move his head because of the restraint that they had put on him back in the ward. As the corpsmen started to push the gurney up the ramp, Jim had this awful feeling that this was his last ride in an airplane. As they went up the ramp, he started to cry. He wasn't wailing but a slow, low sob, when he realized that he was extremely hurt, a lot worse than he had imagined.

Halfway up the ramp, one of the corpsmen asked Jim if he was okay, being concerned that he was in a lot of pain. Jim assured him that he was fine but he just felt a little weepy. He told him he didn't know why he acted like that but it came over him when the Commander left. The gurney came to a stop right next to this perfectly white bed. As the nurses came up to the gurney, both the corpsmen and nurses transferred Jim onto the bed.

As they continued working to make him as comfortable as possible, the pilot came out of the cockpit and walked to the bed. His name was Navy Commander Joseph Sterphone, an Italian from Toms River, New Jersey. He wasn't a big man but he had a great smile. As he shook Jim's hand, he started to explain the type of plane he was flying and the route he would be taking.

"This is a Lockheed C-140 Jetstar. We have a crew of five, two pilots, a navigator and two cabin crew. You must be incredibly special, Marine. This plane has been outfitted just to carry you, the doctor and the two nurses. There is a sleeping area for them but you're going to be stuck in this bed for the duration of the trip. We will be traveling at a cruising speed of a little over 400 hundred miles an hour. We will be making two fuel stops on our way. We will be taking off from here and going to Guam, which is about twenty-four hundred miles. We will be on the ground no longer than thirty minutes. We leave Guam and fly to Wake Island for another fuel stop, again not longer than thirty minutes on the ground. From Wake, it's a straight shot into Honolulu and the Marine Corps Air Station at Kaneohe Bay. Have you ever been to Hawaii, Corporal?" letting go of his hand.

"Yes, sir. About sixteen months ago I landed at Kaneohe for a few days on my way back to Headquarters Marine Corps in Washington, DC," not telling him too much about his past.

"Then you know how beautiful the island can be. The head nurse will explain what will take place after we land there. Corporal, I have no idea who you are or what you've done but it's an honor to have you on board. If there is anything you need from the cockpit, just yell out and we'll do the best we can to get it for you," turning and walking back to the front of the plane.

"Jimmy, how are you feeling? Does it hurt anywhere? You'll let me know if you are uncomfortable, won't you." Ronnie squeezed his hand that she has held since leaving the hospital ward.

"Ronnie, if you have ever loved me as you said you did you'll tell me the truth? What's wrong with me? If I were just on the mend, you people wouldn't be going through all this. Tell me the truth. Am I going to die?" almost pleading with her to tell him the truth.

"One thing, James Coleman. Who-ever said I was in love with you?" trying to feign embarrassment.

"You did, when you were explaining me to Bridget."

As he spoke, the head nurse's face started to go red with real embarrassment. "I thought you were asleep. You're not a nice person for doing that. That was a private conversation with my colleague and had nothing to do with you. I mean, it had to do with you but you weren't supposed to be in the conversation." She really turned red as she realized what she had just said.

"Never mind that. What's wrong with me, Ronnie? Am I going to die?" trying to hold her hand but she has now pulled away.

"Jimmy, I will try to be as honest with you more than you were honest with me but that's a subject we will get to once in Hawaii. We have been given orders from some people in Washington to do everything in our power to keep you alive. It's not going to be easy but you have the best surgeon, two of the best "charge" nurses in this man's Navy. This plane has been outfitted to function as a small operation room. If something does go wrong after we leave Guam, Dr. Pfister will be able to fix it. Jimmy, you are in serious condition and for some reason nobody knows how or why but you lived. God has something special for you somewhere down the line." With this Ronnie turned to sit down and prepare for take-off but she never released Jim's hand.

As the plane taxied down the runway, Jim's back was really starting to hurt and the pain was now started down his both legs. Jim was going to say something to Ronnie but she was really paying attention to all the gadgets that was next to his bed.

The Medivac came to an abrupt halt and Commander Sterphone got on the intercom to apologize, "Sorry about that Corporal. These aren't the best runways and sometimes I miss the markings. Won't happen again. Everyone else, please secure for takeoff. Let me know when the Corporal is secured and ready to go." With that the intercom went dead. There were all sorts of lights about the door of the cockpit and all of sudden a red light started to blink. A few seconds went bye when the red light went out and a yellow light started to blink. As the yellow light went on, the Lockheed, C-140 Jetstar started to move down the runway. Now a second went by than the blinking yellow light went out and a solid green light was above the door. As the green light went on, a sudden rush came as the plane lunged ahead, traveling down the runway as fast it could picking up speed as it hit every bump on the ground. As they finally were airborne, Ronnie leaned over quickly and said to Jim. "What's wrong, Jimmy? Are you in a lot of pain?" then yelling for the surgeon to come forward to check Jim out.

"What's wrong, Corporal? Are you feeling discomfort?" And now turning to the two nurses, Captain Pfister starts to bark out a lot of orders, fast and furious. "Be incredibly careful but try to turn him on his side. I need to look at his back. Bridget try to get that portable x-ray up here. I have an awful feeling that they didn't do something back at the hospital."

With Pfister still barking orders, Ronnie reaches around Jim's shoulders, which brings her head and Jim's head in the same vicinity. As they come closer, Ronnie brushes her lips to Jim's cheek and whispers, "Darling, please don't die. I love you so much."

As Jim's side comes up, there is a massive amount of blood on the sheets.

"What the hell is this?" Ronnie screamed.

As Ronnie still had Jim on his side, Dr. Pfister took a scalpel and tore his Johnnie up the middle. What the doctor saw almost shocked him.

"Get that x-ray machine up here, stat," looking down at a hole about two inches wide in Jim's back that blood was flowing from.

The x-ray machine was put in position and a few "pictures" were taken. It would take about fifteen minutes to get a clear look at what was causing this infection.

"Those stupid ignorant butchers. They never checked his back, too busy worrying about his head. This is what was causing the rise in the Corporal's temperature. It's your fault also that you never checked his whole body. We will address that as soon as we arrive in Hawaii," speaking directly to Ronnie.

Ronnie knowing better never answered his accusation. All she could do was work on the open wound and wait for the x-rays to be developed and go from there.

"There is a fucking bullet lodged in his back. We will have to get that out before we proceed to Honolulu. Let me go and ask how long it will take us to get to Guam and the hospital there." He left Jim's side and he made his way to the cockpit.

Coming back from the cockpit, the captain says, "The Commander says we are at least three to four hours from Guam and the weather doesn't look that good up ahead. He said he may have to gain altitude to keep this plane comfortable for our passenger. It looks like I may have to take that bullet out now."

Without being ordered, the two nurses jumped into action setting up the operating room which was starboard of the main cabin. It looked like any operating theatre in any large hospital on the mainland. One thing remarkable about these two nurses, never an order was given or any correction to what they were doing. Within fifteen minutes of the doctor's orders, the operating area was ready, sanitized and Jim was being prepared for surgery.

The two interns that really hadn't had anything to do up to now sprang into action. With Ronnie and Bridgit's guidance, they lifted Jim's now limp body and carefully moved to the operating table and gently placed him in position, face down.

Bridget kept looking at Ronnie knowing how much she was hurting and scared to death that Jim would not come out of this. Doctor Pfister was also concerned about Commander White but for different reasons. The kiss on Jim's cheek from Ronnie did not go unnoticed by her fiancé but he was a professional and he would never let a little thing like that get in his way in saving this Marines life.

"How did this ever happen? Commander, do you have any explanation why you didn't see any blood leaving the hospital or when this patient was transferred to the plane?" He was beet red while he was speaking.

"The only thing I can think of is when he first was taken to the hospital, his blood pressure was extremely low. They couldn't even hear it at first. With that low, blood would not be flowing. Even when we arrived, Jimmy, excuse me, I mean the patient's blood pressure was still low. As we were on the flight line and I kept monitoring it, it was starting to come up but not that quickly." Stopping when she thought she should.

"That does make sense. All I can say is thank God I caught it in time," as he turned to prepare for this difficult operation.

As the doctor finished talking, Bridget bent over the limp body of Coleman and whispered to Ronnie, "What a complete asshole. If it weren't for you, Jimmy would have bled out," still shaking her head.

"Bridget, we are his team and he's the man in charge. He's the one who saves lives; he's in charge so he takes the credit. No big deal. Let's make sure this man doesn't die on the table," fighting back the tears that are welling up in her eyes.

As the team was about to dive into Jim's back, the pilot came over the intercom. "Hold a second, Doc. I am going to gain some altitude where it will be a lot smoother sailing. Once I level off, I will let you know." With that the plane seemed to go straight up in the air. Everyone had to hold on, but Jim was fine because they had secured him about ten minutes earlier.

As the pilot came back on the intercom to confirm leveling off, Dr. Pfister proceeded to make a four-inch-long incision in the bottom of Jim's back, right near the spine.

"Let's pray this didn't do any damage to the spine or the nerves around it. If so, Corporal Jimmy may be paralyzed from his waist down." With that, Ronnie could feel herself getting lightheaded and she almost fainted.

The operation seemed to take forever. Bridget thought he may be a pompous son-of-a-bitch but Dr. Pfister is one hell of a surgeon. The pilot came back on the intercom telling everyone that "we're about fifteen minutes from Guam. If you need more time, I can circle for about another hour."

Captain Pfister was just finishing up stitching the last of the opening in Jim's back and yelled to the cockpit. "I'm done so if you'd like to land, it's okay with me." He stepped away but still admired his work.

As the plane hit the runway, nothing even moved and slowly they came to a stop on the far side of the airport, next to the fuel dump. The pilot finally exited the cockpit and came up to the captain. "Do you want to lay over until the Corporal is fit to travel, sir?"

"No, I think we can continue on. His vitals are good and there isn't anything here that we would need to comfort him. He'll be asleep until we actually arrive in Hawaii. Oh, nice flying." That was the first and last time Commander Sterphone would ever hear those words out of the captain's mouth.

After getting some well-received food for travel and fuel, the Jetstar once again was in the air after being on the ground for 27 minutes. Commander Sterphone said that it should take anywhere between three to four hours until they landed at Wake Island to refuel. He said they would be on the ground no more than thirty minutes and then it was a clear shot five to six hours to Hawaii. He got the forecast while in Guam and for a small weather system east of Wake, and there wasn't anything to be concerned about.

As the plane was on final approach to Wake Island, Dr. Pfister once again checked on his patient. Checking his back and then his head, he never said a word to his head nurse. Bridget thought that was very odd, because in the past, they worked so well together. He was tired, 36 straight hours since landing in Vietnam, retrieving his patient, surgery on board a moving plane and now just sitting around until Hawaii.

Ronnie suspected something. She knew her fiancé better than most and he had a jealous streak a mile long. Ronnie knew he was upset with the attention that she was showing Jim. She had been with him for some time and with some of the remarks he was making, a long and tumultuous battle was looming. The problem was that she didn't know how Jim felt about their relationship but she knew she couldn't continue with Ben.

As the plane was rapidly heading for Hawaii, Bridget could sense something was about to give. Ronnie was too good of a nurse and an officer to put up with the "crap" that the captain was handing out. Here she had the love of her life on a bed soaring through the heavens with happiness waiting at the end of a long trip, and she had to worry what this "fool" had to say.

Out of nowhere came the pilot with his final announcement. "We are on our final approach to Marine Corps Air Station, Kaneohe Bay, Hawaii. Please secure all materials and prepare everyone for landing. I know he's still asleep but I would like to tell him what a privilege it has been to bring him back to "the world." My flight crew and myself want to wish him all the luck in the world and he will always be in our prayers. Semper Fi, Marine." With that the intercom went dead for the last time.

As the plane came to a halt in front of a very white ambulance with the US Navy symbol on its side, the back of the plane started to open. The orderlies were preparing Jim to move to the gurney that had brought him on the plane. Once everything was finished, they started to roll the gurney down the ramp to the waiting ambulance. As they hit the ground, Captain Pfister was out front and the two nurses on each side of the gurney with the orderlies pushing. Suddenly the Marine Band that was also on the tarmac started playing the "Marines Hymn" and an honor guard fell in on both sides to escort this Marine to the ambulance. No one knows why or who arranged this, but even Captain Pfister had to wipe away the tears.

As Jim was put in the ambulance and secured in position, Captain Pfister got into a staff car with Ronnie and Bridget. Ronnie leaned over and said something to the captain, he nodded and with that, she got out of the car and got into the ambulance. Bridget would reflect later that once the rear of the Jetstar closed in Vietnam until the plane came to a stop in Hawaii, she never let go of Jim's hand.

After a few more surgeries, four if you 're counting, to his body, Jim was coming around to his old self. Still at Tripler Army Hospital but instead of being bed ridden as he had for the past three months, he is now up and walking around. Ronnie has been assigned to his care, along with a new assistant, Mary May who took Bridget's place. Bridget was reassigned back to Vietnam and was based in DaNang. Mary was right out of nursing school but she was a hard charger and wanted to learn everything Ronnie could teach her. She would arrive at the ward at 0700, make sure Jim had breakfast and then would get him dressed and they would walk the wards. It became such a routine that if Mary weren't available at 0700, Jim would start to worry. Jim found out from Mary that Ronnie and the Chief Surgeon had broken their engagement. Captain Pfister would visit Jim daily when they first got to Tripler, but after about a month, Jim never saw him again. He would see Ronnie in the morning and in the evening, and when he was available to go off base, he and Ronnie would go to the beach or walk around the hospital grounds. He was having the time of his life. Ronnie was so sweet and when he was with her he couldn't be happier. When he wasn't with Ronnie, he would start thinking of Linda and wondering what she must be going through. He had gotten a letter from the Commander reminding him that he was still top secret and that he was not to contact anyone on the outside, especially Linda or his family. He also reminded Jim that Commander White has never been investigated so he should be careful in what he says to her.

MY HEATH IS BETTER
BUT NOT MY LOVE LIFE

Two months has gone bye and Jim is starting to feel like his old self, except for one minor thing. Periodically his head feels like it's going to explode and he has trouble focusing. His new surgeon, Commander Pearce says it's due to some of the bullet fragments that are still floating around in Jim's head. He told Jim that it's not "life threatening" and they should pass through his system but he wouldn't give a definite period.

Ronnie and Jim were scheduled to go to the beach Tuesday morning. Ronnie had checked Jim out and they drove to a secluded part of Waikiki Beach, just outside of downtown Honolulu. Ronnie didn't like the seclusion but she understood that Jim was still "top secret" and if she didn't go along with this, then two things could happen. Jim wouldn't go out on their daily trips with her but worse, the Commander would appear at any time. That would be worse than death.

As they started down the pure white sand of the beach, Jim suddenly stopped and fell to his knees.

"What wrong?" Ronnie running to wear Jim had fallen.

"It's nothing. I get this terrible pain in my head every once in a while. You are not to say anything to anyone. I will talk to Commander Pearce when we get back." With this Jim gets to his feet and starts walking toward the water.

"Jimmy, I am really worried about you. I know you want to go back to Vietnam but if you're not 100% then I really think your risking your life. Jim, I couldn't live without you." Putting their blanket out on the white sand and grabbing his hand.

"Do you know what this beach reminds me of?" trying to change the subject. "Vietnam." At night, when the moon is full and there is not a cloud in the sky, with millions of stars shining, the glow from the moon and the white sand makes the night into day. They call it a "shooters moon." That means you don't need a sniper's scope to see your target." With that last word, Jim suddenly stopped and looked directly into Ronnie's eyes. "Forget I even said that. It's classified. If the Commander knew, I'd be out of here, yesterday."

"I would never mention anything we talk about. That pompous ass will always come between us. I have resigned myself to that. He'll be there even after the war is over," trying to show a smile but she couldn't.

"Let's talk about happier things. Okay?" showing a smile that has come few and far between since Vietnam

"I love your smile. Jim"

And with that Ronnie stops talking and just looks down and starts to cry. "What are we doing? Is this going anywhere or am I just wasting my time? I know you haven't mentioned the teenager but you also haven't said it's over either. You know I broke up with Ben as soon as we returned to Hawaii, but you haven't done a thing about her. I can't wait around forever," sounding serious which surprised Jim.

"I haven't heard from Linda in almost eight months. I haven't written her because no one is to know I'm in Hawaii. When the time is right, I will write her and tell her about you. Okay."

"No, it's not okay. I want to know if you are as serious about me as I am about you. I am willing to give up my commission for you. I will do anything and everything to make you happy. You just have to make a commitment to me." Ronnie was now crying.

"What kind of commitment? I can't commit to anything until I speak with Linda. That's it, final." Turning over on his side away from Ronnie's gaze.

"Then that's it. I have been offered a promotion and transfer to Bethesda if I re-up for another four years. I was willing to give this all up for you but I guess I know where I stand. I want to go back to the hospital, now," getting off the blanket, picking up her stuff and almost running back to her car.

Jim wanted to say something but he knew if he did then there would be a long fight and it would be worse. He decided to let it go and by tomorrow it will be forgotten.

When Jim finally got back to his ward, there were all sorts of mail and packages on his bed. Kneeling on the floor he started to go through them. Thinking to himself; *"I guess my mail finally caught up with me. I know some of these boxes are cookies and pies my mother sends me. Guess I will throw those out. Here's a letter from Linda. Might as well see what's up with her."*

Jim looks at the letter to see if one of her tapes is inside. It also is the only letter from her in all this mail. Opening he starts to read.

"My dearest Jimmy:
I haven't heard from you in a while so I hope everything is all right. I

read every day in the Globe what is going on in Vietnam. At school we have a lot of people who are against the war. I have gone to a few of their rallies and they make a lot of sense. But this is not the reason I am writing this letter.

Jimmy, I have loved you from the day I first saw you at Aunt Adelaide's house when I was five. I have always wanted you to be my husband. Before the prom when we first started dating was the best time of my life. I started planning our life together after you got out of the Marines and I graduated college. This letter is hardest thing I will ever have to do.

I have met someone else. He belongs to one of those groups I just told you about. They really hate this war. They are called SDS, "Students for a Democratic Society." He's a nice guy. I didn't mean for this to happen but you haven't been home in over a year. I miss you so but I'm young and need someone who will be there. I don't know from one day to the next if you are alive or dead. You were supposed to be home this past month but they extended you. Your parents have become very secretive about you so I know something is wrong. You love the Marine Corps more than me.

Therefore, I don't think we should write to each other again. What I'm trying to say, is that it's over between us. I will always love you but it just isn't working and it doesn't look as if it ever will.

Goodbye and stay safe.

Jim just sat on the floor and kept staring at the single piece of paper in front of him. He must have been in this position for quite a long time because Fred, the orderly came down and asked if he was all right or did he need a hand to get up.

"Get the fuck away from me. Leave me alone." And with outburst, he puts his face on his bed and starts sobbing uncontrollably.

He must have stayed on the floor for some time because when he woke up, he was laying on the floor with Linda's letter on his chest.

Sitting straight up he thought to himself, "Ronnie. I have to contact Ronnie. It's all good now. I can make a commitment to her. I won't tell her about the "Dear John." I will just say I gave it a lot of thought and I wrote to Linda and told her it was over. That should work. It's just a trivial lie and it won't hurt anybody."

He stood up, tried to straighten his clothes, but after all the wrinkles and things, he concluded that this was a lost cause. He opened up his trunk at the foot of the bed and took out a clean pair of pajamas. After putting them on he walked up to the duty desk where another orderly was on duty.

"Hey, Clyde. Do you know what time Commander White will be coming on duty?' asking Clyde Donald the new orderly on the ward.

"Jim, Commander White left last night for the mainland. I think I overheard her talking to Lt. Commander May that she was going to take the promotion and would be billeted in Maryland. Do you want me to get Mary up here?"

Jim was almost knocked off his feet. I knew she was angry but to leave all of a sudden like this just isn't like her. I don't understand. I didn't mislead her. I told her I had to speak with Linda and we would go from there. I knew she loved me but if she really did she would have stayed with me. I got to contact the Commander and have him get me out of here. Mosh Skosh.

About five minutes went by when Jim could hear the beat of feet coming his way. It didn't sound happy.

"What do you want?" standing at the foot of the bed is Lt. Commander Mary May, the happiest nurse at Tripler.

"Where's Ronnie? Clyde says she went back main side. Is that true?" speaking and in tears.

"What do you care where she is? You told her how you felt yesterday, even after she told you about the promotion and transfer. She decided you weren't worth it and left," spitting out what she was saying.

"I broke up with Linda. It's done. I am now available to her."

"Isn't that white of you. You're available to her. You received a "Dear John" from that high schooler and now your available to her. You arrogant and ignorant so-and-so. She is a Commander in the Navy. She is going to be promoted to Captain and be in charge of all nurses stationed at the Naval Hospital in Bethesda once she arrives on post. She was willing to give that all up for you and now you say you're available to her. You're the most exasperating person I have ever met." Now she was almost crying from rage.

"Mary."

"That's Lt. Commander May to you, Marine, and don't you ever forget it. From now until you are discharged, you will start cleaning up your own area. You are no longer designated "no duty." You will learn, Corporal, the nurse's corps has a much stronger bond than your precious Marine Corps." With that she twirled and stomped away.

I don't care what she says. I can get Ronnie back. She loves me. I will write to her and express my feelings. I better wait a few days to write that letter though. Don't want her to think that she's a rebound. God, I wish the Commander were here.

"Corporal, you have a secured phone call in the head surgeon's office. It sounds as this is really important." Corpsman Clyde said in a hurry.

Running down the hall, Jim crashes through the surgeon's door. Before even picking up the phone, he knows who's on the other end.

TIME TO GO

"Yes, sir. I understand. Report to MCAS Kaneohe Bay on Thursday, May 20 leaving at 1000 hours. I will be traveling on an Air Force Lockheed c-140A Jetstar. I will leave Tripler at 0830 hours and stay in a secure place that has already been designated. I will arrive seventeen hours from take-off at DaNang and will be met by you. Thank you, sir. No, I have no commitments anymore." Silence was on the other end of the phone.

Hanging up, Jim wondered how he was going to get to the airfield. It was now early Wednesday morning and he didn't have much time. Sitting down he started a letter to his parents. Vaguely describing his last six months but never really saying what he was going on. At the end he did say how he is looking forward to being home and sleeping in his own bed. He also told them that Linda and he had come to a mutual understanding that their relationship just wasn't going to work.

After finishing that letter, he sat and started the hardest letter he would have to write.

Dear Ronnie:
I just don't know where to start. To say I miss you is an understatement. The last time we were together it didn't end well. You asked me for a commitment but I couldn't give you one because of Linda. Well, there's no more Linda. I wrote her that night stating that I had met someone else and that the relationship I had with her just wasn't there anymore.

Ronnie, I love you so much and miss you every minute. Please give me another chance. I know I can and will be the man you expect that I should be.

I am going back to Vietnam in the morning and I don't know when I will have a chance to write to you but I know we still get letters. If everything is good between us, please write. If it isn't, don't.

Love you always,
Jimmy

"Well, I got those out of the way. Hopefully, she's not that pissed at me and everything will be good. If not, what the hell, I still have the Marine Corps," thinking to himself as he packed what little clothes he had. He was issued a regular "tropical" uniform when he first came to Tripler. 'I hope it still fits.' Taking it out of his sea bag where he had folded it exactly as he was taught way back at Parris Island. Looking over the uniform he thought how amazing there wasn't a wrinkle to be found. Trying it on he also found that the shirt was a little loose but the trousers were very loose but he could get away with it. He didn't have any dress shoes but got a pair of black shoes from the box in front of the ward. No cover, no tie but he did have a belt again, not the basic issue but it would pass. In about an hour, he was packed, showed, shaved and ready to get back to the war.

Dressing early Thursday morning was nothing new to him. Anxious isn't a word that Jim would use a lot but today is different. He's finally on the way back to where he was and a mission he needs to complete.

"Corporal Coleman? I am Gunnery Sergeant Jeremiah Smith and I am here to escort you to your next destination. Are you ready to travel?" as he stepped into Jim's area and looking him up and down.

"Nice to meet you, Gunny. Do you have any other identification outside of the uniform?" now looking up at one of the biggest and blackest Staff NCOs he's ever seen.

"The Commander said you wouldn't accept me at face value," taking out his wallet from inside his left sock. He had his military ID and of course his Geneva Convention card. Jim took the wallet in his right hand and holding the ID up next to the Gunny's face he just stared at it. All of a sudden they both started laughing hysterically due to the fact that Gunnery Sergeant's picture looked like a black blob on the card.

"I'm sorry, Gunny, I didn't mean anything by that but it sure was funny," sticking his hand out handing back his wallet and to shake this massive man's hand.

"No sweat, Corporal, it's not the first time. If you're ready we can proceed. There are a few things you must know and act accordingly. You will have a four-man protective unit assigned to you as soon as we leave this facility. Also, you are to do exactly what you're ordered to do, without hesitation. Is this understood?"

Grabbing his small sea bag, Jim was right behind this huge man. As they were walking down the ward, no one said a thing. As they approached the orderlies' table, Corpsman Clyde looked up, winked, and said, "It's been a pleasure, Jim. May God keep you safe." And they walked out into the hot sun light.

Waiting at the bottom of the stairs, in formation were three Marines as big as the Gunnery Sergeant. Gunny took his place on the front right side and Jim moved to the middle. Without command, they all stepped off and went toward the Navy staff car in unison. Coming to the rear door, which was open, Jim was ushered into the middle seat, where his back was to the front seat. The Gunny stepped over him and sat on his right. Then two E-5 Sergeants went right across from Jim. No greetings were given, no handshakes, no nothing just all business. The four guards were sitting on swivel seats and as soon as the staff car started up, they each turned the seats facing their respective windows. Also, in front of them, on the both doors large holsters that held 2 HK MP5A2 machine guns with a thirty-round clip in each one. These were similar to the ones that Jim used in Vietnam but a newer model.

As the large vehicle pulled out, the Gunny did not turn from his window perch but said out loud, "Corporal Colman, United States Marine Corps, you are now under my unit's ultimate protection. As you can see we are completely armed and this vehicle is made of four-inch steel. Windows are bullet proof and each weapon on the door has a thirty-round clip ready to go with five extra clips in the shoes for each weapon. If we do come under attack, if you reach under the seat in front of you, there is another machine gun and I have been assured you do know how to use it. Once you secure the weapon, you are to lay prone on the floorboard and await further orders. Please try not to engage my men in conversation because they will not answer. Any questions should be directed to me. Are these orders understood or do you have any questions?"

"Yes, sir, Gunny. Do you expect any problems?"

"You never know. You are a "top secret package" and we are sworn to protect you at all costs. If nothing else, we will be at the airfield in 25 minutes."

As they went down the road toward Kaneohe, these four men never let their glance roam from what they were doing. In the front passenger seat was one other Staff Sergeant but Jim couldn't tell what kind of weapon he was carrying.

It was amazing, no sirens, no speeding, just a perfect pace under the speed limit. Suddenly the Gunny picked up a walkie-talkie, similar to the one we used in the Canada mission.

"Starship to home base, over." Still looking out of his part of the limo.

"Home base to Starship. Do you have the package?"

"That's affirmative, Home Base. We are seven minutes from arriving.

Package is getting a little anxious. Looks like he wants to play with his new toy. Over and out, slightly turning in my direction and there was a slight smile on his face.

"Gunny, that voice sounded familiar. It wouldn't be the Commander, would it? Is he at Kaneohe, waiting for me?" trying to get the Gunny to confirm.

"Unit, be on your guard. We are approaching the guard shack. Protocol 12 will be going into effect in, 3, 2, 1, mark." With that the ceiling of the limo started to open and, what looked like an M-50 machine gun came into place.

As the M-50 locked into place the limo suddenly picked up speed and we went flying past the guard shack. The guard on duty never moved as we passed the shack. At about fifty yards past the gate, the limo once again came back to the speed limit. As it did, the M-50 started to retract back into the opening in the trunk and the roof also came shut.

Within five minutes they were on the taxiway and moving toward an Air Force Lockheed c-140A Jetstar. As they approached there was a platoon of active Marines, at the ready, circling the aircraft. The stairs were down, but no one was either at the bottom of the stairs or the top. As the limo came to a stop, opposite the stair, still no one there to function as a greeter. As the vehicle door opened, the seats that were in a side-ways position suddenly started to straighten out.

"Same as coming out of the hospital, Corporal. No deviations. If anything jumps off, you hit the deck and hug it until told otherwise. Is that understood?" getting out without waiting for an answer.

"Do I get a weapon to defend myself?" asking the Gunny who just turned a little and shook his head.

As the Gunny and Staff Sergeant got into position, which is right against the limo, the Gunny called out, "Come out." With that Jim could feel a gentle nudge on his butt to move. Putting his left foot out first, he feels a hand on his right elbow giving him a helping hand so he wouldn't stumble or fall. It actually helped, as Jim was standing with both hips right on his guards back legs. Right behind Jim Coleman as he moved into place were the two other guards and they were emerging from the vehicle.

"Corporal, take two steps forward on my count. Unit, 3,2,1 march." With that Coleman took two steps. As they were standing at attention, the guard who was in the front passenger seat, got out of the limo and was now on the top step of the plane with his HK at the ready.

"On my command, we will march to the bottom of the stairs. Unit, forward march," and with that all five men stepped off just if they have been rehearsing this for weeks. All Jim thought was how Corporal Johnson, his junior drill instructor at Parris Island, would be so proud. Of course, he would have found something that Jim did wrong.

Once at the foot of the stairs, the two Staff NCOs stopped and took two steps to each side. Now Jim was looking up at the guard at the top of the stairs. A nod from him, Jim started ascending the fourteen steps to the door of the plane.

As he turned and looked at all the Marines at the bottom and surrounding the plane, a voice came from inside the plane.

"Welcome, home, Marine." With that a huge hand came out of the dark and started shaking Jim's hand profusely.

"Thank you, Commander. It's nice to go home and to be with you." With that they both gave a big hug to each other. It seemed to last minutes but only seconds went by. Now Jim was wondering, should I break or wait for him. No need to worry, he broke right after Jim's thought.

"How are you doing, Jim? You look great. A lot better than the last time I saw you. You had a rough going but I knew you'd pull through. Can't keep a great man down. Sit and relax. Gunnery Sergeant Smith will be up in a minute. He and his unit are going around the plane with the two pilots to make sure everything is still on the up and up. The platoon of Marines have surrounded this plane since it came in yesterday afternoon. When the mechanics and refuelers came to work on the plane for our trip, they had four Marines surrounding them. They had to put on an extra fuel tank for our trip. That took two men to do it and ten Marines to make sure they did it right. Sit down and make yourself comfortable. In the rear there are two bunks, one for you and me. This flight should take about 22 hours, but if we have to stop, it can take up to 44 hours."

As the Gunny arrived at the top of the stairs, Jim could hear the engines starting up. The commander had taken his blouse off and he was sitting in an extremely comfortable looking seat in trousers and T-shirt. Jim took off his tropical shirt and sat down in his trousers and T-shirt. The Gunny leaned over and said something to the Commander. Finishing he snapped to attention and saluted, turned and he was down the steps in no time.

The plane slowly started to move and Jim looked out the window. The Marines had made a large opening so the plane could pass through.

As Jim stared out the window, all the Marines that he could see were at "present arms" which is similar of a hand salute but with a rifle. As Jim was going to say something to the Commander, the Commander spoke first, "That salute is for you, Marine. They don't know who you are or what you did, but they know you're something special. You know your Marine brothers; they dig stuff like this." And with that he let out the loudest laugh than you can imagine.

ALWAYS EXPECT THE UNEXPECTED

As the Jetstar went flying through the sky, Jim tried to close his eyes to get a little sleep, but he knew the Commander wasn't tired, so the questions start.

"Okay what happened between you and Linda? Was it you or a Dear John?"

"Dear John. Guess she couldn't stand waiting around for the word that I was killed in action or injured. After I read the letter I concluded that in our line of business regarding this war, we should be orphans," trying to make something painful, funny.

"I agree in some ways, Jim, but in another way I think having someone home waiting for you should help keep you alive. You have something to live for, Jim. You knew deep down that Linda was much too young for you. Not necessarily in age but in the maturity thing. Look who she's dating, a fucking traitor. Some big short with the SDS, the fucking Students for a Democratic Society. Can you believe that? A fucking protestor. Like to have a bunch of them here in Vietnam. They'd piss all over themselves."

"How the hell do you know who's she is dating? Have you been following her all this time? She's a great girl, just looking for something special. I hope she finds it and can be happy with whomever she marries."

"Yeah, yeah, yeah. Great for her. We'll be watching her and her hippy boyfriend for a while. Has nothing to do with you. The FBI is keeping close eyes on the SDS. There is rumor they are going to try to shut down all the colleges in the US. We'll see whom does what," fuming as he thought of what he just said.

"Again, she's a good girl and please don't make trouble for her." Jim was about to say something else but the Commander cut him off.

"Okay enough about Linda. What about that bossy bitch Commander who thought she could give me orders," laughing as he spoke.

"Ronnie had you backed down a few times. She's wonderful. I blew that in a big way. She told me what she wanted from me and what she was willing to do to get me. I never acted on it because I was still with Linda and I couldn't tell her anything until I spoke with Linda. We had a big fight over Linda and the day I get the Dear John from Linda is the same day she left Hawaii and went back east. Have you had her followed also?" sarcastically because he really did know the answer.

"Are you kidding? I had her eating right out of my hand. I had her where I wanted her. Okay, she's one tough dame. Yes, of course we know everything about her because I have an agent right next to her. All she seems to talk about is you and how she is still willing to give everything up for you. I debated whether to confiscate the letter you wrote her a couple of days ago, but I thought better and let it go," acting like he did such a great deed.

"You read it, didn't you?"

"No, because I was here, but when it arrived at Bethesda, my insider read it to me. I told you not to contact anyone. Your folks are okay but not your lover."

"She's not my lover but hopefully, God willing and I come back alive, my wife."

"Have you told your folks about her, now that they know you broke up with Linda? Maybe Ronnie could go up and visit and get to know them and there would be some kind of link between you and them. I do expect you to keep everything top secret. I am willing to bend the rules a bit if that is what you want," tapping Jim on the knee.

"That's a great idea. The next time I write to her and my folks I will run it by both. Tell me. Does Joe know I'm coming? What did he say?"

"Joe doesn't even know you're alive. I thought about telling him but he'd drive me crazy about coming with me or going alone to see you. Especially when you were in the country. He'll know soon enough. We are in the midst of moving from DaNang to a new base the Seabees are building. It's 65 miles southeast of DaNang. Going to be a Marine Corps Air Station with MAG 12, flying A4s and VMO-6, a helicopter detachment. They are calling it Chu Lai. It will be staffed by the 9th Marines under the infamous Colonel 'Bull' Fisher, at one time Chesty's right hand man. (Chesty Puller the most decorated Marine Officer of all time.)"

"Sounds great. Can't wait to see Joe and the other guys. How many did we lose at Dogpatch? Twenty or more?" Jim asked but he really didn't want to know.

"Counting you, twelve are alive. You know about Rosey and Dewey. Seu was lost right after he returned to the ROK Marines. Bando went to the Philippines to recuperate but he's back now. I'm just not sure if we can use him anymore. I think he's lost in the head since Rosey saved his life and such. Messed him up right proper. We lost all the Korean scouts. Mutt and Jeff are the only Montagnards left. Two CIA agents lived including Sean. They are all setting up camp at Chu Lai. We got some new blood, not as good as your used too. The Brits were supposed to train them as they did your group. Something political happened and they have been recalled to London." With this the Commander leaned his seat back and closed his eyes. Conversation over!

The rest of the flight was uneventful. They had to stop in Guam because something was wrong with the extra fuel tank. Took about two hours to fix and that gave Jim and the Commander time to get off the plane and stretch their legs. He wasn't hungry because they had some great sandwiches on board and that beat the hospital food.

As they got back on the plane, Jim thought that this was the end or it was the beginning of the last chapter of his life.

As the Jetstar was descending into the airspace of both Chu Lai and Vietnam, Jim happened to look out the window at the sunset and to his amazement a Marine A4 was on the side of the Jetstar.

"Commander, did you see the plane on our wing? It's a Marine A4."

"There is another on the other side. They have been with us for the last one hundred miles. They will take us right into the airbase at Chu Lai."

As the Jetstar landed and started to taxi down the runway, the Commander leaned over to Jim. "Everything all right with you? Any hard feelings need to be left right here on the plane. I can't have you holding a grudge with anyone. If so, what we are about to do won't work. Is that understood, Corporal?"

"Everything is fine. I just want to know what happened right after I got shot. I remember stuff on the chopper but I just would like to confirm it." Jim was lying through his teeth. He wanted to know why Joe let them put him in a body bag.

A jeep was there to pick up Jim and bring him to the VIP tent at the 9th Marines where he would be staying for a couple of days. Jim couldn't figure out why he was going to the 9th Marines but he could use a good night sleep.

The next morning, Jim got up at 0600 and dressed and went to breakfast. Finishing his breakfast, he got some coffee and headed back to the VIP tent. The Commander told him he'd send a car to bring him to his permanent residence.

"Hey, you Coleman?" A runner from headquarters was at the entrance to the tent. "They want you up at headquarters with all your gear. You're being transferred. Better get there in a hurry. The Colonel isn't in that great of a mood." And he took off before Jim had any chance to ask a question.

Jim started to laugh, thinking, 'That's why they call them runners, I guess.' There were a couple of others in the tent and they started asking questions but all Jim said is, "Your guess is as good as mine." And he got what gear he had and headed toward HDQ. He started to think, 'I guess all the VIP treatment I've been getting is all gone.'

Approaching headquarters, Jim noticed that the whole building was a raised floor, with wooden sides and windows and a tin roof. Thinking about how much Vietnam had changed in just six months. Entering the building, Jim noticed two clerks seated at two metal desks in front, left of the entrance.

"You Coleman?" the one on the far left asked with a half smirk on his face. "Colonel Fisher is expecting you. He's not in the best of moods so do everything by the book. You can go right in," without even announcing

Walking to the door, Jim centered himself in the middle of the door and pounded twice, yelling, "Corporal James Coleman reporting as ordered."

"Get your ass in this office, Marine," came a very gruff voice

Jim pushed the door open, entered, and marched straight to middle of the desk that the Colonel was sitting behind. Stopping and snapping to attention and another report was given. Looking straight ahead, there he was Colonel Joseph "Bull" Fisher from Dedham, Massachusetts. He joined the Marine Corps in 1942 and was a combat hero as a Staff Sergeant in the Battle of Iwo Jima. Between WWII and the Korean War he attended Officers Training School. In Korea he was a 1st Lieutenant where he commanded Company I, 3rd Battalion, 1st Marine Regiment. Legendary Marine, Colonel Lewis "Chesty" Puller was the Commander of the 1st Marines. "Chesty" was the first one to call him "Bull" and he called Lieutenant Fisher a Marine's Marine. This was quite an honor coming from Colonel Puller. He had all the faith in "Bull" and put him in charge of the right flank at the invasion of Inchon. This led to the recapture of the capital city of Seoul and the beginning of the North Koreans thinking of an armistice.

"Sir, Corporal James Coleman reporting as ordered," saying with a crisp voice and standing as straight as an arrow in front of this Marine legend.

"At ease, Corporal. I'm sorry that we are meeting under these circumstances. I've heard remarkable things about you but as you know things have been hectic around here since we landed. I'm sorry to see you leave. I know you know the Commander over in the dark," pointing to his finger at the figure standing in the shadows in the corner of the room.

Turning his head, Jim saw the Commander. "How are you today, Corporal?"

"Never better, sir," turning back in the direction of the Colonel.

"The Commander here has given me a brief history of your background. He also told me that we are pretty lucky you are still with us. That last mission you spearheaded sounds really hairy. I am sorry we won't have more time for you to tell me the details. Oh, stand at attention again." As he rose from his seat behind the desk and came around and stood in front of the Corporal. Screaming right in Jim's ear, the Colonel let loose, "Albert, get your ass in here and bring all that shit with you."

Immediately the door flew open and the Corporal was in the room with an envelope, one of those big ones in his hand.

"I'm sorry we have to do it like this and not as formal as I would like it to be," looking at both the Commander and Jim. "Corporal James Alan Coleman, serial number 2046282 of the United States Marine Corps. You are being promoted to Staff Sergeant E-6, this day of May 30, 1965." The corporal took two collar chevrons from the package and handed them to the Colonel. The Colonel pinned them to the collar of Jim's utility shirt. Finishing that, he stood back and stuck out his right hand and he grabbed the new E-6 and shook it like he was using a pump.

"Before you leave, Staff Sergeant. I wish I could promote you to Captain but I understand you're not to fond of Officers. I don't blame you, neither am I. Do you know exactly how many of the enemy you have killed?"

"I really don't, sir. I do what I do. I go where I go. I know it's more than two," smiling as he was speaking.

"Colonel, his body count so far is seventeen kills," the Commander said without being asked.

After a few more non-significant questions, Jim was dismissed and the Commander and he left the Colonel's office. As they came into the sunlight, the Commander put his hand up to Jim's chest for him to stop.

"Jim, I need to know the truth. Something big is coming down and I need you at your best. No, joke. How do you feel?"

"I feel really great. I get headaches every once in a while but nothing serious. I haven't fired a weapon in six months but I would imagine it's like riding a bike. Can I ask you a question? What's with this body count thing? What does that mean?"

"All of a sudden, someone in Washington has convinced the President that the general public would want to know how many enemies are killed versus how many soldiers are killed in the same day. It's like it's a competition. Now before you high tail it out of the area after you shoot someone, you must make sure the target is dead. It doesn't matter if the whole North Vietnamese Army is after you, you must get the body count. They are going to count everything, even the ones and twos. It just makes your job a little more difficult. Any other questions?"

Getting into the passenger side of the jeep, Jim asks the most important question of the day. "Why Staff Sergeant? Why not just Sergeant E5?"

"I was trying to get you Gunnery Sergeant but they said a three-tier jump without knowing what you did would be hard to prove. They were willing to give you First Lieutenant but like Bull said, you don't like Officers, so it never went anywhere. Be happy with Staff Sergeant because it is well deserved and accept all the congratulations that will come your way. Now let's go freak everyone out."

"How is this promotion going to set with everyone? I don't think it's going to go over with Joe and the others. Hopefully, it's going to work out." Jim for the first time was letting the Commander know how he felt.

"Jim, it really doesn't matter what they think. If anyone has a problem and can't get by it then it's time for them to move on. You are the only one who will not be replaced."

With that the Commander puts the jeep into gear and drives right across an active runway. In five minutes, the jeep comes to a stop at this beautiful new compound. It has four wooden buildings, built up on a wooden platform. The compound was in the middle of a square surrounded by a barbed wired fence ten feet tall with bunkers in the middle of the fences on four sides.

Before going into the compound, which also had guard towers on four sides, the Commander shuts off the jeep.

"Before you go in and meet everyone, let me explain some things that have gone on since you have been away. We have formed new units. Only half the size of the past group. We had ten back then; this time you will be working with five units. The same arrangement still is the format, shooter, spotter, Korean interpreter, two Montagnard scouts and a CIA handler for each unit. You will be in charge of all the units. It's a lot different now because you outrank them all and you are the most qualified.

"I know they were having trouble filling Dewey's shoes as #1 spotter but I did produce a replacement that I think you'll approve. Corporal Joseph Tomelli will be your spotter on this one highly secretive mission. I know I told you that we lost Sergeant Seu to the ROK Marines. He was given a field promotion to Captain and left about three weeks after they came back from Dogpatch. Seu was on an easy search and destroy up by the DMZ when attacked. They lost twenty out of 25 members of his unit, with Seu being one of the first killed. Before he went to the ROK Marines, he did send a very capable replacement from his unit that I believe you will like. His name is Sergeant CK Kim, decorated and wounded so he's no stranger to combat and an expert in tai Kwan do, karate and jujitsu. Oh, I forgot, he speaks perfect English being that he was raised in Seattle. When he got out of grade school his father who is connected to the Diplomatic Corps moved his whole family back to Seoul. Also, Sean was wounded up in the DMZ also, but he's all healed and is on his way back here today."

As the guard opens the double gates to the compound, the Commander starts and drives the jeep up to the front of a large building in the middle of the other four buildings.

"This is our meeting, mess hall and half-ass hospital when needed. Everyone is in the hall waiting for me to go over our next assignment. They do not know you are here, so lay back until I get their attention and then I will introduce you," not waiting for an answer but jumping out of the jeep and up the stairs.

Jim could hear someone that sounded a lot like Tomelli yell, "Attention on deck." With chairs sliding out so they all could stand at attention.

Jim moved up to the door, his heart beating a little faster. He thought about how they had left him on the tarmac to die. How was he going to treat them, even though a lot of them were no longer here? How will Tomelli act when he sees his old partner and a Staff Sergeant at that? Well, in about five minutes the wondering will stop.

"I told you all the other day that a new Staff Sergeant was going to join our ranks upon his release from the hospital in Hawaii. Well, I went to Hawaii to get him and he's just outside. He is a decorated combat veteran and one of the best sharpshooter in this man's Marine

Corps. He's been in country for well over a year, even getting here around or even earlier than some of you old salts." With that Jim could hear the laughter. "I want you to welcome Staff Sergeant James Coleman back to where he belongs."

With that Jim opens the door and steps inside. All you could hear were gasps and a coffee cup hit the floor.

"Did you all miss me? No, that couldn't be true because none of you knew I was still alive." His sarcasm couldn't be hidden by this last statement, as he walked to the front of the room.

"God am I glad to see you. The last time I saw you was when they were about to put you in a body bag. Wow, a long time ago. How are you feeling? You look terrific and a E6 to boot. It's great to be an American." Sarcasm was never lost on Tomelli.

The Commander knew it had to come out sometime and this was as good of a place to do it.

"Joe, why did you leave me there to die?" The smile was gone and it came out as suddenly as Jim was thinking of it.

"Jim, I didn't leave you to die. When we pulled out of Dogpatch, the corpsman on the chopper declared you dead. When we got back to DaNang they dropped the healthy off and they were taking the bodies and wounded to Cam Ranh Bay. The Commander said that I couldn't ride with your body and I had to say goodbye on the tarmac. Before they left, I had them check one last time to see if they could find a pulse. They tried for over ten minutes and then a doctor declared you dead. Jim, that was the worse day of my life to see someone that I admired, almost worshiped and I never in a million years thought you would be killed. You know I would have never left if there was even a slight chance you were alive. You're more of a brother to me than my own two blood brothers." Tears come down Joe's face.

"I know you wouldn't leave me but it sure felt that way. You wouldn't believe what I was going through once we left Dogpatch. I kept yelling at you but I thought the rotor blades were too loud for you to hear me. I could feel someone had a hold of my throat but then he stopped. I am yelling and I am freezing. When we got to Cam Ranh Bay, I was still yelling but again no one, and then I was put in this heavy blanket where I had trouble breathing. I must have been in there for hours because I couldn't breathe very well, so I started pushing on the top of the blanket. Suddenly, I was out in the sunlight and I was being whisked away to the hospital. I was operated on in country and then flown to Tripler Army Hospital in Honolulu where they have a Naval ward or two. I've been there for almost three months and got out about two days ago. The Commander came and picked me up and we landed in country about ten hours ago. Got promoted five hours ago and here I am and I am so happy to see all of you. The ones I know and the ones I will get to know. Joe calls me brother and before too long I will be calling all of you brother. Semper Fi, and let's get this circus on the road." As he finished everyone came around him, patting him on the back and Joe gave him the biggest hug since Ronnie in Hawaii.

"It's great to see you also. What have you been doing with yourself since they put me in the bag?" Jim asked with a little sarcasm that he could muster.

Joe could feel that not everything was all right. As Jim talked he was looking daggers at his friend. "Been training the new guys. Good bunch of Marines, you'll like them. We went to another island just off of Guam for a month or so. Nothing like what we went through. The Brits were supposed to be training them but for some reason they never showed. Brando and I ended up doing the training but you could tell Brand wasn't into it," trying not to look at Jim as he spoke.

They were walking toward Tomelli's hooch, not talking. As they entered, Jim noticed the first bunk on the right was made up. The box that Jim used for his personal stuff was next to the bunk. The chair that was in the old hooch in DaNang was on the other side of his bunk. Looking at the area, Jim started to get the chills.

Suddenly, Jim turned and his nose was about two inches from Tomelli's.

Jim grabbed Joe by the shirt. "Why did you leave me there to die?" Jim started to cry.

"I didn't leave you to die. I would never leave you anywhere without me if there was one chance in a million you were alive." Tears streamed down his cheeks.

"I know you wouldn't. You wouldn't believe how scary the ride from DaNang to Cam Ranh Bay was. I could hear the rotors from the chopper but I couldn't see anything. I couldn't move either. When we landed someone must have opened the body bag because I could see this light but couldn't open my eyes. I thought I was yelling all the time the bag was open but nothing was coming out. The chaplain that found me said that he saw the bag move a couple of times. He then got a corpsman or whatever the Army calls their 'pecker checkers.' He came over and went all over my body with the scope. He heard something so he ran and got a doctor. The doctor listened for what seemed to me

96

hours but was only seconds when he heard my heart slightly making a sound. After a couple of surgeries and a lot of rehabilitation, here I am. Staff Sergeant James Coleman, USMC," trying to ease his conscience and put everything that happened behind him.

"Enough about that. I am so glad that you're back. All kidding aside, any side effects for that whole ordeal?" Tomelli said with a little hesitation

"No, I've been cleared for active duty. I can't wait to get going again. The Commander says that you're the only one left from the old unit. How's your shoulder? What happened to the other guys?" very curious but not really wanting to hear the truth.

"My shoulder is fine, no problems at all. They wouldn't let me go to Cam Ranh Bay with you because they needed to patch me up in Da-Nang. Couple of stitches here and there on both sides of my body and I was good to go. Now for the others. Nichols and Torres were reassigned to a recon unit out of DaNang. They are with 3/9 but I'm not really that sure. I know the Commander asked me about them. I gave them glowing marks and he put in for their transfer back but they never showed. Brando was sent back to the world. He was shot up pretty bad so they were talking about a Medical Discharge. You die and you stay in but he gets shot a couple of times and now he's living the good life back in 'gritsville.' Joe in his way was trying to make light of Jim's ordeal but the joke just died there."

Continuing, Joe goes on about the other's in the unit. "Haven't seen or heard anything about our favorite Irishman. Scuttlebutt has it that Sean is back at the DMZ but no one will confirm that. I've seen Mutt and Jeff a few times and they are living here but doing special stuff for the Commander. I know they've gone out on patrol with a few of the new units. I did hear that Seu was killed in some action while back with the ROK Marines. Other than that, it's all about the same," hoping that this will be the final questions that Jim asks about the "Old Days" but deep down, Tomelli knows that this is not the end of it or will it ever be.

DIDN'T SEE THIS COMING

Joe continued to ask Jim about his folks then he got to Linda. Jim told him what was going on but he never mentioned Ronnie. Jim also told him he just didn't know if Linda was the type in age or make-up that could handle what they have been doing.

"Then why don't you give her the deep six?" meaning why Jim didn't just break up with her.

"I don't think it will matter. I got a Dear John from her just before I left Tripler. She has started college and is involved with some kind of protest group that's at UMass called the 'Students for a Democratic Society.'" Jim tried to be as truthful as possible.

Joe sat up and started looking under his rack as he said, "Oh. I've got a bunch of mail for you. Since you were supposed to be dead, I thought I'd hold them till I got back home and then send them to your folks. I also thought of giving them to the Commander but he was so upset with you dying, I thought better of it. About four months ago he became so upset with everything. I couldn't figure out what was wrong with him and now that you're here I understand." As he said this he went way under his bed and brought back a small bag which looked full. Walking over to where Jim was lying, he handed the bag to his friend. As Jim opened it he could see that there were letters and small tape reels. "This will keep you busy for a while. I have your tape recorder in my draw."

Jim picked up the sea bag and envelope that contained his promotion and chevrons that someday he'd put on his uniforms. He knew Joe well enough that he could tell Joe had something on his mind but couldn't get it out.

Pulling the miniature tape recorder from the foot of his bed Joe handed the item to Jim. Looking at the tape for a few seconds, he then puts the tape through the spools. Linda would always send him a tape because it was better hearing her voice than just reading words in letter form. Once this was done, he sat back, leaning against the side of the hooch, and listened.

My dearest Jimmy:
I haven't heard from you in a while so I hope everything is all right. I

read every day in the Globe what is going on in Vietnam. At school we have a lot of people who are really against the war. I have gone to a few of their rallies and they make a lot of sense. But this is not the reason I am making this tape.

Jimmy, I have loved you from the day I first saw you at Aunt Adelaide's house when I was five. I have always wanted to be your wife. When we first started dating it was the best time of my life and I just knew that you and I were meant for each other and we would be together forever. This is what makes this recording the hardest thing I've ever had to do.

I have met someone else. He belongs to one of those groups I just told you about. They really hate this war. They are called SDS, Students for a Democratic Society. The members are all college students. He's a nice guy and I know under different circumstances you two would be friends. I didn't mean for this to happen but you haven't been home in over a year.

I miss you so but I'm young and need someone who will be there. I don't know from one day to the next if you are alive or dead. You were supposed to be home this past month but they extended you. Your parents have become very secretive about you so I know something is wrong. You love the Marine Corps more than me.

Therefore, I don't think we should write to each other again. What I'm trying to say is that it's over between us. I will always love you but it just isn't working and it doesn't look as if it ever will.

Goodbye and stay safe.

Jim sat there for a few minutes staring at the machine. The tape had worked its way to the end of the spool and was just flapping around. Jim finally started to think to himself that this tape was exactly like the letter she sent.

Finishing listening to it over again really didn't help the situation. 'I know I hadn't written to her like I should have. I know I had my doubts about the way the relationship was going. To send me a Dear John letter and a tape too, "What a bitch." She said she couldn't live without me. I guess she must have gotten a magic elixir when she met this scumbag. He's a damn protestor. A no-good asshole communist. Well, wait till she hears the tape I'm going to send her,' talking to himself and really getting angry.

All of sudden he started to cry. Again, he starts talking to himself, 'Is this the way it's going to be as long as I'm in the Marines? Ronnie left me in Hawaii without even saying goodbye. A goddamn Dear John letter and tape. I just can't believe it. I thought she needed me. I was so sure no matter what ever happened she'd be there.' Suddenly it occurred to him that the tape was the ultimate insult. The letter was bad enough, but to hear her voice, with no sound of remorse, just a matter of fact that "I met someone and you're history" was too much to endure at this moment.

"Sorry, Jim. I couldn't help but hear the tape. First a letter and then sending a tape with the same message. Was she making sure you didn't misunderstand the letter?" as Joe moved over and sat on the box next to the cot. "I didn't tell you but I got one from Susan about a month ago. I guess for what we do we shouldn't have a relationship with anyone," putting his arm around Jim's shoulder.

"Joe, I'm really sorry. Weren't you two getting married this Christmas? What happened?" Jim forgetting his troubles and trying to comfort his friend.

"The same thing. She got a new job at a company in Anaheim. Somewhere near Disneyland. She was working there for a few weeks and met some guy. They had coffee every morning and one thing led to another. She sends me this letter that says, 'We have drifted so far apart that nothing would put us back together.' Can you believe that? I bet she's been banging this guy since I left California." Joe started to tear up as he was talking.

They both sat at Jim's bunk for a long time. They didn't speak. Every once in a while Jim would just shake his head. Finally, Jim finally stood up, picked up the tape recorder and threw it across the room. It smashed against the back wall into a million pieces.

"I guess I won't be sending that tape to Linda after all."

A BIG ONE COMING UP

After feeling sorry for themselves for about an hour, both decided to go to the mess hall. As they arrived, the place was full. Joe walked around the tables introducing Jim to the new guys. He was still thinking of that damn tape so when Joe gave the names he wasn't paying attention. All of them said that it was great meeting the "famous" Jim Coleman. As they took some food and moved to a spot where there were two empty chairs, everyone at the table started to talk at the same time.

"Staff Sergeant. What was it like in that body bag?" a Lance Corporal from across the table asked the first question.

"Dark. It was dark and the air was funky. I don't know how to describe it. I know you're curious of what it was like, but I really don't like talking about it. Makes me think of what would have happened if they didn't see the bag move. You know a lot about me but I know nothing about any of you. Where you all from?" trying to change the subject a quickly as he could.

This one Corporal came over from another table. "Vince Sweeney, Jim. May I call you Jim? I'm from Lubbock, Texas and I shot 249 on the range. You're a legend. How you could shoot that well for so long? Unbelievable," standing there like a big Texan.

"You can call me anything you like. Just don't call me late for chow." As he started to laugh the others looked at him for a while and then laughed.

They all stayed in the mess tent a lot longer than usual just shooting the shit. One of the best times is when you're telling a lot of sea stories. (*Sea-story is telling an unbelievable tale that the teller will often swear that it's true.*)

One story went from one place to another when Joe decided to tell how Jim and he met. He went on and on about Headquarters Marine Corps and what their first assignment was. He didn't give the most secretive parts of the shooting of Diem but enough to upset Jim. As he continued, Jim excused himself and went back to the hooch. Sitting on his cot, he kept thinking of what he was going to say when he wrote to Linda. As he was getting his writing material together, Joe came back from the mess tent.

"How come you came back so early? We were about to get started in on some of our most exciting assignments." Joe sat down on his box still at Jim's cot.

"You may have forgotten because I was dead, but the Diem thing still upsets me. I just don't like talking about that. I don't think the Commander would be to happy either," still trying to get into the writing mood.

"Sorry. I was just trying to show the other guys what kind of 'Super Marine' you were, fearless and one with the big balls," trying to make emends.

"Don't worry about it. I just don't like the first one. What do you mean what I was like? How do you know I'm not still like that? I am no Super Marine, I am Superman," laughing now and still trying to get into writing mode.

Figuring out that the time had flown by, Jim decided to put his writing stuff away for the time being. It has been a long time that he has had the opportunity to just sit back and listen and talk. Standing up, motioning to Joe to follow him to the mess tent where they spent another two hours just being with Joe and the guys.

It was only minutes when all hell broke loose. The VC decided to attack with a full mortar attack. It lasted for about thirty minutes and for the first time that he could remember they were extremely accurate. Two of the hooches were blown up along with the mess tent. Nobody was injured, but for the next couple of weeks they will be eating sea rations outdoors.

The Commander returned a week later. Within an hour of his return, Team # 1 was ordered to report to him in the briefing tent.

"Gentlemen. It is great to see you back together again. I know you've had time to catch up with each other. Jim, I'm sorry about you and Linda. I know that must have hurt a lot. But that's water under the bridge. You and Tomelli have a mission, but this time it's not shooting anyone. Laotian friendlies have located your target traveling around the border of Laos and China. He's a full Colonel in the Chinese Army named Bai Chin Cheng. He has been aiding the Pathet Lao in Laos, the Khmer Rouge in Cambodia, and the Viet Cong and NVA in Vietnam. He is well educated. He did his undergraduate studies at Villanova University in Philadelphia and graduated with a law degree from Columbia University in New York City. He had spent about ten years in the states, even got his American citizenship, but he is one hundred percent Chinese communist. We will be going over all the particulars in the next couple of days. You should be ready to go on Friday, three days from now."

During the following days, the two marines met with the Commander from eight to ten hours daily. Going over and over all the maps, learning the "pluses and minuses" of the area. Where the best pick-up area would be to get the target on board without any problems. This was going to be a little different because they weren't going to be dropped inside Laos as was usual, but this time the drop will be in the furthest northeast quadrant in Thailand. It looked as if they would fly into Chiang Mai, Thailand on the Burmese border and then travel east through the upper north of both Thailand and Laos, crossing into the Republic of China at Jinghong and then onto the village of Simao, Republic of China, where Chin Cheng calls home. Starting at Chiang Khong, Thailand to Simao, China it is two hundred miles. Figuring they travel at twelve miles a day, it should take them a minimum of seventeen days to reach the village.

After figuring out where and how long it will take, they then got into how they should capture the Colonel without causing any international incident. As they were looking over the diagram of the village, the door opened from outside and both looked up when they heard a familiar voice.

"How are you fine gentlemen doing this fine Tuesday afternoon?" in the best Irish accent you could imagine.

"Well, well. The Duke of Dublin has arrived," Jim said as he jumped up and racing across the hooch to hug the man who was like a brother to him. "Where have you been? I heard you were back home in Belfast. What's going on?" Jim asked as Joe finished his hug. Jim knew he'd tell him what he could and nothing else.

"Just coming back from where we are about to go. I've been up there for a couple of weeks trying to get the lay of the land. I think I know how to catch this guy with his pants down, if you know what I mean," sitting down and pounding Joe on the back.

Turning to Jim, Sean says, "You are looking well, Boy-o," turning back to the maps and the finishing touches on today's briefing.

The next morning all three were ending their breakfast when the boss yelled out to join him in his hooch. As the meeting began, the Commander asked Sean to detail what he found out while in China. Sean related what he had told the two the night before. As Sean sat down, the Commander started up again. "You three leave here in less than forty-eight hours. Your two Montagnards will be joining you, but as you know Seu was killed a few months ago. A Staff Sergeant Young-Su Kim will be joining you tomorrow afternoon. He's a veteran of the

Korean conflict and has been in country for over six months. He's not Seu but he's a great replacement. He speaks perfect English."

As the Commander was talking Jim started thinking of Seu, 'Staff Sergeant Seu was one of the best scouts that the unit could ever had. He worked so well with everyone, especially Mutt and Jeff. He wasn't afraid of anything. He was one step ahead of us when anyone in the unit needed to know a specific thing. The first mission, the shooting in Saigon, wouldn't have been as successful as it was if it weren't for him. A truer hero never lived. Rest in Peace my friend," as Jim got back into the meeting.

As the meeting continued, it was decided that they would leave Chu Lai at 2200 hours. They would be traveling on two UH-1E VMO 2 (Marine Observation HELICOPTER) which were equipped with rocket launchers and an M-60 on the doors. One will be carrying the unit and a second UH-1E will be following for support.

On a mission such as this, secrecy is the most important objective in getting to the LZ. A UH-1E can travel up to three hundred miles but it's been decided that they will not go more than two hundred and fifty at a time. The two ships will travel at "tip" level, meaning they will be at "Treetop" level. The reason being is that the helicopters may bring a lot of ground fire from the enemy but they will not be able to use rockets.

As Jim was discussing the flight with his team, the two pilots came into the meeting. Both of them were Marine Captains with VMO 2 Squadron. Captain Michael Rocha from Amarillo, Texas was the pilot of "Chopper #1" and Captain John Tracey from Dublin, Ohio was piloting the support helicopter, which was designated "Chopper #2." They had decided that two stops would be wise on our way to Chiang Khong, Thailand making running out of fuel would be impossible. The Commander hadn't said a word during the entire briefing letting Jim run it by himself. After the meeting broke up, the Commander and the pilots broke away for a few minutes to go over their maps.

While they were talking, Joe and Jim decided to ask Sean a few questions.

"What happened to Seu?" was the first question Jim had.

"After you were killed—by the way you're looking good for a corpse—they sent everyone back to their units. Seu was sent back to the Blue Dragon of the ROK Marines. They had done extremely well against the VC and they kept fighting up around the DMZ. For what I was told, Seu and his platoon went out on a very routine search and destroy mission. They got caught in a trap around Con Thien where the majority of the platoon being wiped out, including Seu. They never recovered his body. The helicopters got the few that were remaining alive." Sean seemed as if he was almost starting to cry

"What do you know about this new guy Kim?" again Jim asked Sean a direct question.

"He's one tough son of a bitch. He lost his whole family when the North Koreans and Chinese attacked Seoul in 1953. He was with the 2nd Marine Division of the ROK Marine Corps when the attack occurred. The North was aided by both the Russians and Chinese which he has never forgotten. You'll like working with him. The only problem is when he gets close to a Chinese captive or Russian you have to watch him. He just wants to cut their throats," giving off with a little chuckle.

"What do you know about this Chinese Colonel we're going after?" Joe changed the subject.

"He's been around that area for about five years. He lives in a village with easy access to Laos, North Vietnam, and the China borders. It's more inland, just north of Gejiu, which is a bigger city. This is more of a hide-out rather than a residence. It's not too far from the border of Burma either. He comes down about once a month to meet with the Pathet Lao, the Khmer Rouge and the NVA/Viet Cong in that order. Stays in our area for a few days, but no one has ever seen him longer than a few hours in one place. He's a military genius who has studied the military battles of General Giap, especially what he did to the French at Dien Bien Phu."

Taking a breath and a slug of whatever he was drinking, Sean continued, "In case you don't know the story, here it is capsule form.

"The battle that settled the fate of French Indochina was initiated in November 1953, when Viet Minh forces at Chinese insistence moved to attack Lai Chau, the capital of the then T'ai Federation (in Upper Tonkin), which was loyal to the French. As Peking had hoped, the French Commander in Chief in Indochina, General Henri Navarre, came out to defend his allies because he believed the T'ai 'maquis' formed a significant threat to the Viet Minh 'rear' (the T'ai supplied the French with opium that was sold to finance French special operations) and wanted to prevent a Viet Minh sweep into Laos. Because he considered Lai Chau impossible to defend, on November 20, Navarre launched Operation Castor with a paratroop drop on the broad valley of Bien Phu, which was rapidly transformed into a defensive perimeter of eight strong points organized around an airstrip.

When, in December 1953, the T'ais attempted to march out of Lai Chau for Dien Bien Phu, they were badly mauled by Viet Minh forces."

Sean was quite sober but he stopped again to take a long belt of that liquid in the bottle. Continuing, not missing a beat he said. "Viet Minh Commander Vo Nguyen Giap, on March 13, 1954, launched a massive assault on the three strong points of the Dien Bien Phu Garrison. Beatrice, being the biggest and largest of the strong points, fell in a matter of a day. Strong points Gabrielle and Anne-Marie were overrun during the next two days, which denied the French use of the airfield, the key to the French defense. Reduced to airdrops for supplies and re-inforcement, and unable to evacuate their wounded, under constant artillery bombardment, and at the extreme limit of air range, the French camp's morale began to fray. As the monsoons transformed the camp from a dust bowl into a morass of mud, an increasing number of soldiers—almost four thousand by the end of the siege in May—deserted to caves along the Nam Yum River, which traversed the camp; they emerged only to seize supplies dropped for the defenders. The 'Rats of Nam Yum' became POWs when the garrison surrendered on May 7." Sean was having fun with this history lesson because he stopped drinking.

"Despite these early successes, Giap's offensives sputtered out due to the tenacious resistance of French paratroops and legionnaires. On April 6, horrific losses and low morale among the attackers caused Giap to suspend his offensives. Some of his commanders, fearing U.S. air intervention, began to speak of withdrawal. Again, the Chinese, in search of a spectacular victory to carry to the Geneva talks scheduled for the summer, intervened to stiffen Viet Minh resolve. Reinforcements were brought in, as were Katyusha multitube rocket launchers, while Chinese military engineers retrained the Viet Minh in siege tactics. When Giap resumed his attacks, human wave assaults were abandoned in favor of siege techniques that pushed forward webs of trenches to isolate French strong points. The French perimeter was gradually reduced until, on May 7, resistance ceased. The shock and agony of the dramatic loss of Dien Bien Phu garrison of around fourteen thousand men allowed French Prime Minister Pierre Mendès Laniel to muster enough parliamentary support to sign the Geneva Accords of July 1954, which ended the French presence in Indochina." As he finished, Sean looked around and asked if there were any questions.

"Thanks, Sean. This really helps us knowing the make-up of the Chinaman," Jim said, smiling to show he really did like the lesson.

As Sean finished his sentence and sat down, the meeting between the Commander and the pilots broke up.

"I heard a little of your conversation and questions to Sean. Yes, we need to capture this Colonel. Only if it's impossible to get him back alive are you to kill him. The higher-ups in the Pentagon feel that he has all the information about what the Chinese have been up too regarding this war. I have laid out a timeline with your pilots. We are going to give you at least a month and a half to get him and bring him back. You're going to be dropped off at Chiang Khong on the border of Laos and Thailand. It's approximately two hundred miles to his village of Jianshui. You will be traveling through the Laotian Highlands which is mostly mountains. Sean has been there for a while so he knows what it's like when traveling through this region. Once you capture the Colonel, try to get him back across the Thai border as quickly as possible. The two helicopters will begin your extraction at 66 days after you are dropped off. You will be dropped off on the 6th of October. The choppers will return on the tenth of December and will wait for fourteen days. If you aren't at the pick-up point by then, it will be assumed that you have been killed or captured. The two helicopters will then return to Chu Lai and there will not be a search for you. If you're still alive, then I am sure, as in the past, you will enjoy the walk. Oh Jim. Happy Birthday, tomorrow." The Commander was always a man of surprises.

"Thanks. It seems the last two major assignments we've had have been on my birthday. Hopefully, I'll have another to celebrate next year." He wasn't really smiling that much.

Everyone stayed in their tents for another couple of hours. Sean said that this mountain range wasn't as bad as the mountains were when rescuing the pilots. The weather Sean said shouldn't be terrible because the monsoon season was about two months from now and that meant that it would be at least dry.

"How are we going to capture this guy anyway? We going to go right into the village and snatch him?" Joe has always been direct with his questions.

"Sort of," the Commander answered.

The Commander then turned to Sean to explain. "He's kind of a horny cat. He likes his nookie. He goes to this one house which is three houses from his place and across the street. Now I don't know if it's a whorehouse or just his girlfriend. I've seen two or three little ones running around during the daytime. I've also seen a female come out and get them at times. Good looking. Around twenty-five to thirty years of age. Tough to tell with gooks. He never comes out in the sunlight. What we need to do is get inside the girlfriend's house and wait for him. We need to neutralize whoever is inside. When he steps in, we grab him up immediately. Now he doesn't have any security around him. There's a small garrison down the hill from the village. About twenty to twenty-five soldiers. They just lay around doing nothing while the Colonel gets his rocks off. We have to keep them where they are. One good thing about where the house is, the back of the house looks out to the mountain range." He took a breath so Jim spoke up.

"What time of the day does he usually go to see his concubine?" thinking the latest would be the best.

"All sorts of times. He's been there in the morning and at night. Most of the time it's at night but never in the afternoon," Sean explaining the Colonel's planned day.

"Is it out of the question to grab him up in his own place? You said that there are two or three kids associated with a woman from that house. To go in and neutralize whoever is inside would be too much. You would have to kill four individuals with them not making a sound. That is out of the question. What I'm thinking is when he goes to the house for some action we could go into his place. We could wait there without worrying about the girl or the kids. We grab him and tie him up and off we go when the sun goes down. What kind of action do they have in the streets at night?" looking directly at Sean.

"Not that much. They all cook outside if the weather is good. They finish around 1700. Some of the older men sit outside and smoke. Everything is done say no later than 1900. The streets are bare and no one's around accept maybe a bunch of dogs. Commander, did you happen to explain the physical make-up of the Colonel?" Now he is looking directly at the Commander.

Shaking his head, Sean continues to talk. "Well, he's over six feet and weighs about two hundred and sixty pounds. He looks extraordinarily strong and while at Villanova he was on the wrestling team. He's not going to be easy to move" Sean finished his briefing.

"Gentlemen, I can't reiterate this enough. This Colonel, Bai Chin Cheng, is especially important to the outcome of this war. He is quite influential with all the Communists organizations in all the countries that surround Vietnam. If we capture him and he talks then this could cut short this war by many months, if not years. One thing and don't forget this. If at any time you feel that this mission is compromised

[Commander's nice way of saying if we are in trouble] then he must be eliminated immediately. He must never be allowed to go back to what he has been doing." Everyone would comment later that they have never seen the Commander so serious at a briefing.

A chalkboard was at the side of the tent. The Commander went over and picked it up to move it to the front of the table. "Gentlemen, this is Bai Chin Cheng," pulling away the cloth covering the board.

There were ten pictures on the board. They were all of the Colonel in numerous kinds of dress. There was one that had him in shorts or a bathing suit. He was well fit and quite muscular. The pictures showed that he had jet black hair, a ruddy complexion, and a deep scar over his left eye. (Sean said that was from a fight he had while attending Columbia.) There was one picture where he was with his children and a beautiful woman. Sean said that this was the woman that he went to see every night.

"Commander. Can we agree that the scenario about capturing him when he returns to his house at night is the right one?" Jim asked the question aloud.

"All in favor of doing it Jim's way say aye," the Commander said keeping his cool. Everyone at the table including Sean agreed that this was the most reasonable scenario to cause less of a chance to be discovered.

Sean nodded but said, "Only problem with this is getting him across the street where the scouts will be."

"What's behind his house? I mean beside the mountain, is there a river, flat areas or gullies? I'm asking because we could use the river or gully to get him out without being seen." Jim looked at Sean then at the Commander.

"Like most of these villages, they are built on flat land between mountain ranges. Behind his house is a flat area for about three hundred yards and then mountains. Behind her house is about one hundred yards of flat and then the hills begin and then mountains. Either way we'll be in the open for a while." Sean finished talking.

"Why don't you discuss both possibilities and conclude on what you want to do? I don't care because I'm not going to be there. You three are. Make the one decision that gets him out of there without any disturbance. We'll meet back here in about two hours. Get something to eat and discuss." All three got up and went out at the same time.

As they sat in the mess tent going over all the different scenarios that could, would or should happen, they decided on the one stumbling block. The Colonel. A much bigger problem was about to be discussed. How to get him across the street and into the jungle as fast and quiet as possible.

During this discussion, Joe asked a question that was really intelligent and well thought out. "How are we going to control him? We going to use ropes, wire, or something that he can't get out of. I would suggest handcuffs. Two pairs for his wrists. We can't knock him out because he's too big to carry." As he's looking around the two others nod in agreement.

"Handcuff his hands behind him and a long rope around his neck. We must be able to muffle his voice. Put cloth inside his mouth and then secure it with a gag," Sean suggested.

"What about his legs? He can run," Joe interjected.

"That's what the rope around his neck is for. If he starts to run, we just rank on the rope. That will stop him." Sean again with the right answer.

"Why can't we knock him out? It is the safest way to put him down. We can have Mutt and Jeff make some kind of litter to transport him away from the village. When he wakes up, then we use the handcuffs and rope around the neck. We just have to decide what time we take him out on a litter." Jim was matter of fact and it sounded as if this was going to be the solution.

"It makes sense, but how do we get him on the litter and across the street?" Joe asked a question that the other two were thinking to themselves.

"We have Kim and the Montagnards to build the litter and have it at the back door at a certain time. We load him onto it, secure him and get out of there, as quickly and quietly as possible." Jim was finally deciding what they were to do, just like a Staff Sergeant should.

"What do you think of this mission?" Joe asked as stood over the urinal.

"Seems simple compared to some of the other things we've done. I don't imagine this guy wants to die. If we explain it to him in a way he knows he's dead if he does something foolish then it should work. Getting him out of the village will be tricky. We need at least a six-hour head start before they realize he's missing. As soon as they realize he's gone, the garrison will notify the Chinese government. After that all hell will break loose. Once we are away from the village and he wakes up, tie him up so he can't get away. Tell him Kim's story quickly and explain that he's better with us than Kim." Jim had that twinkle in his eyes knowing this could work.

Jim and Joe kicked around a few other small problems that could arise with this mission, then started to discuss the Korean scout. No one asked or even mentioned Seu. Seu was the type that sensed a problem and was one step ahead with a solution. The trouble being was Sergeant Kim was an unknown, being this is his first mission with the first team. They knew how he felt about the Chinese and what he'd do if he got hold of this Colonel. Being outside their comfort zone, meaning Seu, it's going to be hard to rely on someone they've never been with. Jim decided that he wanted to meet with Kim prior to leaving for Thailand.

Kim was much taller than Seu. He was almost six feet and well set up physically. He was around the same age as Seu, forty something. One thing about Koreans, you could ask how old they are and you never got an answer. He came into Jim and Joe's hooch and just stood in the doorway. Not saying a word just looking around.

"You want something, Sergeant?" Jim asked not realizing who he was.

"I am looking for Sergeant James Coleman," he said in perfect English.

"You got him and that's Staff Sergeant. What can I do for you?" still not realizing who the Korean was.

"I am so sorry, Staff Sergeant, I was told Sergeant. I should have checked. I have been ordered to come and speak with you. My name is Young-Su Kim, Sergeant from the 2nd Marine Division of the Republic of Korea Marine Corps. What may I do for you, Staff Sergeant?" putting out his hand for Jim to shake.

"Ah, Kim. Thanks for coming over early. This is Joe Tomelli, our second in command of this mission. Now to get down to business. As you may or may not know our unit has had a Korean ROK soldier before. Someone who was really close to us. We are really sorry for what happened to him. What I need to know from you is how different are you, if anything, for Sergeant Seu?" offering him a seat to sit down.

"Sung-min Seu was a dear friend of mine. I had known him since I was a young man joining the 2nd Marines. He was like a big brother to me. I also will miss him very much. Believe me, Staff Sergeant, if I thought there would be problems with me taking his place I wouldn't. I would never disgrace his name," in tears.

"That's all I need to hear. We are going to meet tomorrow in 1900 to go over final details. The final briefing that the Commander likes to run. Our Montagnards will be here also. I look forward to working with you. See you tomorrow. Do you have any questions for me?" shaking his hand again.

"Mutt and Jeff. Seu used to talk about them and you two a lot. He was so happy when he was working with you people. You made him a better man," again shaking Jim's hand with all the gusto that he could muster.

The following day was like no other. The Montagnards arrived around 1800 hours and Kim came about ten minutes later. As usual, the scouts didn't have a lot to say, but when they did they went through Kim. Sean came around five minutes before we were to start our final briefing.

"Gentlemen. Remember what happened the last time we were together. I don't want to go through that again. If it does come to that, the prisoner is to be eliminated with no prejudice. Kill him like the dog he is." Jim thought he had never heard the Commander speak like that before.

TIME TO JUMP OFF

The final briefing finished at 2115. Jim and Joe walked over to the mess tent to get some coffee and Jim's concoction for their camouflage. The "drum" of coffee was right where it should be, right to the left of the front stair of the mess tent. Taking out his little metal box, and taking the ladle, Jim pulled up this awful looking drink and he put as much coffee grounds as the box would take. For some reason, Jim always smelled the grounds before putting the top on. He had found a handkerchief that his mother sent him and he used that to wrap the medal box tight so it wouldn't leak. He then grabbed a cup from the table beside the barrel, scooping up some coffee, putting into his medal cup and starting back to his hooch. Picking up his gear, making sure that he didn't spill any coffee, he starts out the door. Halfway there he hears the Commander start yelling that the copters were ready to go. Looking around to see if the others were coming, he picks up his pace and moves toward the tarmac. Approaching he sees the #1 helicopter with the crew chief standing to the right of the open door.

"How you are doing now, Staff Sergeant?" he said to Jim sticking his hand out.

"I'm fine. Do I know you?" Jim said with a quizzical expression on his face.

"I know you won't remember being that you were dead. I was the crew chief on your last flight on a helicopter. My name is Bob Coughlan from Phoenix. I'm glad they made a mistake on your diagnosis. The guys told me what you did out there. I really take my hat off to you and your unit. After the last time and you're going out again into the unknown. Wow, you are my heroes," still shaking Jim's hand.

"Thanks, Sergeant. It's all in day's work. I'm glad they were wrong also," pulling his hand back.

"Okay, let's all get in and buckle up. We'll be out of here in five," he said as he got into his chair at the door and brought the M-60 down to him.

Just as he said that the rotors that had been silent started to move very slowly. Looking around and making sure everyone was secure, Jim tried to relax, seeing this was his first flight since leaving Dogpatch. Just as he felt relaxed, the copter lifted about a foot and started to turn.

Once in the right place, it proceeded straight with the propellers picking up speed. Within ten seconds they were in the air, heading north.

Jim seemed fine when the rotors were slowly moving but when the "huey" started to rise and turn, so did Jim's stomach. Sweat started to emerge on his forehead and his right leg wouldn't stop shaking. For about five minutes, Jim had his eyes clenched tight until Sean leaned over. "You all right, Boy-o? You look a little green around the edges. If you have to throw up, do it up-wind," trying to lighten the moment.

Shaking his head to let him know he was all right, Jim looked out the door where he could see the chase copter, which seemed to come out of nowhere.

It was a uneventful flight except for a few times being shot at by ground fire. Flying "tip high" made it easy because by the time "Charlie" heard the copters and looked around or was trying to set up, they were gone. When it was time to stop and refuel, the copters would swoop into the location. There were two fuel trucks at the ready; they fueled and then they were gone. Right outside Bangkok at a Thai Air Force Base, something very unusual happened. It was decided by the pilots and Jim to spend the night at this base and leave in the morning at first light.

Approaching the airbase, the two copters were directed to the far side toward a compound similar to the one in Chu Lai. It had the large fences and four or five wooden structures with four towers at each corner. As the helicopters came to a stop and the propellers slowly came to a halt, the men jumped out of "Copter #1." All of them started stretching and moving their legs up and down, as if they were running in place, just to get the blood moving again.

Not noticing what was going on, the men mingled around each other when Joe finally looked up to see six exceptionally large MPs standing around them. Jim and Joe went to speak with them and after two minutes everyone was escorted to this fenced-in prison which was their "hotel" for the night.

Once settled in, they were escorted to a building on the far end of the compound which was a mess hall. They were served some sort of meat, rice, a biscuit and a cookie. Once they were finished eating, the six MPs escorted them back to their sleeping hut.

Laying down it seemed just seconds to get to sleep then the lights went on and everyone was awoken. Again, for breakfast the same meat stew and coffee and then walking to the helicopter and in the air again. This time the flight didn't seem so long. During the flight, Captain

Rocha would get on the headset and tell Jim what was going on. As they approached their final fuel stop, Captain Rocha suddenly made a turn to the right. He didn't tell Jim why the detour happened but he did say that it was necessary.

As the #1 helicopter approached the LZ, Jim could see a small military camp at the base of this huge mountain range. It was now 2215 so it was dark enough for them to come in almost undetected. As the helicopter touched down, there was no hurry to get off or watch out for the rotors. They landed and the copter just shut down. Again, eight large army MPs escorted the group to another compound that was similar to the night before. This time there wasn't wooden barracks but tents which they entered and each of grabbed a bunk.

The pilots came over to where Joe and Jim were settling in and started to talk. "Staff Sergeant. Remember we'll be back on the tenth of December and won't leave here till Christmas Eve. Good luck. God speed and Semper Fi," as they shook hands with everyone in the tent. As the flight crew left, Jim called everyone together on the far side of the tent.

"Kim, ask the scouts when we should leave. I would think dusk would be the best time. They know this kind of terrain so I will do whatever they think is best. I just pray it's not like the last mountain range we had to traverse. Straight up and the weather was awful. Kim, get back to me as soon as possible. If we are to leave in the daytime we need to be really careful not to be seen." As the time went by, Kim came back and said the Montagnards had decided that dusk would be the preferred time.

Starting out at 1945 on October 7th for a journey that no one could ever imagine becoming as difficult as any other they had done.

For some reason Jim had never asked this question of the scouts, "Why is it in all our travels through jungles and mountains there are always little pathways? No matter where we are there seems to be paths or even roads where there shouldn't be," imagining it has something to do with all the wars that seem to go on in these regions all the time. He wasn't complaining. It's definitely much easier with pathways than hacking the brush as they did in WWII.

As they started out, the weather was absolutely wonderful. The daytime temperatures averaged around 76 degrees with almost no rain. Night temperatures were in the upper sixties which made travel great. Proceeding out of Chiang Khong, they headed for the border, which they passed at 2300 that same night. As always they traveled at night.

The weather was clear, no clouds with the moon was as good as the sun, a "Shooter's Moon." They were averaging twelve miles per night. If they continued at this pace they would be a Chin Cheng's village within fifteen days.

Approaching the Nam Tha River, it was decided not to cross right away. Jim wanted the scouts to recon the area. Passing his wish onto Kim, the Korean had the scouts gone in seconds. They returned about two hours later, sat and spoke with Kim. When finished Kim came and spoke to the others.

"Mutt and Jeff say that no one is around where we will cross. They went two miles each way and saw nothing. They suggest that we cross now, not to wait till moon is high. Sergeant, I tend to agree with them." Jim liked the way he used their nicknames, something Seu would never do.

"They know best. Let's get ready to go," motioning to all to get up and get going.

As the unit approached the river, it looked shallow. The scouts did tell everyone to watch where they stepped because of "holes" in the water. Kim explained that the "Nam Tha" has areas all over that it becomes deep all of a sudden. The natives call this a "hole" in the river.

As they approached the river, the scouts went into a defensive mode, bent over, on all fours but not quite. They waded into the water approximately ten feet from the shore.

Kim said that everyone should go in single file and head toward Mutt and Jeff. He also emphasized that they should try to step in the same place that the person in front stepped. As they entered the water and moving in single file, the water for the longest time didn't seem to come halfway to their boots.

Mutt had already gone across and laid out the path that all would take crossing. Jeff was halfway across in the middle of the river, waving for people to come directly to him. The river's width at this point was no more than one hundred yards. Sean was the first to start across from the group with Joe and Jim following with Kim taking up the rear. Kim stayed on the Thai side waiting till everyone made it across. The water never got deeper and they all made it without incident.

Once everyone was across, Mutt waived for Kim to start crossing. As he started, Jeff was waiving frantically. Kim had his head down and couldn't see that he had wandered off course by five feet. As he was about halfway across, suddenly he disappeared. One moment he was walking, the next he was gone. Without hesitation the scouts were in

the water running to where Kim disappeared. As Mutt approached, he dove face first into where Kim had disappeared. Jeff, who was right behind, grabbed ahold of Mutt's ankles. Everyone was at the water's edge watching what was taking place.

Still holding Mutt's ankles, Jeff started moving back slowly. Mutt's waist came up and then his shoulders. Straining to see what was going on, Jim could see Mutt's arms and two sets of hands. Mutt had a hold of Kim's hands and was holding on for dear life. The strength of these Montagnards simply amazed him. They look like "skin and bone" but they are the strongest when something like this happens. As the two scouts pulled Kim out of the "hole," they picked him up and rushed him to the side where everyone was waiting.

Sean instantly went to Kim's limp body and started to push on his chest. Then suddenly he leaned over and it looked as if he was "kissing" Kim.

"What the hell are you doing?" Jim yelled.

"Mouth to mouth. I'm trying to get his lungs cleared," as he went back to "kissing" Kim.

Turning to Joe, Jim said, "We're close but don't fall in a hole. If you do and I have to do that, you had better kiss your ass goodbye," trying to lighten the situation.

Sean continued this for what seemed to be hours but it was only a minute or two. All of a sudden Kim started to cough and water came flying out of his mouth. He was breathing again. Sean sat back and he looked exhausted. In a few minutes Kim sat up. After finding out what had happened, he turned to the scouts and nodded. No thanks, no handshakes. It's what military men do. A nod of the head was all the thank you they needed.

Turning to Sean, Jim said, "Where the hell did you learn that stuff? What were you doing kissing Kim?"

"You are really a creodont. It's not kissing, you ass. It's called mouth-to-mouth resuscitation. I blew air into Kim's lungs to make him cough up the water that was there. The pushing on his chest is something new we learned in training a year or two ago. It's called 'CPR' which stands for Cardiopulmonary Resuscitation. You push on his chest where his heart is located and this makes the heart start working again. It doesn't always work but it's worth a try. This time there was success." He still was looking exhausted.

Jim turned to Joe and whispered, "What the hell is a creodont?" as Joe just shrugged his shoulders.

"Good thing for Kim you knew about this," turning and walking back to see how Kim was.

"How are you doing, Kim?" as he leaned over to him.

"Much better now, Staff Sergeant. I owe my life to the Montagnards and to Mr. Sean. I am forever in their debt."

"Are you able to travel? We're kind of out in the open here. Don't want some unwanted visitors. If you can, let's get going," looking at the scouts who nodded they were ready to go.

As this small little band got back on the trail, they started heading up the Laotian mountain range which starts just east of the city of Louangphrabang. As they headed northeast, passing the village of Muang Xay from the west side. They continued toward the Chinese border, going past the village of Phongsali, east of the North Vietnam Border and just south of the Chinese Border. Crossing over into North Vietnam at midnight, north of Dien Bien Phu, continuing to Lao Cai, on the Laotian, Chinese border. The travel so far was extremely uneventful.

Arriving at the Chinese border, there were no crossing guards. No bridges as they have in other parts of this region. There was nothing. The scouts as usual were a half day ahead of them but they waited at the border. Determined that there would be no problems, Jim decided not to cross immediately but waited till after midnight. The unit did what they always have done. Each person was to have a twenty to thirty-foot separation from the person in front.

After leaving the border, they came upon the city of Gejiu. Giving it a wide birth going to the east at least ten miles away. They then turned directly north knowing that their final destination was only forty-six miles.

As Joe and Jim checked with Kim, they discovered that their estimated travel time was off upon arriving at Jianshui. They arrived above the village four days early and that could cause a problem. Jim had to rely on CIA Intelligence to determine that the Colonel will be in the village. Never had his units had great success with their intelligence. Jim and Joe put their heads together on how to tell if the Colonel has or has not arrived.

Jianshui was a small village, eight houses at the most. It was right at the base of a mountain range which ran all the way to Kunming, which is the first major city in China from the North Vietnam border. One strange thing about this village that was different from any other they had seen in our travels: no dogs barking. All villages, whether it be in Vietnam, Laos, or Cambodia always have dogs that are barking when the sun comes up.

Settling in on the hillside which was on the far west side of the village, Jim sent Kim out to make sure the Colonel was in the Village. It took two hours until Kim came back.

"Staff Sergeant. The Chinese pig is in the village. He's located at the second house from the left. There are no doors in the rear, only two windows. The windows are for one large room in the rear. It looks as if he sleeps there. There is a side door on the right side of the building. Again, two windows on the left side but no door. A door and two windows in the front. There is no dog attached to that house. No guards either. I looked through the windows and saw a pig who lives a simple life. It also looks as if he lives alone. There is a big bed, cupboard, chest of draws and a closet. He wasn't in the house and I don't know where he went. I decided I would wait for an hour until he came home. A little time later, I looked through the window again and suddenly he was in the house. I watched him for a while to get a sense of what he does prior to him going to bed. When he was asleep I went around the outside of the house to find the best way in." Jim thought this was a perfect report.

Kim continued, "Sergeant. I believe the best way is wait till this abomination is asleep. We will then be able to get in and subdue him without much trouble. We will all be involved with attacking him. He's strong, so you and Corporal Joe will grab him around the arms and waist. Mr. Sean will grab his legs. The Montagnards will stuff something in his mouth so he can't yell out. Once he is controlled then you can inject him with the sleep juice. The scouts will position the litter before we go in. Put the pig on the litter and we all carry him across the street. Do you like this so far?" He was happy with himself.

"Sounds good to me. What time do you think he will be going to bed? What if we go in before he comes back and wait to grab him then?" asking everyone that was there.

"Asleep may be the best. He'll be groggy when waking up. He won't be able to fight as hard as when fully awake," Joe making a good point.

"Should a few of us still be in the house until he goes to sleep? It cuts down the possibility of making too much noise coming in," Jim asked in general.

"Two maybe but where to hide. Everything is out in the open. No doors. I will send the scouts back. They can check again to see if there is a place to hide." Kim started to stand up.

The Montagnards were gone on a mission for Jim. Intelligence had said that a small unit of Chinese soldiers was just east of the village, about fifteen miles away. Jim wanted to know where and how many were there and if they had any heavy equipment, such as a tank. Within the hour, the scouts were back and talking to Kim in a fury. Their conversation lasted about fifteen minutes and then Kim came over to the other three.

"Staff Sergeant, Mutt and Jeff have seen the Chinese contingent on the other side of the hill, eight klicks from here. They counted over two hundred Chinese regulars and three tanks." As Kim stopped, Jim was shaking his head and Joe and Sean were laughing.

"Kim, we are not laughing at you. Jim hates anything that has to do with klicks. He wants miles and he doesn't care if you don't know miles. We know you were raised on the metric system, but he doesn't care. He wants everything in miles. I will make it easy for you this time. Jim, it's five miles, not twenty-five as intelligence told us." Sean finished and Joe was still laughing.

"Damn those assholes in Intelligence. Can't they get anything right?" Jim sounded as frustrated as usual with the information given out by "the Company."

"Okay, let's get back to snatching the Colonel. We can worry about the Chinamen's army eight klicks from here later." Finishing, Jim turns and smiles at Kim.

As Jim finished speaking, Kim had the two scouts at his side and was explaining what was needed. He told them to go back to the house and see if there is any place that two people could hide.

As quickly as Kim finished explaining what they had in mind, the scouts were gone. Seeing them go down the hill, Jim wondered what kind of thoughts they must have regarding everything transpiring in their country.

Jim was getting anxious. Waiting was not his strongest suit and he wanted to pace but there was nowhere to do it. After about two hours, he starts asking where are they or do they think they've been captured. Within minutes after he started his questions, the scouts simply showed up from nowhere. Coming in right behind their waiting colleagues. They have always been quiet re-entering any concealment, but this time it was different. They just appeared with no one hearing them. Jim thought that he would use them in the future with this kind of technique. They sat around the circle talking to Kim for an hour, but it was only ten to fifteen minutes. As they spoke, they were drawing things in the dirt. When they finished they were smiling.

120

"What did they say? Can we get him without much noise?" Jim was almost shouting.

"They say that it won't be easy. There is absolutely no place to hide in the house. But they found something that could work in our favor. There is a trap door in the front room that leads under the house. It's not locked. We can go up into the front room without a chance of being heard or seen. Once inside, the scouts will get a rope around his neck and pull. This should cut off any chance for him to yell out," still squatting and pointing to the drawings in the dirt.

"They know not to pull too hard on the rope. We don't want to snap his neck," looking at Kim knowing that's exactly what he would like to do.

"They know. I do not agree but they know," Kim said sounding unhappy.

"Kim. You must leave your personal feelings aside. This man, no matter what you think of him, is special to the United States. He has information that could actually help stop the war. So, make sure that we get away clean but with him intact. Don't want to go through all this for nothing." Jim looked directly into Kim's eyes.

The sun was up and the village was busy. Everyone stayed in the covered perch overlooking the village when something unexpected happened. The Colonel came out of his house. It wasn't that he just came out but in full uniform.

YES OR NO!

"Why is he in uniform?" Jim asked in a whisper

"He may be expecting someone?" Sean spoke up for the first time. "Usually, the only time Chinese officers get decked out in their finery is when someone of higher rank is coming for a visit."

Just as if on cue, a gray sedan with an NVA flag on its front bumper came into sight. Four motorcycle escorts, two in front and two in back, came roaring through the village, stopping directly in front of the Colonel. The driver jumped out, turning he opened the back door. The Colonel started to move toward the car with a big smile on his face. As he marched toward the back door, he continued saluting as he moved. As he got in place to greet whoever emerged from the back seat, the passenger appeared.

"Holy shit. Do you see who it is?" Sean said out load.

"I see it's a General but I can't make out who it is," Jim said in response straining to see the face.

As the General turned to greet the Colonel, Jim finally saw his face. Sean and Jim said his name in unison, "Giap. It's General Vo Nguyen Giap."

"General Vo Nguyen Giap, the man responsible for the destruction of the French in Vietnam and the main person responsible for all the havoc and killings in this current war with the USA. To say he was a military genius would be an understatement."

"How do you know all about him?" Sean said with curiosity.

"We had to learn everything about him and Ho Chi Minh. Joe and I have spent many hours reading and re-reading everything there is about the both of them. Giap is considered one of the greatest military strategists of all time. He kicked the crap out of the Japanese during World War II, serving as the military strategist for the resistance," shaking his head and now trying to figure out what to do.

"What the hell is he doing here, now?" Jim still shaking his head.

"Why does he only have the motorcycles with him? According to all reports I've read, when he travels, there is a two-hundred-man detachment assigned to him at all times," Joe piped up.

"That must be the army the scouts saw the other day. You know the ones that are eight klicks from here. If they are NVA, then I'm amazed the Chinese would allow him to bring a force into their country. I need to know if the ones the scouts saw are either NVA or Chinese regulars," trying to make some sense of Giap being alone.

After the formal greetings, the General and Colonel went into the Colonel's house. The soldiers that were on the motorcycles stood guard at the front door. A lot of things started to go through Jim's head. 'Should we try to capture Giap instead of the Colonel? Should I shoot the both of them? What would the Commander say if I came back and told him I had a chance to take Giap out and didn't?' as he just kept looking at the house .

"What are you thinking about, Jim? You know we may never get this close to him again. His soldiers must be around here somewhere. We'd never get him back to DaNang. We should just do what we've planned on. Snatch the Colonel after Giap leaves and head back." Sean made a lot of sense, but what would the Commander say?

"You know if we tried to grab the General it's going to be an all-out fire fight. It's not going to be like getting the pilots at Dogpatch. We are only six and he's got hundreds. There is no way we can get him. We can shoot him but capturing him is out of the question. Get that out of your mind, Jim." Joe was again making sense.

"I agree with what you're saying. The only thing I keep thinking of is what will the Commander say?" looking at both of them.

"Jim. You will be damned if you do and damned if you don't. You're not going to win with him. If we grab or even kill him he'll go crazy because of the international shit that may happen. If we don't do anything and let him get away he'll go nuts also. It's a no-win deal. I think we wait for him to leave, grab the 'Chinaman,' and find out what they talked about. Safest and best way for this to turn out right," again Joe making more sense all the time.

"When we get him back to the boys in Chu Lai, they will be able to find out what Giap wanted with the Colonel. No sense in tipping the apple cart," Sean chiming in with more positive advice.

"Let's see what the scouts find out. If his force is nowhere to be found then maybe we should give it some thought. This is being dropped right in our laps. Getting him out of here would be impossible. I just don't know what ramifications would develop if I shot him. Let's just wait and see," as Jim turned back to look at the house again.

As they waited, the scouts returned. They were gone for about four hours. They went directly to Kim who after listening brought them up to Jim, Joe, and Sean.

"They say that many NVAs are camped about twenty miles southeast of this village. They say that it doesn't look more than fifty men. Mutt went further down and found the rest of the NVA about ten miles past. He says there are about one hundred fifty to two hundred NVA soldiers. Many trucks and a tank. He says that they acted as if they were going to go into battle. He says he couldn't get that close to hear anything. He says that they had patrols circling the encampment at all times. Very strange for the NVA to do that," as Kim continued explaining what the Montagnards had told him.

"Kim. Ask Mutt if he felt that they were getting ready in case of an ambush or were they going to fight the Chinese?" looking at Mutt as he spoke to Kim.

As he translated Jim's words, Mutt became very animated and said, "He thinks they are getting ready to fight someone. He says that there were no signs of any ambush. He did say that we are right on the border of Burma and they sometimes send in the military to fight the Chinese." As Kim finished his sentence; he stares right at Jim.

"I remember the Commander saying that the Chinese weren't that happy with the North Vietnamese. The Chinese were upset that Ho and Giap have relied so much on the Russians and not enough on them. He also said that Russia wants to make Vietnam one of their puppets like Cuba or Yugoslavia. They can govern themselves but come under the control of the USSR. China is afraid of this. Also, the Burmese government is controlled by the military and they are also close with the Soviet Union. The Chinese are trying to do everything to persuade both of their leaders to come to their side. The funny thing is that the Vietnam War could end up in a battle between the Republic of China and the United Soviet Socialist Republic. You didn't think I knew what USSR meant did you?" Jim looking at his comrades and laughing but thinking this was serious.

"Kim. Ask them what they think. Do they think they are going to attack this village or somewhere else?" Joe getting involved in the discussion.

As Kim started to talk to Mutt, Jeff joined the conversation. As usual they never sit down. They squat on their haunches with their asses almost hitting the ground. During the conversation, the scouts again became quite animated. When they finally finished, Kim turned to all to translate.

"They believe that the North Vietnamese are going to fight the Chinese. They said before we left Da Nang they heard the Burmese Army was built up on the border. Now Burma doesn't have that big of an Army but we are a long way from Peking. They said that the Burmese Army is only six hundred miles from Kunming, the largest Chinese city in this part. If the Chinese end up fighting the Burmese then the North Vietnamese would side with Burma. You would have the NVA, Patet Lao and Khmer Rouge along with the Burmese against the Chinese. With all these countries being on the side of the Soviets, this would give them the right to fight the Chinese. But why is Giap here? He's close to the Soviets and if a fight is coming, why talk to the Colonel? This is getting to be very confusing. Kim, ask the scouts about the army they saw five miles from here. Is it the same ones they saw today but in another location?"

Kim turned to the scouts and started talking in the perfect Montagnard language of Autronesian, which is a mixture of Malayo-Polinesian, and Jarai, Roglai and Rade. After he finished asking the questions, the two scouts turned and started talking to each other. When they finished they only said a few words to Kim. Kim turned to the others and said, "They are different. One hundred and fifty NVA about ten miles from here and two hundred Chinese are just five miles," speaking with no expression on his face.

"What Chinese? I thought you both said that the soldiers that were five miles from here were NVA. Now they are Chinese and there are two hundred of them. What the fuck is going on? We have two hundred Chinks and one hundred fifty to two hundred NVA and God knows how many Burmese are on the border. I think the idea of taking out Giap is gone bye-bye. Now we are taking the Colonel with two hundred of his homeland buddies just sitting a stone's throw from here is going to be quite a feat." Jim was shaking his head and cussing under his breath.

As dusk came, the front door of the house opened and the General appeared.

"I got that cocksucker in my sites and there is nothing I can do about it. I wonder what he would say this minute if he knew he's this close to death. That motherfucker should be dead. He's going to kill a lot more of our brothers before this is all over." Jim was working up a hate that got the others worried.

"Hey, buddy. Lighten up! You know if you killed him that another would pop up and the Colonel would get away. Let it go, Jim. There will be another day down the road," as Joe took the rifle from his buddy who was crying his eyes out.

As the General went to his car, the Colonel was nowhere to be seen. The motorcade started up. The two motorcycles that were stationed in front of the sedan started to move. The two bikes who were stationed behind the car remained with the riders now guarding the front door. Jim turned to Kim and told him to have the scouts go down and look into the window to see what was going on.

"Kim, make sure you tell them to make sure the Chinaman is still alive."

As they were waiting, Jim tried to get some sleep. Laying there thinking of his folks, his brother, Bob and his wife, Gayle and the baby Marylou. He also started thinking of Linda for about a few seconds and then Ronnie came into his thoughts. He was thinking if he would ever get out of this forsaken country and be able to go back to her. Realizing how stupid he was the last time they were together. All she wanted was a commitment but he just couldn't say it. Know he's thinking that all this is going to stop when he gets home. Just as he was going into a deep sleep, the scouts returned.

Again, they huddled with Kim first and then they came over to join the rest of us.

"It looks as if the Colonel is a prisoner. He isn't tied up but they have two guards at the front. The scouts couldn't see any weapons in the house. It looks as if he's under house arrest." Kim was still listening to the scouts and talking at the same time.

"If we are going to get the Colonel it has to be tonight. He may be more willing to come with us now than a few days ago. Let's get ready. We'll move out in fifteen minutes." Jim stood and gathered his equipment.

CAPTURED AND ARROGANT

Fifteen minutes does go by quickly. The scouts had already departed and were on their way down to the house. It was decided that they would take out the two guards. Seeing the house was on small stilts, the scouts would put the bodies under the house. As the rest of the unit was coming down the hill, the clouds started to part and the worst possible thing happened. Behind the clouds was a "Shooter's Moon." A full moon that gave off an overabundance of light. It took about fifteen minutes to get to the bottom of the hill. They came upon the house across from the Colonel's. Moving around to the front, they could see the two scouts on each side of the Colonel's house. The two guards were still at the front as the two scouts got ready to minimize the problem. They had their crossbows in their hands, half crawling to get to their vantage point. Suddenly as if by cue, they both lifted the bows and fired. Both guards went down in unison. Within seconds the scouts were on the bodies and dragging them under the house. As they were doing what they do, the unit started to run across the street one at a time. As they approached the front door, Kim burst through and was on the Colonel before he knew what hit him. Kim had his K-bar in his right hand which was at the Colonel's throat and his left finger up to his lips telling the Colonel to be quiet. The rest of the unit was right behind him. Sean followed Kim and he got to the left of the Colonel and had his pistol barrel at the side of his head.

'Well, I guess the idea of not making noise was forgotten. What happened to the trap door into the living room? We will have to discuss this when we get back to Chu Lai, half smiling and wanting to laugh but he couldn't chance it.

"You know by now not to say anything. If you make any kind of noise, you're dead. I know you speak English. Nod if you understand?" As Jim was talking, the scouts put a cloth on the Colonel's mouth.

After they gagged him, the scouts tied his hands behind him. They put his pants on and tied his sandals. Taking his coat, they put it over his shoulders. When finished they made him sit on the floor.

"Colonel. It looks as if you're in a world of shit with the Vietnamese. This is what we are going to do. We will be leaving here within twenty minutes. We'll go up over the hill across the way and then over the mountains. If you give us any problems whatsoever, I will kill you. The bottom line is that either you come all the way back with us or you die. Those are the only options. Also, if we are discovered by the NVA and Giap, my orders are to make sure you're dead. Now, nod your head if you understand," trying to be tough but understanding.

He nodded as if he understood but his eyes had the hatred of a thousand men. Picking him up, they let him go for second. He lurched forward toward the door, but Kim was on him in a second. Tackling him, and as the Colonel was going down, Kim kicked him in the side of the head. The Chinaman just laid there not moving. Jim thought he was dead. Kim had this look in his eyes that resembled the hatred that was in the Colonel's.

"Kim. Nice going. Do you know this man? You have a look in your eyes that you two have run into each other before," just getting quizzical before everyone leaves.

"No, Staff Sergeant. I don't know this pig, but I've seen many like him during our war. The Chinese Army came into Seoul and killed my family. I have sworn vengeance on all Chinese," again with the look of a killer with no feelings.

As he finished telling them all about his feelings about the Chinese, the Colonel started to stir. Jim leaned down as he was shaking his head.

"You see, Colonel, it's almost impossible for you to get away. I still think you have a better chance with us to stay alive than with the NVA. You must have done something really terrible for Giap to come himself. Well, I don't care right now what it is. I care that we get across the street and into the hills. If you do anything like you just did, I'll kill you." Turning to the others, Jim ordered, "Let's get him ready to travel."

As he was talking to the Colonel, the Montagnards came back into the room with a three-foot pole they found. Turning the Colonel around, they placed it between his back and upper arms. They then tied his arms to the pole as tight as they could. This restricted his balance if he decided to run again. It also gave them a better way of controlling him as they traveled.

In five minutes, everyone was ready to leave. The scouts left by the trap door. As they waited, which seemed like forever, a knock on the side door was the signal for everyone to move out. As they did before, each person went one by one through the side door and then into the road. Usually, Sean and Joe would be in the lead, but with the Colonel all tied up, they got on both sides and physically carried him into the back of the house that was across from the Colonel's. Jim was right behind them with Kim as usual taking up the rear for safety sake. As Jim was starting to clear the back of the houses, he saw someone standing in what would be called the backyard. Not seeing and really not caring if it were a man or woman, he fired in that direction. The silencer on the HK-54 machine gun worked well and the figure fell where he or she stood. This time collateral damage counted. Hitting the bottom of the hill within fifteen minutes of leaving the Colonel's house, they started to climb. Jim noticed that the Colonel was having trouble keeping his balance especially at strategic locations where he could leave clues to the ones who would follow.

"If you fall one more time, I cut both your ears off," Jim said directly into his right ear.

At the foot of the hill, they started to run. Four hundred feet straight up and then down the other side as fast as they could move without stopping. The Colonel was not helping the situation at all. He would stumble as he did going up the hill but he didn't fall. Picking him up for the umpteenth time, Jim noticed that Kim was picking up twigs and leaves behind the group. Slowing down just for a while, he looked at Kim to find out what he was picking up.

"Every time that pig falls he leaves clues to which way we are traveling. I'm cleaning up as much as I can. We need to be careful with him. He does not want to go back with us. He knows what the South Vietnamese will do to him when they are finished questioning him." He still had that steel look in his eyes when talking about the Chinaman.

Coming down the other side of the hill, the Colonel fell pushing down the bushes all around him. Stopping to rest and for Kim to fix up the area, Jim took the gag off and spoke to the Colonel directly.

"I want you to listen and understand what I'm going to say to you. My orders are to get you back to Chi Lai in one piece, if possible. That is the key words, 'if possible.' If it looks as if we are to be overrun then I will kill you. Those are my orders. But thinking it over, I will not kill you, Colonel. I'll leave that pleasure to the man that hates you more than anyone here. Staff Sergeant Kim of the ROK Marines, who is a survivor of the Chinese attack on Seoul in 1953. I can assure you that he will take great time and pleasure in making you pay for that attack." As he was speaking the Colonel turned his head and looked at Kim.

"I wasn't even there in 1953," he said rather loudly loud. "You're Chinese and you're in the Chinese Army. He really doesn't care if you were there or still in your mother's womb. He hates the Chinese. Figure it out. You're here and Chinese." As he spoke to the Colonel, Kim had taken out his K-bar and was sharpening it staring directly at the Colonel, with fire in his eyes.

"I know Americans. You won't let him do anything to me. You're more humanitarian than that. Also, I am an American citizen. I have rights," defiantly speaking but not looking at the Korean.

"You can believe what you want. You have no rights out here and for you being an American citizen. You lost that right as soon as you put that uniform on. You don't know me but I'm sure you've heard of us. I'll just give you a few examples. The Vietnamese female Colonel Dung Thi Phong shot and killed during a Chinese attack on her village of Lang Son. I put a bullet in her head as she held her baby. What about the two Air Force pilots held by the Chinese border the beginning of this year? We were the ones that freed them. No, Colonel, I'm not here to brag about what we do. I'm just here to tell you that if you're to be killed, the Korean will do it. I will feel absolutely nothing if he does and I may even watch," trying to speak matter-of-factly so he'd understand that *he* was telling the truth.

As he was telling the Colonel about their exploits, Jim could see in his eyes that he believed him. Also, Staff Sergeant Kim just had this look that he really wanted us to be compromised. Jim knew that whatever he had planned it wasn't going to be pretty.

As they were getting ready to move out, Jim once again stopped and said something to the Colonel. "Colonel, I know as a Marine we are obligated to always try to escape. As a Marine who has you captured it is my obligation to kill you if you try to escape," grabbing him and pushing him toward the rest of the unit that had started to move out.

Before departing their location, which was about fifteen miles from the village, Jim had been talking to Joe and then he wanted to get the rest of the units opinion on which way to get back to Chu Lai.

"All right, everyone pay attention and have an opinion. Don't take too long deciding or we won't have to worry about anybody's opinion. Originally we would go into Laos and then down to Thailand to a friendly base and wait to be picked up. I was thinking that if Giap has that many men behind us, he would surely call ahead and tell everyone to get out and find us. Then we have the Pathet Lao who also will be called and told to man the border. Now the NVA and the Viet Cong will also be notified and they will be coming up from the south. This is what I propose and if one person disagrees we do the original method," taking a deep breath and continuing with his idea as he takes a small piece of paper out of his one and only pocket. "We go directly east skirting the Chinese-Vietnamese border till we come to a familiar place called Lang Son. There we go directly south over the mountains coming out between Hanoi and Haiphong. We hug the water's edge at Haiphong then make it down to Ninh Binh, Thanh Hoa and then make it east past the villages of Vinh and Ha Tinh, then down past Dong Ho, where the NVA has a huge presence. After Dong Ho it is just a skip and jump to the DMZ and Quang Tri. We then will arrange for a pickup to Chu Lai. What do you think?" as he sat back and waited for Joe to piss all over his idea.

"It's brilliant. They expect us to stay in the jungles with the trees and high grass as cover. They will never expect us to head east instead of southwest. I agree with Jim." Joe was actually excited about the new plan.

The scouts in about ten minutes had figured out it was six hundred and sixty-five miles to the city of Hue. Jim thought, 'All most seven hundred miles. What the hell, it isn't that we are not used to walking.'

ON THE RUN AGAIN

Jim once again and for the last time had to explain to the Colonel emphatically how important it was for him to follow orders. Not using Kim this time, he explained that he was getting tired of the falling, stumbling, breaking of branches, etc.

"I don't think you understand the problem we are having and I am getting sick of telling you how important it is for you to cooperate. Giap has called Hanoi by now to send out everyone available to find us. I don't think he cares about us particularly. He only wants you. You know too much and if you get killed, it is fine with him. You must know by now he's not afraid of your government. He's up against a greater force than you people can muster and he's doing a fairly good job fucking with us. So, if you delay us from getting to our destination, you won't have to worry a bit about the South Vietnamese because we'll leave you here dead or tied up like a stuffed pig so you can wait your fate with the NVA."

Stopping to rest, Kim would always have his K-bar and stone and start sharpening it. As he moved the knife back and forth on the stone he'd just stare at the Colonel.

They had been traveling for about sixteen or seventeen nights when they came to the village of Ninh Binh. It was a typical, small, unexcitable piece of land in the middle of a mountain range. They came in on the northeast side so not to arouse the village. The scouts had found a perfect place to stay for the night. As usual it was a third of the way up a mountain. It was a perfect cut out that overlooked the village and areas beyond. Jim decided to let them rest for a day or two and then force march to the DMZ.

Jim was sleeping for a long time. Joe came over to wake him which was quite unusual because Jim was always the first one up. Joe said that there was only thirty minutes till they left. As he was talking, Jim kept shaking his head.

Joe noticed that Jim had this horrible look on his face and he knew something was wrong.

"Joe. I can't see. Nothing. I'm blind." His hands waved around trying to touch something as he was screaming.

"What do you mean you can't see? Look at me. I'm right in front of you. What do you see?" Joe was screaming also.

"Not a damn thing. It's black as can be. This is what the doctors in Hawaii must have been talking about," Jim said trying to remain calm.

"They told you that you would be blind. Are you shitting me?" Joe was getting extremely upset.

"They told me that there is still a piece of the bullet in my skull. They said that it could float around and could hit some nerves and cause me extreme discomfort. I would have severe headaches or loss of sight. It's not permanent and within days I would be fine again. They also said that it may never happen. Well, I guess they were wrong," trying to show a little humor in his explanation.

Jim was trying to give off the attitude that this really didn't bother him, but in reality he was scared to death. As Joe was peppering him with questions, all Jim could think of was what if this doesn't go away? How am I ever going to get back to Chu Lai? The one thing about this mission was that the Colonel had to get back alive, no matter what. Now this. Jim knew that the NVA with General Giap would be trying to get the Colonel back. He wanted to tell Joe to stop talking but he could tell he was also scared for his friend.

"And you never said a word about what the doctor's had told you. Do you think they would have said something to the Commander?" listening to him in mid-sentence.

"Joe. Stop talking and let's figure out what we are going to do. You must take the Colonel and get him over to the other side. I'm not the primary worry right now. It's getting him back. Leave me one of the Montagnards. After this thing subsides we will be right behind you," still not seeing a thing but really trying.

"Brave American. You will be dead in days once the General's troops get to you. Let me go and your buddies can get you back to your base." The Colonel was now talking since they took off the gag.

"You shut the fuck up or we will not have to worry about you getting to the south. Put that gag back on him and don't take it off until we get to Chu Lai." Joe wasn't in the mood to put up with the "chink."

"Jim. He's right in a way. We just can't leave you here. How do we know your sight will ever come back? You'll be going through the woods at a snail's pace. They will catch you come hell or high water. You know what they will do to you if you're caught," this coming from the CIA field handler, Sean.

"It really doesn't matter what you all think or not. I'm still in charge of this mission and what I say goes. You will leave when it gets dark.

Make your way to Quang Tri. I will keep Mutt and we will be right behind you. I know this is going to go away. If it doesn't then we'll cross that bridge when we get to it. Now get ready to get out of here. I need Kim to tell Mutt what's going on. If he's all right with my decision that's great but do not order him to stay," closing his eyes hoping that when he opens them he can see.

"You should stay here until you're really feel that you're ready to travel. Everything has been explained to Mutt and he seems to understand. Once you're ready to go he is to try to get to us as soon as possible. While you're in this cave you should make sure no one knows you're here. Jim, make sure you're almost perfect before leaving. Mutt knows all about Giap and the NVA looking for us. The scouts have spoken and each knows the route we will be taking. Hopefully, it'll be only a few days before your sight comes back. We will be traveling at eight to ten miles per night because of the Chinaman. You should be able to catch up with us before we hit the DMZ. Do you have any new orders or anything else we need to know before leaving?" Joe and Sean alternating talking made them sound really serious.

"Nothing new, just the same ones. Make sure you get him back alive. If you don't think you can get back in one piece, make sure he's dead. Also, don't deviate the route going back unless it's necessary. Other than that, I'll see you when I see you," holding his hand out for them to shake.

Lying there in the dark, his eyes are wide open but nothing. Not a shadow. They are all gone and he doesn't know where Mutt is. What a horrible feeling. He knows not to yell out because he doesn't know how far away the village is and how far sound travels. Just as he was getting really fidgety a hand was on his arm.

"You okay. I take care you. You, number 1." It was Mutt speaking "Pidgeon." Mutt sounded exactly like Sergeant Seu.

"Mutt. I'm sorry but I don't know your real name. How long have you spoken English?" What he would call English.

"Me, Mutt. We stay here long take. I stay you. We back Chu Lai, pretty damn quick. Learn speak, nun school. Boy." He's telling Jim that he could call him Mutt. They will stay as long as it takes for Jim to get well and Mutt learned English at a parochial school when he was a boy.

As he finished speaking, Jim could feel him pushing his body back to lie down. As he did this, a wet rag came over Jim's eyes. Knowing from this point on that he had nothing to worry about. Jim was in the best hands.

"I have never realized how much your eyes mean to you. You have absolutely no idea what time of day it is, morning or night. The only thing being blind is that it is always nighttime. Mutt is so attentive. He told me in his way that he was going out to get some food and would be back in an hour. He also gave me a code word "Pleiku" so I would know it was him. He gave me a grenade and told me to pull the pin and lob it straight, then duck. I didn't know how to feel being alone or not. I know he wouldn't leave me alone if he thought there was imminent danger so that made me feel a little better. When he left I had my back against the furthest wall but facing the entrance. I have heard people say when you lose one of your senses the others get better. The only problem was I started to imagine I heard everything. Many times, while I was waiting for Mutt, I thought I heard troops coming up the mountain. Thank God no one came in the cave."

"Pleiku, Mr. Jim," were the nicest words he heard for a long time.

"Mutt. That didn't take you long at all. What's for dinner or breakfast or whatever? Did you see anything going on out there?" Jim just wanted to talk to someone even if Mutt had trouble understanding him.

"I got medicine. Help see. Some fruit. Eat then medicine. May yes, may no." As he talked Jim knew he was busying himself around the cave. His voice would be on the right, then the left and then back to the right. Jim thought, 'I never realized how fast he moves.'

He brought back some guava fruit and kiwi. Also, something that tasted like a potato but didn't smell like anything he ever had. He also brought back some fresh water. After they had finished, Mutt had Jim lie on his back. Jim knew Mutt was mixing something because of the little noise he made. When he finished he came over and said, "Smell shit, good you."

Jim thought, 'You're not lying.'

It was the worst smelling stuff ever. Jim always thought the outside "shitters" in Da Nang were the worst smelling, but this made them smell like perfume. Mutt placed the compound over both of Jim's eyes. In seconds both eyes started to get really hot. Jim said something to Mutt but he only grunted. He had tied the compress around Jim's head so he wouldn't remove it when it became uncomfortable. As the compress got hotter, Jim really started to feel tired.

Jim must have been asleep for hours because when he awoke a light was shining through the entrance. A light was shining. He could see some light. It wasn't clear. It was better than the night before. Jim said something out loud, but Mutt wasn't there. He couldn't see him or anything but he knew he wasn't there. Within minutes Mutt came into the cave. Jim could see his shadow and he said, "Pleiku?" He answered with his high-pitched Pidgeon, "Okay, Mr. Jim. Can see good?"

"I can't see anything, but I can see bright lights. What the hell was in that awful stuff last night?" trying to smile to show him how happy he was.

"Old Montagnard medicine. Mother put cut. Go away. We are more later. You be okay pretty damn quick."

Jim could imagine that smile on his face. Not knowing if he just got used to it but that stuff didn't seem to smell as it did the night before. Again, Mutt had Jim lie down and then he wrapped the compress around his head covering the eyes. Tying it with a long rag, Jim again got very sleepy. The rag had slipped off his eyes so the light from the entrance woke him up. He could see the entrance and all the rocks around it. Looking around, he could make out everything but it was a little hazy. He did notice in his exhilaration that Mutt wasn't in the cave. Trying to stand but the pain from his head was almost unbearable. That with his eyesight returning he now has developed severe headaches. Thinking back at what the doctors had told him that with his eyesight possibly returning, a severe headache may develop for a few days.

As he was lying in the glow of light from the entrance, he heard something from outside. Reaching for his machine gun and snapping a round into the chamber, he was about to lift the barrel toward the entrance when Mutt appeared. Looking at Jim quizzically, he then realized that Jim could see again and a smile came to his face. He brought some fruit back with him so they would have something to eat. Trying to explain to Mutt that he could see but his head was really hurting. Once he understood, he went about mixing more of that horrible smelling stuff to put back on Jim's eyes.

"That's got to be the worst smelling stuff ever. Its smells like what my niece leaves in her diaper but worse," talking to the Montagnard knowing he has no idea what I'm talking about.

As he laid on his back with the compress over his eyes, Jim started to think of the past. Wondering what Ronnie was doing. His folks. His brother. His favorite aunt. Wondering what all of them are doing this moment. He even gave a brief moment thinking of Linda and what the radicals were doing this very minute. Moving his head a little to see if it still hurt but finding there was no pain. He started to sit up but fell back down. There it was. A severe pain right behind his right eye. Damn. He thought it was gone but again he was wrong. At least he can see but this pain is really severe. Closing his eyes hoping that in a few minutes it would be gone.

As Jim took the compress off his eyes, the cave was completely dark. He knew he could see because he could see the lights from the village. Jim debated for a while to try if he could sit up without pain. Moving to rest on his left elbow there seemed to be no pain. Pushing himself up, still no pain. Now sitting up and actually shaking his head, still no pain. He tries to stand as Mutt enters the cave. Not saying anything, the scout just stands there watching him. As Jim gains his equilibrium, he could see a big smile on his friend's face. Still being a little shaky on his feet, Mutt comes over and grabs his arm. Directing Jim to walk around in a little circle with him holding his arm tight. Not letting him fall but wanting Jim to know he was there all the time. Jim's legs were getting stronger and he couldn't wait to get going.

As they sat in the dark eating some fruit, Jim started to talk to his friend. Asking him how long he thought it would take them to catch up with Joe and the rest.

"Mr. Jim. Other go fifty-mile front. They go ten-mile night. We go fifteen night. Maybe catch twenty day." Jim's starting to understand everything he says.

Mutt explained that they should rest for a couple of hours and then set out to meet up with the rest of their party. He said that he wanted to put another compress on Jim's eyes while they rested. He didn't explain why but he was quite insistent. As he placed it on his eyes and tied it on the back, the smell was worse. Lying down, closing his eyes, he was quickly asleep. Jim was having a great dream when all of a sudden he was shaken out of his sleep.

"VC. Number 10. Come trail." Mutt was leaning over Jim with his hand over Jim's mouth.

"How many are there?" trying to remove his hand.

"Six, seven, no more. Come trail. You shoot. No noise," pointing toward the cave entrance.

Getting up and going to where the haversack was lying on the ground, Jim takes out the Remington and quickly starts to assemble it. He then takes out the scope, snapping in place on the top of the rifle. He then screws the silencer to the front of the barrel.

Jim thinks to himself, 'I missed you. Now it's time to take care of business.'

Taking a box of bullets from the pouch of the haversack, Jim makes his way to the entrance. Looking over the ledge, he couldn't see anything. The sun hadn't come up yet so it was still quite dark. Mutt came next to him and pointed down the mountain toward the right side. He strained to see something but it was difficult. Looking in all directions, Jim shook his head in frustration. Looking halfway down the mountain, Jim saw something move. Taking his rifle, laying it on the ledge, looking through the scope. There were six black pajama Viet Cong patrol. They were slowly walking behind each other up the trail. Putting the box of cartridges on the ledge, he takes ten bullets out and places them in order next to the box. Taking one, Jim puts it in the rifle and then snaps it into the chamber. Now he was ready and anxious to fire. One of the hardest shots you have to take when being a sniper is shooting down on something. The VC were about three hundred to four hundred yards down the mountain. There were six to ten feet between each man and Jim decided to take out the last VC in line and work toward the front. As he sighted in on the last soldier, Jim slowly squeezed the trigger. Suddenly, the rifle recoiled and the VC dropped right where he was walking. The soldier in front didn't even flinch. Taking another round, putting it in the chamber, and snapping it shut, Jim once again is sighting in on the last soldier in line. When ready, he squeezes the trigger but unlike the first kill, this VC fell just as the soldier in front turned to him. Turning around again to yell something, but Jim's third round hit him in the base of his neck and nothing came out of his mouth. Three down and three to go. Jim started to think, 'If I am that lucky I would again have a clear shot at the fourth VC.' He wasn't that lucky. The last two soldiers turned just as the fourth soldier's neck blew up. They scrambled into the brush. Thinking they were safe entering the trees, the last VC happened to wait a second to long. Jim's next bullet hit him in the right temple and he was dead before he hit the ground. Now there was one VC halfway down the mountain, firing up to where he thought Jim was.

One thing about positioning yourself above your prey: You have the advantage in both looking down and seeing them better than they can see you. The second advantage is that you can wait them out. You can see if they are going to circle your position trying for a better advantage. Waiting was not one of Jim's stronger suits. He found out that the remaining Viet Cong had less patience than him. The VC decided to go closer to where his partner fell. Coming from behind the tree where he was hiding, he turned onto the trail and died where he turned.

Mutt gathered all their gear and he decided that they would go up over the mountain. Jim never felt that he should ever check the bodies of those who had been shot. He knew that if he shot anyone they were dead. No need to waste time checking on something that he already knew the answer.

Going up the mountain was worse on Jim this time than any other time that he could remember. His head was beating like a big bass drum. His eyes were burning but Mutt said, "More normal," or at least something that sounded like that. As they kept going up and up, Mutt stayed closer to Jim than usual. This almost cost them their lives.

As they were going up, neither noticed that on their right side were about ten eyes on them. It was an NVA patrol, but for some reason they decided to follow at a distance. Mutt was more concerned with Jim and he didn't notice anything. Reaching the summit of the mountain at 1400, Mutt suggested they should take a rest.

THANK GOD FOR FRIENDS

As they rested, Mutt decided to recon the area. Jim was lying on the grass right on the top of the mountain looking up into the sky. His head was still pounding but his eyes didn't hurt as much as before. Closing his eyes what seemed like a second he fell asleep. Jim started to dream when all at once Mutt was shaking him with his hand over his mouth.

"NVA. Downhill. Ten. Two klicks. [One klick = .4 mile.]," still holding his hand over Jim's mouth as he tried to stand.

"Are they moving up?" finally asking as Mutt pulled his hand away.

"No. Wait. No why." He said translated they were just waiting down below and Mutt didn't know why.

"We've got to get out of here. Do you have a trail laid out?" asking as he was picking up his equipment.

All of a sudden a shot rang out and Mutt screamed. The bullet ripped into his left shoulder. He hit the ground like a rock but he was close enough that Jim knew that the bullet had gone all the way through his shoulder. Ripping his shirt, Jim made a bandage for his friend. This was not easy because Jim never raised his head more than three inches from the ground. He didn't return fire because they were too far away to use the machine gun and using the Remington would be useless.

"Can you travel?" asking Mutt who nodded his head.

The top of the mountain was flat so they crawled to the edge where it started to go down. Nodding to Mutt, they stood and started to run down the mountain. Jim could hear firing behind him but they just kept running. Jim again thought, '*When you have a headache and your partner has a bullet hole in his shoulder, running is not the best thing for us to be doing. Fortunately, we are near to the edge of the forest about one hundred yards. After that we will be in amongst the trees. That means, "Advantage us."*'

Dodging between the trees, the bullets became more frequent. The sun was going down in the west so it was much harder for them to hit the runners. Just as they came to a clearing, bullets started to be fired from down below. The rounds were not being directed at them but at the NVA. Joe and his group had come back when they heard the firing and figured it had to be Jim and Mutt being chased. The NVA didn't stay around long. They turned the way they came over the top of the mountain and down the other side.

"Am I glad to see you but you don't listen to orders very well," hugging Joe as Jim chastised him.

"What are you talking about? And you are welcome for saving your ass," he said still hugging Jim.

"I gave you an order that you were to get the Chinaman guy out of here in one piece. One piece means not coming back when you hear rifle fire. But we are really glad you did. Have Jeff look at Mutt's shoulder and see what he can do," turning to Kim and giving the order.

Jim lets go of Joe and starts over to look at the Colonel who still had that air of arrogance around him.

"I bet you thought you'd never see me again. We will get you to the south and then I want to see how arrogant you are then," Jim wanting to kick him in the teeth.

Later that afternoon, after resting for some time, packing up and with the scouts well in front of them, they start out for the border and safety.

The scouts have told Kim that it should take no more than two weeks to get to the DMZ and a day to arrive at the Marine Base in Khe Sahn. During that long two weeks, the group has encountered three VC patrols and one large NVA squad. After a short fire fight with each, the enemy would pull back and disappear.

After the last encounter with the NVA squad, Jim decided to speak with the Chinese Colonel once again.

"You know, Colonel, during all these skirmishes with the VC and NVA, I couldn't understand why they would pull back. They had overwhelming numbers than we, but after ten minutes, they were gone. Then it hit me like a lightning bolt. They want us to get back to the south. They want you to be tortured by the South Vietnamese. You really must have pissed off the General. He wants you to suffer worse than he can do."

Fourteen days to when the scouts told Kim it would take them to the DMZ. Arriving at night, they went through the two miles without a problem. Now they had only fourteen more miles to Khe Sanh.

- - - - - -

Khe Sanh was the last Marine Corps outpost prior to going into the DMZ. It housed different elements of the Third Marine Amphibious Force. (III MAF)

In 1968, Khe Sahn would become the most famous of all battles during the Vietnam War. The Battle of Khe Sanh would last from January to July 1968. It would involve not only the III MAF but also the 1st Calvary Division, the US Seventh Air Force, the 1st Battalion Ninth Marine Regiment along with minor elements of the South Vietnamese Army. (ARVN). They would be coming up against two to three division size elements of the People's Army of Vietnam (referred to as the North Vietnamese Army or the NVA). In July 1968, the Americans would destroy all of the base complex of Khe Sanh and withdraw from the battle area. The North Vietnamese only gained control of the Khe Sanh region after the American withdrawal.

Upon arriving at the base, the six had to go through security. Without any military IDs, they were put in a room until the MPs could contact the Commander or someone in authority. After that, they went over to the Officer's Club. One of the main problems going into any of the clubs outside of Da Nang was the rules. The main rule was to leave all weapons at the door. They could not or it was just they would not do this. Throughout their time in Vietnam and going into many "O" or NCO Clubs throughout the country, they never once left their weapons outside. Now this also caused problems with the MPs or SPs on the door, whether it be a Marine, Army, or Navy. They would want them to leave their weapons but they wouldn't comply. Bottom line is that they became quite familiar with the brigs and stockades throughout the country.

RELAXING WITH JUST THE WAR

"General meeting in the mess tent at 1630 hours. Everyone is to be there. Commander is in a good mood. We're screwed." Joe just came back from breakfast.

"Wonder where he's going to be sending us now. Hope we at least get a few days' rest. My head is still killing me and the blindness. Wow," Jim said to Joe as he swung his feet over the cot and on to the floor.

They had just got back at 0200 this morning. Most of the guys were still asleep but others like Joe went to breakfast. Joe had brought back some coffee for Jim. Sipping his coffee, he listened to Joe wonder what was next.

As Jim was listening and laughing, the Commander's clerk, a Marine Lance Corporal, came in with a huge yellow bag and yelled, "Mail Call." Now there are only two people in this tent so every time he does that Jim and Joe wonder why.

"Hey, John. How come you go into all the tents and scream 'Mail Call?' Now there are only two or three four tops in each tent and everyone can hear you if you whisper. Why do you yell?" Jim asked laughing. John Davenport was supposed to be a spotter in this last group the Commander put together. When they were at training in the Philippines, he shot himself in the foot. Now most people thought it was an accident but the Commander didn't. He thinks Davenport was trying to get a ticket home. The Commander was damned if he was going home on "his" ticket. So, he put in for a clerk and was given permission and he kept John as his. Davenport was and still isn't too thrilled about being a clerk but here he is.

"Hey, Coleman you got a bunch of letters. None from your fiancé though," throwing a bunch of letters and a package on his rack.

Jim looked and saw Joe saying something to Davenport. He yelled back, "Sorry about the remark, Jim. Didn't know but I shouldn't have said anything. Sorry again," as Davenport left by the far door.

"Don't let him bother you, Jim. He's a jerk and everyone knows it," Joe trying to fend off a tantrum.

"No problem at all. I've got over it. I keep thinking if it were me in her shoes what would I do? Well, I concluded the same thing. I don't think I could wait a year or two," trying to show a strong face

"Good for you, Marine. You're full of shit but good for you." Joe was laughing as he spoke.

Jim went to his cot and started to look through the mail. Must have been ten letters and two small packages. Opening one of the boxes which contained food from his mother. Salami, pepperoni, cheese and two boxes of crackers. Yelling out to the whole camp that he had food. The other box was filled with small, about six-inch pies. Blueberry, apple, and mincemeat were all packed real tight and nothing leaked. As he starts to look through the mail, he wonders to himself if there will be a letter from Linda. Nothing.

Continuing looking at the letter, there were two from addresses he didn't recognize. One was from Davenport, Iowa. It was from a little girl in the tenth grade in high school. Jim thought of the irony seeing this girl's name is Linda and she goes to high school.

Jim opens the envelope and takes out the letter.

She writes:

I am so proud of all of you in Vietnam. We should not pay any attention to these demonstrators because they are cowards and jerks.

It was a great letter but he was wondering why it was addressed to him. Not "any marine" but to Staff Sergeant James Coleman, USMC. He will write back to her and find out.

The next letter that he opened again was from an address he didn't recognize. It came from Philadelphia and he started to think of anyone he's met that comes from the City of Brotherly Love. Opening the envelope, the smell of perfume starts to fill the tent.

The letter starts.

My Dearest Jim:

I have wondered for so long how stupid I can be. I let you get away from me because of some stupid thing you said about you "girlfriend" in Boston.

I love you with all my heart and have since the first time I saw you. I hope you feel the same but if you don't, so be it.

If there is no hope for us, please don't write back. It would just kill me knowing that I blew the best chance in my life for happiness.

Again, I love you so much.

Ronnie

Sitting on the edge of his bunk, holding the letter in his hand, sweat coming from his forehead, he lets out a yell that the whole world may have heard. His left hand started to shake uncontrollably as he started to look around. The tent just was getting dark. 'Oh, my God, I'm not going to lose my eyesight again. I got to call Joe.'

"Joe are you in the tent. I need to see you right away," as he laid down full length on his bed.

"What's up, Jim? What do you need?" coming over to Jim's bunk.

"Read this letter and tell me what you think?" holding the letter out but not telling him about the darkness.

As Joe finished all he could say was, "Wow."

"What do you think? Do you think she's just playing?" looking up to where he thought his voice was coming from.

"It sounds like she's got it bad for you. I can't understand why but that's what it sounds like. Why don't you write her back and ask her. Tell her about Linda and go from there. Hey, what the hell is wrong with you?" Joe stood at the foot of the bed.

"Nothing wrong. I just didn't know what to make of the letter," knowing exactly what he was talking about.

Leaning over to his right ear, Joe whispers, "You can't see anymore can you?"

"How did you know?" Jim was frightened now.

"When I got off the cot. I saw you move your head. Your eyes never moved with me. How long has this been going on?" He sounded quite concerned and angry.

"Right after I read the letter and called you over," he tried to explain. "The headaches started in earnest when we got to Khe Shan. The eyesight was going in and out when we waiting for our ride back."

"I thought this was over after this last mission. You said you were fine when we met up on the path. You lied to me. You not only put yourself in danger but all of us were in danger because you could go blind at any minute." He was getting louder which meant he was getting angrier.

"Joe. You can't say anything to the Commander. They'll kick me out of the Corps on a medical discharge. That's no way to go out for what we are doing. Please. I'll work this out before the next mission. Please. I'm begging you." That's all he could say.

"Jim. I love you like a brother. You're more of a brother than the ones I've got. But you have to take care of this. This is going to get you killed and us along with you. If this doesn't improve by next week, I'm going to have to tell the Commander. I'm sorry but that's the way it has to be," knowing he was right but it really hurt coming from him.

"I'll take care of it with the Commander. I don't need you to do my dirty work," as he turned around on the bunk.

As the days went by, the eyesight started to get better. Mutt would sneak his home-grown remedy in at night. Joe couldn't stand the smell and finally he went to bunk with one of the other guys. The headache remained but his sight was now at one hundred percent. He still couldn't move that well with his head feeling as if it would explode at any minute.

On the sixth day after his discussion with Joe, the Commander called the two of them in for a meeting. As Jim moved to a chair, the Commander could tell something was wrong.

"What's bothering you now?" was a question that should have been put another way.

"What do you mean by that? I never have anything bothering me. It's you people who make a big deal out of everything." Just as Jim finished he could hear a snicker come from Joe's direction.

"Is that so? Is that the reason you weren't going to tell me that you lost your eyesight during the last mission?"

Jim was dumfounded that he knew that. He quickly jerked his head to look directly at Joe. "Why in God's name did you tell him that?" Jim was now beyond being mad.

"I didn't say a word to him. I don't know who told him but I know I didn't. Drop the fucking attitude also. You are not in the right in any way with this," as he started to stand up.

Jim tried to stand but his head hurt so bad he fell back into the chair. Jim just knew the rest of this meeting was not going to go in his favor.

"Why didn't you tell me that you've been having trouble with your sight? How long has this been going on?" The Commander seemed concerned.

"Just that one time," waiting for Joe to contradict him with news of the one last week.

Joe said nothing. It was as quiet as it always is when the Commander has the floor.

"Jim. You can't go out in the field if you are having problems. You can hardly move now with these headaches. How long have you had them?" again showing concern.

"They started in Hawaii. The doctor said they weren't dangerous. He said that they wouldn't last more than three days. I've had a couple of episodes but nothing this bad. Today is the worst. Oh. I had a sight problem about six days ago. Mutt has some home-made remedy that cures it within two to three days," trying to get him to forget any restriction he's about to put on Jim.

"It really stinks too," Joe spoke up.

"You knew about this and didn't speak up? That's twice you haven't told me about what is going on with the group. I'll discuss this with you later. Jim, you will be confined to this compound until I can get you to Japan to see a specialist," turning and walking out of the tent.

"I owe you an apology. I thought you told him about what happened on the mission. I'm sorry," holding out his hand hoping his brother would shake it. "I told you I wouldn't and I didn't., shaking his hand but not with the vigor Jim thought he'd have. "Then if it wasn't you who was it? It would have to be either Sean or the Korean." Jim couldn't think of anyone else.

"The Commander was in with the Chinese Colonel for a while until the MPs took him away. He could have said something about what happened on the trail," making some sense.

Jim thought that Joe may have had the right idea. The Colonel may have said something off hand about what went on. 'I don't think the Korean would say anything about an NCO to an officer.' Sean and Jim are friends and he knew Jim told Joe not to say anything so he didn't think it was him. It really doesn't matter anyway the Commander knows and that's not good.

THIS DEVASTATION HITS HOME

No one said anything for the next few days. Jim's headaches were starting to subside and his eyesight was once again perfect. Not wanting to mention anything to the Commander was accomplished since he hadn't been around for the past few days. While he was gone the group decided to take a trip to the local village of An Tan, which is just down the road from Chu Lai. It seemed when they would go to the village the Commander was always away in Da Nang.

The routine was that they would load the truck with all the guys who wanted to go to the village. It was easy to get out of the compound because this truck was used daily to go to the dump. They then would drive to about a half mile of the village, flip a coin to see who would remain with the truck and then walk down Highway 1.

As they approached the village there was a sign above the dirt road saying, "Entrance Gate." In the middle of the sign, in Vietnamese writing was the name of the village. "An Tan." Going through the "gate" all you could see were the many shops selling their goods to any passersby, especially military personnel.   As they were going down the main street, Jim noticed a church on the right side. It was further in than the other buildings. On the front, above the front door was a swastika just like the ones the Germans had during WWII. Jim grabbed a couple of his people and pointed it out. Sean came up to see what was happening and Jim told him what he saw. Sean explained.

"It's not the same thing. The Nazi swastika was on an angle. This emblem is straight up and down. It's a symbol of luck for many Eastern religions such as Buddhism, Hinduism and Jainism. The origin comes from a Sanskrit work 'svastika' meaning 'auspicious object,'" looking at all of them and smiling.

"You know something, Sean?" Joe yelled over to him. When Sean turned to give Joe his attention, Joe continued, "I really don't give a shit. Still looks like a Nazi swastika to me," almost falling over laughing.

As they left the church area and started to walk down the center of the road, they were giving off this air of superiority. Knowing they were good and for some unknown reason they wanted all the villagers to know it too. As they walked they came to this one "store" with a folding table in the front. There were sorts of trivial objects on it. As they were looking over the items, a little girl came out of the house in back. She was three to four years of age, jet-black hair, dark eyes, and the sweetest smile you have ever seen. Jim was stunned in how this little girl could capture his attention. Without thinking he placed his weapon against the table and leaning down, he picked the little girl up. She was adorable. She reminded him of his niece, Marylou. She took his soft cover off his head and put it on her head. With her right hand, she started to play with his mouth and nose. Jim was definitely in love.

As she continued, a man came from the house. He looked around and then walked over to the table and picked up Jim's machine gun. With this the others in the group stood straight up and started to raise their weapons. The young man, seeing what was transpiring, lowered the weapon but kept it in his hands.

"Bab co noi tieng Anh Khong?" ("Do you speak English?") Sgt. Kim asked the father in Vietnamese.

"Vang mot chut. ("Yes, a little."), smiling all the time as most Vietnamese do.

"Put down the machine gun slowly. No fast moves," Jim said as he pointed his .45 at the man's head while still holding the little girl.

Still smiling, he put the weapon down where he found it. With this, Jim put his weapon back in the holster and then stuck out his hand and said, "Hi. I'm Jim Coleman with the Marines. What's your name?"

"My name, An Dung Troung. Daughter Fuc," as he pointed to the little girl still cuddled in Jim's arm.

"What are you selling here?" looking at his table of crap.

"Oh, very good stuff, suitcase, sunglasses, Vietnamese lighter, cards, postcards." He was getting excited at the prospect of selling something.

"Tell you what. You give me one of everything you sell. How much?" feeling sorry that he scared the shit out of him a few minutes ago.

"Lot dong," he said in return while almost shaking apart from being scared.

"I only got MPC [Military Payment Certificate]. I have no dong, no American money. This is Marine Corps money."

"Dong, no Marine, dong. No more," as he started to get angry.

"I only have MPC, you shithead. I don't have and won't have dong. These people just don't want to listen," getting frustrated beyond reason.

"Let's go. He doesn't want to do business," turning and starting to walk down the road.

"I take, I take," his hand straight out looking for the money.

After Jim paid him, the man put everything in the Air Vietnam travel bag which Jim also purchased, and the group started to walk down the road.

"I just can't get that little girl out of my head. She was so cute but she looked like she didn't have a thing. When we get back to the compound, I'm going to write my mother. I'll tell her everything about this little girl and ask if she could send some clothes for her. I will give her the little girl's approximate sizes." Jim was excited just talking about his new love.

A couple of weeks went by and then the mail clerk came to the entrance of the compound and left this huge box for Jim. Taking it back to the tent and opening it, Jim saw that it was filled with little girl's clothes. He showed all the guys what his mother had sent for little "Fuc." Jim couldn't wait to go out to the village with the little girl's stuff.

As fate would have it, the Commander left for Saigon two days later. As soon as they saw his helicopter take off, everyone was out the gate and on the truck. Jim loaded the box of clothes on the truck and then commandeered the duty officer's jeep and headed out the gate.

As they entered the village, it seemed like a hundred kids came from nowhere begging for stuff. Jim gave out a few of the outfits his mother sent and they went away. Making his way to the store, he noticed a man was sitting in a chair in the front of his house and he looked like the guy who sold him the stuff a few weeks ago. The little girl was playing to his right.

"Do you remember me?" Jim said as he approached him.

They must have looked scary to him because he had this look of fear on his face. Lifting the box onto the table, Jim started to take out the outfits but he started to shake his head profusely.

"This stuff is for your daughter. No charge. Free. It's a gift from my mother in the United States," trying to calm him down.

"No take. VC see. No take." He was out of his mind screaming.

"Okay, okay. Relax. VC won't see anything. I'll take them back to the base."

"Thank you. No. Thank you." He really sounded sincere.

As they left the village, Jim decided to give all the stuff to the kids at the dump. As they approached the vehicles, Jim whistled loudly and suddenly like the "Pied Piper" there were at least fifty kids standing in front of him. Giving all the outfits away, he even gave some of the boys the girl's shirts. Knowing that they will sell them, he didn't care. He was so disappointed that little Fuc didn't get them.

A week went by and the Commander once again was on his way to Saigon. Everyone was going to the village but Jim didn't feel like going. Two days later, on Tuesday, the Commander returned and scheduled a meeting at 1400 to discuss why they hadn't had any missions.

Early peace talks were going on in Saigon and Washington and the higher-ups in both governments didn't want anything to hamper a chance for this war to end. None of the top North Vietnamese generals came to the talks so everyone knew it was just a waste of time. That evening everyone was sitting around outside talking about what they were going to do back home.

- - - - - -

The 1965 proposal

The first major proposal came from North Vietnamese premier Pham Van Dong in April 1965. Pham's four-point plan called for a return to the provisions of the Geneva Accords of 1954, along with the withdrawal of US military personnel:

1. Recognition of the basic national rights of the Vietnamese people – peace, independence, sovereignty, unity, and territorial integrity... The U.S. government must withdraw from South Vietnam U.S. troops, military personnel, and weapons of all kinds, dismantle all U.S. military bases there, and cancel its military alliance with South Vietnam. It must end its policy of intervention and aggression in South Vietnam...

2. Pending the peaceful reunification of Vietnam, while Vietnam is still temporarily divided into two zones, the military provisions of the 1954 Geneva agreements on Vietnam must be strictly respected...

3. The internal affairs of South Vietnam must be settled by the South Vietnamese people themselves, in accordance with the program of the NLF, without any foreign interference.

4. The peaceful reunification of Vietnam is to be settled by the Vietnamese people in both zones, without any foreign interference.

US Secretary of State Dean Rusk, responding to Pham's proposals, declared that he could live with points one, two and four—but he interpreted point three as a demand for Viet Cong *control of* South Vietnam, a condition the United States could not accept.

Rusk claimed that he could find no member of the North Vietnamese government willing to "give up their aggressive ambitions or to come to a conference table," so he would place his trust in "our own men in uniform."

- - - - - -

Suddenly the sirens went off which meant that the VC were attacking the airfield. Having assigned bunkers, everyone went running to their "hooches" to get their weapons and then to the bunkers. Joe and Jim had to run to the far side of the runway to their assigned bunker that overlooked the airfield. They could see one of the F-4s on fire as they both jumped into the bunker. Jim got his Remington out and set it up. Looking down the runway, they both saw a man dressed in black pajamas running around the planes. There were Marines in foxholes above the planes firing down on this "suicide squad," as they were called. As the firing got intense, the VC started running toward the end of the runway. Jim noticed two VC side by side standing right beside a burning A4 at the end of the tarmac.

As the firing increased, the two VC looked around as if expecting someone else. It looked as if they were going to run to the end of the runway and into the woods. Jim saw them when they were next to the A4 and he sighted in on the one on the left and fired. He dropped instantly. The other stopped immediately, which saved his life for the moment. Joe had fired right after Jim but because the VC stopped, the bullet went right by his head. Sighting in on the enemy Jim saw that he started to run. As the VC started, he took just two steps and that was all he took. Jim dropped him before he could take the third.

When the sirens sounded again that meant it was all clear. Joe and Jim left their foxhole but they took the standard precautions going down to the bodies. Many times, the VC when wounded would put a grenade under their bodies. When the Marines went to turn them over, the grenade would go off killing the Marine and anyone that was close to the body. The two went to the first VC that Jim killed and gently pulled on one of his legs. Whoever was not pulling on the dead man's leg would watch closely to see if there was any kind of bomb under the still body. This time there was nothing. As Joe finished pulling on this VC's legs, Jim suddenly called to him, "Is it just me or does this VC look familiar to you?" as he pointed his flashlight on to his face.

"It's the shop keeper. Remember he held my weapon as I was playing

with the little girl. I'll be a son-of-a-bitch," shaking his head in utter disbelief.

"Thank God they told us to empty our weapons before we went into the village. Wonder what would have happened if we hadn't," still shaking his head in disbelief.

"Well, let's put it this way. You will never have to wonder about him again. My question is what's going to happen to the little girl?" For the first time Joe seemed to really care about something else but himself.

"I really feel bad about the little girl. I wonder if she has any family in the village?" Jim was still shaking his head.

After checking out the second downed VC, they finally got back to the compound around 0600 hours. Jim went directly to his tent. As he was taking his utilities off, he couldn't stop thinking about the girl. As Jim was cleaning his Remington, Joe came and started to talk. "What are you up to?" he said as he watched him clean his rifle.

"I'm building a fucking bridge. What do you think I'm doing? I'm also just thinking of that little girl. I can't help but worry that she doesn't have family in the village. What is going to happen to her? I can't stand this shit anymore," just staring into space not really looking at anyone or anything.

"What can you do about it? If she has relatives, they will look after her. If not she will be put into an orphanage run by the nuns. She will be well taken care of." Joe was really trying to figure out what was wrong with Jim.

"Put in an orphanage. Just like that fucking crazy female Colonel I killed a few months ago. The nuns raised her and how did that turn out? She was the worst killer in this fucking country. I have to do something about that little girl. We are going out to the village tomorrow," Jim said with authority as Joe just shook his head.

They couldn't go to the village for a couple of weeks. The Commander had them doing some patrols around the perimeter of Chu Lai just to keep them from going crazy. Before the time came to go to the village, the Commander summoned Jim to his tent.

"So, you killed that little girl's father. What's the big deal, he was VC. You've killed VC before. Now what do you think you are going to do with her? She is either gone to a relative in the village or another village. Worst case is that she was probably picked up by Catholic charities and is in an orphanage somewhere down south. There is nothing you can do about it now," sitting back in his chair as if he has just passed some hot law.

"I just got to know what is happening with her. I really feel bad about what I did that may cause problems for her. Leaving her all alone without a father with nobody to take care of her." Tears started flowing from his eyes.

"Okay, you can go to the village tomorrow but don't get involved in anything that would make us look bad. Take Tomelli and Sean with you." For one brief moment the Commander had a heart.

He left the compound at ten hundred hours but this time instead of taking the dump truck, he commandeered the Colonel's jeep. It was just sitting in front of the operation tent so he jumped in, started it and off he, Joe, and Sean went. This time Jim brought one of the other Korean scouts, Staff Sergeant Choi, to act as an interpreter. Parking the jeep out front of the entrance to the village, they walked directly toward the little girl's house without stopping or browsing at any of the shops along the way. As they came to the house, Jim noticed that the front of the shop was not there and the house looked empty. He asked the Korean to ask around and find out what happened to the little girl. He was gone for only a few minutes when he returned.

"Gone, Da Nang. Nuns, take. Stay Da Nang little time, go Saigon. Stay long time." It seems all Koreans speak English the same way, pidgin.

"When did they come to take her? Is she going to an orphanage?" With that last question Choi had a strange look on his face.

"Two day. Bus take her Da Nang. Home Saigon. Live long time." He was quite adamant about what he had found out.

Turning to Joe saying, "Well, I guess that's all I can do. Hopefully in ten or fifteen years she doesn't kill everyone in the convent," turning and starting to walk back to the jeep.

"He won't let you go. You know that don't you?" Sean said as they walked back to the jeep.

"Won't hurt to ask. If I can just go down there," getting into the driver's seat.

"Better you than me. I know exactly what he is going to say and you do too. To be honest, Jim, I wouldn't be in total disagreement with his decision. You can't save everyone in this fucked up country. He's going to have a conniption fit when he hears your request." Jim knew Joe was right but he still was going to ask.

As Jim knocked on the Commander's open door, he looked up and motioned Jim to come in.

"What can I do for you today, Jim?" As he spoke, he had something unusual on his face, a smile.

Sitting down without him telling Jim to do so, Jim proceeded to go into an exceptionally long dissertation on what he wanted to do. Jim told the Commander about how his mother had sent over a bunch of little girl's clothes but the father was afraid of the VC seeing them. Jim continued on what they found out in the village. The little girl was going to DaNang but would end up in Saigon in an orphanage. He just rambled on knowing that the Commander was not going to approve of him going to Da Nang and definitely not Saigon looking for her. Finishing his dissertation, he just sat there not saying a thing.

"If you find this girl, Jim, what do you intend to do? You can't bring her back here and it will take forever to try to send her home to your mother," making more sense than Jim really wanted to hear.

"I just want to know if she is alright and maybe find out what I have to do to adopt her," waiting for the screaming to start.

"Jim, I don't really know how you feel so I'm not going to tell you I do. One thing I do know the Marine Corps will not let you do this. You killed her father and when she gets older, she is going to want to know about her parents. You going to tell her that her 'Daddy' was the enemy so you blew his head off. I really don't think that she will accept your explanation and you can't keep it a secret. I tell you what. I have a friend of mine that is a chaplain in Da Nang. He may be able to help you find her. I have a big meeting in a couple of weeks in Da Nang that will last a couple of days. You can go with me and while I'm busy, the good chaplain can help you find her. I will call Commander Galvan and tell him we are coming." As he stood up he stuck out his hand for Jim to shake it which was unusual for him.

As Jim headed back to his tent, he was really trying to figure out what just went on with Commander Damon. He has never acted like that before. Anytime any of them wanted to do something out of the ordinary, he would always say no and would never change his mind. When Jim finally got into his tent, he grabbed Joe and told him the whole story.

"He's been in country too long. He didn't even say 'no' once in your conversation?" Joe was just shaking his head as he spoke.

"Nothing negative. He was just listening most of the time. We are leaving for Da Nang in ten days, just him and me. I am going to have a meeting with some chaplain down there and he is going to help me find her. This is really weird." Jim tried to figure out what was going on.

The next ten days seemed to drag but finally it was here and they were going to leave. The helicopter flight was nothing spectacular and they landed within thirty minutes of taking off. The Commander and Jim went directly to the chapel to meet with Commander Galvan. As they entered the chapel, a young, thin man in utilities was fixing the altar and whistling something neither recognized.

"Commander Fausto Galvan, don't you have helpers who could be doing the menial work instead of you?" Commander Damon said running up and hugging this man with emotions I've never seen before.

"Jim, say hello to the greatest chaplain in this man's Navy. Fausto, this is the young man I was telling you about, Jim Coleman," as they shook each other's hands.

"Jim, this is a great pleasure to meet you. The Commander has spoken often about you and what a great job you are doing for our country."

Jim automatically spun his head to look directly into the Commander's eyes. How many times has he told him never to divulge what we do? Now here is a friend of his, no matter that he's a chaplain, telling him how much he brags of how Jim does his job. Rank definitely does have its privileges.

Commander Damon then excused himself from both men saying that his meeting was going to be on the hour and he didn't want to be late. As he left the chapel, Father Fausto asked Jim to sit and talk for a while.

"Let me tell you a little about myself. I was born in San Fernando, California in 1939. After high school, I attended the University of California, San Diego. Upon graduation, I really didn't know what I wanted to do until I took a trip to Boston. I met a priest at the Holy Cross Cathedral who just got out of the Navy as a chaplain. He told me that it was the best life in the world to be a chaplain. Without even going home, I went to the St. John's Seminary in Brighton and entered the priesthood. After being ordained, I put in for the Chaplain Corps, asking for the Navy, which I got. Upon graduation from chaplain's school, I had my choice of duty stations and I chose Da Nang. Now you've heard my story and I think I know what you want, let's sit down and discuss how I can help," moving to the front pew.

Jim sat there for the next thirty minutes explaining what he wanted to do and why he wanted to do it. Father Galvan never said a word but just nodded occasionally. As Jim finished speaking, the chaplain got out of his position and stood over him.

"Are you out of your mind?" He did not scream but was direct. "Do you just think that because you shot her father that you can come in here and adopt her? You are going to ship her back to Boston to live with your parents. Your parents have raised their children and now you want them to raise a young child at their age? Do they know what it is going to take to raise a foreign child in an area such as Boston? Tolerance is not a strong suit for those people. Jim, think about what you are trying to do. If this happens and when she becomes of age, she will want to know about her heritage. You are white as snow and Irish so I would conclude your mother and father are as well. She is Vietnamese. Her father was Viet Cong and was killed during a suicide attack on Chu Lai. Now you come from Hingham and I imagine there are not a lot of non-white people who live there. She will not have anyone who she can relate to. She will be an outsider for all her school years. When you receive your discharge from the Marines, you are going to go back home and raise her as your daughter. What will happen when she finds out how her real father died? Do you think she is just going to look at you in the same light as before? Of course, she won't. She will look at you as the one who ruined her life. You took her from her homeland after you killed her only living relative. Jim, you had better give this a lot of thought. Have you even talked to your parents about this?" Finally he stopped talking.

"Father, I know what you are saying is one hundred percent true, but I have to do something. I took her father as you have said but I am the one that has also put her in an orphanage. No, I have not spoken to my parents about this but I know it will not be a problem. My hometown is one of the greatest towns in Massachusetts to grow up in. I know it will not be easy, but she is little and by the time she realizes what is happening she will be an American. Father, I really want to do this. It's important to me," finishing his rebuttal to what the priest had said.

"Jim, listen to the last word you just said, 'important to *me*.' Not her but me. You sound like that you are the only one that is involved in this whole thing. For God's sake man, think of the little girl before you think of yourself. The only thing I can get out of this whole conversation is how selfish Jim Coleman is." As he finished Jim was looking daggers at him.

"How dare you call me selfish? You don't even know me. Look what I'm going to do for this little girl. I'm willing to share my family with her. I'm willing to spend as much money as I have to send her home and raise her. I'm even willing to change my life for her. How can you call me selfish? I'm going to do all these things and more for her." Jim stood to leave.

"You sit your ass down in the pew and don't move until I dismiss you. I am still a Commander in the Navy and I outrank you. Jim, listen to what you are saying. All you said in this last ridiculous rebuttal was I am or I'm. You did not say her or your parents, all you are worried about is you. Do you really think that what you are feeling is the way to go into this adoption? In addition, are you sure your fiancé would want an Asian adopted daughter to raise?" looking at Jim with all the passion he could give.

"Don't have to worry if she'd want an Asian daughter or not. She doesn't even want a white Marine as a husband. Got a Dear John the other day so that is one thing I—I mean *we* don't have to worry about. I hear what you are saying, Father, but I have to do something for this little girl. I took her father away from her. She has nothing and I do not want to live the rest of my life thinking how I screwed up her life. If I can get my folks to adopt her will you help me push it through?" on his knees begging.

"I really think you are making a serious mistake, but if your family says they have no problem with it then I won't stand in your way. The orphanage is just a few hundred yards outside the gate. Would you like to see her?" standing up and leaving the pew.

As they left the base and entered the outskirts of the city of Da Nang, Jim could see the difference of his hometown and this dump.

Jim started to think to himself, 'We have big homes with grass all the way around our property. She could run and play with her friends. She would never have to worry about this war again.'

As they approached the orphanage, the good padre reminded Jim not to interact with the girl. The nuns had agreed for Jim to look in on her but not to talk or play with her. As they approached, Jim was starting to get a terrible feeling in his stomach.

"Something's wrong, Father. I have this terrible feeling something is going to happen," starting to yell at the priest.

Just as he went to turn and run, a blast went off in front of them. Jim could feel the sudden heat from the bomb and he felt himself flying through the air fifty feet to the rear. As Jim landed, he knew he wasn't dead but he didn't really know what had happened. Staggering to get up, he started to look for my chaplain. The building that they were walking towards was no longer there. It was the main building of the orphanage. Jim just kept staring at the rubble when Commander Galvan came up to him.

"What the hell was that? Why would anyone blow up an orphanage?" he was asking a lot to absolutely no one.

"The VC just blew up the orphanage. I have to see if there are any survivors. Come and help me." Jim started running toward the fire and destruction. .

As they ran toward what was left of the orphanage, the city people were also starting to run toward the building. Jim got in the rubble and started to pick up boards and toss them aside. Many of the Vietnamese men were calling out, "La len neu banco the nghe chung toi," which means "Yell, if you can hear us," but nothing came from the rubble. They stayed there for hours trying to find anyone still alive. They dragged out a number of nuns who were severely wounded and maimed. After finding the nuns, Jim discovered some children who had the roof come down on their heads. As the medical teams from the base were working on the living, the Vietnamese were putting the dead bodies aside. Commander Damon had appeared out of nowhere and was helping the two go deeper and deeper into the debris. They were tossing everything aside when Jim came to an open room just under the burnt wood. As he kept pushing and pulling the debris he jumped down into an open space. In front of him were a number of small bodies, five or six little ones. One of them was "Fuc," his little girl lying there, as she was asleep. A little blood was coming from her mouth, and he took his handkerchief and cleaned it immediately. He stood there not knowing what to do next. Tears started welling in his eyes but he didn't care who saw them. Talking to himself he kept asking the same question repeatedly. 'Why? These are little children. I don't shoot their children, why would they blow up mine? They are so little. They have nothing to do with this war. Why? Someone tell me why. I will kill every one of you little motherfuckers. I will kill you, your wives, children, and any other thing that is precious to you. I will, I'm telling you, I will." With that Jim started crying uncontrollably.

"Let's get out of here, Jimmy." It was Commander Damon with the chaplain right beside him.

"I need to get a blanket for her. I don't want her to be cold. She is so small and she will be cold down here. Let me get something to cover her," as he started to look around.

"She's gone, Jim. Let's get out of here. That's an order," as the Commander took hold of his arm.

"You touch me again and I'll blow your fucking head off," as Jim pulled his arm from the Commander's grip.

As Jim stared into the Commander's eyes, he could see absolute fear. Commander Damon knew how serious Jim was and he just backed off. As Jim looked around, he couldn't find anything to cover her. Jim handed his machine gun to the chaplain, took off his blouse and put it over "his" little girl. Kneeling by her still body, for some reason he started to say the Act of Contrition. When Jim finished, he wiped his eyes, took his weapon back, turned and left the area never saying a word to either of the two officers. The Commander and Jim went back to the airstrip and boarded a helicopter going to Chu Lai. They did not talk from when they were in the basement of the orphanage to landing in Chu Lai. Jim got off the copter and went immediately to the compound and his hooch. It was late at night when they got back and Jim laid on his bed never taking off the rest of his uniform. Every time he closed his eyes, he saw his little girl lying there in the rubble. After a few hours had passed, Jim finally cried himself to sleep.

BACK ON THE HORSE

As days became weeks, Jim had not spoken of what had happened in Da Nang to anyone. All he could think of was that little girl. A three-year-old who had harmed no one and these animals blew up the building where she lived. Not only did they kill her, but they killed thirty-two children and nine nuns.

Weeks went by and nothing was going on. Jim just could not get that little girl dying for absolutely nothing out of his mind. Why would the Viet Cong blow up an orphanage for no reason at all? Didn't they realize that doing such a dastardly act would cause everyone in the free world to be against them? They are not stupid people; they must have known that pictures of a destroyed orphanage and little coffins would be in every newspaper around the world. Why in the world would they risk such criticism for such a stupid deed?

"What if the VC weren't responsible for the orphanage explosion? What if it was someone else who was trying to make them look bad in the eyes of the world? What if the CIA was behind such a thing?" Joe had come into the tent with his new theory.

"Why would the CIA do such a thing?" sitting up on the edge of his cot.

"To make them look bad. Lately in every paper and magazine around the world there has been pictures of the south or the USA doing some crazy things. Like the police chief putting a pistol to the side of a VC head and pulling the trigger. In the picture, you can see the start of his brains coming out the other side of his head. Then there was the picture of the young girl on the cover of *Life*, running down the street naked after her whole body was blistered by napalm. I'm just saying that we've had some bad press recently so blowing up something like an orphanage and then blaming the other side makes sense."

Jim sat there listening to Joe and realized he was making a lot of sense. "You are crazy with all these conspiracy theories. I can see the CIA blowing something up that would make the VC look bad but not a convent. They knew that there were only children and nuns in there. They can be bad but I really don't think they would do that," trying to make his mind believe what he was saying aloud.

"Just think of it. All over the world the headlines will say, 'Viet Cong

Blow Up Convent. 32 Innocent Children Killed.' Don't you think that's going to change a lot of minds regarding us coming into this war?" Joe's expression was smug after this salvo.

"I can't afford to even hear talk like this. I work for them, just as you do, and if I even thought they would do something as despicable as this it would be all over regarding what I do. The best thing for the both of us is to get a mission that will take us away from here for a couple of weeks. I wonder how the peace talks are working out. I think we should have a talk with the Commander and see if he's got anything coming up that we can do." Jim stood up straightening his utilities to see the man.

As he and Joe entered the Operation Tent, the Commander was standing by his desk just staring out into space.

"What can I do for you gentlemen this fine and glorious night?" still staring out the tent window.

THE MISSION OF A LIFETIME

"Joe and I were wondering if you had anything coming up that would take us out of here for say two weeks?" as they both moved closer to him.

"How would you two like to lead a mission that would take you to Hanoi? What you would have to do is break out a number of Navy pilots from the Hoa Lo prison," looking straight into both of their faces.

"We just wanted to be gone a couple of weeks, not the rest of our lives. A regiment could not break anyone out of that place. I heard that they have a regiment guarding that place and it is in the middle of the city. They call it "Hanoi Hotel." Whose great idea is this one?" trying to chuckle while he was speaking.

"Well, to be honest it is my idea. I proposed this while you and I were in Da Nang that horrible day," trying not to look them in the eye.

"Speaking of that and I wish we didn't have to. Do you think or do you know who actually blew up the orphanage?" staring him in the eye looking for any strange movement.

"The VC blew it up. You know that. Why the stupid question, Jim?" He never called him Jim in a briefing.

"Well, if we are being honest, Joe and I were talking and it came around to the orphanage. We started to say that why would the NVA blow up an orphanage? What advantage would it be to them for the world to hate the VC for killing those little children. The US couldn't to do it so wouldn't it be beneficial if the CIA did it themselves and then blamed the VC?" tears coming to Jim's eyes as he spoke.

"That's crazy talk, Staff Sergeant. We don't do those things. Enough of that bullshit, let's get down to business." The Commander for all the time Jim has known him really didn't sound that convincing.

As usual there was a big board in front with a blanket over it. As they started to take their seats, the Commander reached around and pulled the blanket having it fall away from the board.

"Hoa Lo was a prison used by the French colonists in Vietnam for political prisoners, and now by the North Vietnamese for U.S. prisoners of war. Hoa Lo Prison is Vietnamese but it has become known in the papers as the 'Hanoi Hilton.' The name Hoa Lo commonly translated as 'fiery furnace' or even 'Hell's Hole,' also means 'stove.' The French built the prison in Hanoi in the late eighteen hundreds when Vietnam was still part of French Indochina. The original name for the prison was Maison Centrale meaning the Central House, a traditional euphemism to denote prisons in France. Located near Hanoi's French Quarter, the Maison Centrale held Vietnamese prisoners, particularly those who were agitating for independence. These captives were often subject to torture and execution. Ho Chi Minh spent a couple of years in this lovely place. We know of two American pilots that are prisoners there. A Lieutenant Junior Grade, Everett Alvarez Jr., and a young man I went to Annapolis with, Navy Commander James Stockdale. The Commander was flying a mission in his A-4 when he ejected over the north in September. Washington wants you to get all the information you can about this prison but it's not going to be like it was at Dogpatch." Again as always the Commander stopped to take a sip of water.

"I don't understand. Not going to be like it was at 'Dogpatch?'" Jim looked at him confused.

"You are to recon the place only. You are to see if it is feasible to get them out without any trouble. Dogpatch was in the middle of nowhere, but the Hilton is in the middle of Hanoi. We know that there are six prisoners in the main jail with Stockdale as the highest-ranking officer. With the information you bring back we will be able to formulate an escape plan and get them all out in one piece. You are not to engage any hostiles at any time whether going or coming. This is strictly a recon operation. You are to get in as quickly as you can and then get back here with the information as quickly as you can," stopping and looking at the two Marines, waiting for a reply.

"You mean to tell us that we are to go all the way to Hanoi, check out a prison for a way in and then come back here? Are you and Washington out of your fucking minds?" Joe was doing well but the last sentence was over the top.

"Watch it, Tomelli. I let you people speak from your heart but watch the disrespect. Is that understood?" looking right at Joe.

Jim felt he had to jump in not only to save Joe's ass but to tell the Commander what Jim thought of this plan also.

"Commander, I don't feel that either one of us is trying to disrespect you. We went through hell at Dogpatch and now the higher-ups just want us to walk into Hanoi, find this prison and then just 'check it out.' Do they realize what they are asking us to do? Hanoi isn't like any city in the US. There are a number of NVA and others up there that want to kill us on sight. I don't really know what we can bring back that is going to be any different than if we went up there and broke the Commander and the others out in one fell swoop," trying to ease the situation.

"It doesn't matter if they know what they are doing or wanting or not. It's not your job to figure that out; it's your job to do what they want without any questions. I don't know what has gotten into you two, but since Jim has returned to the unit you question everything. I hear you with the others. This isn't a union shop where you have a right to your opinion. Your opinion doesn't count and if you ever thought it did you have been drastically misled. You will do what you are told and go to Hanoi, find out about the prison, and come right back. If you have a problem with this order a couple of months in the brig on bread and water will help change your mind." With that he got up and left operations, slamming the door behind him.

The two just sat there looking at the door. Joe slowly turned to Jim saying, "I guess that could have gone a lot better than it did. I don't think we question everything that comes down but it's our asses on the line, not his."

"You know we'll have to do this so we might as well do it with a smile on our faces. At least we won't be fighting half the NVA brigade this time. All we have to do is reconnoiter the prison, find out all the in's and out's and then come back and give him the information. Sound easy to me," just trying to calm Joe down before he goes off and does something he will regret.

They met with the Commander for the next four nights going over all the maps and pictures that he had of Hanoi and the prison. Going over the list of prisoners that Washington knew were being held in Hanoi. As they sat at the table, Jim suddenly became quite ill. He dashed out of the tent, got as far away as he could when everything that he ate came flying out. As Jim stopped throwing up for the time being, he suddenly made a mad dash to the head. Getting there just in time feeling as if he was going to die and then felt that he wasn't. He would say that he didn't think he has ever been that sick in a long time. A half hour went by and then he made his way back to the briefing tent. He felt terrible but didn't know what was wrong. As Jim entered the tent, the Commander looked up and said, "You look absolutely terrible. I want you to go to sickbay right now and get an aspirin or a short because I really think you have malaria. Have you been taking your salt pills," with more concern than he has ever shown.

- - - - - -

Malaria is a mosquito-borne disease caused by a parasite. People with malaria often experience fever, chills, and flu-like illness. Left untreated, people may develop severe complications and die.

- - - - - -

Salt pills that the Commander mentioned are large pink "horse" pills that everyone is supposed to take at least once a day. The only problem with that is when they are on a mission for weeks at a time there is no room to carry salt pills so everyone is susceptible to malaria.

Jim was feeling as if he'd like to die this instant. Leaving the briefing and making it back to his bunk, Jim climbed under the covers and Joe put a couple of more blankets on him because he was freezing even if it was almost one hundred degrees outside. A corpsman came to his tent and gave him a couple of pills. He said that Jim had malaria and if he stayed in bed it would be gone within two weeks. Jim complained that he never felt worse even when he was shot in the head. Jim said he felt better then than he did right this second. The Commander came in and of course, he had spoken to the corpsman.

"It looks as if you're going to be laid up for a while, Jim, with this wonderful decease. Make sure you take the quinine pills and get plenty of rest. You are on the shelf for the next couple of weeks. You can use the rest." As he usually did he turned and left the tent not waiting for any kind of reply.

For the better part of the next week, Jim slept the whole day. He couldn't even get out of bed except to go to the head which he almost had to crawl to. At least twice a day he would shake so much he thought he would shake right off his rack

One night after sweating and shaking for hours, Jim finally dozed off. It was terrible. At first Jim dreamt that President Diem was standing at the bottom of his bunk. Half his head was missing with blood all over his white suit. He kept asking Jim, "Why did you do this? I have done nothing to you." Repeatedly he kept saying this. Then he just disappeared and then Lt. Diamond the pilot they rescued from Dogpatch, who had died before the helicopters came, was standing there. "All I needed is for you to get here quicker so I'd still be alive. It's your fault that I died. You had one job and you screwed it up," pointing his finger at Jim and then he was gone. Closing his eyes and when he opened them again Jim was in a very dark place. Trying to get out, but wherever he was wouldn't open but then he realized where he was. Jim was in the same body bag that the chaplain had found him in. He wasn't scared because he knew he was coming. He then heard some rounds being fired and they were in a series of three. Series of three that sounds like a twenty-one gun salute that they do at a military burial. After a few minutes, Jim heard something falling from outside on the top of a piece of wood but not the bag. It sounded like dirt being dropped but it couldn't be because the chaplain had rescued him. Again, the noise and then he heard a voice talking to someone else saying, "It's getting cold out here. We need to fill this grave quickly and then we can go home for the day." Starting to yell but nothing was coming out. Jim tried to rip at the body bag but nothing moved. "Oh, my God, I'm going to be buried alive and there is no one to find me." Closing his eyes again and he started to pray asking God for forgiveness for what he had done. Again, a picture came into view. This time he could smell the scent of burning flesh with a little girl standing in the distance. As he walked closer to her, he recognized his little "Fuc" and he started running toward her. As Jim ran, she was moving further back. Suddenly stopping, and looking around, there were hundreds of children surrounding Jim and they all had guns. They started to shoot and bullets just came raining down on him putting holes in all parts of his body. As Jim was falling, a sudden light shone and someone was saying.

"Jim, are you all right? You were tossing and turning, mumbling something about children and weapons. You were screaming, 'Don't shoot, I'm your father.'" It was the Commander kneeling next to Jim's bunk.

"Yes, sir, I'm fine. I just had a bad dream that was worse than a nightmare. You know what was strange about this whole thing. Do you remember the movie *Serenade* I told you I went to see while recouping in Hawaii? That song "Nessun Dorma" that Mario Lanza sang in the movie kept playing all through my dream. I wonder why that happened and what does it mean?" just shaking his head in disbelief.

Joe brought in clean sheets because the ones that were on the bunk were soaked from sweating. As they changed the bed sheets, Jim sat on Joe's bunk just watching them but thinking of what had just happened in his sleep. Jim thought that the malaria caused that and the dream would never come back again.

He was sitting on the edge of his bunk when Mutt and Jeff came in with a jar in their hand. It was a greenish yellow color and once they took the top off the most horrid smell filled the tent.

"What in world is that?" Jim tried to stand up to get away from that horrible odor but fell back on Joe's bunk.

"Fix up. No sick. No more," Mutt said in his pidgin English.

"What the hell is in it? It smells terrible. I couldn't get that down without throwing up. Is this the same shit you gave me in the cave?" Jim kept shaking his head "no."

"No, not same. Hold nose. Go down well," Mutt said with both scouts holding their noses.

Mutt held the jar out for Jim to take it. He didn't want to hurt Mutt's feelings, but the odor was a combination of old socks, dirty feet, and ass. Jim took the jar and looked around. Some of the men who were in the tent looked out the sides of the tent. Some were standing down at the far end of the tent at the back door. All the men in the tent were holding their noses. Now Jim knew he couldn't chicken out. Taking the jar, holding his nose, he swallowed the contents.

As he finished, Jim could feel something coming up quickly. Jumping up, he staggered out the front entrance and hurled most of the stuff he just drank out on the ground. Thinking that he was going to pass out because he felt so sick. He couldn't get over his stupidity, when he was just feeling better that he drank that crap and he was now sicker than ever before. Going back to his bunk he noticed that everyone had left especially his two Montagnard "friends." As he laid down on his bunk, the whole room started to spin and he thought he was going to fly right out of the bed. He finally fell asleep and must have been out cold for at least twelve hours. When he woke he didn't want to do anything because he was afraid he would be in worse shape than he was right now. As Jim went to sit up, he fell back a little but grabbed the sides of the cot and pulled himself up in a sitting position. Swinging his legs over the side, he tried to stand up for a second time. As he moved to stand he thought to himself, 'I am feeling great.' Turning to walk to the door and down the stairs, he was waiting for the worst. The aches and pains from the malaria were gone. Jim started to yell for his scouts and they came running.

"I don't know what was in that crap you gave me but I feel great. Thanks a lot for saving my life. When we all get back to the states, we are going to market that shit and make millions of dollars," shaking both of their hands and laughing at the same time.

Another week went by until he was feeling better so he could resume the briefing that had been aborted due to him being sick. While sick, the corpsmen estimated that Jim lost about ten to fifteen pounds. Losing weight anyway while being in country was common because everyone lost at least ten pounds. Jim started to work out with Joe doing PT every chance they had. Running around the outside of the landing field but well inside the perimeter of the base at Chu Lai was one thing they did every day.

The Commander called them in one day. "You know that running you do every day around the landing field? Stop it. You two are starting to get predictable and 'Charlie' likes those things. They can see you are getting in shape for something. Either they will try to get you or they will shoot you both while jogging. That is all. You two are dismissed."

After about ten days of minimum physical training and eating better, the Commander called both of them into his tent. There was no small talk or bravado. He said it was time to finalize the plans to go to Hanoi and check out that prison. Again, sitting at the table, they were looking at a number of maps and pictures of the area.

"Wouldn't it serve us better to have the scouts in here looking at these maps?" Joe speaking directly to the Commander.

"I have already gone over all the maps pertaining to the direction you'll be taking once dropped off by helicopter," he said matter of fact.

"Just to be curious, where will we be dropped and how far do we travel before getting to Hanoi? I imagine the drop zone won't be inside the North." Jim was looking at the maps once more and speaking.

"You will leave this evening at 2200 hours heading to Ha Tinh just north of the DMZ. The distance from Ha Tinh to Hanoi is seven hundred miles. The terrain will be typical North Vietnam with hills and rice paddies intermingled throughout your journey. There should be no trouble for your unit because you all should be used to it. When you get to Hanoi, you are to do one thing and one thing only. You are to get as much information possible about the prison. One particularly important item is how many soldiers are guarding the outside of the prison. How often do they change guards? Things like that. I know you so don't even think of trying to rescue the prisoners. You'll get yourselves shot or even killed and then it would look bad for the US," smiling for the first time in a long time.

"Jim, I need to speak with you alone, now." looking at Joe to leave.

THE RUG IS PULLED FROM UNDER ME

"What's on your mind, Commander? I have to get back to the tent and get my stuff together. You said we were leaving at 2200 this evening, right?" walking back and forth in front of the Commander's desk.

"I need you to sit down and listen to me carefully. You are not to say anything until I finish. Is that understood, Staff Sergeant?" The Commander was in a serious mood, Jim thought.

"They are leaving at 2200 this evening for Hanoi but you're not going. Instead, you are going to Tan San Nut airbase at 0600 tomorrow morning to connect with a flight back to MCAS El Toro. From there you will start a thirty-day leave with a flight back to Boston. When your leave is finished, you will proceed to the Naval Hospital in Bainbridge, MD for observation and surgery on your head. You will be able to come and go at your leisure from the hospital and the only time you need to be there is when you have appointments. I do believe that you are familiar with the head of the trauma unit, Commander Veronica White. The only advice I will give to you regarding this matter is that you be extremely cautious in your activities. Remember it is against military regulations that an officer, male or female, has a romantic relationship with enlisted personnel no matter male or female." As he finished Jim just sat there in what one would call disbelief.

"Am I allowed to say something about this or as usual, am I to keep my mouth shut and take it in the ass? I would like to talk about this without any regulations or rank getting in the way." As Jim was starting to speak the Commander could see that he was in for what is usually called a "shit storm."

"I have no problem with that as long as you know how far you can go without me 'pulling rank'." The Commander didn't have a choice and he knew it.

"Where in hell do you get off pulling me from the most important mission that we've had in two years? I am built for this and we have gone over all the information regarding the prison and the city. Why would you put me through that when you knew I wasn't going? I know you have a mean streak, but this is going all out to be a prick." Jim's head was starting to hurt and his eyes were becoming blurred.

"The decision wasn't made until last evening and I didn't make it;

the doctors did," trying to explain but he knew Coleman wasn't going to buy it.

"Are you trying to tell me that you couldn't override their decision and who are these quacks anyway? I haven't seen a surgeon in months. The only one I saw was a couple of doctors here for my malaria." Jim was still upset, he was starting to yell, and his head was beating like a drum.

"The doctor you saw for your malaria was a neurologist. Before you asked what a neurologist does, I will tell you. A neurologist is a medical doctor who specializes in diagnosing, treating, and managing disorders of the brain and nervous system including concussion, migraines, and strokes amongst other things. Dr. Wilkinson was interested in your temporary blindness and headaches more than anything. He came to his diagnosis late yesterday afternoon after observing you in the briefing session we were having. He noticed that your eyes were fluttering and that you had to sit down at certain stages of the briefing. He became alarmed and after you and Joe left, he came out of hiding and expressed his concerns. We came to this agreement for your welfare and for the good of the mission. Joe will be teaming up with Corporal Light. I have been going over all the information with him these past few weeks as a precaution that you didn't get over the malaria and I needed a back-up. I'm sorry, Jim, but this is out of my hands and I feel it's the best for you. You've been out here a long time, almost two years, and it's time for you to go home. I wish it were as a hero because you deserve it, but as you know, no one knows about us and medals are out of the question. With medals come questions and you can't and won't answer. When you get back to your folks' place, please remember that you are still required not to say anything about what you did over here. If there is a problem of any kind, you are to call CIA headquarters. Ask for Lieutenant Commander Delores Elder, she is my assistant at Langley. She will walk you through any problem you may have." Finally the Commander stopped talking and Jim was ready to scream.

"I think this whole thing is bullshit. I could have gotten out six months ago when I was shot. I came back because of you and what we created and I want to see it finished. I've gone through a lot for you without ever saying anything. I saw a lot of good men die and never said a word. I gave up two women for you. My life has been turned upside down and sideways for you. Now you do this to me. How fucking ungrateful you are. You are a two-faced son of a bitch. Throw me in the brig, why not. You've taken everything away from me anyway. I have no more to give. If something goes wrong on the Hanoi mission it's your fault. Light is a good man but he's not me. I have worked with my team for all these years and now you're taking it away. All I got to say is fuck you," getting up and starting to head for the door.

"You sit your ass back down here, Staff Sergeant. You listen to me and listen well because I will not repeat myself. I have told you over and over you are the best I have ever seen. There is no one better in any service than you are. You didn't lose your will or desire to perform but your body has finally called it quits. I would be risking everyone in your unit if I let you go. In the last mission with the Chinaman, you were lucky you came out of that alive and you know it. You can rant and rave, call me all sorts of miserable things, but you are still not going. I want you to go back home and get better. You have one year left on your enlistment and then I expect you to come to work for me at the Company. But you have to get better. You can't have these headaches that knock you to your knees and the blindness, this is just unaccept-able." The Commander stopped suddenly to catch his breath.

"When you get to Bainbridge do exactly what the doctors tell you to do. They all will have your best interest at heart and they will make you well. Grab that girl that really loves you and marry her. She's willing to give up everything for you," again stopping to catch his breath and wipe the water from his eyes.

"Get better, Jim. Make everything work again for you as it has in the past. Agent Simon will be at your disposal while you are in Boston and Maryland. He will contact you after you have settled in at your folks. When you are ready to go to Maryland, he will drive down with you. He will be back at Langley but he will still be at your beckon call." This time the Commander sounded sincere and in some way miserable.

"After today, what makes you think I'd ever come to work for you. I have had it. I'm done. I'll go back home, go to the hospital and then I'm gone after next May. I will be done with the Marines, the CIA, Viet-nam, and anything that I've been associated with these past years. Now can I get ready to leave," getting up and not even waiting for an answer.

"I know he's upset but it's for his own good. I also have to think about the mission. Tomelli is very capable and he will get the job done. I love Jim but he can get a little restless and go in and try to rescue ev-eryone in Hanoi. God, I hope everything goes all right and they don't run into any trouble. One thing about Coleman. He may get into trouble but he has a way of getting out of it quickly. I hope I'm not making a mistake in sending Jim home and not on this mission."

The Commander sat in his chair just thinking to himself.

As Jim left the Commander's office he was in tears. Not wanting to see anyone, he decided to walk around the airbase. As he was walking the far side of the runway, he noticed two men running across the tarmac about one hundred yards in front of him. 'Who the hell is that?' Jim thought to himself. 'VC. They must be a suicide team. They are here to blow up as many planes before they die. There in black and running bent over so they can't be recognized. All I got on me is my sidearm. Wonder where they are running to? There is nothing this side of the airport. Only thing is the end of the main runway where the planes take off from. I think I'll follow them to see where they are going or what they are up to.' Jim took out his .45 and started to jog in the direction that the two VC went.

At the end of the runway there isn't anything but mounds of sand leading to a little cove on the east side of the base. Only other thing that's around here is the Seabee base, which is right on the ocean.

As Jim came up to a high mound, he peeked over the top trying to see the two culprits before they did anything. Peering over the mound, it was difficult to see anything now that dusk was coming upon the area. Jim thought he saw movement just outside the Seabee compound.

"There they are. Just looking around the new cement mixer that the Seabees just got in and were quite proud of. They drove around the whole base these past ten days showing it off. It was the first of its kind anywhere in southeast Asia," Jim was thinking to himself.

As Jim just laid there watching the two, he noticed that one of them took out a small satchel and opened the driver's side door and put the satchel inside and then shut the door. Suddenly the two started running in the direction that Jim was lying and waiting.

'Oh, shit. Here they come. I hope I have enough rounds in this weapon,' as he laid as still as he could and waited.

Just as he finished talking to himself, the two VC came flying over the dune, just left of where Jim was. As they landed and started to run, Jim fired five shots, hitting both invaders in the upper torso and the neck. Both dropped dead about ten feet from where he was waiting.

Suddenly sirens started to blare from the compound and rounds were being fired toward the sand dunes where Jim was lying.

'One good thing with the Seabees being the only ones shooting. They couldn't hit water if they fell out of a boat. Worst shots in the world. I should know because I spent an awfully long week trying to teach them to fire a rifle.' Jim started to giggle to himself.

Lying on the other side of the dune and waiting for the compound to stop shooting, a large explosion happened. Jim crawled up to the top of the dune and peeked over. The once elegant and pride of the Seabees, their cement truck was now in pieces all over the front of the compound. The satchel that was put on the front seat by the VC was a bomb. Later Jim found out that the VC didn't know what it was but they thought it to be some kind of tank so they blew it up.

When everything settled down, Jim came out of his hiding place and walked to the compound to explain what he saw. The Commander was summoned to the debriefing and after about two hours, the two were on their way back to the compound. Nothing being said between the two compatriots but now enemies.

"Tomelli and Light are moving out in two hours. Plenty of time to say goodbye. After this mission, Joe will be heading home also. He's going to spend his last six months at Twenty-nine Palms, just outside of Palm Springs," stopping the jeep just outside the gate.

Jim jumped out and started to walk slowly toward his tent. Going up the three steps, he pushed open the screen door and he noticed Joe and Larry Light sitting on Joe's bunk. As he stepped in, Joe turned and nodded in his direction. Jim nodded back and went to his bunk and pulled his sea bag out from under the rack.

"I'm sorry, Jim. I found out this morning. I asked the Commander if we could postpone for a couple of weeks so Larry and I could get familiar with each other but of course he said no. Larry is good and he is up to date with all the plans that you and I worked out. The Commander said that he's sending you back to Bethesda to work out your health problems. Isn't that where Ronnie is based? I'm going to miss you, buddy. I'll be out of here in about four months and he said that he got me stationed at Twenty-nine Stumps. At least I'll be close to home. Are you going to spend some time with your folks? They will be thrilled. When was the last time you heard from them? I am rambling because I don't want you to go. I love you, Jim." With that Joe came over and hugged Jim like a huge bear.

"I don't want to go either. Yeah, I'm going to be home for thirty days but I will have a watch dog while there. Remember Josey from CIA Headquarters? Well, the Commander has him meeting me in Boston. While I'm on leave there, he also will be around Hingham, just in case I would need him. He'll be around Bethesda too because Langley isn't that far from the hospital. I haven't heard from or sent a letter to Ronnie since that last one where she professed her love for me. Hopefully, she will still have the same feelings," stopping to catch his breath.

As he stopped to wipe the tears from his face, he continued, "Joe, Larry will do a great job. The only thing I insist on is that you come back in one piece. I wish I were going because I really wanted to see if we could break the guys out of that prison." With that last sentence Jim started to laugh and cry at the same time.

Joe and Larry left the tent around 2130 to walk to the tarmac and the waiting helicopters. Jim decided to stay in the tent because he had already said goodbye to Joe. As he kept looking at his watch, he became quite melancholy. As the clock came closer to 2200, he jumped off the rack and ran down the stairs and off to the tarmac.

The unit was standing around waiting for the Commander as Jim came running up to them. He went to the scouts first and told them how much they meant to him and thanked them for saving his life numerous times. He then went to Kim and told him that he never thought anyone could take the place of Sergeant Sue but he was the one and thanked him also for saving his life. Sean was next and Jim told him how much he meant to him. Sean said that he has a feeling that he and Jim would be working together in the future. Lastly, Joe was standing off by himself as Jim came up and started talking. Suddenly, Jim burst into tears and turned and ran back to his tent.

Jim was laying on his rack when the Commander came in.

"Better get dressed in your tropical uniform. You can go without a tie and you have dress shoes. The plane will be leaving in about an hour. Don't miss it because you will screw everything up upon the way," turning and leaving as quickly as he arrived.

"What the hell time is it?" yelling after the Commander.

"Time to go home," was all Jim heard as the Commander yelled back.

Jim got out of the jeep in front of the operations building, just east of the C-130 waiting on the tarmac. Grabbing his sea bag and holding a large envelope in his right hand, he proceeded to walk up the four steps to check in before going to the plane.

Handing over the envelope to the Lance Corporal at the desk, he stood there and looked around. He noticed a colored Marine sitting, slumped over. He had dirt on him from head to toe and a huge red circle on his utility blouse. The Lance Corporal gave Jim back his envelope and said that he should go to the waiting room until his name is called. Picking up his sea bag, Jim steps into the waiting room and sits across from the Marine. As he takes his place, all Jim can hear is the Marine moaning.

"Are you okay, Marine?" Jim asks looking at this large man with a muddy gray complexion.

As time went by, the Marine sitting across from Jim said nothing but continued moaning. Wrapped around one of the buttons on his utility shirt was a tag, stating his name, service number and blood type. As the Marine kept moaning, Jim got up and crouched in front of him. A familiar smell was coming from the Marine but Jim couldn't put his finger on what it was. On his shirt was something that Jim was quite familiar with, dried blood. One button held his shirt together and Jim decided to unbutton it and see what was going under the shirt. As the button fell away and his shirt opened, Jim almost screamed. There was a hole in this Marines chest as wide as a football.

"Can we get some help over here. This Marine is really hurt and needs assistance," screaming for someone to come and help.

"Don't worry, Staff Sergeant. An ambulance is supposed to be here any minute now," the Lance Corporal replied.

"When was the last time you contacted them?"

"I called about 30 minutes ago. He'll be all right. He just a…"

"I hope you weren't going to say what I thought you were. Call down to headquarters and get an ambulance up here quickly. Keep calling every five minutes until they come. This Marine is bleeding to death." Jim was now screaming at everyone or anyone in the vicinity of this building.

As he finished, the Lance Corporal said that the plane was ready for boarding and he had to be on it within five minutes or they will leave him here.

Jim was torn whether to stay with this Marine or get on the plane. As he was thinking, he remembered two things; the Commander saying don't deviate his plans because he would screw everything up down the road and the smell he got when he went to see what was wrong the Marine in Operations. The smell was Death.

Leaving the building was a difficult decision. As Jim approached the plane, he stopped and looked back at the Operations Office. An ambulance had pulled up and they were taking the Marine out on a stretcher. The only thing wrong, there was a sheet over his entire body, meaning that this Marine, who was left there alone, had died.

Tears suddenly came down his cheek. Shaking his head and dropping his sea bag, Staff Sergeant James Coleman, USMC stood at attention and saluted.

Looking up as they placed the Marine in the ambulance, Jim said as loud as he could, "Semper Fi and I will see you on the other side," wiping the tears off his face.

As he was getting ready to board, he heard a jeep's horn. It was the Commander and he drove the jeep right up to the front of the stairs.

Jumping out of the jeep and running up to Jim, "Have a great flight. Don't do anything I wouldn't do and if you do, name him or her after me. Once Joe and Larry return and we debrief, I will be on one of these babies and heading back to the world. I'll see you in Bethesda in over a month. Your girlfriend will be thrilled to see me. Semper Fi, Marine." With this he gave Jim a huge hug and salute.

Jim boarded, and with the seats all against the bulkhead, he picked one in the middle. As he tried to get comfortable and seeing he was the only one on the flight he closed his eyes and thought, 'In about two more days, I will be home in Hingham.'

WINDOW SEAT ON THE LEFT, PLEASE

Jim was the hundredth person to check in for the flight to the "World" (rather than say USA or Home, the Army started "Back to The World") and a way of life he hasn't had for over two years. Waiting in line wasn't that hard for him because he just kept thinking of the end prize, home and freedom. As he got closer to the check-in desk, Marines in line started asking if everyone had there shot card up to date.

'I never had a shot card. I remember when we first arrived in country [rather than say Vietnam, they decided on "in country"] someone mentioned that we would have to get our shot cards brought up to date. When we mentioned this to the Commander, he told us not to worry about it. Well, now I'm starting to worry if I'm held up in any way from going back home today, I will hunt that Navy jerk down and rip his scrotum out.'

"Coleman, Staff Sergeant James Coleman, front and center, please," a corpsman was screaming his name and he even said please. Jim thought that word was replaced in the dictionary because no one uses the word "please" in the Marine Corps.

"I'm Staff Sergeant Coleman. What can I do for you?" with a big smile on his face.

"It isn't what you can do for me. It's what I am going to do for you. I'm Doc Honaker, we met about a year ago in Da Nang. Do you have your shot card handy or did they *forward* it to El Toro?" As the corpsman emphasized the word "forward" Jim knew what he was saying.

"Yes, Doc. They forwarded that with the rest of my papers. I only have the ones stating that I'm to be on this plane and into the world I will go." Jim still had that same silly smile on his face ever since he got off the C-130 about two hours ago.

"Very well, Staff Sergeant. You won't have to stand in line. Just go over under the trees and wait for your name to be called. Have a safe flight home and God bless you for what you have done over here. Oh, your uncle Damon sends his regards." As the Doc picked up a few papers and walked away, Jim still had his mouth open from that last sentence.

Jim started to think, 'Where aren't I connected? I know if I go down to see Ronnie before I report to the hospital, I'll have someone there.

That could cause a big problem because Ronnie doesn't like the Commander or anyone connected with him. I wonder how Josey will fare as soon as he introduces himself and for whom he works. I'll worry about that when it happens.'

Jim was just settling in on his bench when a Lance Corporal came up to him and asked if he was James Coleman. No rank, just his name, which is very odd for the Marine Corps to do this because they are into rank and respect of that rank.

"It's Staff Sergeant James Coleman, Lance Corporal," standing and looking down because he was six inches taller than this young Marine.

"Sorry about that, but you are wanted at the main building of this terminal. Just go straight into the building and take a quick right and go up the stairs to your left. It's the second door on your left," turning and not saying a word, he walked away.

Picking up his sea bag and envelope, Jim straightened his uniform and headed for the terminal. As he got to the stairs, his head was starting to hurt again and his eyes were becoming blurry. After stopping at the bottom of the stairs for a while, he trekked up very slowly and as he got to the second door on the left he stopped to catch his breath. Dropping the sea bag, Jim straightened his uniform once again and knocked on the door three times.

"Enter and center yourself in front of the desk, Staff Sergeant." It was a familiar voice but Jim couldn't place it. Or at least not yet.

Opening the door; the room was very dark but he could see the desk in front of him. Walking straight for the desk, stopping, and centering himself, he proceeded to sound off in true Marine fashion.

"Sir, Staff Sergeant James Coleman, reporting as ordered."

"At ease, Staff Sergeant and a very impressive opening. They would be proud of you at the Recruit Depot in San Diego."

Jim listened and suddenly he knew who was talking. "Thank you, Colonel Fisher. It's a real honor to be told you did something right from someone as you. But I need to correct you on one item if I may." Not waiting for an answer, Jim continued, "I am not a Hollywood Marine, sir. I am a true Marine who is enormously proud to have graduated from the one true Recruit Depot, that being of course, Parris Island."

"That's what I love to hear from my Marines. They don't worry about rank or anything, if they graduated from PI and someone mistakes them as a Hollywood Marine, they set the person straight. You made my day, Coleman. Relax and have a seat. Someone is here that for some reason wants to stay in the dark. Jim, I got you a ride on a private plane leaving here in about one hour. It will get you to California about six hours before the one you're scheduled on. Do you want the ride?" The Commander loves to play his games.

Jim looks at the Commander and then at the Colonel before he says anything. "Commander, I am eternally grateful in everything you've done for me and I'm sure you will continue in the future. But I would like to fly back with my brother Marines. I haven't had any contact with anyone outside of our units for two years. Even when I spent that time in Hawaii I was in quarantine. I'm sorry, Colonel, and this has nothing to do with you, sir. I just feel coming home with all the other Marines on that plane, well, it will mean something to me."

"Son, I would have been disappointed if you didn't choose the plane. I told Damon here that you would go with your brothers and not the luxury of a small plane. Good for you, Marine," as "Bull" stuck out his hand to shake it with Jim.

"Well, I am not that surprised, but if it were me, comfort over everything else," as the Commander started laughing.

"Well, Commander, that's the difference between a Marine and a Squid, with all due respect," Jim said as he and the Colonel gave out a great roar of laughter.

"Before you go, Jim. Make sure you call your mother from Alaska. You'll be stopping there to go through customs. Have her book an American Airlines flight for Thursday around noon. You'll be arriving El Toro on Wednesday evening and it will take you awhile to get your orders, money, etc. Don't forget to call her."

With that over, Jim picked up his sea bag, gave his final farewells and headed for the plane.

There it was, a Pan American World Airways 707 Clipper America, mostly white with a big PAN AM on both sides with a blue strip running from bow to stern. Men were just standing around with their sea bag right next to them. There must have been three hundred Marines standing and waiting to get on the plane. An Air Force General was at the top of the stairs with the pilot of this particular plane.

Jim was in the front of this mass of humanity and he could hear the conversation between these two men very clearly.

"Captain, I really don't care if your company is on strike or not. I have three hundred Marines down below who want to go home after spending at least a year here in this hell hole," the General was almost screaming at this pompous pilot.

"General, I feel for you and your people but what is right is right. I am ordered by my union to cease all movement during this work stoppage. Once we land at our destination we are to lock down the plane and leave." He has an air of superiority that just isn't going over with the General.

"I have an idea, Captain. Why don't you go down these stairs and explain to all these men that because your company is on strike you're not going to take them home. Oh, I will commandeer this plane and fly it back to the 'World' because I am qualified to fly this type of aircraft. How's that sound, you arrogant asshole?" with this the General is just staring at the Pan Am Captain.

"Very well, General. I will be filing a grievance with not only my union but with the Department of Defense when I return to the States. Is that understood, General?"

"You do what you think is right, Captain. Oh, if you don't have it, would you like Robert McNamara's personal phone number?" with that the General starts walking down the stairs with a huge smile on his face.

Jim turned and looked at the massive amount of sea bags piled at the stern of this plane and no one was loading them. He walked over to one of the Air Force enlisted men standing there watching everything.

"Excuse me. Can you tell me why the bags aren't being loaded on the plane? Is it our duty to load them or the Air Force?" trying not to be too strict in asking.

"Your bags, you load them," was the sarcastic answer he got in return.

"If it's not too much trouble to answer me in a civil tongue. How do we do that? Is there a container they go in or do we just throw them any which way?"

"Get a couple of people up in the belly of the plane. Start loading at the rear and move forward. Stack about four high and as many bags fit from wall to wall. I would do this really quickly if I were you," trying to sound a little friendlier.

"Why is that?" Jim asked but knew the answer.

"That pilot is pissed off because the General made him look like a fool. He'll want to get this bird in the air as soon as possible. He has to take the men but he doesn't have to take the bags."

With this, Jim made his way through the crowd to the aft of the plane where there was a huge door open. He yelled for three other people to get up in the plane with him and start stacking the bags in a hurry.

As Jim was in the belly of the plane and the bags started coming up, two men at the door caught the bags and threw them in Jim's direction. As he bent over to get the next bag, another hand touched his. Looking up he couldn't believe who it was. Colonel Greene, the Commanding Officer from MCAS Beaufort and the son of a bitch who busted him from Sergeant to Corporal because of that fucking cat.

"Nice job, Coleman, in getting this bag thing put together. It's hotter than hell in here," the Colonel smiling at Jim

"I can get an enlisted man to do this, sir."

"Not on your life. I can't wait another second for us to get out of this forsaken shit hole. Oh Jim. That damn cat of my wife's was rabid. You really had an enemy in that First Lieutenant. He wanted your ass really bad. Too bad he got killed up on the DMZ," turning around and throwing another bag up on the pile.

"I ran into him at Camp Pendleton when I first left for Vietnam. He was a real hard on but a great Marine. I didn't know he was KIA," trying to sound concerned.

"I have always wondered if he was shot by his own men. He was a ball buster and he gave no quarter. Just see what he did to you. Found out about three months later that he opened the door to your truck and took the safety off the riot gun. Not the right fit for a combat officer," as the Colonel got back to his job of lobbing those bags.

Jim and the Colonel finally reappeared as the last bag was thrown toward the front. Jim turned to the Colonel and said, "It was pleasure working with you, Colonel. We'll run into each other somewhere down the line," trying to say something nice and get away from the man who almost derailed his Marine life.

"I don't think it will be down the line, Jim. I will be seeing you in a few months once you get clearance from Bainbridge. My new duty station after my thirty-day leave will be Commanding Officer, MCAS Cherry Point. I understand from the Commander that you are scheduled to be the Staff NCO at the MCAS Cherry Point brig. Also, my wife no longer likes cats but she has one big ass dog," as he walked away laughing.

'The pompous son of a bitch never said he was sorry for busting me a stripe and confining me to the base for thirty days. I'm glad that prick Stasky isn't with us anymore and the Colonel is right, he was shot by his own men.' Jim was talking to himself as he watched the Colonel walk away.

It was quite hot and humid out, and after spending about thirty minutes in the belly of this 707, Jim's clothes were soaked with perspiration. Everyone was given a number and Jim's was four, so he figured he'd be right up at the front.

An Air Force Master Sergeant came to the stairs and walked halfway up. In his hand was a clipboard with quite a few papers attached.

"Listen up and stop the jibber jabber. I am going to read off names and numbers to board. Please pay attention and when you hear your name or number come quickly to these stairs and go up to board. There will be a stewardess at the top and she will tell you where your assigned seat is. Don't take too long. The quicker this gets done, the quicker you're on your way home." A huge roar came from everyone waiting to board.

"Number 1, John Michell. Number 2, Rudy Cordero, Number 3, John Coley, Number 4, James Coleman, Number 5, Robert Jennings." Jim heard his name and he bounded up the stairs to the top.

"James Coleman, Number 4, ma'am," standing in front of this beautiful human being and screamed his name.

"Do I look like a ma'am, Marine? How would you like me to call you a soldier?" as she smiled the most beautiful smile.

"Wouldn't like that at all, ma—miss. Marines never like to be called soldiers but you must know that. I'm just excited to be going home. It's been two years," trying not to cry.

"Well, James, you go all the way in the back and you have that window seat in the last row. I'm so happy and proud to be one of the stewardesses to be taking you home. Semper Fi, Marine, and the Commander says to have a great trip," smiling that perfect smile until she mentioned the Commander and then there was fire in her eyes.

'It's beyond me how he gets to know everyone around here. Colonel Greene and now this stewardess. Wonder what other surprises he has in store for me. He is on a first name basis with the pilot,' Jim was thinking to himself about how far the Commander can reach out. Taking a quick left, Jim walked all the way to the end of the plane and the window seat on the left.

As the plane started to fill from the back to the front, it was getting extremely hot and clammy. Jim started to think, 'With all these souls on this plane, I don't know anyone except the 'ball less' Colonel. How many have I walked by in all the bases and outposts and didn't know their names or even cared? Now we are all in the same boat and we still won't talk to each other.'

It's about 45 minutes since the first Marine boarded and they were ready to take off. The stewardess got on the intercom and explained about smoking only in the designated rows. The life vests under the seats and how to and when to use them. In case something happened to the pressure in the cabin, a facemask will fall down from the ceiling, put it on and hope we don't all die.

They were pulled out from the boarding area and then the Boeing 707 started all the engines and started down the taxiway to where they would take off. The cabin was full but the Marines behaved themselves with the stewardesses and the stewards. Suddenly they stopped and you could hear things going on down below but they couldn't see anything. They were being put in position for takeoff by what is called a "tug." It's like a plow but it hooks up to the front of the plane. They were being pushed backwards, and as Jim looked out the window, he could see that from where he was seated, there was water below.

Again, all four engines started up and water was blowing everywhere. Slowly the big plane started to roll, the water disappeared, and the tar of the runway could be seen by him. Suddenly, Jim closed his eyes and said a "Hail Mary" as the big plane was moving as fast as it could toward the end of the runway or into the water at the end of this long takeoff. As the plane started to lift, Jim looked out the window and there was water. As it was straining to get up, there was complete silence in the cabin. No one coughed, sneezed, or spoke. It was a strange feeling but when the smoking light went on, a huge roar came from the cabin. This meant that everything was good and they were on their way to reentering the "world."

As the flight was at the right height, sandwiches were being handed out by the flight crew. You could have a ham and cheese or turkey and cheese. Jim decided to get a ham and cheese, but when he opened the box, it was turkey and cheese. The turkey was like shoe leather and the cheese was nothing like he remembered but he didn't complain and he ate the whole sandwich. Jim just kept thinking, 'By tomorrow we will be in California and the next day I will be home.'

As Jim closed his eyes to try to get some sleep, he started to think of both Ronnie and Linda. First he thought he'd run into Linda or at least her family when he visited his favorite aunt Adelaide. They lived next door to each other and he would be going over to see her the second day he is home.

Then he thought of Ronnie and what he would say to her when he got to Bethesda. He thought he'd wait the month before seeing her but he'd call her as soon as he got home. Then he thought he might just jump in his car. What car? He has to buy a new car because the old one wasn't any good anymore. He'd get the car and drive down to Maryland for a weekend. One that Ronnie would be off. He thought he'd die before he got to see her again. Then a dreadful thought came to him.

'It's been months since I got that letter professing her love for me. What if she met another surgeon who could sweep her off her feet? What do I have to offer her? I'm just a grunt, uneducated and a killer. Am I crazy to think she would be satisfied with me? I may just call her and say that it can't work and she'd be better off without me.' He decided to get that thought out of his mind and concentrate on just seeing her and to wait to see where everything turns out.

The steward came on the intercom and after all the boos because he wasn't female he explained to the masses that they will be flying directly to Alaska. Everyone will have to deplane to go through customs. The reason being the steward explained that it is US policy that a plane coming from Vietnam will have to go through customs at the first airport inside the United States. He said that this should only take an hour but everyone will be on the ground for two hours. There are a number of telephones in the Anchorage Airport and you will be able to call home, collect. With this announcement everyone started to cheer again. Jim decided to try to get as much sleep as possible.

VIETNAM ISN'T THE ONLY WAR

Closing his eyes, Jim starts to dream about an unknown mission.

We're coming back from Canada, Josey and me. Everything had gone as planned in Shawinigan Falls with a few "hiccups" but nothing that wasn't handled. Crossing over into the United States at Penobscot, Maine was a lot easier than when we entered Canada because I wasn't asked any questions. Once we left the checkpoint, we decided to drive into the town of Penobscot to get something to eat. As we were finishing, Josey said he was going to call the Commander and tell him that we were on our way back and should be in Langley within twenty-four hours.

As Josey came back to the table, you could tell he had something on his mind and it wasn't good.

"You look like you swallowed a bug," trying to be funny.

"There was a church bombing at the 16th Street Baptist Church in Birmingham, Alabama. Four little girls were killed and one seriously injured. This is the church that my family and I have gone to ever since we moved there when I was five. I know all of the girls that were killed and their families. The Commander said it was the work of the Klu Klux Klan. He said he has a job for you so we have to get back to Langley as quick as we can." Gathering our gear, I paid the bill and went to the car.

We drove all day and night and I even got a chance to drive Josey's beautiful Ford Galaxy. Pulling over on the other side of Hartford, Connecticut, Josey said he was really tired and wanted me to drive. At first I drove the speed limit on the Saw Mill River Parkway leading into New York City. Once getting over the George Washington Bridge and onto the New Jersey Turnpike, I opened it up. What a ride!

We traveled the Jersey Turnpike with no problems and after leaving the last tollbooth on the border of Delaware, Josey once again took over driving. We were at the gates of Langley nine hours after we left the restaurant in Maine.

Entering the Commander's office, there was no one to greet us but the Commander's office door was open. As we moved forward, the Commander yelled to come in and forget the formalities. He was sitting behind his huge desk with only the small desk light on.

"You made great time. Did you drive straight through?" were the first words out of his mouth. I was thinking, 'Like he really cares about our health or our well-being.'

Josey spoke up, "Straight through, sir. Jim drove from Hartford to the end of the turnpike just outside of Dover."

"Everything went well in Canada. You made sure he was dead?" looking straight at me.

"Yes, sir. Right in the temple. He didn't survive," answering him just matter of fact.

"Corporal, I have a big job for you that just came across my desk minutes before Agent Simon called me." He is not going to forego the formalities when addressing a subordinate.

"Josey, I mean Agent Simon told me about the bombing in Alabama. Does this have anything to do with that?" looking directly at the boss.

"It has everything to do with that. This is one of the dastardliest deeds ever done against the colored people of the south. It has KKK all over it." I never saw the Commander so somber and with no emotion.

"What can we do about this one thing?" I asked without really expecting an answer.

"This is a Klan thing and we must retaliate swiftly without them knowing where it came from and by who," again, with no emotion showing.

"I don't know anything about Alabama or the Klan. Is someone going to meet us down there or is he there already?"   "The agent in charge will meet you in Atlanta. He has already been briefed in what his part will be. You, Agent Simon and I will be going over every aspect of this mission. A lot of it will be by the seat of your pants. There is no time to bring any of the other agencies in on this," looking at us like his head were a lighthouse.

"It doesn't matter to me but who is the target?" I wanted to know a little more than the Commander is wanting to tell me at this time.

"He is the Grand Cyclops of the United Klans of America, Blanton George Thomas, Jr." As he spoke, the Commander was looking directly at Josey.

"Is he the boss of all the Kluckers?" was my next question

"Kluckers. I like that. Yes, he is the big kahuna of all the Kluckers," the Commander said with a little smile.

"I don't want to sound stupid, but what's a kahuna? Is that another title the Kluckers use?" trying to sound at least one tenth intelligent.

"No, it's just an Hawaiian expression when talking about someone

of authority. It doesn't have anything to do with anything. Just forget it." Now he sounds a little exasperated.

"You didn't answer my question, sir. Who is going to be with me or am I on my own?" As I spoke I could tell the Commander was starting to get angry with me.

"If you'd just hold your britches, I'll tell you. First I wanted to see the reaction from Agent Simon here. Are you all right accompanying the Corporal down to your hometown and dealing with everything that is going on?" the Commander always asking the direct questions.

"Yes, sir, I am. I knew these young girls who were killed and their families. I also am aware of Mr. Blanton Thomas, Jr. and what he stands for. I just don't understand how someone can blow up a building with youngsters inside." Josey was in tears as he spoke to the Commander.

"When you find out what makes these people tick, please let me know. Alright, Coleman, here is your answer. Agent Simon will be accompanying you. He knows the area. He knows these people and he will know what you have to do by the time you leave here, which will be two days from now. Coleman, why don't you get some shuteye at the motel across the street. You have a reservation and the room is paid for. Simon, you just live down the street, so I will see both of you at 0900 tomorrow morning," turning in his chair as he does when he dismisses you without a word.

"Do you want to stay at the motel with me or are you okay to go home alone?" I asked my friend as we left the main building and headed toward Josey's car to get my bags.

"No, I'm fine. I'm only about fifteen minutes from here and it will be good to sleep in my own bed after what we just went through. I will see you around 0800. We can have breakfast together if you're up for it," shaking my hand, getting in his car, and driving off.

All these rooms start to look alike after a while, I thought. I have to take a shower because I'm starting to smell like a "goat." Staying under the water for about thirty minutes just trying to relax. As I got out of the shower and dried off, I started to think of the new mission. What kind of people would do such a thing? Flopping on the bed naked, I closed my eyes and fell asleep.

Josey showed up around 0800 but he didn't look as he got any sleep. The first thing he ordered was a pot of coffee. As we were eating, I asked if he had spoken with his folks down in Birmingham.

"Yes, for most of the night. I also spoke with the parents of all the girls that were killed. Do you know that they were only 13 or 14 years of age? They had their whole lives in front of them and this piece of trash ends it all. I just don't understand how someone can hate that badly," as he started to choke up.

"Well, if everything goes the way it should, he's going to find out how much I can hate him and I'm white," almost yelling it out loud.

"I know you will and I told the parents that justice would come to the ones who perpetrated this act of cowardice," looking at me but not looking at me.

"Let's finish up and see what the Commander has for us," I said while paying the bill.

"You should let me pay for this."

"I get reimbursed and you don't," walking out to the front of the café.

Crossing the street, we said nothing to each other. As we entered the main building and got into the proper elevator, again nothing is said. As we approached the Commander's office, Josey suddenly stopped and grabbed my arm. "This man has to die. You need to kill him so he suffers just as those little ones did. I don't want him to die instantly but suffer. That's all I want from you, Jim. Please do what you do but don't make it easy on him," as we pass into the outer office.

As we were ushered into the "inner sanctum," the Commander was at the window just staring out.

"Coleman, what do you know of the Klu Klux Klan? Do you know where it originated? What do you know about Alabama?" now turning and looking at me.

"I know that you can't be a Marine if you are a member of the Klan. I would guess it started in Alabama or Mississippi because of them being in the south. I don't know shit about Alabama but I would think this is why Josey is coming with me," puffing out my chest with the answers I gave.

"You don't know anything about anything let alone Alabama and yes, that is why Agent Simon is accompanying you. The Klan, you would think started in the Deep South but it didn't. It started in Pulaski, Tennessee, which is in the South but not the Deep South. The first Grand Wizard was a Confederate General, Nathan Bedford Forrest. There are three separate Klan dates."

- - - - - -

The 1st Klan - 1865 to 1871 which folded because the Congress passed the Klu Klux Klan act authorizing Ulysses S. Grant to use military force to suppress the KKK.

The 2nd Klan – 1915 to 1944. William Joseph Simmons of Stone Mountain, Georgia was the Grand Wizard. They were primarily anti-Jew, anti-Catholic, and anti-Negros.

The 3rd Klan – 1950s to present was a post war opposition to civil rights. The current Klan just wants to scare and kill Negros anywhere they can find them. After that they were put down by the many politicians and finally they hooked up with the White Supremacists and the Nazi brigade.

- - - - - -

The Commander is always pleased with himself when he thinks he knows more than anyone else.

"Wasn't the 2nd Klan actually started in Indiana rather than Georgia and they collapsed within a year of starting because their founder was convicted of killing a white woman school teacher?" Josey asked but I should have told him not to. The Commander never likes to be up-staged.

"They weren't around that long so they never were credited with starting phase #2 but it doesn't matter. That's a little background for you to understand what Agent Simon has been dealing with since he was born. These people just hate. They hate Negros most but they also have a hard-on for Catholics, Jews, Northerners, and people who aren't white, Protestant and Southerners. Some people call them 'WASP.' Are you all right with that explanation, Simon?" as the Commander had his evil smirk on his face and thankfully Josey decided not to say anything.

"You will be meeting up with our Senior Agent when you arrive in Atlanta. He will have a car and equipment and ya'll will be driving to Birmingham. Coleman, you will be in charge but all three of you will be well versed about what is happening there," as the Commander finished.

"I thought we couldn't operate in the United States," I asked very innocently.

"I will read the quote Congress gave for participation within the US borders.

- - - - - -

While the primary operational grounds of the CIA are indeed outside the US, it is permitted to act within the US to address the specific areas of foreign intelligence, counterintelligence, and terrorism. The CIA has branch offices in several cities in the US. Some of these are simple liaison with critical industries on issues such as security. Others serve to keep watch on international espionage efforts, intelligence defectors, and the like.

- - - - - -

"The Company doesn't like to operate within the US because we are a clandestine operation, which means what we do is kept secret. It is secret because it's especially illicit, which means forbidden by law, rule or custom. Most of all of our operations are covert, meaning not openly acknowledged or displayed. This is right out of Webster's Dictionary.

"Now you have the $100 explanation why the CIA shouldn't operate within the US boundaries. Let's say 'It's not good for business,'" stopping, sipping and continuing. "You will leave tomorrow morning and fly out of National to Atlanta on a Eastern L-188 Electra, where you will be met by Jonathan Duke. He will drive you to Birmingham which is only 150 miles. Once in Birmingham, I want you to be quite outspoken, ask a lot of questions to the local police. Go around to the businesses around the 16th Street Baptist Church and ask more questions. I want you to be as transparent as you can without anyone really knowing who you work for. Agent Simon will handle the colored sections of town because he knows all of them anyway. Corporal, you will handle the white section. I don't think you'll have an easy time, especially with that Boston accent." With this last statement, Josey almost fell on the floor laughing, as did the Commander.

The briefing went on for about five hours and the Commander even had lunch brought in. Overall, he said that he wanted to make a statement so these racist, bigoted, motherfuckers will know if they do such a thing again, they will face dire circumstances.

Leaving the office of Commander Damon was never as difficult as it was this time. Along with the boss, we took the elevator to the sub-basement of the main building, which housed the armory. The Commander walked around as if he was shopping at the local Piggly Wiggly. Pushing his "shopping cart," he proceeds to gather as much artillery as he could see. First he takes ten hand grenades, twenty sticks of dynamite, blasting caps, timing switches, ten blocks of C4 military grade explosive and a myriad of other things that will make one hell of a noise. Josey and I didn't take a thing and there were a few things here that I wanted to remember just in case Vietnam ever kicks off.

As he finished "shopping" he turns to us, "These things will be in the freight section of the Hartsfield Atlanta International Airport. You gentlemen are excused and I would recommend an early evening because you need to be up early tomorrow morning," just turning around and walking off without a goodbye.

A knock came on my door around 0430 and it was loud. Josey was standing in the doorway with a cup of coffee in each hand. Straightening his right arm and offering a cup of coffee to his "partner."

"Why are you not dressed? Our flight leaves National at 0830 and we need to get going," looking around the room to see where my clothes were.

As I stepped out of my pajamas and walked into the bathroom, I thought. 'It's 0430 and I still have to take a shower. It is approximately ten miles to the airport and at this time of the morning, we will be the only ones on the road. It should take us all of thirty seconds to check in because we have reservations. Let me take a quick shower, grab a decent cup of coffee from the diner and we will be off no later than 0500.'

Ten minutes later, I came out, dried myself off and got dressed in a blue suit, white shirt, striped red and blue tie, and black shoes. Everything looked perfect to infiltrate the south accept for one thing. With the short haircut that I had, everyone would know I was with either the FBI, US Marshals, or the Marine Corps.

I picked up my suitcase, which the Commander acquired at the armory, and Josey and I headed out the exit of the motel and into a company car that was waiting to take us to the airport.

"I told you that we'd be the only ones in the airport at this time. Let's check in at Eastern and then we can find a restaurant to get some breakfast. Do you realize it's not even 0530 yet? You are unbelievable," half laughing and half being angry.

"We have reservations under either James Coleman or Joshua Simon. Can we get the tickets here or at the boarding gate?" I asked the pretty young girl behind the counter.

"Mr. Coleman, I can print your ticket now, but Mr. Simon will have to get his at the gate," as she turned to get my ticket.

"Your name is Kimberly, isn't it. I saw your name tag on your jacket.

Now tell me something, Kim. May I call you Kim? Please answer this question as honest as you can or dare. Why does my partner here, Mr. Simon, have to wait until we get to the boarding area? Is the plane that full or is it something else? Now these reservations were made by a Federal Agency and we do a lot of traveling and I would hate to report back to my superiors that Eastern Airlines didn't want to give Mr. Simon his ticket. Now, Kim, you can try to answer my question or you may get a supervisor and see if he can answer the question to my satisfaction," as I watched the agent suddenly start to cry.

"Jim, let it go. I'm used to it and it's not a big deal," Josey started to beg me.

"It's a big deal to me. You and I are partners, not a white agent and a colored agent; we are agents. Now, Kimberly, what's it going to be? Issue a ticket to both of us and have your supervisor issue it. Your call," just staring with no expression on my face.

"Excuse me, gentlemen. I will be right back," as she wiped her eyes and went through the door that was right behind her.

When Kim reappeared, there was an older woman right behind her. Pushing past the agent, she comes right up to the counter which was separating her from both of us. "Gentlemen, I hope there won't be a problem."

"There is no problem and I hope I didn't give the impression that I was upset. I just have a question and hopefully you have the answer. I would like to know why is it that I have a ticket in my hand and Mr. Simon doesn't. Is it because the computers are down or the printer is broken? Now those are two excellent excuses and there would be no reason at all that anyone could object to having someone go to the gate and get Mr. Simon's ticket. Isn't that right, Supervisor Blunt?"

The supervisor took about two minutes to answer and you could tell by her standing position which moved at least ten times that she didn't have an answer. Finally, she cleared her throat, turned to the ticket agent, and said. "Kimberly, be a love and go to Gate 6B and get Mr. Simon's ticket and boarding pass and bring it back to me. Thank you, dear," with a half-smile on her face.

"Thank you so much, Supervisor Blunt. You are a love as is that sweet girl Kimberly. Now we will wait right here and make sure everything is in order. Hopefully, we won't have a problem with our seats. We do want to be seated together," again, staring right at her eyes and the supervisor on the verge of crying along with her agent.

Ten minutes went by and I was about to reach over and drag this pompous, racist pig across her counter when Josey said Kimberly was coming up the concourse.

"Was there any trouble, you sweet thing?" I was looking at Kim hoping she didn't have any bad news.

"No trouble at all, Mr. Coleman. You will be at a window seat in first class, 2B. Mr. Simon, you also will be in first class, with an aisle seat, 2A. Is that satisfactory with you, Mr. Coleman?" I could actually see the perspiration falling from Kim's forehead.

"This is excellent. I will make sure my supervisors know how helpful you two have been. Now y'all have a wonderful day and thank you for your kindness." I picked up my bag and motioned to Josey to head toward the gate.

"You know, Jim, you didn't have to do that. I'm used to sitting in the back of the bus. It comes with the territory," as Josey motioned to his skin.

"Yes, I did need to do that. These people have to realize that we are all humans and should be treated as such. As long as you're with me, you will never sit in the 'back of the bus,'" sticking my hand out for Josey to shake it, which he did vigorously with a huge smile on his face.

Standing at the gate, waiting for everyone to board before we headed for the entrance. We discovered that first class was wide open. All the stewardesses greeted us with smiles and handshakes and the one that was covering first class asked if we would like a mimosa before take-off.

"I don't care for one, but I'd sure like a hot cup of coffee and my partner here would love one of those things you offered." I was smiling at the stewardess and then at Josey.

"My name is Terry and I will be your lead stewardess for our flight to Hartfield Atlanta International Airport in Atlanta, Georgia. When we reach our altitude, I will be serving breakfast. We have scrambled eggs, bacon, sausage and home fries or a fruit plate. The eggs come with biscuits and gravy. What would you gentlemen prefer?" with the sweetest smile, coming out of that light chocolate face.

"What do you think? Do you think I have a chance with her?" Josey whispered to me as I almost spit up my coffee.

"Sure you do. Girls always love going out with guys who haven't said a word," laughing as I spoke.

"How can I talk? Nobody could get a word in with you always hogging the lime light." Now my "man" was laughing.

"Terry, can I see you for a minute before we take off?" looking over

at Josey as I rose from my seat and met her in the aisle right above where Josey was sitting.

"You wouldn't dare," he said with a plea in his voice.

"Terry, this is my partner and my absolute best friend, Joshua Simon. Josey, this is Terry and she's our lead stewardess," looking down into Josey's uncomfortable eyes.

"It's a pleasure to meet you, Joshua. Do you live in Atlanta or DC?" a perfect question to ask if you seem interested in the person you're talking to.

"I live just outside of Langley, Virginia and yes it is a pleasure to meet you," sounding more relaxed with each word.

"Now, Terry. Are you married? Have a boyfriend? Available to date?" With these questions, I knew that Josey just wanted to sink into his seat but not before he killed me.

"Are you asking for yourself, Mr. Coleman, or is it your partner is too afraid to ask me himself? No, I am not married nor do I have a boyfriend. I am 26 years old and a graduate of Howard University. I have been flying with Eastern since I graduated, and I am based in DC." Terry had that look on her face for Josey to ask her.

"Where do you live in DC?" now Josey is getting with the program.

"Just off of Mt. Vernon Square with two other stewardesses. It's on 7th and M Street. Are you familiar with the location?" Now I feel like the third wheel.

"I know exactly where Mt. Vernon Square is. My cousin used to live around there a couple of years ago. She was working for the State Department at the time. I would love to take you to dinner. Please give me your phone number and we should be back in ten days or so. I can give you a call and we can finalize the details," looking like a kid at Christmas.

"That would be great, Mr. Simon, sir."

"It's Josey or Joshua. I love how you say Joshua." If I didn't know better, my partner here is blushing.

"Then it's Joshua. May I call you Jim?" turning to me and smiling.

"You can call me anything you want. Oh, as if you care. I live in Jacksonville, North Carolina," chuckling as I said that.

"Are you a Marine? I dated a young man for a while that always said he was from Jacksonville, NC. You have the haircut for it," still smiling but Josie seemed to have stopped. "I have to make the takeoff announcements and then get your breakfast. Both of you want the egg breakfast," as she turned without really waiting for an answer.

"She dated a Marine. Wow!" Josey was shaking his head.

"Is that a deal breaker? I'm a Marine and I'm harmless," chuckling at that statement.

"I know you are, but not all Marines are like you. Most of them are dogs," still shaking his head.

"Call her when we get back and take her out. She seems nice and you will have a great time. Dating a stewardess is the best, because they are on the road or in the air most of the time.

Breakfast came and after eating we both fell asleep and awoke after hearing the engines slow down for landing. I had to go to the bathroom and throw some water on my face. Coming back, Josey and Terry were in deep conversation, so I took seat 1B for the rest of the flight.

As the airplane taxied into position to let the passengers off, Josey and I stood up and retrieved our belongings from the overhead bin. As the stairs came into place, Terry opened the huge door and motioned for us to deplane.

"If she says, 'the Commander sends his regards,' I will scream," speaking to Josey who had no idea what I was talking about. "I'll explain later. Did you get her phone number?"

"Yes, and much more. I have her itinerary for the next month," smiling and giving her a peck on the cheek on the way out.

As we went through the door to the outside, the heat and humidity hit me right in the face. I started to sweat all the way down the stairs and into the terminal.

Entering the terminal, I noticed this huge individual standing in the back and watching everyone who came through the door.

"You should get along with Agent Duke," as I pointed to the large colored man standing against the bulkhead.

"Are you Duke?" as we walked up to this man extending our hands at the same time.

"That be me. You are Agent Simon and you are Jim Coleman. Do I call you Agent Coleman or Corporal Coleman?" extending his hand to me following shaking hands with Josey.

"Just call me Jim, it's less confusing. What do they call you?" looking around the airport to make sure nobody is watching us.

"Most people call me Bubba."

"Are you ready to travel to Alabama?" turning and noticing Terry the stewardess grab Josey's hand on her way by.

"Nice going, partner. Now, Bubba, let's get your car and get out of this ungodly heat," as I continuously wipe away the sweat from my forehead.

"We need to pick up a box at the freight office. Something the Commander sent after you two left his office yesterday."

As Josey, Bubba and I come out of the terminal, there's a black 1963 Chrysler 300 right where it says, No Parking. As we get into the car, I jumped in the back seat.

"You afraid to be seen with two colored gentlemen?" Josey said.

"No, not really, but what I have been told about the South, it isn't the safest thing for me. Also, I'm tired and it's a long ride. Good night," as I laid on the back seat.

As we approached Birmingham, I sat up and asked where we were. Being told right outside of Birmingham, I suggested that we get something to eat because I was hungry.

"That may be a problem, Jim. Whites and coloreds can't eat at the same table in any of the restaurants here in Alabama. These people are still trying to get over the riots and bombings that happened last May here," Josey was relating to the unrest in the South.

"How come I never hear of these things that are going on? Give me a little background, please," almost begging for information.

Josey thought for a while and then he started to speak, "In April 1963, the Reverend Martin Luther King and the Southern Christian Leadership Conference (SCLC) joined Birmingham's local campaign organized by Rev. Shuttlesworth and his group, the Alabama Christian Movement for Human Rights (ACMHR). The goal of the local campaign was to attack the city's segregation system by putting pressure on Birmingham's merchants during the Easter season, the second biggest shopping season of the year. On May 2, 1963, more than one thousand colored students attempted to march into downtown Birmingham where hundreds were arrested. The following day, Public Safety Commissioner Eugene 'Bull' Connor directed local police and fire departments to use force to halt the demonstrations. Attorney General Robert Kennedy sent Burke Marshall, his chief civil rights assistant, to negotiate between the black citizens and Birmingham city business leadership. The business leaders sought a moratorium on street protests as an act of good faith before any settlement could be declared. Marshall encouraged the campaign leaders to halt demonstrations and accept this interim compromise. King and the other leaders agreed in 1963 and called off further demonstrations. Their victory, however, was met by violence. On May 11, 1963, a bomb damaged the Gaston Motel where King and SCLC members were staying. The next day, the home of King's brother and Birmingham resident, Alfred Daniel King, was bombed. Luckily, no one *at the bombings was injured. Dr. King's brother, his wife and five children were in the rear of the house and managed to escape any injuries.*

"Here is where it really gets interesting." Josey continued. "On June 10ᵗʰ, President John F. Kennedy federalized National Guard troops and deployed them to the University of Alabama to force its desegregation. The next day, Governor Wallace yielded to the federal pressure, and two Negro students—Vivian Malone and James A. Hood—successfully enrolled." Josey sounded like a history book as he took a break.

"Wow. You really know your history when it comes to the facts regarding what is going on in the South. Thanks for that. Now I know what I will be dealing with," smiling and slapping Josey on the shoulder.

"Now this is what I am thinking when we walk around Birmingham. You and Bubba should go to the colored section to find out what you can. What I'd like to know is when the next Klan meeting is going to be. Find out where, when how many attend and if any attending are big shots. What I mean, 'Are they something big in the Klan.' Also, find out who the other three who were with Blanton Thomas. Find out what buildings the Klan members own. This is going to be one federal visit these people will remember for a very long time." As I finished I was almost giggling.

"What about having lunch? I would suggest we drop you off at the edge of town and you walk to Ollie's Barbeque. That's where most of the Klan meet for lunch. You can find out a bunch of stuff but remember, don't talk." There was a big grin on Josey's face but Bubba didn't understand what was going on.

"Bubba, he seems to think if I open my mouth and talk it will give me away as a federal agent. What do you think?"

"Corporal Jim, I knew you were a Yankee the first time I saw you in the airport and you hadn't said a word to me." With that we all laughed.

Bubba dropped me off just south of town. As I started to walk down Main Street, everyone who was out on the street looked at me. It was the blue suit I was wearing or the highly polished shoes. Of course, it was the haircut, shaved sides and flat on top. Marine all over me. Ollie's was right in front of me, but before going in, I peered through the window. It was crowded but there were seats at the counter. Checking to make sure the .45 caliber that was under my armpit was ready to fire.

Pushing the door open and walking in, many of the customers turned and looked in my direction. Strolling to the counter, motioning to the waitress that I should sit here.

"You can sit anyplace you'd like. It's a free country," the waitress with a bit of fire in her voice was almost yelling at me over the complete silence.

"Thank you very much," straddling the stool and trying to get comfortable.

Trying to situate myself on the stool, the person that was sitting next to me got up and moved. As soon as he left, a young man around twenty came over and sat down. He was dressed in jeans, white T-shirt, and a ball cap with the Confederate flag on it.

"You the guy who drove in with the two niggers?"

"No, I drove in with two colored gentlemen." I could feel the hate coming out in this so-called open restaurant.

"Where are the niggers now?" came the question as the young man turned his stool into Jim's thigh.

"You say nigger one more time I will blow your fucking racist head off," as I turned my seat and caught the young man in the groin. In the same motion, my jacket opened so he could see the weapon I was packing.

As the young man got over being hit in the balls, he stood up and yelled, "Hay, y'all. We got us a federal agent down from Washington, DC visiting our fair city. He drove up with two colored gentlemen as he calls them. I just call them niggers."

With that last word, I jumped from my seat, taking out the .45 and hitting the young man with the Confederate hat right across the side of his head. In the same motion, I started looking around the restaurant to see if this man had any friends who would want a piece of me.

"I told him not to use that word anymore or I'd blow his head off. Now I see you all have lunch plates on your table so rather than shoot him, I decided to hit him. If I blew his head off, all your food would be ruined with blood and brain matter," finishing speaking, I noticed a lot of women customers were starting to turn green.

I started to sit down again, when a policeman came flying through the front door with his pistol out. "Don't move or I will shoot," were the first words out of the policeman's mouth.

"You talking to me, Officer? I'm just sitting here trying to get this young lady to take my order. This young man was being quite disrespectful and he needed a lesson taught to him. My name is James Coleman and I am a federal officer," turning and trying to get the waitress's

attention.

"I don't give one goddamn for whom you work. You could have killed Billy Bob here."

"Billy Bob. Are you shitting me? His name is really Billy Bob? Oh, my," was my reaction to a typical movie name for a Southerner.

"His full name is Billy Bob Thomas. His father is Blanton George Thomas, Jr. and he's the Grand Cyclops of the Birmingham Den for the United Klans of America. He's going to be upset for what you did to his son," standing over Jim in the restaurant.

"I was on my way to meet the head 'Klucker' here in Birmingham, so I guess I will wait here and see how long it takes him to arrive. Oh Officer. If you don't move and stop standing over me, young Thomas won't be the only one on the floor," turning around completely and looking up at the officer.

"He'll be here all right. You just wait and see," as the officer turned and headed for the door.

"Now what can I get you, sir. The pot roast is great. It comes with mashed potatoes, greens and grits," now the mouthy waitress was now trying to be my friend.

"What's your name? I'm Jim," smiling to an extremely attractive sixteen-year-old.

"My name is Melanie Troup and I'm seventeen years old and a senior in high school. How old are you?" They are direct in the Deep South.

"I'm 20 years old and I'm from Boston"

"What brings you to Birmingham?" She's really trying to be friendly or quite nosey.

"Came here to investigate the bombing of the 16th St. Baptist Church. Terrible thing and I'm going to find out who is going to pay for what they did." Now Melanie starts to back up into the kitchen.

Just as Melanie passed out of view, the front door of the restaurant came flying open and this little man five foot six or seven inches comes through like Napoleon. As he approaches, I notice that he has a bat in his right hand.

"Unless you're on your way to the baseball field I'd drop the bat." I start to stand.

With this, the senior Thomas decides he's going to take a swing with the bat at me. As he swings the bat, I grab it in mid-air and snap it out of Thomas's hand. "You are lucky you're still standing. Why in hell are you trying to hit me with a bat? I have done nothing to you to make you do that or at least not yet. Before you pick up junior here, please come outside with me. I need to speak with you in private." I head toward the front door with Blanton Thomas right behind him.

Taking a right and going to the end of the restaurant's building and into the ally. Turning quickly so my jacket opens so Thomas can see the "bad news."

"Now I didn't want to say this in front of all the people at the restaurant but here it is. I know you and Mr. Frank, Mr. Chambeau and Mr. Wallace blew-up the 16*th* Street Baptist Church killing Denise McBride, Adie Mae Brady, Carole Richardson, and Cynthia Wellesley who were only thirteen or fourteen years old. I know if you go on trial you will be found not guilty by your peers. Your peers are white, Baptist, and fucking Klan members. You're wondering right now what's he talking about? If I'm found not guilty I will be free to go and blow something else up. Well, Mr. Thomas, I am here to tell you that I'm going to kill you. Within the next week, you and your other goons will be dead. So, get as many bodyguards as possible because you will need them. It won't save you but it may give you some idea of safety." Finishing my soliloquy, I turn and walk back into the restaurant.

Walking toward my seat and sitting down as Thomas come in right behind me with his deputy not far behind.

"Johnny, I want you to arrest this crazy man," Thomas is yelling at the officer.

"What did he do, Mr. Brantford, sir?" The officer was taking out his handcuffs.

"Unless you want the Federal Government to come up your ass, I would put those back on your belt." I start to stand.

"He threatened my life and the lives of three other outstanding citizens of this community. Arrest him I'm telling you." Thomas was almost purple in the face.

"Officer Johnny, I did not threaten Mr. Thomas and his friends. I am here to investigate the 16*th* Street Baptist Church bombing and make sure that those four little babies get justice. I have not yet decided what that will be but they will get it," now talking directly to Officer Johnny.

"Johnny, he just threatened me again. Arrest him, I'm ordering you to arrest him. I am your Gra—"

"Do you want me to finish that sentence for you? Let me see. I guess it would go like this: 'I am your Grand Cyclops of the Klu Klux Klan.' Is that what you meant to say, Mr. Thomas? So, by that, Officer Johnny, you must be a Klucker too," almost laughing in their faces.

"I didn't say that at all. You're putting words in my mouth, you fucking Yankee," almost spitting the last word out.

"Now, now, Mr. Blanton, sir. Your face is about as red as those satin sheets you wear at your cross burnings. Didn't think I knew that much about you Kluckers," now in my glory screwing with these "Johnny Rebs."

"I demand you do something immediately, Deputy." Blanton Thomas was as angry than any man could be. Right where I wanted him.

"Now, Mr. Blanton, sir. You know that this deputy is part of your inner circle but there isn't a fucking thing he can do. You see, Mr. Blanton, sir, you're a Klucker and that's against everything I and anyone else in the Federal Government stands for. So, when your day comes and it's coming, you or better still, your relatives won't have a leg to stand on and you'll die and nobody is going to give a shit." Turning immediately, I walk slowly out of the restaurant. "Have a great day, Melanie. I'll see you for breakfast tomorrow," hollering back to the cute waitress who is going to give me some important information but she doesn't know it yet.

Walking down the sidewalk in front of all the storefronts, looking around, seeing who is interested in a "federal agent." Just as I was going to cross the street, a car comes careening around the corner and heads for me in the middle of the street.

As the car is bearing down toward me, I reach under my left armpit and take out the .45 that is in the holster. Turning to face the car head on and taking my position, bent over at the belt and aiming my pistol at the driver of the car. The car was now fifty yards away from me when it veered to the left and stops.

"What the hell is the matter with you? Were you really going to shoot us?" as Josey, half laughing opened the back door so I could get in.

"Do you see how many of these rednecks are looking out their windows to see who is in the car? This will definitely be the topic at the next Kluckers meeting. Let's get out of here. After talking with these folks, I need to take a shower," sitting back in my seat and putting the pistol on the seat next to me.

Leaving the city of Birmingham, I finally remembered that I didn't have anywhere to stay.

"Where am I staying tonight? I need to be close because I have a breakfast date with a pretty young waitress," talking to the two men *in the front seat.*

"We already have a room at the Gaston Hotel. That's a 'Coloreds Only' hotel just south of the city. Now the Elyton Hotel is one of the oldest hotels in Birmingham. Sixteen floors with suites on the top floor. I have never been in it. They don't let my type come in the front door but it's supposed to be really nice," Josey said over his shoulder.

"Turn around and drop me off at the Elyton. Give me about an hour and then come pick me up. I want to go look at the church and then I would like to meet with the families. Can you arrange that, say 9 p.m.?" yelling to the front seat and still thinking of what transpired earlier at the restaurant.

"We must find out where the other three are. Also, where does the Klan hold their meetings or where is the place that they keep their records. Bubba, once we find out where everyone or everything is, then you can go to work in blowing them up. I will handle the three others but I need that information fast. Also, find out if they are married and how many kids they have." I finished talking as we pulled up to the hotel.

As the car comes to a complete stop, the colored hotel bellman jumps up and runs to help. Stopping on a dime and looking in the window as Josey waves at him, he looks at me like I am the devil.

"Don't worry, kid. You can take my bag. I'm white enough for y'all to stay in your fine establishment," leaning in the window and smiling at my compatriots.

The bellman leads me up the front stairs and into the hotel which is quite elegant and dark. Walking to the front desk, I turn to the young man giving him a five-dollar tip and saying, "You impressed my brothers in the car. They'll be back in about an hour. Will you call me when they arrive?" turning and addressing the girl at the desk. "Hi. I'm James Coleman with the Federal Government and I will need a room for the next six days. I'd like one in the middle of the hotel and at the end of the hall. What do you have available?" smiling at the girl with the name tag of Beverly.

"Can you give me a minute? I need to ask the manager what is available," as she turns and goes into the door that was just behind her.

I know exactly what is going to happen. With the list of rooms right in front of her, she will get the manager who will come out and tell me they are booked for the rest of the week or something like that. That's when the fun will begin. As the manager, a short, fat man of fifty came through the door with Beverly right behind.

"Now before you start and tell me you're sold out, let me explain who I am with and why I need the room." I was about to explain when the manager held up his hand.

"Mr. Coleman, my name is John Jeffries and I am the owner of this hotel. Rest assured there will be no problem with your room. Now I was told that you would like one of our rooms on the 16th floor. Billy will be glad to take your bags up to room 1632. It's at the end of the hall and there is only one exit or entrance. Dinner is being served in our dining room and will be served till nine this evening but you will be able to get room service till midnight. We are proud to have you stay with us." I was about to say something, but Mr. Jeffries with his hand held up again bends over to say something. "Rest assured, Mr. Coleman, we are not all rednecks in this fair city. Oh, by the way before I forget, the Commander sends his regards," smiling as he started to come around from in back of the counter.

"I'll be a son of a bitch." I was dumbfounded as usual with this last statement.

"I beg your pardon, sir." Beverly was horrified to hear such language or at least that's the way she came across.

"I'm sorry, Beverly, but Mr. Jeffries caught me by surprise." I could feel my face heat up.

"Mr. Jeffries, I will be going out for a couple of hours. Is there anyway someone who is not staying at the hotel or on the 16th floor can get up there?" making sure some unwanted visitors won't be waiting when I come back.

"No, sir, no one can get up there without a key. Our elevator operators know to ask to see the key before he shuts the door. Would you like to meet the elevator operator?" as Mr. Jeffries starts to walk toward the elevator.

"Arnold, this is Mr. Coleman and he will be staying in room 1632 for the rest of the week. He is concerned that there may be some undesirable characters coming to his room," as Jeffries talks to this old colored elevator operator.

"Mr. Coleman, sir. I can guarantee you that no one will be to the 16th floor that doesn't belong there." I noticed while Arnold is speaking he opens the small cabinet door in front of him and takes out a .45 caliber pistol.

"Thank you, Arnold. You have put my mind to rest."

As I turned to leave the elevator operator Arnold speaks up, "The Commander said that you cover all possible problems," smiling and *shutting the elevator door behind me.*

"Isn't there anyone that the Commander doesn't know?" not speaking to anyone.

"The Commander has stayed with us a number of times. He is a gentlemen and a wonderful judge of character." Mr. Jeffries moved to the front desk.

"Can I speak to you in private for just a minute?" moving Mr. Jeffries to the far end of the front desk. "You have heard that I had a bit of a disagreement with Blanton Thomas this afternoon at Ollie's. I would expect some blow back from that and I wouldn't want your establishment damaged in anyway. These people seem to like blowing things up." I decided to tell Mr. Jeffries what had happened so he could make some kind of arrangement for protection. I didn't mention the killings of the four teenagers or the arresting of the men responsible for the bombing of the 16th Street Baptist Church. "Mr. Jeffries, how come you are not Klan? Your family has lived here a long time and you grew up with most of the people that are Klan. How come?"

"Jim, may I call you Jim? My great grandparents came from up around Minnesota in the late 1800s and settled here. One thing the Klan is aware of is the feelings toward them by the true families of the South. They would never dare blow up a hotel in downtown Birmingham, especially a 'white' hotel. They will try to get you coming or going but believe me that will not be as easy as it sounds. Just keep your eyes open and don't trust anyone in the police department. They are all Klan." Jeffries finally stopped talking. Jeffries had one request, "Will you do one thing for me tonight? Please tell those families of the girls that if they need anything have them contact Arnold. He will tell me what they need," again smiling and bidding me goodnight.

As I started to walk out of the hotel, I kept asking myself, 'How do these people know what I am going to do? I know Josey or Bubba wouldn't tell them and I don't think the Commander would but who knows. It's good to have a friend on the inside.'

As I walked down the hotel steps, I noticed a man in the shadows. Not wasting time, I turned and walked quickly toward him before he could run. It was the deputy that I met at Ollie's.

"What are you looking for, Johnny? Thomas tell you to follow me and see what I was up to? Tell him I am going out to the 16th Street Baptist Church to check out the crime scene. Then I'm going to meet with the parents of the four dead girls and then I am coming back to

the hotel. I am staying in room 1632 and I will kill the first person who tries to get into my room without an invitation. You go tell him that and then I don't want to see you again outside of you walking you post. If I do, I will kill you," turning and walking back to the front of the hotel to wait for my ride.

As I stopped in front of the hotel, I turned to see if the deputy was still there and he wasn't. Deputy Johnny was high tailing it across the street and going into the tire shop. I thought that I have to find out who owns the tire company when I get back unless Josey knows.

Just as I thought they were going to be late, up comes the Chrysler from the other end of 1st Avenue North. Being on the other side of the street, Bubba decides to make an illegal U-turn but nobody noticed or even said anything.

You are going to drive these deputies crazy with your driving. An illegal U-turn, how can I face the Commander?" as they all had a good laugh with this statement.

I filled the other two in on what was going on at the hotel. Josey knew where the church is so he went directly there. As we pulled up to what used to be the 16th Street Baptist Church, I felt sick to my stomach. The whole church was a charred mess with the big beams still smoldering. As we got out of the car, we could smell death from down in the street.

"They are going to pay for this," I said out loud but to no one in particular.

"How could anyone in their right mind do this? They must have known that there were children in the church but they couldn't care less. I am going to make them all pay, but the ones responsible, I will have something special in mind for them." As I finished talking the two other men noticed tears running down my cheeks.

We walked in and around the rubble, and I noticed something that I almost stepped on. It was a medal of St. Jude. In the Catholic religion St. Jude is the patron saint of desperate cases and lost causes. What was it doing in a Baptist church?

"Hey, you two, look at what I just found. It's a medal of St. Jude. Someone who was in this church, before or after, dropped this. If it was the bomber who set up the explosion then he's a closet Catholic and he doesn't want the others to know. What do you two think?" as I passed around the medal.

"I think you're right, but who would it be? If he wore the medal while going to Klan meetings then he was looking for trouble. This also

*could be someone trying to throw us of the Klan and start looking at
Catholics instead," Bubba said as he held the medal and looked at Josey,
who was also nodding his understanding.*

*"If we can find out who this belongs to, we can turn him into an
informant. If not, then we will use it against him. Shake the bushes and
see what falls out." Josey sounded excited.*

*After sifting through the rest of the rubble, Josey told me that the
families should be at the Gaston Motel by now.*

- - - - - -

[*The A.G. Gaston Motel offered accommodations, food, and entertainment to black travelers. A fixture of black businesses in
Birmingham, the motel was the choice for headquarters of the local
civil rights campaign that shaped the city and the nation in 1963. The
modern Civil Rights movement followed southern-state defiance of the
Supreme Court's* Brown v. Board of Education *decision in 1954 that
ruled segregation was unconstitutional. While some state and local
governments tried to maintain the status quo of systemic racism and
oppression, including racial segregation of public accommodations,
civil rights groups and allies organized to address racial injustice and
promote equality. In Birmingham, the Alabama Christian Movement
for Human Rights (ACMHR), founded by Reverend Fred Shuttlesworth
in 1956, was key in organizing resistance to segregation and discrim-
ination within the city. Encouraged by Rev. Shuttlesworth, Dr. Martin
Luther King, Jr. and members of the* Southern Christian Leadership
Conference (SCLC) *joined forces with other civil rights figures in Birmingham in 1962. Dr. King believed desegregation in Birmingham
would have national effects and was thus a logical site for a large di-
rect-action campaign. In Rev. Shuttlesworth's words, «If you come to
Birmingham, you will not only gain prestige, but really shape the country. If you win in Birmingham, as Birmingham goes, so goes the
nation." Together they conceived of a protest campaign to work toward
the desegregation of the city. The campaign, known as the Birmingham
Campaign or Project C – C for confrontation – consisted of a four-
part strategy including small-scale sit-ins, a generalized boycott of the
downtown business district, mass marches, and finally a call on out-
siders to descend on Birmingham.*]

- - - - - -

As the Chrysler came around the corner of 16th Street North, they could see the motel down at the corner of 5th Avenue North. Out in front of the motel was a sight to be seen. There had to be at least five hundred Negro men, women and children just standing and waiting for something.

"What are all these people doing here?" I looked at Josey.

"They're waiting for you, Mr. Coleman, Sir," as Josey smiled back.
"Why me?"

"You are the 'Great White Hope' that they are waiting for. I know that most of the folks that live in the 'Bottoms' [colored section of town] know that you are meeting with the families of the girls that were killed. I think they just want to come down here and see what you look like," pulling the car up in front of the motel. The people suddenly parted so he could park.

When we got out of the car, nobody said a word but they made an opening so we could walk up to the entrance.

Entering the motel and walking a few steps inside, I could see in front of me a very elegant dressed colored man. Walking up to him, I stuck out my hand and said, "Good evening, my name is James Coleman and I am here to find out who killed your children and rectify this situation," finishing with a somber look on my face.

"My name is A.G. Gaston and I own this establishment and it is my pleasure meeting you, Mr. Coleman. I know Joshua here, but I'm sorry I didn't catch the other man's name." A.G. Gaston had a huge smile on his face as he turned to Bubba and stuck out his hand.

"My name is Jonathan Duke but most people call me Bubba. It's a real honor meeting you, Mr. Gaston," Bubba grabbing A.G.'s hand and shaking it quite a long time.

"Gentlemen, everyone calls me A.G. Before you go in and meet the families let me explain a few things. Down here, when a white man promises something, it is usually something bad, so be careful what you promise. Along with that, most coloreds down here don't trust anyone that doesn't live in the 'Bottoms.'"

As they entered a conference room, four colored ladies were sitting across from the entrance, with four colored men standing behind them. To the left and right were children aged from five to fourteen sitting in chairs. Everyone was dressed, as Josey said later, in their "Sunday Go to Meeting Finery."

I was the first to speak. "Good evening. My name is Jim Coleman and these are my associates, Joshua Simon and Jonathan Duke. We have come down from Washington, DC to discover who are the perpetrators of this dastardly deed which happened days ago. I promise you that we will not be leaving until these cowards are identified and dealt with accordingly," tears coming down my cheeks.

"What is your intention regarding punishment for these men?" one of the colored gentleman behind the second chair asked.

"My intention, as you call it, is to make each and every one pay for killing your babies. If you want me to kill them all then I will look into that and see how feasible that would be. I will guarantee that the man in charge will meet his fate by the end of this week." I knew I shouldn't have said that but these people have to know that I wasn't down here to see the football game on Saturday afternoon.

After the meeting with the families had come to an end, Josey, Bubba and I got into the Chrysler and headed toward the lumber mill just north of downtown.

"Two of the accused work at the mill and a former Grand Cyclops is part owner. The third owns the garage and Thomas is owner of the tire shop." Josey found out everything I wanted to know.

"It is now Sunday night and I would like to see these go up early Wednesday evening, say around 10 p.m. We must make sure that there are no employees in this mill, or the garage, or the tire company when they go up. Do you two think you can have everything ready by then? I would also like them to go up within five-minute intervals, say 2000, 2005 and 2010. This should get their attention quickly and it gives me to Saturday midnight to complete our mission," explaining what I wanted from the two bomb experts.

"Jim, why is it so important to have everything finished by midnight Saturday?" Josey looking at me with a quizzical expression.

"I told that blowhard Thomas that I would kill him within the week. I told him that last Saturday outside the diner. I would hate him to think I was a liar." With that all three of us started to laugh.

Dropping me off at my hotel, the two men headed back toward the Mill to try to finalize what they would need to blow it to smithereens.

I walked through the lobby looking around to make sure some of the undesirable members of the Birmingham community weren't there waiting for me. Walking toward the elevator, I could see Arnold sitting on his stool inside.

"How you doing this evening, Arnold?" as Jim entered the elevator.

"Fit as a fiddle, Mr. Jim. No one tried to get to the 16th that wasn't *supposed to. Are you really going to take care of those men that blew up my church and killed those four little babies?" tears starting to fall down his cheek.*

"I'm going to bring them to justice, Arnold. It all depends on how they react once confronted with the evidence," looking at the colored man and giving the operator a little wink.

"Arnold, before I go to my room I have a question to ask you. Do you know of anyone in the Klan that could be Catholic? We found something in the rubble that makes me think that a Catholic may be involved," looking at this little colored man who knows what is going on before it happens.

"I don't know for sure if he's still a practicing Catholic but the dep-uty's parents were Catholic and he was baptized and confirmed in the Catholic Church. If you really want to find out if he's still goes to church, you need to talk to the pastor, Monsignor Ronan. Have a great night, Mr. Jim." As the buzzer starts, Arnold goes to shut the elevator door after I exited.

As I walk down the hall to my room, I'm having a strange feeling that someone is watching me. Opening my door, I once again look around down the hallway to make sure I'm alone. As I enter and click on the lights, I start to walk slowly to the living room. Taking out my weapon and holding it in my right hand, I hug the wall as I enter the living area. There is nothing out of the ordinary but I still have this strange feeling. Once again hugging the living room wall with my weapon now in my left hand, I slowly head toward the master bedroom. Slowly opening the door and flipping on the lights, again nothing. Walking around the room, I come upon the walk-in closet, and I notice the sliding doors are closed. I think I left them open but am not really sure. This would be a great place to hide. Slowly, I slide the right-side door open just a little. Reaching in I pull the chain at the opening to turn on the lights. Again nothing. Turning, I walk out of the master bedroom and head for the second bedroom which is across the room. Noticing that the lights are on and the window shade is up, I immediately fall on the floor and quickly scoot across the living room rug as quietly as is possible. Getting to the bedroom door, I slowly stand against the wall and place my hand on the doorknob, opening it slowly. The light switch is against the far wall meaning I will have to cross over the door sill, with the whole room in front of me, my back against the wall and the lights switch ten feet away.

"If there is anyone in this bedroom or even in the suite, you better

come out now if you know what is good for you," standing with my back to the left of the bedroom door.

Waiting to see if anyone would come out, suddenly there's a knock at the door. I almost jumped out of my skin. Walking very slowly with my back still against the wall, I open the front door slowly. I am to the right side still against the wall and my right hand holding the pistol, cocked and ready to fire.

"Hey, Jim. What's you doing?" a sweet young voice is asking.

"Melanie, how did you get up here?" shocked that she was here and thoughtful in how I was going to get my gun from down at my side, up to the shoulder holster under his left arm.

"My daddy is the Manager in Residence, so me and Mommy live with my daddy just two doors down. I heard the elevator and opened my door a speck and saw it was you and I thought I'd come over and keep you company," pushing her way in and going directly for the couch.

"Melanie, it isn't safe for you to be here. You must go back to your room, now," trying to be as emphatic as I could be.

"Oh, don't worry about my folks. They went to a meeting tonight and won't be home way after midnight," flipping her shoes across the room.

"What kind of meeting, Melanie?" now sitting on the chair across from the sofa.

"It's an emergency meeting and I think it has to do with you and what you are doing here in Birmingham," looking as cute as a button and as dangerous at the same time.

"What kind of meeting is it, emergency or not, to discuss me?" watching her every move just in case she decides to do something stupid.

"It's a Klan meeting, silly. My daddy is the Grand Exchequer of the Birmingham or Northern Alabama den. They were talking about you tonight at dinner and how you threatened to kill Uncle Blanton. Is that true? Are you really going to kill him?" She looked twenty-four but acted like a ten-year-old girl.

"Holy shit, your father is a big shot in the Klan. What does your mother do for the Klan or should I ask?'" with a slight grin on my face which Melanie didn't catch or even understand.

"She the Executive Vice President of the Women of the Invisible Empire or better known at the WKKK, Women of the Klu Klux Klan. She's at all the meetings that my daddy goes to," just staring at me and smiling with a lot of her robe open.

"Who told you that I was going to kill your uncle?"

"Uncle Blanton, he's not really my uncle but I've known him since birth so I just call him Uncle Blanton. He was talking to my mommy and daddy Saturday night and he said that you told him that by next Saturday, he would be dead. Did you really say that? Was it when you took him outside when you were in the diner?" leaning forward that she almost comes off the couch and out of her robe.

"One, I never threatened to kill anyone. I told him that I was here to make sure justice was enforced to the perpetrators of the bombing. If he interpreted that this meant I was going to kill him then he must be one of the bombers. Don't you think?" looking deep into her eyes and trying not to look down.

Sitting there talking to this teenager and looking into her eyes I saw something that I never thought I'd ever see in a young girl. Hate!

"Are you alright, Melanie?"

"I'm fine but I don't see why everyone up North feels sorry for the niggers. They don't do anything to better themselves and when something happens to them, all the Northerners come down and try to change things around here. That's what you're here for, to change Birmingham to Boston. That's not right. Leave us alone or take the niggers with you back up North." Now there is fire in her eyes.

"Wow! Do you really believe that shit? That's the biggest piece of crap I have ever heard. Melanie, how old are you? Do you really think blowing up a Baptist church is going to change things down here? The United States Congress has said that the coloreds will have the right to vote. There isn't a chance in hell that blowing up a church is going to change that. If you people keep it up and continue to blow things up, the government will send down the military to keep peace. Do you understand that?" I could feel my face getting hotter and I am speaking a little louder than before.

"One thing, Mr. Yankee, those kids weren't even supposed to be in the church that late at night. How would my uncle know that? He doesn't go there. If they send down the military, we will go underground and just wait for y'all to leave. That's when the fun will begin. Oh, you asked how old I am. I just celebrated my sixteenth birthday last month," smiling at Jim while she spewed this horrific memorandum.

"I think it's time for you to leave. Your folks should be back by now. Let me explain a couple of things to you as you leave. If you tear your dress or scream rape and before the police arrive, I will kick in the door of your parents' apartment and put a bullet in each of their heads. Also,

you just confirmed that Blanton George Thomas, Jr., your uncle as you call him, is responsible for the bombing of the 16th Street Baptist Church. You may want to tell your father and your uncle to be quite careful this coming week. Now get the hell out of here and remember what I said. Also, if I get one knock on my door before the sun comes up I will shoot first and then answer the door. Oh, our breakfast date this morning is canceled due to you being crazy. Now scram," turning and slamming the door in her face.

As the sun came up, the Chrysler was waiting at the curb. Walking out of the hotel, I saw Melanie's father standing behind the registration desk. Walking over to where Mr. Troup was standing, I wanted to talk to him. As I approached and before I could say anything, the Resident Manager started to turn toward the door slightly to his right.

"Don't run, you son-of-a-bitch. You must be as low as they come to set your sixteen-year-old daughter on me. There are places in hell for fathers like you. I know Melanie told you what I told her. Tell your Grand Cyclops and you take heed to be exceptionally careful where you go this week. You never know what kind of accident may befall you. Also, I will be checking out on Saturday and I don't expect there will be any problems," turning and not waiting for an answer that never came but everyone in the lobby heard what I had to say. "I hate this place. You won't believe what happened to me last night after I got to my room," as I start to explain what happened including what just transpired at the front desk.

"Did she come on to you or was it a gut feeling what was going to happen after she left?" Bubba asked

"She was dressed in a robe and the front was open from her belly button to the top. She didn't come onto me but I knew something was going to happen to either embarrass me or put me in jail," trying to make sure I mentioned everything to them.

"Okay, let's forget that and concentrate on the mission at hand. Are you set with the explosives and when are you two going to set them?" getting back to talking about what was coming in the next few days.

"I was thinking and I will run it by the Commander about killing all four of the bombers. If I do kill them it will cause major problems for the Negroes down here. I thought I'd cripple the three and just kill Blanton, because he's an unbelievably bad person and secondly, I just don't like him. What do you think?" looking at the two men as we drove toward the mill.

"I think the orders from the boss were to kill all four. I hear you

about the fallout of all of this, but they deserve to die for what they did to the little girls." Josey becoming quite articulate as he drove.

"I will make sure that the three will never be able to make another bomb or even pick up a cup of coffee in their predominant hand. There are all sorts of nerves in the arm leading to the hand and I know where they are. I will kill Thomas but to maim the other three will definitely send a message." As I finished the other two men nodded but I knew that they weren't in agreement with me.

As we passed by the mill, Josey said he wanted to show me something that I may find interesting. Just outside of Birmingham to the north was a massive forest with a small dirt road leading into it. Josie took the Chrysler and drove for four miles to a smaller dirt road that went another two miles. When the car stopped and we all got out, we started to walk down an old path still heading north. Sweating profusely, we seemed to have walked to Georgia and the mosquitoes found a new eating place when we came to a clearing.

"Where are we and what are we doing here?" I asked between wiping the sweat from my face and slapping the open places on my body.

"This is where they hold their meetings. See the burnt cross laying to the right there. They are supposed to have a meeting this coming Wednesday night. It will start at 9 p.m. and it lasts till midnight. We can get here about 4 or 5 and wait for the Kluckers. The reason for us to be here early is that they start putting the cross up around 6 p.m., after everyone is out of work," Josey explained.

"Who told you about this place?" asking with curiosity.

"You won't believe it but it was the deputy. Seems he's not only the town's deputy but he's also an undercover agent with the FBI. He wants to meet with us at 7 p.m. tonight at the Baptist Church."

"I'll be damned. Contact the Commander and find out if this is true," looking at Josey, knowing he already had done that.

"It's legit. He's been under for over two years. I guess he's really decorated with the bureau and you'll like this. He's a former Marine sniper. I don't know his real name but he just goes by Deputy Johnny. The Commander said that the bureau is really high on this guy and has tried to get him to come in but he says he's still got things to find out about the Klan here in Alabama and Mississippi." Josey finished as the three of us start out of the forest.

"What time are we supposed to meet Deputy Johnny?" I asked as we all got out to have some lunch at a Negro diner.

"7 p.m. at the 16*th* St. Baptist Church. He says if anyone sees him with us , he'll just say he was making sure the Feds didn't find anything they shouldn't have."

The diner was crowded but I thought it was noon time and everyone was here to have lunch. As we came in, everyone stopped what they were doing, turned and looked not at the two black men but the white one who just entered. As we came to the counter, a young man came up and showed us to a booth in the far corner of the diner, away from any windows or doors.

"Now I know how a Negro must feel going into an all-white diner. Every eye is on the white man," speaking with a little nervousness in my voice.

"Let's not get over ourselves, Master Coleman, sir. They are looking at all of us because they all know why we are here. Just wait and see what happens next," Josey said with Bubba nodding in agreement.

"Okay, but I'd hate to die here and not finish what we came down here to do," trying to laugh but nothing was coming out.

Just as I finished talking, the same young man who had seated us came up to get our orders. As he was waiting he finally said, "Everyone in the Bottoms knows who you is and we are grateful for what y'all are going to do. This meal is on us; your money is no good in here," smiling as he waited for Bubba to finish his order.

"The food here is terrific. They should open a place up in Jacksonville, NC. Every Marine based at Camp Lejeune would be there every day. Great call on eating here," pushing my plate away and staring at Bubba.

"What's wrong? Haven't y'all ever seen a man enjoying a 'scrum shish' meal?" We all laughed at the same time.

"I expect that we will be going to the mill and the car repair shop some time tonight?" asking the other two while riding back to my hotel. "We will pick you up at 10 p.m. Dress in black and try to find a way out of the hotel in the back. No one can see you if we want this to be a booming success." Bubba doesn't say much but he knows explosives.

As we pulled up to the hotel, all the people sitting on the veranda stopped and looked at the white man getting out of a car driven by a Negro.

Running up the stairs to the hotel, taking them two at a time, and when on top I yelled at the top of my lungs, "Hey," to everyone on the porch. Going into the hotel lobby, I noticed the owner Mr. Jeffries and I start waving to get his attention. Seeing me, he quickly moves toward me.

As we shake hands I start to talk, "Good afternoon, Mr. Jeffries. Is there some place that we can talk in private?"

"How about your suite? No one can get to that floor and my office isn't the most secretive place in this hotel," starting toward the elevator.

Upon entering the suite, my hand as usual is always on my weapon which is under my left arm. Looking around and seeing nothing has been disturbed, I offer Mr. Jeffries a seat. "Mr. Jeffries, do you know you have the Grand Exchequer working for you here in the hotel?" sitting in the chair opposite the couch that Mr. Jeffries was now occupying.

"Son, there isn't anything that goes on in this city that I don't know about. Mr. Troup and his wife have been members of the Klan since they were eighteen years old. Their daughter is too young to join but when she does, she will be worse than the other two combined. If I were to take out anyone it would be her. She's a bitch on wheels. She had a Negro boy whipped to an inch of his life because he had the audacity to say hello to her. I heard that she came to your room last night and tried to seduce you. Is that true?" sitting up in his seat.

"She was there to seduce but we only talked. She must not have been particularly good at seducing anyone in the past. I just explained what would happen to her parents if she started to scream and carry on because nothing happened. She was the one who told me about her parents being in the Klan. She did say some awful things about Negroes. Let me ask you a question and I need an honest answer. Before I ask, I will tell you that I've been sent down here to eradicate the four people responsible for the bombing of the 16th Street Baptist Church. If I do just that, how much trouble will come down on the Negroes in the Bottoms?" Now I was sitting up in the front of my chair.

"I know why you are here. The Commander filled me in long before you got here. He asked me the same question and I told him what I'm going to tell you. The Negroes will feel the wrath of the Klan no matter if you kill one or one hundred. It's just the way we do things down here." Jeffries was now sounding matter of fact.

"I need some information on the working hours of the mill, the tire shop and the auto repair. Do they have cleaning crews? What time of the night are all three empty? I will need this information as soon as possible but before Wednesday night."

"I know the mill shuts down at 5:30 p.m. I don't think they have a nightly cleaning service but the Negroes in the Bottoms could tell you.

They do all the cleaning of all the offices in town. Can you tell me what you are going to do to those businesses?"

"No, I can't tell you. I also want to know if the Klan is going to have a meeting on Wednesday night and when the first person gets there. This is extremely important and I would need to know that as soon as possible," standing up and walking toward the door.

"Thanks, Mr. Jeffries, for everything you have done to make my stay so comfortable. Hopefully when I return next month, you'll have room for me," motioning to Jeffries that the door to the Troup's apartment was open a couple of inches.

Jeffries walks out to the hall and then turns back, winking and saying, "You are welcome, Jim. It's been a pleasure having you with us. Call me directly when you think you will be coming back and I will make sure you have a room with us." Turning he puts his one finger to his lips and smiles.

As Mr. Jeffries starts to walk down the hall to the elevator, he passes the Troup's apartment and says, "Did you hear enough?" and then continues to the elevator.

As the night approaches and everything outside is getting dark, I am dressed in a black sweatshirt, black trousers, black sneakers, black gloves, a black watch cap and old coffee grounds for my face. While Mr. Jeffries was in my room, I did ask him how I could get out of the hotel without being seen. He said that on the 12th floor there is an exit door with stairs that will bring anyone down to the back parking lot. It opens with the room keys so when whoever comes back they can go to that door and get in. I called Josey and told him to meet me in the back parking lot around 10 p.m. 'Mondays shouldn't be that busy at the mill,' I thought. 'When we get there hopefully no one will be around. I'm concerned if they have any watchdogs on premises but I thought that Jeffries would have told me.'

As ten o'clock was approaching, I turned off all the lights in the room, opening the door slowly, looked down the hall to the Troup's room to make sure that door wasn't open. Closing the door behind me, making sure there isn't a sound. Slowly, I unscrew the light just left of my room and about six feet down the hallway. Moving slowly, I can hear the night noise coming from outside. Another light bulb just in front of the Troup's room but this time it's on the right side. Slowly crossing over, I unscrew the light but leave the bulb in so it can't cause any notice. Once past the Troup's' room, I start to run on my toes toward the elevator. Hitting the down button, I wait to see who is in the elevator with Arnold. Thankfully when the door opens, it's only Arnold.

"Going for an evening stroll, Mr. Jim, sir? Mr. Jeffries says that you were going to visit someone on the 12th floor but you weren't sure that was the floor. If it isn't, just go to your right of the elevator and the door to the stairs is right there. When you return, get on the elevator on the fourth floor. That way I will know it's you and I will pick you up right away. You have a nice evening and do be careful," opening the door on the 12th floor.

Getting out I go to my right to the exit door. Opening the door to the outside, the Chrysler is there waiting. Jumping into the backseat, I start to straighten my sweatshirt so the holster won't show. Sitting back, I proceed to tell my two compatriots what had transpired earlier in the hotel room, relating how the door to the Troup's room was opened about two inches.

"I'm amazed that they let Jeffries exist down here. I would think that they know he's not on their side, him being a Catholic and all. I don't think there is one of them that's open minded. If you are not a WASP (White, Anglo-Saxon, Protestant) then you are nothing to these people." Josey is explaining the Klan once again.

After he finishes talking the car grew quiet. All our minds are thinking of Wednesday night and what a surprise these "Kluckers" were going to have. Approaching the mill, Josey shuts of the car lights and the car slowly glides into the main parking lot and stops.

"Why are we parking here out in the open? Don't you think you should find a better place to hide the car?" I'm starting to get nervous that something would go wrong.

"I'm just sitting here and looking around to make sure no one is in the mill working. If they are not working tonight, then it's a good bet they won't be working on Wednesday night either," turning in his seat to face me.

After about five minutes, Josey puts the car in drive and he slowly points it to the back of the mill where all the logs are kept before being processed. Slowly driving up in the dark takes a lot of skill, especially with the tight quarters that the stacked logs make. Stopping, we get out and move to the back where Bubba is opening the trunk. On the floor of the trunk are ten bombs made from a block of C4 and wired to a timer. Scratching my head thinking that there was supposed to be twenty bombs shipped from Langley.

"Where are the other devices that came from Langley?"

"We already set them earlier this evening," Bubba spoke up

"Okay then, let's get started. What do you want me to do?" asking the two demolition experts.

"Under that blanket is what you are good at," Bubba again speaking as he pulled the blanket down and showed me what was there.

"All right. A Heckler & Koch MP5 sub-machine gun. It's like Christmas has come to Birmingham. There's three cartridges, thirty rounds each fully loaded. Are you two not telling me something? Do you expect a war? This is a lot of fire power," looking at my new toy.

"No, we aren't expecting anything but just in case something comes down unexpected, then you can scare the hell out of these rednecks. You position yourself somewhere out here and we will do the rest. If someone comes, just make the sound of a hoot owl. Let me here you," Josey said with no conviction.

I let out what I thought an owl sounded like but the other two couldn't stop laughing, "Have you ever heard an owl sound like that? Better still have you ever heard an owl, period?"

"In the movies I think but a real owl, hell no." I started to laugh also.

"That call is no good because no one would believe it was an animal, let alone an owl. If someone comes, try to talk to them but if not, shoot up the place, we will know what that means," Josey grabbing up the rest of the devices and following Bubba into the basement of the mill.

Nervousness was starting to settle in because it was taking longer than I expected. While waiting, a patrol car slowly came into the parking lot. I put the SMG through the open window and onto the front seat. Standing at the side of the car, the patrol car came right up to me. As the officer in the car proceeded to roll down his window.

"Good evening, Mr. Coleman, sir. What a fine night to blow something up," chuckling, Deputy Johnny started to drive around the parking lot and then went left onto the main street.

Thinking something may have gone wrong with the others, I started to pace. Walking back and forth, suddenly I could see two men at the furthest part of the mill running up the long row of stacked wood as they came quickly toward me. Suddenly they disappeared behind the logs and I was going crazy until they appeared thirty feet from where I was standing.

Not saying a word, we jumped into the car and slowly, with lights still off, left the front of the mill and onto Republic Blvd. When everything was clear, I finally had to say something.

"Everything go okay. You were in there for a long time. Deputy Johnny came by and said, 'What a fine night to blow something up.' I thought I was going to choke laughing," talking to the two men in the front seat.

"When this thing goes up they won't find a board bigger than an inch, just like a whole bunch of toothpicks. Hopefully, it will be empty Wednesday night because if it isn't they will never find any bodies." Bubba was almost giddy with the thought.

"I know you two have a personal thing with these people and I don't blame you. We are down here to make sure they understand they can't blow up a church or anything else without paying the price."

"I didn't say you should kill everyone just the ones that need killing. We know who blew up the church so they should be taken care of first. Then we've seen some strange people walking around this city. If I had my way I would tell you to blow up the city of Birmingham because it breeds all that is wrong with the south." For the first time Josey is so outspoken and enthusiastic over something.

"There are some good people in this city. Just consider Mr. Jeffries from the hotel and his family. Arnold the elevator operator who works twenty-four hours a day. We haven't met many others but I'm sure there are some who would fight on our side," trying to calm Josey down before something goes wrong.

"You forget I grew up here. It hasn't changed in thirty-two years and it won't change for another thirty-two. There has to be change. Dr. King has the answer but I doubt they will listen. JFK wanted change and they killed him. When is it ever going to stop?" looking at me and beginning to tear up.

"I don't know, my friend. In the next few days, I do know that Birmingham will have changed forever. I also know they are going to take it out on the coloreds but it can't be helped. I don't know this Dr. King, but if you think he has the answer, let's get him down here to teach these fucking rednecks the truth." Now I am starting to get emotional.

I sat on the veranda of the hotel for most of the day. I was going to be picked up at 5:30 p.m. to go to a barbeque down in the Bottoms. My two friends arrived around 5:20 p.m., stopped in front of the hotel and yelled to me to get in the car. I asked them why they did that and they said to "watch the faces of the white folks sitting around was worth the price of admission."

Arriving at the barbeque, there had to be over one hundred people *here. Now as I got out of the car, Josey and Bubba came around and walked with me where the most people lingered. Everyone was in a good mood and they all came around me and just looked. It seemed to me that they acted as if they had never seen a white man before.*

Mentioning this to Josey, he said, "They have seen a lot of white men but they have never seen one at a barbeque. You're the first and last white man to come and break bread with them for an awfully long time," as he laughed when finishing what he had to say.

It was a meal that I would like to but would never forget. Many delicacies, pigs knuckles, rocky mountain oysters (commenting how good they were until I found out they were bulls testicles), fried chicken, smoked beef, greens, hominy grits and other stuff I just wouldn't try. Josey and Bubba were having a good time trying to feed me anything that would make me throw up.

One thing about a party in the Bottoms. These folks really know how to party.

It was late when we finally drove back to the hotel. Not a lot was said between the three of us. I thought to myself that this will be the last happy occasion that will go on down here for a long time.

As we pulled up to the front of the hotel and I was saying my good-byes to my friends, a white Plymouth came flying down the street. Two men were in the front seat and two in the back. All were dressed in white robes and hoods. As the car came close, Josey and I jumped into the street with our guns drawn and pointed right at the vehicle. The car swerved to avoid us, sped up and continued down the street with no shots fired. Josey swore he saw a fire coming from the passenger seat meaning they were ready to throw a "Molotov cocktail" at me and my friends. When order was restored, Josey said he'd pick me up at 5:30.

Coming through the lobby and into the elevator still shaking a little for what almost happened, I greeted Arnold with as much of a salutation that I could muster.

"How the hell can you people live down here? They hate you, your color and your attitude. They just came driving down the street with their 'Klan stuff' on and a Molotov cocktail in the front seat. They were willing to die just to throw that but the driver got smart and just drove by. They risked their lives for what. To kill three federal agents and for what? Everyone around here knows who killed those four children. They hate Jews, Catholics, Northerners and anybody else that disagrees with them. As God is my judge, they are in for a rude awakening to-

morrow night. All bets are off. They will get what they deserve and no ones to blame but themselves," smiling at the elevator operator as I got off on the 16th floor.

Passing the Troup's' apartment, I stopped and started to talk in a loud voice.

"If you are smart, you'd stay in your room all day and night. People are going to die and even if you are racist pigs, I'm giving you a warning. Don't blame me if you get shot," turning and walking to my room, I started whistling "Dixie."

Wednesday morning was like any other day in the South, hot and humid with this late September. All everybody was talking about was the game between Alabama vs. Georgia this past Saturday. The Tide beat the Bulldogs 32-7. They also were talking about the upcoming game this Saturday in Mobile against Tulane. Alabama football seemed the only subject the white folks around Birmingham talked about other than the possible retaliation by the Negros against the white folks who were responsible for the bombing of the church.

I spent most of the day reclining on the veranda and listening to the old gentlemen discuss Alabama football. As the sun started to set in the west, I decided it was time to go to my room and get ready for a long nights work.

It was now 5:20 p.m. and ten minutes before I was to be picked up at the rear parking lot. Opening my door, I went through the same ritual I did a few days ago accept this time I have my suitcase with me. Unscrewing the light bulbs, slowly moving past the Troups' apartment, making as little noise as possible and quickly moving to the elevator. Arnold was there before I could push the button to summon the elevator.

"Good evening, Mr. Jim, sir. Are you going to have a busy evening? A beautiful night for whatever you have to do. Be sure that you and your friends are careful and you come back to us in one piece." as he stopped his elevator on the 12th floor.

Taking the stairs two at a time but stopping suddenly at the door that led to the back parking lot. Slowly opening the door, the black Chrysler was just waiting at the entrance. As I jump into the back seat, Bubba turns and hands me the same machine gun that he had a few nights ago in front of the mill. Bending over I check the magazines for the Heckler & Koch MP5 submachine gun, making sure there are three full magazines of thirty rounds each.

Quickly our car speeds out of the back of the hotel and onto 1st Avenue North heading toward the forest and my first Klan meeting.

Taking the final dirt road, I notice a number of cars in the distance. As we take a left, the other cars have already gone right and are parking around the meadow. The sun is setting in the west behind a number of pine trees, so it is hard to see what exactly is going on.

Pulling off the dirt road and going into the woods for a half mile, Josey pulls the car into the middle of pine trees and shuts the engine off. Getting out, I take the SMG, pull back the bolt, and let it go, pushing a live round into the chamber. Quickly, my two compatriots have their weapons in hand and we are on our way to where the Klan will hold their meeting.

Approaching an overlook to the meadow below, we crawl the last fifty yards to the edge. Looking down I can see at least ten men in coveralls just standing around where the cross would be put up. Over to the right side and about twenty feet from the gathering are four men working on the cross. After about fifteen minutes have gone by, the four men stand and start to lift this big cross. It looks very awkward and the section that goes across doesn't look that secure. A few of the men who were just standing there go over to help the others with this heavy monstrosity. Finally, the cross is in position to put into the ground. As the huge cross fits into the hole, two men on each side of the now positioned cross grab ropes and move out twenty-five feet and tie the ropes to two stakes already in the ground to stabilize and secure this symbol of hatred.

As we watch what is transpiring down below, I recognize one person who is standing around watching this display, Blanton George Thomas, Jr. Not giving any kind of orders, he just stands there, off to one side, smiling.

Josey gestures that we should move back because he's got something to say. "Jim, I know you have your doubts in what we are about to do tonight. Let me tell you that the Negroes in the South have been going through this mess for over two hundred years. It's got to stop. Now I know that whatever comes out of this night, it's not going to change anything soon. I really believe this will be the fuse to instigate some sort of a change in the way we are treated down here. Jim, I love you like a brother and no matter what happens in the next few hours, I'm sure it's in the best interest of the people and the United States. God be with you my brother," with this he grabs me and gives me a huge hug.

As we get ready for an interesting evening, I take my haversack from my back and put it on the ground. Opening the top, I take out the three pieces of my ever-present Remington 703 Sniper rifle. Quickly. I start to assemble the stock to the barrel to the operating system, snapping everything into place. Reaching into the bag, I take out my scope and place on top of the operating system. Again, reaching into the sack, I take out a box of thirty cartridges and place it on the ground. Finally, I go back into the bag; reaching to the bottom, my hand emerges with the sling for the rifle. Sliding the strap into the loops at the front of the stock and at the base, I pull it tight. Suddenly I remember Parris Island and how my shooting instructor told us that the sling should be tight against the stoke when traveling through brush, so it won't get caught on something. When ready to fire it is when you loosen the strap and then fit it around your left arm. Placing the now assembled rifle against a pine tree, I go back and pick up the box with the rounds in it. I turn the box and let the cartridges fall on the grass. I start to count the shells to make sure I wasn't missing any. Picking them up. I put them in a pouch that I was carrying in my pocket. Sitting there, looking at everything I go back to the haver sack and take out the most important part to a sniper rife. The silencer. As I was putting everything together I noticed my two partners watching everything I was doing. Standing now, I hold the rifle barrel straight up and start to screw the silencer into place. When finished I look at the other two and smile knowing that my time is near to put these "bastards" in their place.

As I finished my preparation, we start to move back to our position right above the meadow. I have a regiment that I go through and Josey knows once I am in this mood, I can't be disturbed. Crawling to the edge I look down to see how many "Kluckers" have shown up. To my guess without counting, it looks as if fifty have shown up so far. It's now 8:35 p.m. in the evening and festivities are due to start at 9 p.m.

Rolling on my back and with the Remington laying on my chest, I close my eyes and try to focus on the job at hand. Picturing the chaos that will begin once the bombs go off and the rounds start to fly, I have in my mind how and when I will shoot the Grand Cyclops. I haven't decided on the other three, but this is the best time to figure out what to do with them.

Turning back to the ridge, I take the scope off the rifle and look through it to see if I can find Blanton's three accomplices. Sweeping the meadow with the scope, I stop and stare at the one person I thought I'd never see. Mr. Jeffries, the owner of the all-white Elyton Hotel. I passed the scope to Josey and pointed down to the left. I quickly motioned for my two friends to move back.

"I'll be a son of a bitch. That man had me fooled from the start. I should have known he wasn't what he said he was. If he were the Klan would have burned down that hotel with him in it. Thank God I didn't tell him what we were going to do tonight. He never did get back to me about the Klan meeting. What do you think we should do? Should we scrap this mission for tonight and come back later when nobody would expect us?" I could feel the heat rising in my face and I would like to let out a scream.

"It's up to you, Jim. You're the shooter and it all depends on how you feel. You must ask yourself if we can accomplish what we are here to do," Josey the everlasting pragmatic.

As I lay on my back just out of sight high on the ridge, I am thinking what the Commander will say when I tell him his friend Jeffries is Klan. He had me fooled, which isn't that hard to do, but Commander Damon, who's been at this a long time, he fooled him also. Now do I kill him for making a fool out of me and the CIA or do I do nothing and let the Commander take care of this? Deep down the question will always be "What would the Commander do?"

Suddenly a huge noise arose from the meadow and the clearing. Looking down I could see two hundred men, women and to my surprise children all dressed in different color sheets and hoods. Now a man dressed in a red robe and hood, the Grand Cyclopes, takes a lit torch and moves toward the cross. He turns to the crowd, holds up the torch (a massive roar comes from the members), turns and lights the base of the cross. In seconds you can see the flames move up the cross to the arm and then the whole cross in enveloped in flames.

As the cross is burning, Blanton George Thomas, Jr. the Grand Cyclops of the Birmingham Den of the Klu Klux Klan, starts his tirade about Negroes, Jews, Catholics, Yankees and any other thing he can think of. Starting at 9 p.m., it's now 9:50 p.m. and he's just starting. I tap Bubba on the leg and as he turns I hold up ten fingers and then point to my watch. Bubba turns and taps Josey on the shoulder and does the same thing. Both turn to me and hold up ten, then ten again and then five fingers. This tells me that the first bomb, which is in the mill, will go off at 10:15 p.m. Realizing that there will be a five-minute spread from 10:15 p.m. to 10:30 p.m., when the cross is scheduled to explode. Thinking to myself, 'I hope he stops talking by then or they will need another Grand Cyclops at their next meeting.'

Right at 10:13 p.m., the Grand Cyclops finishes his lengthy speech of hate. I have my rifle at the ready but I won't point it until the first bomb goes off. Waiting these past couple of minutes is excruciating. It seems more like an hour than two minutes and then it happened. The earth shook when the first bombs went off and everyone down in the meadow turned toward the city. As they did, I took the Remington and sticking out over the ledge, I sight in on the Grand Cyclops. As the picture of him comes through the scope to my right eye, I start to squeeze the trigger, then the recoil and I see that the front of the Grand Dragon's face right at the jaw explodes and he goes down. Instantly, four or five members in all black robes take out their side arms and start shooting up the hill. The only thing about this is they are firing up the wrong hill. Again, I sight in a figure in a white robe with a green stripe going down the left side. I point the rifle at this figure and start to squeeze the trigger again. This time Cash Frank's right shoulder explodes and blood is now running down his clean white robe. As he goes down he is laying straight out when the next round hits his left hand, shattering it into hundreds of small pieces.

As they start to pick up Thomas, I squeeze the trigger for another round to go into Blanton's right kneecap. Turning back to Cash, I start to squeeze the trigger again, as this bullet hits the ear of a man in a solid green robe and hood. As the bullet slices through the hood and part of the ear, the man rips off his hood and holds his hand to his right ear.

Thinking to myself, I say, "You're lucky, Mr. Jeffries. It could have been a lot worse. Now you have to explain what happened to the bottom of your ear, you racist pig."

Just as I hit Jeffries, another bomb goes off in the city. This time the body shop should be level with the street. Now all the people that were in the meadow are running helter skelter toward their cars. It's around seventy-five yards to their cars so I take the SMG, pull the bolt and start firing over their heads. Everyone hit the ground at the same time. Bullets start coming our way, so we know that they have figured out where we are.

"Time to go," I yell to the others who are now starting to fire their weapons.

As we start to run down toward our car, the third bomb now goes off in the tire shop. Three minutes later, we all jump into the Chrysler and start going out the back way of the clearing.

Turning to get on a main dirt road, the fourth bomb goes off under the cross. Without thinking we said the same thing at the same time, "Wish I could have seen that."

Coming in from the east of the mill, Josey pulls off in a side street and stop. We get out with our weapons still at the ready. Deciding earlier that we would go up on the city hall roof to get a better look at whoever comes out to see the rubble from the three explosions.

As I take my scope and start from the left and slowly go to my right, I am looking for two individuals. Far to the right, I am disappointed that neither Chambeau nor Wallace are in the crowd. Thinking that I may have missed them, I start now on the right and quite slowly start to the left. Scoping to the right at what used to be the front of the Mill, Chambeau and Wallace are standing next to each other.

"This is much too easy, fellas," telling the others that they are in front of the mill.

Putting the scope back on the Remington and taking out four cartridges, I put one in the chamber and snap it shut. Pointing the rifle over the edge of the City Hall I look for both of them but they have moved. Quickly I start where they were and go left until about fifty feet away they are walking back to a blue Plymouth Fury. As Chambeau gets to the passenger side of the car, my rifle recoils and he falls where he stands with his right kneecap blown away. As he grabs for his knee, the rifle recoils again and I see his right hand explode.

For some reason, Wallace decides to check on his fellow Klan member as the round finds its target and his left shoulder explodes and not seconds later his right hand also explodes. Both men are lying beside each other in excruciating pain but they have their wits about them to try to crawl under the car. Taking the rifle and scope back to the front of the mill, I'm looking for someone that I expect to be in the crowd and there she is. Quickly I reload and point the rifle right at the neck of this poor unfortunate girl. As she turns, I squeeze and then the recoil. Looking through the scope I can see that her voice box is now gone. She won't die but she will never be able to speak that hate that she did in my room

"Let's go guys. As the Lone Ranger says, 'My job here is done.'" I start policing for brass from the cartridges. This is done so no one will know who was here and what kind of weapon was used.

Jumping into the Chrysler, Josey guns the engine and we roar out the back of City Hall onto 19ᵗʰ street. Taking a left, the car lurches toward Route 20 which is only a block from the city limits. Getting on the highway and checking to see if we didn't have anyone following. Atlanta being only 147 miles, it was a clear shot all the way on Route 20. I didn't break down the Remington right away just in case we had some unexpected visitors driving up behind us.

Josey was driving at 65 miles an hour and he started to slow down when we passed East Birmingham. I started to dismantle the Remington and as I did, I took a rag from my haversack and cleaned my weapon. As I started to put the three major pieces of my rifle in the bag, I started to think about what had transpired these past few hours. Was I wrong to shoot Melanie in the neck? She just had so much hatred for a young woman and I knew she wasn't going to change. Now she'll have to write stuff down if she wants to let anyone know who she really hates.

We arrived at 6 a.m. at the Atlanta National Airport and after saying our goodbyes to Bubba, we went directly to Delta Airlines. Checking in at the gate, we didn't have the problem that we experienced in Washington the week before.

"Mr. Coleman, you have a message. Please wait until I can pull it up. Here it is. Have a nice flight." An incredibly happy and attractive young lady was the ticket agent.

"A message from guess who. He wants to see us as soon as we get in. Oh, joy," turning and heading for the gate and our flight out of this God forsaken place in the world.

Walking into the Commander's office, I noticed he was sitting with his back to us and looking out the window.

"What the hell happened down there? I got a call that Jeffries was in the hospital due to him catching some shrapnel from the tire shop blowing up. Didn't you wait to make sure the streets were clear from innocent citizens?" starting to get his blood pressure up.

"Well, Mr. Innocence is a tried-and-true member of the United Klans of America and an officer of the Alabama Klan. He was at the Klan meeting in the meadow and he was wearing a green robe and hood, designating a state officer. I shot him in the ear because I wanted him to explain why he was there and why he was wearing all that stuff," usually feeling a little nervous when he's loud but now I wasn't.

"Are you shitting me? He's a member. He's a Catholic and the Klan hates Catholics. Are you sure he's actually not a plant from some other agency here in Washington?" trying to justify his major mistake that seems to have come out.

"I found a St. Jude medal in the rubble of the 16th Street Baptist Church and I went to him thinking he would know of any ex-Catholics that may belong to the Klan. He suggested I speak with the pastor of the local Catholic Church in Birmingham, a Monsignor Ronan. I did speak with him and he told me that the only one he ever saw wearing

a St. Jude medal was Mr. Jeffries. I didn't think much of it because he was so helpful and he knew you. The only thing I thought was weird was when I asked him to find out some information about the Klan, meeting times and members, he never got back to me. Hope you're not that upset but I could have killed him," just sitting there waiting for him to explode.

"No, you did the right thing. How many people know that he knew me?"

"No one that I know of. He told me but he never spoke to Josey or Bubba," watching him and the quizzical look on his face.

"Bubba is Agent Duke. That's his nickname and I'd work with him again anytime. He really knows how-to blow things up."

"Hey, Staff Sergeant, it's time to get up and go through customs. We just landed in Anchorage, Alaska in the good old US of A," the Lieutenant that was sitting next to me said.

Going through customs was quite easy after everyone retrieved their sea bags. The one question everyone was asked if we had brought back any VC or North Vietnam weapons that was not authorized. I didn't have anything, but I know others that had all sorts of "souvenirs" that they had collected in the time they were in country. I remember one Marine who was a couple of spots in front of me when they asked that question. "Did you bring anything back home that you got in Vietnam?"

His answer was, "Does the Clap count?" We all got a good laugh from that.

After I went through the line and made sure my sea bag was going back on our flight, I just had time to call home and tell my mother to make sure I have a ticket from Los Angeles to Boston. We were told before we deplaned that we should be arriving in MCAS El Toro around 9 p.m. PST. We would have to get our bags inspected and get our new duty station orders. There were to be plenty of taxis to take us to either LAX or SAN for flights to our home destination. I told my mother to book the earliest flight to Boston, around 10 a.m.

Getting back on the plane and into the same seat I was anxious to get going and home as soon as possible. As the plane started to move off the gate and down the taxiway for takeoff, I started to fall asleep again.

"Well, they arrested that son of a bitch Jeffries yesterday evening. He didn't put up much of a fight and he will end up serving at least ten years in federal prison. the other five didn't fare so well," as the Com-

mander was almost gleeful when he gave me the news.

Blanton George Thomas, Jr. will be a cripple for the rest of his life with his kneecap shattered and his lower part of his face was injured beyond repair and he can only breath through a hole in his throat.

Bobbie Ed Chambeau will also be crippled and have a severe limp as his right kneecap was shattered and he has no use of his right hand.

Bobbie Frank Wallace fared a little better than the others. He has use of his legs but his left shoulder was shattered along with his right hand. The doctors had to remove his hand because it was too far gone to be saved.

Cash Herman Franks lost his left arm due the severe wounds and he also lost his right hand. He is using a prosthetic hook where his left hand would be.

Melanie Troup will never be able to sing in the school choir due to her voice box was shattered and she can never talk again.

"I feel a little bad for the girl. She is only sixteen and somewhere down the line she could have seen the light and repented," knowing deep down none of these pigs will ever change.

EL TORO TO LOS ANGELES AIRPORT

As the plane was slowing down, I woke up and the Lieutenant told me that we were over some place called Simi Valley, California. The pilot came on the intercom and said, "For the folks on the right side, just look out and down and see what you've been fighting for." As I looked out I could see a drive-in movie screen and a cheer rang all through the cabin.

The large 707 landed and started to taxi toward a huge hanger where we could see many Marines standing around and waiting to greet us. Deplaning was easy and the on-duty Marines had all the sea bags out of the hole, placed at six lines of fifty with room to move to recover our bags. Once I got my bag, I walked over where there were a number of tables with alphabetic letters in front for the first letter of your last name.

There was one person in front of me and when he finished I walked to the desk and said loudly enough, "Coleman, James. Staff Sergeant." They retrieved a large yellow envelope with my name on it. Then this woman Marine asked what my serial number is. I gave it to her and she handed over this envelope. As this was being done, a civilian had opened my sea bag and with a large pointer was going through the contents. He asked me a few questions and then he closed the bag and sealed it with a piece of wire. The final word both the WM and the civilian said to me was something I will never forget, "Welcome home, Marine."

Now from the tables to the taxi stand was around one hundred feet. There were a few Marines standing at the front of the line as I approached.

"You going to LAX, Staff Sergeant?" one of the younger ones asked.

"I'm going to Boston so if LAX is going to take me there, then yes I am."

"We three are going there too. Want to ride with us and we can split the fare?"

"If you let me ride with you, I will buy everyone breakfast at LAX," as we gave our bags to the driver and piled into the cab.

We are about to leave El Toro and an announcement is being made that "The anti-Vietnam protestors are at the front gate. They are blocking the exit and are not allowing any cars to leave the base. Until further notice and to prevent any hostilities upon your departure, you are confined to this base until this situation can be rectified."

"Let's go toward the front gate and when it's open we will be one of the first cars out," I said to the others in the back seat.

Driving toward the exit I could see a number of young people with signs walking in front of the gates. Most of the signs said, "Get out of Vietnam," "Make Love not War," and my favorite "Send Johnson to Vietnam, not Soldiers."

We sat at the gate for thirty minutes until suddenly coming up from the main street were approximately twenty-five motorcycles. As they came closer, the bikes had a driver but also a rider in back with bats. Henry the cab driver said, "this will be fun. Those are the Hell's Angels and they don't like the protestors. This has happened before and the amazing thing is that the police never come because this is federal land and no civilian authority is allowed."

As we slowly start toward the exit, we could see the Hell's Angels jump off their bikes and start hitting the protestors over their backs and heads. In a few seconds, there were bodies lying all over the cement. The Angels started to drag the limp bodies to the side of the road so to allow all the cabs to proceed out of MCAS, El Toro. As we passed the Main Gate, we could hear this cheer come up from our protectors. Henry the cabbie told us that most of the Hell's Angels in California are former Marines. All I know they did us a great favor in getting rid of these people who just don't understand what we did in Vietnam.

As we start to approach the airport, Henry suggested that if we want breakfast, the bowling alley is the best place. Pulling into the parking lot I noticed a huge sign on top of the building: "CAFETERIA - TOP-LESS WAITRESSES."

Looking at Henry I must have had that look of "Are you shitting me?"

"Read the sign. We don't lie here in Los Angeles. Come on, you will really enjoy your first breakfast back in the states. Something you will never forget," walking in and laughing as he walked.

We found a booth right away and the four of us sat down with me at the end because I was going to pay. Fortunately, I had turned my Military Payment Certificates (MPC) in for real US greenbacks. As I was reading the menu and deciding what I wanted I heard this voice say, "Can I get you something to drink?"

Not looking up I sat, "Milk, please."

The voice came back saying, "Do you want it in a glass or out of one of these?"

I looked up and here was a twenty-five-year-old blond standing not three feet from face with her bare breasts just standing straight out and about a foot away from my mouth.

"Holy shit," was the only thing I could think of saying.

"I've heard worse responses. Hi, I'm Honey, and I will be your waitress today. Are you fellas just back from Vietnam? Well, welcome home and you can look all you want but you must not touch," giggling as she walks away.

It was one of the best meals I've had in my life. Pancakes, eggs, bacon and sausage, home fries, toast, orange juice and Coffee for $1.99 each. We all had the same thing so the check came to $7.96. I left a $20 bill and as I walked by Honey on the way out, I said, "That tip is for a great view."

I was the only one flying on American Airlines so I was the first to be left off. As I said goodbye to everyone, I grabbed my sea bag and turned to go into the terminal.

"Excuse me, Marine. Are you Staff Sergeant James Coleman? My name is Earl Thomas and I need to bring you to the General Manager's office the minute you arrive," grabbing my bag and walking quick step through the terminal and starting down a long hall way.

As we were about to enter the first rotunda, a middle-aged man and woman were coming the other way toward the exit. As the woman passed, she yelled out, "Baby Killer," and spit right in my face.

Shocked, I didn't do anything immediately, but Mr. Thomas grabbed her around the arms and had them pinned as he yelled for security. The man, who I assumed was her husband, started to move toward the "sky cap" as my wits came back to me. As the man was about to grab Mr. Thomas, I jumped in and pushed him against the far wall.

"I will sue. You fucking killer," as I still held him against the wall as Mr. Thomas was screaming for security.

Mr. Thomas aloud the woman to straighten up but he was still holding her arms as the police came running down the hallway.

"What's going on here?" an airport police sergeant was asking Mr. Thomas.

He was about to explain what happened when this woman started to talk.

"My name in Mrs. Thelma Woodson from Iowa City, Iowa and me and my husband were just walking down this hallway when this *person* just jumped us." While talking I thought Mr. Thomas was going to burst a blood vessel.

The Sergeant turned to face the woman directly and he softly spoke so not everyone passing by could hear him.

"My name is Sergeant Maurice O'Toole of the Los Angeles Airport Police. My badge number is 1573489 and I want to explain a few things to you, Mrs. Woodson of Iowa City, Iowa. If you lie to the police you can go to jail and then prison on top of paying a huge fine. If you attacked this young man who is fighting for you and your loved ones, you will go to jail and then prison. So, Mrs. Woodson, I will give you another chance to change or amend your story," as the Sergeant turned and told me and Mr. Thomas to let go of the Woodson's.

"Well, Sergeant, this is the way it was. My husband and I were walking down this hallway and I saw this soldier. I've been reading about all these atrocities that have gone on over there and I snapped. I just knew I had to confront this young man who has killed hundreds of babies," almost crying as she was telling her story to the policeman.

"Well, Staff Sergeant, what do you want to do? I can arrest Mrs. Woodson of Iowa City, Iowa and her husband for aggravated assault but you would have to testify at their trial. You also could not press charges and go on your way. It's up to you, Staff Sergeant." The policeman gave me no idea of what I should do.

"I have been away from home for two years and nothing against your lovely, city but I just want to get to Boston. Let them go, Sergeant." I think I made the right decision.

"Mrs. Woodson, not all soldiers kill civilians, especially babies. The newspapers and television are firing up the people back home that are against this war by telling stories that have never been proven truthful. Now this Marine only wants to get home and I'm going to let him. If I hear of you doing anything like this while you're in our city, I will throw the book at you. Do you understand?"

"Yes, sir, Sergeant, and I want to thank you. I promise I will try to control my disgust for this war and the people who are fighting it," as she and her husband walk away.

"Marine, hopefully you will never have something like this happen to you again. I thought you handled this as any good Marine would," smiling and then shaking my hand.

"Sergeant, thank you for taking my side. I now realized that this isn't the most popular thing you could do. Again, thank you," still holding onto the Sergeant's hand.

"Have a safe trip and Semper Fi, Marine," smiling as he started walking. "Oh, Staff Sergeant. I was with 'Chesty' and the 1st Marine Division in Korea. Semper Fi," as he let go of my hand and started walking toward the street entrance.

"Let's get you up to the General Manager," Mr. Thomas said as he grabbed my bag and tossed on his shoulder.

We came to a huge open area they called the "Number One Rotunda" due to the fact there was "Number Two" about one hundred feet away. Getting into the elevator and going to the second floor. Walking into the waiting area, Mr. Thomas goes to the far door. Knocks then he opens the door.

Ushering me in, Mr. Thomas closes the door behind him. Sitting at an exceptionally large desk was a man, bald but with a great smile.

"Good morning, James. May I call you James? My name is Paul Haney and I am the General Manager of American Airlines here in Los Angeles. I have been speaking with your mother since last night. From our conversations, I came to the conclusion I better get you home today or else. What a lovely lady and I came to the conclusion, a wonderful mother. As you may or may not know, most airlines are on strike, all but American. We are booked to the gills and most of our flights are wait listed. You are waitlisted on our 9 a.m. flight to Boston but to be honest it doesn't look good. If everyone shows up who has a ticket then no one on standby will get on. If only one person doesn't show up for the flight then you are on it." As he finished the phone rang.

Picking it up, he started talking about the flight to Boston and how it looked for me to get on it. As he was talking, I started to look around his office. There was a large bay window overlooking what looked like a lot of planes. Behind his huge desk was a bookshelf with books, trophies and a record player. As I was looking over to the left, he hung up the phone and screamed, "Mr. Thomas. Get this Marine down to Gate 64B. His ticket will be at the counter with his boarding pass. I'm sorry, James, I could only get you a first class seat. Enjoy your flight and we are proud to be the carrier that reunites you and your family. Give my best to your mother."

Mr. Thomas once again grabs my bag and starts out the door. I turn to Mr. Haney and thank him for everything and shaking his hand he says one thing I will always remember.

"Welcome home, Marine. It is a pleasure to have met you," with that I turn and run after Mr. Thomas who had decided to take the stairs instead of the elevator.

Approaching the gate, I reach into my pocket and take out a twenty-dollar bill to give to my Sky Cap.

"This is Staff Sergeant Coleman and Mr. Haney told him he has a seat on this flight. Will you make sure this bag is on the flight?" Mr. Thomas is doing all the talking and then this young lady grabs the bag from him and starts walking down the stairway.

"Mr. Coleman. It's been an honor to have served you today. I don't think I've had this much fun since my father got me the job. Have a safe trip and if you ever come back to LAX, please make sure you come by and say hello." As he goes to turn and leave I grab his arm and spin him around.

"First, Mr. Thomas, what is your first name? Here is just a small token of my gratitude for getting me here and watching my back."

"I'm sorry, sir, but your money in no good today. If you'd like, just write a nice note to Mr. Haney and tell him what you think of my service." With this he gives me a hug and then turns and starts to trot back toward the entrance of the airport.

"I'm sorry, Mr. Coleman, but you need to board now because we are holding the plane for you," this lovely little lady with a terrific smile is apologizing for interrupting me.

Running down the terminal stairs and across the tarmac, I get to the stairs leading to the plane and I take these stairs two at a time. Entering the cabin, the big door slams behind me meaning I was the last passenger. The stewardess pointed to a seat right in front on the right.

ONE MORE FLIGHT THEN HEAVEN

Sitting down, the gentleman next to me stands up. Thinking to myself and remembering what had happened in the airport, I get ready to have a scuffle.

"My name is Jeffrey Jacobson from South Weymouth, Mass. I am so proud that you will be sitting next to me on this trip. When we gain our traveling height I want to buy you a drink," sticking out his hand for me to shake.

"It's nice to meet you, Mr. Jacobson. My name is Jim Coleman and my family lives in Hingham."

"Please, Jim. May I call you Jim? Call me Jeff. I was in the Army during the Korean War but didn't get to see any action. What is like over in Vietnam? Do you think we can win this war and how long will it take?" Now my new friend Jeff is starting to get excited.

"Vietnam is such a beautiful country. It has beaches and lots of sand. But when you get into the north there are mountains that you can't believe. Up there it gets quite cold and the monsoon season is something you would never believe. It rains about four months steady and all you're walking in is mud. I do think we can win the war and quickly but we need the support of the American people. It's quite lonely over there and when we hear about the protests and such, it's demoralizing." I'm feeling I should be on a soapbox.

Sitting back, I continue to answer his questions and some I just ignore rather than telling him it's classified. He doesn't press me for an answer to these questions and as we go along I feel quite comfortable talking to him.

"What would you like to drink, Jim?" as the stewardess comes around taking drink orders.

"I'm not much of a drinker, Jeff. I do like sweet drinks though. You order what you'd think I'd like," closing my eyes and thinking of us landing and who would be there to meet me.

"Claire, I'll have Dewar's and water and my friend Jim will have Jack Daniels and Coke," Jeff gave our orders to the stewardess.

When the drinks arrived, I picked it up to take a sip but Jeff wanted to toast me saying, "I am so glad you're on this flight. I am so proud of what you guys are doing over there and don't pay any attention to what's happening back in the states. It won't last long," tapping my glass and he takes a huge gulp. I take a sip and it burns my throat going down.

When we finished our drinks, Jeff orders another for him, but I tell him one is my limit. He then asks me if I'm being met by anyone at the Boston Airport. I tell him my parents, brother and his family, and my favorite aunt. He asks me if I have a girlfriend but I tell him that I broke up with one I had for a few years. I would really like to see her at the airport, and he has this funny look on his face but I let it go.

I fell asleep right after lunch and didn't wake up till the pilot got on the intercom to tell everyone to put all their stuff away because we would be landing in fifteen minutes.

"I was more tired than I thought. We got in about 9 p.m. last night but didn't leave the base till around 3 a.m. We stopped at a bowling alley right outside of LAX which also had a restaurant with waitresses topless. It was hard to enjoy my meal when you got two lovely tits staring at you at all times," laughing just thinking of what I had just said.

"So, you've been up all night. No wonder you fell asleep but it seemed very peaceful. Well, Jim, once again it's been a pleasure and enjoy your thirty days off before you head down to North Carolina," shaking my hand once again as we taxi into position for us to deplane.

I must have looked stunned because he turned his head but I could see he was chuckling. How did he know I was going to North Carolina after my leave? I never mentioned anything about that.

As I was standing, the pilot once again came on the intercom.

"Ladies and gentlemen. We have traveling with us today Staff Sergeant James Coleman of the US Marine Corps. The Staff Sergeant is returning home after spending two years in Vietnam. He has family waiting for him so if you will, please let him deplane first." Finishing with the announcement a roar and clapping came from the whole cabin.

"That's for you, Jim, and well deserved. Have a great time at home with your family," patting me on the back as I start toward the exit. "One more thing, Jim. The Commander sends his regards."

I snapped around that I thought I cracked my neck. Jeff had this huge smile on his face.

As I come down the stairs I can see my folks, my brother and his family, my Aunt Adelaide and the one I was hoping to be there.

* * * * * * * * * * * * * *

"Sergeant, I am going to count to three and then you will wake up and you will remember nothing that has transpired this afternoon," as Dr. Cushing starts to count.

"One, two, three," snapping his fingers and I open my eyes.

"How are you feeling, Sergeant?"

"Great, Doc. How did I do? How long have I been here?"

"You did exceptionally well and it only took three hours," as the doctor helped me stand up and move toward the exit.

"Sergeant, you shouldn't have any more bad dreams. If you do just call me directly. You won't have to go through the Commander."

Leaving the doctor's office, I go down the stairs to the underground garage. I am feeling great but I'm wondering what happened in there for him to say I won't have any more nightmares.

FINALLY, EVERYTHING IS GREAT OR IS IT?

It's been two years since I left active duty, but I'm still working for the Commander. It's now Captain and he is now waiting on his appointment to Admiral. With all my bitching and moaning about him and what I did while assigned to his unit, I couldn't have a better boss.

When I left the Marines, the Commander got me a job with Pan American Airways as a Purser on flights from Boston to London and beyond. When I go beyond London it is usually because the captain has an assignment for me. I am still doing the same thing but this time I get paid as an "Undercover Operative."

To date I have had three missions within Europe. I get the call from Langley, not necessarily the captain, and they tell me where and when to go. There is "no why." I then contact Pan Am to schedule a trip to whatever destination. Then the CIA agent assigned to that city or district will contact me to arrange a meet. I get the flight I want and I carry my Remington on without anybody ever thinking of going through our luggage. Airline people are immune at security. We do have to go through customs but no one ever touches my belongings.

Everything is going terrific at home and my wife is pregnant again with our second child. Our son, Ricky, is now three years old so we are hoping for a little girl. Sometimes I think of what it would be like having a girl but with everything that is going on with "free love" I think I'll stick with having boys. We live in a "Cape" house in South Weymouth with three bedrooms, one large bedroom I converted into two small kids rooms. We never parked our cars in the garage so we converted that into a TV room. Then having some extra money, we lived on a slab but we decided to dig it out and make a cellar. When it was finished we had a laundry room, a play room for the children and a large entertainment room. Everything was as perfect as could be until I got a call from Langley.

Picking up the receiver I heard, "Jim, call immediately. Your father needs to speak with you regarding your vacation," then nothing on the line.

One thing about the CIA, no one trusts anyone. The message "Your father needs to speak with you" means that Captain Damon needs to speak with you immediately on a secured line.

Going to the basement, I retrieved the phone that I was given when I left the Marine Corps and became an employee of the Central Intelligence Agency. Dialing the number to Langley, I start to think how this all started. Trying not to get nostalgic, the phone suddenly stopped and the same recorded voice says to say your code. I start to answer, "8055294433" and then silence.

"Good afternoon, Sergeant Coleman. What can I do for you today?" a stranger on the other end of the phone.

"Delores Elder, please?" wishing to speak with the one person I loved talking to when I called.

"Chief Warrant Officer Elder has retired, sir. She's been gone for three months. I'm sure we sent out notification to all agents who she has dealt with. Is there anything I can do for you?" a nice male voice but not Delores.

"No, I never got notification about her retirement. Do you know where she has retired to?"

"I can't give out that information, sir, but I know she and her husband and her three children have moved down south where they are from. Again Sergeant, what can I do for you?" I didn't know she was married with kids and now her replacement is getting upset with my questions.

"I got notification that Captain Damon wanted to speak with me as soon as possible. Will you patch me into him, please. Oh, what is your name?" seeing that I will be dealing with him from now on.

"I am Petty Officer Second Class Angus Stratton and it's a pleasure to make your acquaintance. Let me see if the captain is ready for you." Again the phone goes dead.

"What do you know about the Pentagon Papers?" No hello or how have you or your wife been. Just a question right out of the shoot.

"Only what I read in the papers which isn't very much? Why? What exactly are the Pentagon Papers?"

- - - - - -

The Pentagon Papers, officially titled "Report of the Office of the Secretary of Defense Vietnam Task Force," is a United States Department of Defense history of the United States' political and military involvement in Vietnam from 1945 to 1967. The papers were released by Daniel Ellsberg, who had worked on the study; they were first brought to the attention of the public on the front page of *The New*

York Times in 1971. *The New York Times* ran an article stating that the Pentagon Papers had demonstrated, among other things, that the Johnson Administration "systematically lied, not only to the public but also to Congress."

- - - - - -

"It really doesn't matter what they are? They're out there and a lot of people have a lot of questions. I need you down here tomorrow before noon and I don't know how long you'll be here," sounding like he was about to cry.

"What do I care about this damn article? Why do you want me? Why should I be worried?" trying to sound nonchalant but now getting a bit worried.

"You better be worried because your name and what you did in Vietnam is in it."

* *

Ingram Content Group UK Ltd.
Milton Keynes UK
UKHW022232160323
418717UK00012B/73